CRAZY
FOR TRYING

CRAZY
FOR TRYING

a novel by
Joni Rodgers

MacMurray & Beck
Denver

Copyright © 1996 by Joni Lonnquist Rodgers
Published by:
MacMurray & Beck, Inc.
1490 Lafayette, Suite 108
Denver, Colorado 80218

Printed and bound in the United States of America
1   2   3   4   5   6   7   8   9   10

Poems on pages ix and 299 by Jon S. Lokowich are reprinted with
permission of the poet.

Library of Congress Cataloging-in-Publication Data
Rodgers, Joni, 1962–
    Crazy for Trying/Joni Rodgers.
        p. cm.
    ISBN 1-878448-73-0 (hardcover)   1-878448-92-7 (paperback)
    1. Women in radio broadcasting–Montana–Helena–Fiction.
    2. Man-woman relationships–Montana–Helena–Fiction. I. Title.
        PS3568.034816C73 1996
        813'.54–dc20   96-23009
                                        CIP

The text for *Crazy for Trying* was designed by Pro Production and set
in Goudy.
Cover design by Tangram Design.

*This book is dedicated
to my daughter,
Jerusha Isabelle Rodgers*

This Dupont dimly moon I see
Through plastic mirror film too cold to touch
Forgets me—forgets you
As every night it floats away
The tattered days—
Then full—forgets forever.
These dials, reels and lights who rule
Evening and my hours remember though.
They remember you in mad electric coils.
In cold transistor souls they brood,
Having known your voice and hands as I do. . . .

Jon S. Lokowich

1

omething made Tulsa Bitters sit bolt up straight and realize she'd been asleep, or something like it, for a very long time. It may have been the doppler rumble and scream of another train on a parallel track or perhaps just that clock radio that clicks in your head, telling you that your neck is stiff and your teeth are wearing tiny sweaters and all the really good dreams are over anyway.

A lady in an indigo caftan sat facing her. She looked up and, before Tulsa had time to recoil from Stranger Eye Contact, tapped knowingly on the front of her newspaper.

"CARTER CAMP PANICS AS HOSTAGE CRISIS DRAGS ON," she announced. "He's doomed now. Never be re-elected. And that pretty wife of his. No more Air Force One for her. She'll be riding the train just like the rest of us."

She folded the paper and tucked it under the seat, glancing over her shoulder as if Mrs. Carter would be along any minute. "I don't usually take the train. This was all my son's idea. I'll make him pay for my hemorrhoid surgery, if I ever make it back." She sighed and pulled a loose stitch from her knitting. "So . . . what brings you out this way?"

"Well," Tulsa paused for a moment, not really wanting to think about it, "I have this fabulous job offer. And my fiancé is from Helena originally, so of course, he'll be joining me soon." Tulsa hated herself for lying but went right on for some reason. "After the school year, that is."

"Ah, how lovely for you."

"Mmm-hmm," Tulsa nodded emphatically, "it will be. It really will."

"When are you planning to be married?"

"Well," Tulsa felt her cheeks warming, "we haven't actually set a date . . . yet."

"I see. A long engagement?"

"Not very." The irony was strictly for her own amusement.

"It's nice to get settled first. Do you have a place there?"

"Yeah—well, no . . . but—" Tulsa felt her chest constricting and started searching for some way to end the conversation without either sounding evasive or physically leaping off the train. "I'm going to get things set up while he's finishing . . . " *What is coming out of my mouth?* " . . . medical school."

"Oh my, a doctor! And is your family there as well?"

"No . . . but Mother and Daddy are flying out from Chicago this summer."

"Is there a grandbaby on the way?" the woman asked conspiratorially and, misinterpreting Tulsa's pained expression, reached across the aisle to pat her stomach. "I wasn't quite sure. Some girls are just heavy, you know. Don't you be embarrassed. It happens. Even to a nice girl from a nice family." Her needles clicked in a moment of blessed silence. "When are you due?"

oh shit this is september october november december

"January. January . . . 29th."

"So of course you'll be married by then."

"Oh, of course." Tulsa rummaged through her bag, hunting for nothing more than an excuse to get out of the high-backed seat.

"Poor thing! In a new town all by yourself. That young man of yours should be taking better care of you."

"Oh, he wanted to come with me," Tulsa chimed in, hoping this was what the woman wanted to hear. "I just couldn't let him take time from his studies just now. He has a—um . . . anatomy exam this week."

Anatomy. He would love that.

"As a matter of fact, my father was a doctor. I know it requires a true sense of dedication."

"Oh, yes. He is. Very dedicated."

"What did you say his name is?"

"It's . . . Aaron." Tulsa spoke the syllables gingerly, as if they might burn her lips.

"I mean his last name," the woman smiled. "I'm from Helena myself and everybody knows everybody else."

"Oh . . . well—that *is* his last name. Aaron. His first name is . . . Hank." When surprise registered in the eyes of her traveling companion, Tulsa murmured, "He gets a lot of kidding about that."

"I'm sure he does. The Aarons . . . hmm . . . maybe they're new to the area."

"Yes." Tulsa struggled to straighten her achy legs and stood to collect all the debris from her carry-on. "Well, I think I'll just—"

"You know, my niece owns a lovely rental property on Benton. A lovely historic area. Just perfect for a young couple with great expectations. Let me jot down her name for you. Perhaps she'll have a vacancy."

"Oh—well . . . "

"Now, I'm Regina, and I didn't catch your name, dear."

"I'm . . . " She caught herself about to say "Bette Davis" or "Hermione Gingold," but fear of incurring any further karmic debt prevented her at the last moment. "Tulsa."

"Well, Tulsa dear, here's Anne Marie's address. You just give this to her and she'll take good care of you. Heaven knows, with that brood of hers, she's always stuck at home, so you won't have any trouble catching up with her."

"This is really very kind of you, Regina. I just wish . . . "

"Not at all, dear," Regina smiled, her knitting needles clicking.

"Well, I . . . I'm just going to run to the ladies' room," said Tulsa guiltily. She began to push her guitars under the seat, but Regina extended her hand.

"Don't bother, dear. I'll watch them for you."

"Oh, I—that would be . . . Thank you." She weaved on shaky sea legs down the narrow aisle to the cramped lavatory, and the door closed behind her with a hydraulic hiss. Tulsa leaned against it, not knowing where to set her bulky purse or her bulky self.

She remembered being on an airplane when she was small. Her mother had nudged her inside and closed the door, leaving Tulsa alone in the dim, steel-walled closet. She was afraid to sit down, thinking if she flushed, a trapdoor would swing away and *ka-roosh* her right out the bottom of the fuselage, under the sucking scream of the jet engines and into the vast, silent atmosphere. She tried to go standing up like she'd seen a man in the park do once but emerged with her pants and kneesocks damp and her chin trembling.

"Mom," she gulped, "I was—I was—"

"You know, Tuppy-my-guppy, I have your burgundy cords in the bag, and I'm thinking they'd be a little more seasonable when we get to San Francisco. Comfort-wise. That's what I'm thinking. Would you mind changing?"

"No, I don't mind," the guppy gratefully shook her head.

The grown-up Tulsa hitched up her dress, missing the scent of baby powder in low-heeled shoes.

Alexandra Firestein: "A woman has no reflection so pristine as her mother; no stronger ally, no greater enemy—except, perhaps, herself."

Tulsa washed her hands, trying to avoid the mirror, then wrestled her gigantic purse onto the sink. She took out her Noxzema and wiped away the smudgy raccoonish remains of her mascara. She rubbed at a smear of blush above each sallow cheek and scrubbed her pudgy neck where the brocade pattern of the seat cushion had left a bold red imprint while she slept. She prodded her heavily padded bra, trying to push it back to semiroundness. Her hair looked like a bad night at the Ice Capades. Her forehead showed signs of premenstrual breakout. She was ugly. She savored the mouth-watering sting of it; it was her uniqueness, her red badge of courage, and the only familiar thing left in her world. Someone at some time had opened some tiny puncture wound on her, and by carefully continuing to peel around the edges of it, Tulsa was able to open it wider, always just enough to prevent it from healing. She had nurtured it through a spotty childhood and into raw red adolescence. It had become easier to lay the wound open during high school as others rushed to reaffirm her worst fears about herself.

She was asked out only once, and it wasn't even by one of the three boys in her class who were taller than she was. Radley Baenmeier was the ill-fated short boy who waited for her after assembly the day Dr. Fursthort called her forward and gave her a certificate for getting the highest SAT score in the history of Lighton Valley Christian Academy. The good doctor was scowling because Tulsa was about to graduate with a D average and was known to cut classes early and often. What's more, the girl was a Jew—a Christmas-concert-shunning Jew—and that mother of hers was a pestilence, God help us, a threat to decent people. Tulsa ran the gauntlet of spattering applause to the front of the auditorium, nicked the embossed certificate from his chubby fingers, wriggled out of a damp handshake, and dodged behind the heavy stage curtain. She hid, heart pounding, in the velveteen forest until everyone was gone.

Everyone but Radley Baenmeier. He was waiting for her.

Congratulations, he told her and did she suppose, he wondered, would she maybe want to go see a play or something sometime, because his mom would drive them on Friday, you know, if Tulsa wanted to go. Tulsa wanted to go. Truly she did. Radley was a known brain and not completely unattractive. He was almost as tall as she was and smelled like he'd just taken a shower with Dial soap. Tulsa even thought she could stand being driven by Radley's gushy mother and sitting close beside him for two Dial-scented hours in the aching, artistic dark of *Othello*. But somewhere between Desdemona's passion and Iago's deceit, she became convinced that this must be an elaborate practical joke and someone was about to pour a bucket of pig's blood on her head just like in *Carrie*, and then she got terribly thirsty and crept down the back stairs to make her way miserably home in the snow. Radley never spoke to her again. He just schlubbed over to the other side of the hall when he saw her, and Tulsa just quoted Alexandra Firestein on the archaic, meat-market practice of dating. It was easier that way. For a girl who looked like she did.

Even Aaron told her that her brain was her most attractive feature. Describing her body as "lucky to be attached to such a beautiful soul," he used words like "statuesque" and "Rubinesque" and "bountiful."

Words like "acquiesce" and "maidenhead."

He gently eased her into her own body that first time he entered her. She felt a kind of worthiness so novel it made her cry. He was soothing and solicitous, thinking it was the pain or the sight of her blood on his sheets. She couldn't speak around the swelling in her throat to tell him how it felt to be living, at last, inside a body that someone wanted to caress, kiss, possess. After years of feeling like a foreigner, this was a moment of homecoming for her.

He spoke haiku during. He sketched her portrait after. They sat Indian-style on the top bunk in his dorm room and shared a can of cola spiked with Bacardi. By the time Tulsa realized in panic that the sun had come up and he was seeing her naked body in broad daylight, Aaron was pulling her on top of him and saying something about the "trepidation of the spheres."

It was two years later, when she was securely, irrevocably in love with him, that he dumped her and she remembered the scar she'd so carefully constructed. Now she wanted to go someplace where nobody would see or speak to her, where she could be alone to lick her wound, nibble at it, keep it for a cherished treasure, a symbol of her unselfish love. She was back where she belonged now, hating her fuddy reflection in a cramped bathroom mirror. She tried to yank a comb through the top layer of her hair, but the auburn strands clung together with grim alcohol-based determination—ultra hold.

Alexandra Firestein: "The look is merely a symptom of the malady: the desperate art of self-deception!"

She selected a wider-toothed model and raked at the dried spray and old perm until it formed something between a fez and a whisk broom.

"Oh, shit anyway." Tulsa's dry eyes suddenly stung with tears.

"We continually struggle to be that which we, in spirit, are not . . . "

"I—give—up!" She punctuated each word with a wrench of the comb.

" . . . until that moment when a woman's only relief is a bold and specific gesture; suddenly she must leave town, cut her hair, kill herself!"

Tulsa dove into her purse and came up with a pair of nail scissors. She raised her eyes to the mirror and saw herself, breathless on the brink of this bold gesture, tiny scissors open and hungry above her head like that baby chickenhawk in the Foghorn Leghorn cartoon.

"Hmmm." She lowered her arm. "Wait! I don't have to cut my hair—I left town!"

"Celebrate each small victory as a great awakening and each small awakening as a great victory."

She triumphantly deposited the nail scissors, then picked up the bag and shook it, hoping to bring some inspiration to the surface, but the Indian-print chasm offered nothing. She picked out a flat eye-shadow palette and a three-shade Blend-a-Blush kit, a Ziploc bag of nail polishes and remover, another palette with lip colors and liners, and two camel-hair brushes, piling the items in the tiny tin sink until, like Alice's "Drink Me" bottle, a little metal flap marked "Waste Disposal" caught her eye. Tulsa poked the blush kit in and quickly glanced at the mirror to make sure she was still there after the fateful *ta-shank*.

She was. She was there all right, and her cheeks held their own organic flush. She pushed plastic cases, tubes, and bottles through the spring-loaded door. It guzzled each item and snapped shut with a satisfying smack. The bag became pliable and giving. It fit easily to the side of the toilet now, still lumpy, but lighter. She found a travel-size bottle of shampoo and spent the better part of an hour washing away her stiffened coif, bowing over the inadequate sink, pouring water on her head one Dixie cup at a time. She pulled fifteen or so paper towels from the dispenser and blotted it dry as best she could, then slid the wide-toothed comb through it, sweeping the layers back from her face, allowing the waves to tickle her shoulders in their own way.

"Last but not least!" Tulsa pulled her arms inside her oversized denim dress and strained to unfasten her squashy bra. It dropped to the floor, and, finding her wide hips left no room to bend down to retrieve it, Tulsa kicked it under the edge of the metal cabinet, figuring she'd never pass the Ann Landers pencil test anyway.

"She walks in beauty like the linebacker," Tulsa spoke lovingly to herself and then sang, "O'er the land of the freeeeeee and the home of the ba-raaaave."

She continued to rifle the bag. Not much there now but linty Chiclets, loose change, and a tampon or two. She thought about trying

to retrieve the nail scissors, since she had to keep her nails fairly short
to play guitar, and then she remembered that she was also going to
need the polish remover, but the idea of putting her arm into the black
void behind the trash flap—the same happy little flap that only a moment ago had seemed so friendly—well, who knew what sort of nose-
blown, moldy condom secrets were concealed in there. Oh well . . .

> *"It must be accepted that there is no freedom gained without some life
> lost."*

Tulsa ran her fingers through her unhindered waves, zipped her
satchel confidently, lowered the toilet lid, and sat down, waiting
silently for Montana.

══════

Whah doncha love me like ya use-ta do . . .
whah must-ya treat me like a worn-out shoe . . .

Hank Williams drifted down the winding dirt road, a distant,
scratchy soundtrack to the smell of whiskey and Montana's evening-
colored mountains. And Lorene's red hair. Mac loved how that red
hair floated back on the open air after he and Ben Sharkey used an
acetylene torch to take the top off her old yellow Caddy. The wind
smoothed and rippled her peasant blouse against her body and took
her laughter trailing off behind them like a long silk scarf.

Of course, Lorene's father was pissed as a newt, but the Caddy's
black roof was peeling anyway, and Mac had always kept this secret vision of himself roaring across the back forty in a sleek convertible.

. . . I'm the same old trouble that you've always been through . . .
so whah doncha love me like you use-ta do . . .

"Because you're not really listening to me right now, are you, Mac?"
"Sure I am, Rex," Mac answered without missing a beat. "Hangin'
on every word."

"Well, I'm not getting any feedback here, Mac. Can you help me out a little? If you help me understand . . . might be able to facilitate . . . "

Terrific.

" . . . organization based on team effort . . . respect for group dynamics . . . "

Interpersonal Horsecrap 101.

" . . . count on a certain caliber of performance—or at the very least, regular attendance. I need to know that those people are really with me."

"And I won't be much longer, I take it?"

"Well, not if that's your attitude, Mac. C'mon, I know your checks are being garnisheed. I know you're behind on child support. You need this job and I'm willing, for history's sake, to give you a chance to turn this thing around before I make any major changes."

Somehow it hadn't occurred to Mac before this moment that this boy was his boss, someone who could Make Changes, or even Call Shots. The kid had been in Mac's unit in Vietnam, though none of that was mentioned when Mac was interviewed for the position of copywriter at Wambler-Belzen Advertising, where Rex's father was the emperor or some damn thing and Rex was dutifully ascending the ranks. The job didn't pay that well, but MacPeters hadn't exactly cultivated an impressive résumé. Rex scanned the wrinkled pages curiously: ranch hand, librarian, road construction, disc jockey? This guy had worked as a liaison for the Montana Bureau of Indian Affairs last summer and spent Christmas as a bell-ringing Salvation Army Santa.

"Two jobs that were not dissimilar," Mac had joked during the interview, but now he removed his cowboy boots from the desk and leaned forward in the swivel chair. "History's sake, Rex?"

"We both know I wouldn't have gotten home in one piece—"

"Well, that's mighty big of you," Mac made a wide, dismissive gesture, "and Christ knows it's been fun, but I'm afraid you're gonna have to shove that 'certain caliber of performance' horseshit." His tone was calm and friendly, and when the young man didn't respond right away, Mac leaned back and stretched, hands behind his head, shaggy salt-and-pepper hair even wilder than usual. He didn't know whether he was daring Rex to fire him or daring Rex to keep him on.

"I anticipated this might be your attitude," Rex sighed. "I had Althea cut you a check." He offered Mac an envelope and then had the audacity to offer his hand. "I genuinely wish you good luck, sir."

"What's that?" With the helicopters thrumming, Mac could barely hear the fresh-faced private facing him on the airstrip.

"I said 'good luck,' sir."

Mac hated this boy for going home first and hated himself for having no home to go home to, but he swallowed the bitter taste and said, "Thank you, private, same to you." He grasped the outstretched hand before he realized twelve years had passed.

"Thank you, sir."

Rex withdrew, leaving Mac with the check in his hand and all the things he might have said ringing in his ears. He should have told that chinless geek to go—

Too late. Rex was already back in his office, where the walls went all the way to the ceiling and a pretty young girl screened his calls. Mac stuffed the check in his back pocket and then hastily pulled it back out to see if they'd taken child support out of his severance pay. They had. At times like this, he seriously thought it would be easier to try to get Lorene back than to keep on paying through the nose until Colter came of age. Not impossible, he thought as he headed out into the dry heat of the parking lot. He'd been separated from Beverly quite a while now. Surely she'd file the papers any day. He rolled his quarter-ton pickup to the hilly part of the lot for a push start, leaped in, popped the clutch, and fed a Hank Williams tape into the 8-track deck. That wouldn't be bad at all: Lorene again.

The first time they were married, Lorene had been a virgin. She even looked like a virgin, just seventeen, doe-eyed and slender, and she smelled fresh and delicate as a single lilac blossom. On their wedding night, she had the sweetest ways he'd ever known. She wanted to know everything about pleasing him. She was limber and willing, and Mac could remember thinking then that this was a woman he'd be a fool to leave. But he'd left anyway, and after he was married to a weathered waitress named Cora for two months, he started thinking how lucky he'd be to get that lilac blossom back. The luckiest SOB on the face of the earth, he knew on their second wedding night, and he remembered thinking the same thing a year later when they were stationed in Japan and he watched her give life to the small and wondrous creature they named Colter O'Donnel MacPeters. Mac felt himself born again at that moment, receiving a new and unspoiled life, free of all the regrets that shackled him like Jacob Marley's ghost.

Back in Montana, they had reveled in Bohemian mid-'60s bliss, wearing sandals with socks and plundering secondhand stores for shelf treasures. Lorene macraméd a hammock for the baby, and they hung it near the Murphy bed, which they never folded up into the wall because they might want to make love just on the spur of the moment. But one night, Mac simply couldn't climb the stairs to the apartment above the Sweet Grass Bakery. He sat in his truck, resting his head on the steering wheel, hoping people passing would think he was only stoned. It was getting on toward daylight when he realized Lorene was looking down at him from the second-floor window. He ground the starter and let her watch him drive away. He circled the block to see if she was still there.

She was.

She was there at the screenless, wide-open window, her hair breezing back all auburn and easy. Just the way it did after he and Sharkey took an acetylene torch to the old yellow Caddy.

Lord, her father was pissed as a newt. But the roof was peeling anyway.

―――――

Known as Big Sky Country, Montana is a state of stunning mountain vistas, friendly people, and natural wonders. . . .

Tulsa sat on the closed lid of the toilet, examining and reexamining the colorful brochure until a sharp rap on the flimsy door caused her to drop it on the grimy floor.

"Miss, are you all right in there?"

He must be the purser or whoever it is that has to take care of things when people on the train vomit or slash their wrists or whatever.

"Fine, thank you," Tulsa called, "I'm just . . . doing my hair."

"I see." Irritation crisped the edge of his sympathetic tone. "Well, I'm sorry to bother you, but there are people waiting."

Tulsa took a deep, cleansing breath and unlatched the door to a man and a woman who stood there in the hallway. Tulsa avoided their eyes. They must be furious at having to wait, disgusted by her preppy-gone-bad appearance. They must be wondering why someone with such a lame hairstyle spent so much time working away at it in public bathrooms, questioning whether she even had any business being on this train at all! Tulsa grasped for an excuse, but the woman giggled nervously and blurted, "'Scuse us," barely getting the words out before the man pulled her into the tiny cubicle and wrestled the door shut. Tulsa stood facing the wood-look contact paper, explanations crowding her open mouth. There were bumpings and rustlings from the other side, then a series of muffled vocalizations, high-pitched squeaks and low moans in bending dissonance.

Resisting the impulse to press her ear to the door, Tulsa made the swaying journey back to her seat. Regina was asleep, her mouth slightly open. She stirred, and a paperback romance novel slid down off her ample bosom.

The Tempest and the Tiger Lily

"Whatcha reading, Tuppy-my-guppy?" Her mother loved to swoop up behind Tulsa and encircle her with her arms.

"Rimbaud," Tulsa said, trying to hold the book out of her mother's sight.

"Ah, Arthur Rimbaud . . . 'les Chercheuses de poux,'" her mother teased with exaggerated French affectation and then, seizing the book and holding it over Tulsa's head, switched to a Peter Lorre imitation, "'The Seekers of Lice,' how enchanting . . . *nye-heh nye-heh!*"

"Mom!"

"*Mah-ahm!*" she tickled and mimicked, "*Maahh-ahm!*"

"Mom, give it back!"

"Eeeeee! Lice! Lice!" she squealed, ruffling Tulsa's hair, but she stopped short and her smile faded when she saw the cover of the book. "Funny, this doesn't look like Rimbaud." The cover illustration featured a lissome young woman in a flowing peach gown, supple back arched, generous breasts thrust forward as a sultry sea captain rose up and possessed her from behind on the windswept cliffs of some Celtic shore. "What *is* this?" Her absolute contempt was undisguised. *"The Seaspray and the Passion?"*

"It's none of your business," Tulsa whined.

"'Seaspray'? 'Passion'? If you want passion, Tulsa, read some Lillian Hellman! D. H. Lawrence! Some Brontë . . . Rilke . . . Donne! This isn't passion—this is pultaceous dime-store drivel!"

"Ally," Jeanne's Southern lilt came softly from the kitchen, "could you please help me in here a minute?"

Tulsa's mother opened the paperback, affecting the captain's brawny brogue. "'Vixen!' he said, laying his rough hands upon her silky, lavender-scented flesh. 'Too long my only lady has been the open sea. This night, I shall have a woman of flesh and blood, as real and stormy as the moors!'"

"Mom!" Tulsa leaned across the sofa, grasping at the paperback.

"Al, honey, please," Jeanne called again.

"No—wait, Jeannie! I think he's about to kiss her hard and make her like it." She continued in the breathy, melodramatic voice of the peach-gown lady, wearing the amethyst words of love like costume jewelry. "'Yes, Bleak, yeeessss,' Miranda sighed, submitting herself utterly and completely to his powerful-a-*lllllipssss*. . . . 'Guppy, how can you read this pulp and call yourself an intellectual?"

"She didn't call herself an intellectual, Ally. You did." Jeanne's quiet assertion brought Alexandra sharply about, and Tulsa pounced on the opportunity to grab the book and head for her room.

"Tulsa, come back here." Her mother charged after her. "Tulsa, I'm speaking to you!"

Tulsa tried to shove the book under her pillow.

"Al, c'mon," Jeanne said, tugging the wide sleeve of Alexandra's shirt.

"No, Jeannie! I won't let her read this drivel and think—"

"Now hold on," Jeanne interrupted. "Aren't you the Alexandra Firestein who testified before a congressional committee not four months ago, decrying the evils of censorship? Or is it only evil when it's your books that are being banned? We are talking book banning here, if I'm not mistaken."

"Well, yew ahh mis-taykin," Alexandra mimicked Jeanne's gentle Georgia drawl. "We're talking *guidance*. I won't allow her to latch onto these myths about invincible, virile men and the sweet, sappy little women who love them. This is not about real life, Jeannie, or real passion!"

"Oh, c'mon, Ally. It's just a book."

"Not to her!" Alexandra pointed at her daughter. "And not to me."

"Ally, honey, the willow is strong 'cause it knows how to bend."

Alexandra stood for a moment, tapping the binding of the book against her breastbone. Then she held out the book but drew it back at the last moment so Jeanne had to take a step forward, close enough for Alexandra to lean down and kiss her. "I love you when you wax metaphorical."

"And I love you when you wax your legs." Jeanne kissed her back and laid the book on the dresser, giving Tulsa a side glance and making an ogre face behind Alexandra's shoulder. She hooked one finger through Alexandra's long string of turquoise beads and led her from the room.

"Or maybe you could read some Firestein." Tulsa's mother reappeared in the doorway just long enough to smile and shrug. "Very passionate stuff."

"Yeah, right . . . " Tulsa mumbled.

Jeanne led Alexandra across the hall, and Tulsa watched her mother extend a graceful leg to kick their bedroom door closed. She was laughing, soft and languid. "Vixen! Tonight, I shall have a real woman, stormy as the moors!"

"Yes, Bleak!" Jeanne was giggling now too. "Oh, *ye-e-e-esss* . . . "

Regina stirred again, and Tulsa set the paperback on the seat beside her knitting bag. Turning toward the window, she stared out at the stars and drifted into a semicomfortable doze where Aaron's haiku ribboned around the rhythmic click of knitting needles and turquoise beads. She wanted to sing with him, but she knew she was asleep and didn't want to risk blurting something out loud.

"Shhhh," Aaron laid his finger across her lips, pulling her into the tiny train lavatory. "My Hippolyte, Queen of the Amazons."

A tight collar of panic tingled around her neck; to wake now would be unbearable.

"When we love, a sap older than time rises through our arms," he recited, nothing more than that trace of Rilke between his mouth and her nipple, *"already dissolved in the waters that make the embryo float."*

Tulsa held herself there, straining to be still and silent, to stay with the swaying of her train.

———

The Joker's Wild was smoky and affable, full of guys with cowboy hats strutting for women with evening-red lips. Mac started feeling better even before Berryl Maclusky clapped a shot glass on the bar for him, drawing the whiskey bottle down close and then high above, finishing with a twisting motion at the very mouth of the glass. It was the only right way to pour a shot of Jack Daniels, official whiskey of country songs, rock quarries, and trucks with gun racks. Mac upended it with an equal and opposite reaction and zinged the empty glass down the bar to Ben Sharkey, who caught it with a rumpled nonchalance.

"Hey, beertender, gimme a bar."

Berryl knew without asking that Mac meant the cheapest thing on tap, but in a frosted stein, which cost ten cents extra. "Lest we forget the hyacinths that feed the soul," he'd said once. She remembered that.

"You are the only woman I ever truly loved, Mrs. Maclusky."

"Yeah, well, tell it to Yak when he asks me why I haven't beaten this bar tab outa you yet."

"Yak's my blood brother, Bee. He knows if I can't pay, he can carve a slab off my ass."

"That's a comfort, Mac. You could buy a round for the house if you weren't so damn skinny."

His barmates laughed, and Mac let them. He was feeling surprisingly mellow just now. Ben Sharkey slid his bony, hunched frame one stool closer and took a cigarette out of the front pocket of Mac's plaid flannel shirt. His hands were shaking pretty bad today, Mac noticed.

"How goes it, Shark?"

"It goes. You know."

"That I do." They sat smoking and tipping their beers for a bit. "On thorazine again?" Mac finally asked.

"Yeah. Went up to the V.A. in Great Falls Wednesday." Sharkey's voice inflected downward but didn't sound desperate or even disappointed, really.

"Maybe you oughtn't to drink that beer with it."

"Yeah."

"Yup."

"Yup."

"Yeah."

"Don't let me interupt the intellectual conversation, gentlemen." Berryl was back, refilling the now unfrosty glasses.

"We just need a mature and voluptuous woman to inspire us, Bee."

"I'll speak to my grandmother."

Ben Sharkey's hunched shoulders lurched in the *fr-frmph* that was as close to laughing as he came these days.

"Where's your monkey suit, Mac?" hailed Brody Fox, not intending or needing to shout.

"Well, Big Bro, due to an appalling lack of corporate vision, Wambler-Belzen has decided to facilitate group dynamics by redelegating—"

"You got canned *again?*" Brody boomed.

Mac felt Berryl's sharp glance from clear down the bar. He baffed Brody's shoulder with the back of his hand and muttered, "Maybe you could speak a little louder so *all* my creditors will be updated."

Brody's laugh was long-winded and hearty. "Well, it's time you got a real job, anyway. I read some of that crap you wrote in the Quality Implements catalog—all that about the nobility of ranch life and all I wanted to know was how many tons of shit can the thing haul!"

"Not as many as you can, Brode." Mac went back to his beer, feeling a little less go-with-the-flow, and they all rested their flannel elbows on the bar.

"So how's the Mrs. MacPeters these days?" Brody inquired.

"I wouldn't know." Mac definitely felt his mood slipping.

"Single man again, eh?"

"Yup."

"Bev clean you out pretty good?"

"Somehow the words 'pretty' and 'good' don't spring to mind when I think about Bev these days."

"Man, I know how that goes," Brody said dolefully.

Berryl was back. "Need another one, Mac?"

"Another what, Bee?" He hated it that she was suddenly being kind. "Are you offering to give me a job or sleep with me?"

"I'm offering you a beer or a belt in the mouth."

"I'll take the beer," Mac sighed. "Put it on my tab."

2

Mac released the emergency brake, giving the truck enough of a shove to get the wheels rolling. He struck the side of his fist on the dashboard and the Hank Williams 8-track burbled back to life. With any luck, he'd be able to grab his guitar and be out of the apartment before Anne Marie could lumber up the stairs. He would have abandoned the rest of his worldly goods just to avoid her, but he had to have the Alvarez. He had to play at least a little every night or he couldn't get to sleep. Sometimes it was hours, because he could never seem to relax when he was lying beside a woman. Sometimes it was just a lick "to scare off the bears" before he and Colter crawled into sleeping bags on the ground. But he had to lay his hands on it. It was a nightly ritual, the closest thing he'd ever known to kisses and lullabies.

"You better eat your potatoes if you want to grow big enough to be singin' in Nashville," his mother had told him, promising her boy he'd have his very own guitar someday.

On his tenth birthday, she kept her promise. She got up long before the light to bake him a cake, covering her good yellow dress with a flour-sack apron. "Johnnycake" they called it, heavy and dark, rich with molasses, sprinkled with confectioner's sugar. Humming a Hank Williams tune, she carefully decorated it with little stand-up cacti and singing coyotes cut from paper. She fashioned a little paper guitar with music notes floating up and a happy boy peeking out from behind a fancy number ten and gently pushed in ten little tallow candles just as morning began to color the dark windows.

She opened the kitchen door, reached above the lintel for her squirrel rifle, and walked out into the cool mountain morning. From the back porch of the big stone house, she could see what seemed like the whole universe, hemmed in by rocky ridges and high pines. She stepped down the rough log stairs into the yard where the chickens were just beginning to scratch. She started to climb the corral fence but remembered the dress and used the gate instead. Behind the stable, she paused at the window to coo at the horses that stamped and shuffled inside. Then, kneeling in the sweetgrass, she placed the hunting rifle alongside her slender neck and flew away with the covey of quail and starlings that rose up, startled by the blast.

Jarred upright by the gunshot, dragged forward by the sound of Satchi's keening, the boy was standing in the chilly morning of his room before he even realized he was awake. The outside of the window was dusty, but he could make out the figure of his grandmother beyond the cloudy brown film; naked, on her knees, she clenched Pa Roy's pearl-handled Bowie knife in her fist. She methodically drew it across her copper breast and stroked it down her arms and stomach in an ancient ritual of grieving, a primitive wisdom that released blood and anguish, redeeming human skin too fragile to encompass such an all-encompassing sorrow.

Hired men, still in their long johns, came shouting and stumbling out of the bunkhouse. Pa Roy was running toward Satchi with a horse blanket, bellowing at her, dragging her to her feet, shaking her until she dropped the knife in the dirt. He tried to bind her within the stained blanket, to pull her to him, but the reedy, high-pitched wailing grew louder as she flailed and struggled. Pa Roy struck her hard. She collapsed forward and he collected her up in his arms, burying his face in the streaming black tangle of hair.

Cheek and palm against the window, the boy watched his grandfather stagger up the steep path, across the front porch, into the house. Pa Roy slid the deadbolt to lock him in his room, but he could still hear Satchi sobbing and babbling that Indian talk Pa Roy forbade. Trembling, he crawled back under the quilt Satchi had made like sunrise on one side and sunset on the other and rocked back and forth till it wound around him like a cocoon. Then he lay still, blood and silence pounding in his ears, his breath puffing pale steam in the cold morning room.

He awoke at dusk. Pa Roy's long shadow reached across his bed. "Get up, boy."

He didn't know his grandfather could speak so quiet. He crept to the kitchen, holding his quilt around him. Satchi was sitting on the floor, smoking her pipe, staring into the fireplace, her eyes swollen and her cheek bruised. Blue thread and dried blood showed at the edges of the white strips where the neighbor woman had stitched and bandaged her.

"Yer ma made ya a cake."

Royal MacPeters laid a gentle—or perhaps just weary—hand on his grandson's shoulder, and then his boots thumped heavily out, across the porch and down.

On the planed-plank table, beside the johnnycake with its singing coyotes, lay the Alvarez, wildflowers and cattails and ribbons all along its slender neck.

———————

Helena sprawled comfortably in all directions but nestled one elegant shoulder against the sloping body of her first great love, and the same mountain that lifted a rocky, undomesticated face to one side of the world supported the city with a protective arm on the other. They lay together beneath a quilt of evening colors, listening to all this life they'd begotten.

Last Chance Gulch furrowed between the hills. Born of a glacier, kidnapped by gold miners and seduced for a bawdy business district, the gorge matured to an American Main Street but was later restored to cobblestones and coffee shops, while modern civilization bled outward from it like tie-dye, spawning houses, stores, schools, suburbs, and all-you-can-eat salad buffets all the way to the valley. Trekking into town, Tulsa was somehow surprised by the life-size laundromats, buildings, and Burger King. She'd sort of expected log cabins and free-ranging cattle and was a little disappointed to realize that, for all its legends of copper kings and Chinese muleteers, this town was still, on a basic, mechanical level, the same as any town, including the one she'd just run away from.

Benton Street was situated well up the side of the mountain, high above and parallel to the Big Dorothy bluster of Last Chance Gulch;

a little farther and she'd have been headed up the Mount Helena hiking trail. Shaded with pines, lined with lilacs, Benton was well tended and nicely restored with windows full of light, yards full of tricycles, and porches full of stonework and cedar gliders.

It was dark when she finally stood on the front walk, breathing heavily and perspiring inside her bulky sweater. The Victorian residence would have been imposing if not for the white Christmas lights strung along the topiary bushes. Japanese lanterns hung from the trees, and luminarias lined the curving driveway. Tulsa reached into her pocket and clutched the note from Regina, those lines of train-swayed scrawl her only excuse for approaching the wraparound porch.

Voices and sound effects came from inside: someone running down the broad staircase, someone calling for help with a keg of beer, someone jingling car keys and shouting they would be right back. Jackson Browne's *Everyman* album ruffled a lace tablecloth hung up for curtains. Tulsa shrank back to the shadowed porch swing. There was a party getting under way, and parties pulverized her. She had spent too many of them sitting on wrought-iron lawn furniture, desperately seeking the first possible opportunity for escape, the back of her neck crawling with a lurking suspicion that the guest of honor had been forced to invite the famous woman's daughter. Even more crushing were the publishing affairs, when her mother's agent filled the apartment with a strategic, faux-kissing blend of black and purple silk—the artsy, the intellectual, the politically promising, and those with money to invest in any of the above. The food was always fresh and bland and attractively laid out, just like the conversation. Tulsa would cower on the sectional sofa, hiding behind her bangs, but people always came over to her anyway, hoping to insinuate themselves into her mother's circle of energy.

"Strings!"

A tall, smooth-faced boy lifted her guitar case right out of her hand and, before she could form an objection, opened it, parked himself beside her on the swing, and started tuning.

"Wow . . . a Framus. This thing is beautiful," he said, and then cocked his head to one side, intently plinking harmonics. "Great action. Easy on the wrist."

"Yes, but—I usually don't—"

"Gotho pegs! Did you have all this mother-of-pearl customized too?"

"Well, my mom had it done in Europe and I really—"

"Oh," he turned to Tulsa as an afterthought, "you don't mind, do you?" His eyes were dark and warm, his smile genuine, his hair pulled back in a maple-honey braid.

"Well . . . " Tulsa had a strict rule about strangers playing her guitars, but she suddenly wasn't sure if that included tall, beautiful, ginger-voiced strangers.

"I'm Colter," he added, as if that clarified things somehow.

"Hi." She nodded and then shrugged. "Have at it. I'll be right back."

She dug Regina's note out and moved toward the door, dragging the heavy duffle, hugging the twelve-string to her chest, and praying no one would ask to touch it. The boy's voice followed her into a front hall. The French doors of apartment 1 stood open to reveal a blazing fireplace and an invitingly overstuffed sofa. Tulsa was marveling at the woodwork and wallpaper when the aroma reached her. It drifted in the back door. Something warm, red, *barbecued*.

"Food." Tulsa didn't mean to actually whisper it, but she hadn't eaten since she got on the train two days earlier. Her keen nose and empty stomach told her to keep moving. Inside door number 2, Bob Dylan sang, weaving and clashing with some sort of buzzing kitchen appliance. Under the lintel, an enormous mastiff-cross yawned, stretched his paws toward Tulsa, and then continued snoring. Voices filtered down from somewhere above the open staircase.

"*Now!* I mean it!"

"Dammit, Anne Marie—"

Out of the jumble of music and voices from all other parts of the house, the name leaped to the foreground. Tulsa strained to hear what was being said. She started up a few steps, then backed off and bit her lip.

dammit Anne Marie I have a note for dammit Anne Marie

She climbed a little farther to the wide second-floor hallway and leaned forward, one hand on the heavy newel post, but still couldn't make out what was being said. She moved up several more steps, almost against her will, to a landing where the staircase turned and narrowed.

I have a note. Dammit Anne Marie, you don't know me, but I have a note from your dear, sweet Aunt Regina and any niece of my close personal friend Regina—

"That's a shitty thing to say! Jack's a good man. Worth ten of *you,* that's for sure!" The woman's voice was ice cold and angry. "Now you get your shit together and get the hell out of here!"

"C'mon, Annie, Bev's lawyer tied everything up. In a couple weeks—"

"You've been saying that all summer! You owe me for three months! I only let you stay this long because Colter begged me to cut you some slack."

"*Colter!*" Now the man was angry too. "Colter needs to mind his own fucking business."

"He was trying to help you out," the woman's voice came down a little, "and so was I. I know things are weird for you right now and I'm sorry, but Jack's gonna be home in less than an hour, and you've gotta be gone."

Whatever the man said in response was low and sarcastic. The woman answered. There was a moment of silence, then the sound of a door closing and footsteps toward the staircase. Tulsa tried to spin and retreat, but her wide body was wedged in the narrow passage between her twelve-string and duffle bag. She tried to back down, but her purse caught on the railing. She felt a wave of panic, knowing she could only go forward and come up with some plausible excuse or stand there and be discovered.

What am I doing here?

"Can I help you?" Anne Marie stood unsmiling above her. Her strawberry-blond hair was woven back with ribbon, sprigs of baby's breath tucked into the sides. She was pregnant and particularly immense from Tulsa's perspective four steps below the hem of her billowy maternity jumper. Tulsa stood gaping until Anne Marie impatiently said, "If you're looking for Mac, he's up there." She indicated the third-floor apartment behind her. "But he's just leaving."

"Well—I couldn't help overhearing and I thought—I mean, if there's going to be a—a vacancy?" Tulsa gave up trying to make a lovely first impression and wretchedly held up Regina's rumpled note. Anne Marie sighed and sat down on the top step, squinting at the pink paper in the half light.

"*Regina?*" She wheeled on Tulsa, and her tone was not one of congenial recognition. "How do you know her? Where is she? *Here?* Not here!"

"No . . . well—I don't think so—"

"You're from the mental hospital, aren't you? You're a nut."

"No!" Taken aback, Tulsa began babbling. "I just—I met your aunt on the train and she said you might have an apartment and so I—I'm sorry. I didn't mean to just—I didn't know you were . . . having a party. . . . "

"My aunt?" Anne Marie was still unsympathetic and suspicious. "Regina is my mother. And she's supposed to be in the Warm Springs mental facility."

Tulsa could see Regina nodding and smiling over her knitting needles.

"Look, my husband is getting home from California tonight. And I planned this big wingding. And everything is pretty much falling to shit." To Tulsa's horror, Anne Marie's face crumpled to cry and she repeated, "Shit!"

"Listen," said Tulsa, instinctively patting Anne Marie's hunched shoulders, "Regina was fine. She was knitting and she had money—I saw her counting it. And she said she was getting off in Whitefish. Maybe you could call the police there and maybe they could . . . you know."

"Round 'er up?" Anne Marie laughed raggedly, and Tulsa did too, though she couldn't imagine why.

"I'm sorry." Rationalizing and apologizing, Tulsa gathered her things to go. "I don't know anyone in town and . . . I just came here because your—um—Regina said you might—"

"Do you have money?" Anne Marie interrupted.

"Well . . . some."

"How much?" she pressed.

"How much is the apartment?" Tulsa asked warily.

"One sixty-five plus your share of the water. We pay electricity and gas heat, but Jack fixed the thermostats so they don't go above 72. I need first, last, and security deposit up front. No waterbeds. No pets. No overt weirdness or making out on the porch 'cause I've got little kids. Other than that, we all mind our own business. Rent is due on the first and that's in cement. No exceptions, no excuses." Anne Marie fired off the facts and figures, cold as a stock ticker, then added, "That's my landlady persona."

"Hmmm," Tulsa was adding and subtracting in her head. "This is my begging persona. I can give you the first month and part of the deposit now. I can give you the rest later. As soon as I start working."

"How soon is that?"

"Oh, soon. Very soon." Tulsa shifted a bit. "As soon as I find a job."

"Ah, geez," Anne Marie sighed at the familiar proposition. "All right, I guess. But I need at least two fifty tonight. All this beer and barbecue stuff left me kind of overdrawn. Jack's gonna kill me."

"I have two hundred forty-seven dollars and seventy cents." When Anne Marie didn't immediately respond, Tulsa added, "And I haven't eaten for two days except for coffee and a Ding Dong."

"Ah, geez . . . " Anne Marie was struggling, Tulsa could tell. "Well, I've gotta have two hundred, anyway. I've just got to, or Jack—"

"Will you let me eat at your party?"

"Will you babysit my kids part of the evening?"

"But you don't even know me!" Tulsa said in surprise.

"Yeah, and you don't know my kids!" Anne Marie laughed again, and Tulsa recognized Regina there. "Nick's in third grade—the bodily function sound-effects stage. You won't have any trouble with Emma; she's just learning to read, and I'm lucky if I can pry her face out of her book long enough to feed her. Mary Laur is three, we call her Pickles, and if she starts doing a sort of two-step dance—get her to the bathroom immediately. Jack and I will be right here along with eight million other people. How much damage can you do?" Anne Marie rested her forearms on her stomach. "I just need some help with crowd control, you know? Just help me corral them in their rooms around nine and read 'em a little of *Sneetches and Other Stories* and it'll be cool."

Tulsa knew the Dr. Seuss volume by heart. Her mother had a different voice for every character. "'I've heard of your troubles, I've heard you're unhappy . . . '"

"'But I can fix that, I'm the fix-it-up chappie!'" Anne Marie finished with her, pleasantly surprised. "Cool," she nodded. "You're hired.'"

Tulsa nodded too.

"And I'm sure there'll be lots of leftovers. We'll stock your fridge tomorrow." Anne Marie struggled to her feet. "So, you want to see the place? It's tiny, but Jack put in a Murphy bed and a cute little kitchenette and the bathroom's actually bigger than mine. We've got the four-bedroom on the first floor. Colter has the studio down there, and Rina and Joey each have a two-bedroom unit on the second floor. But up here—this one's my favorite."

"What about—um," Tulsa glanced uncomfortably at the closed door.

"What—him? He knew weeks ago he had to come up with the moolah and be out before Jack got home. It's cool."

"Maybe we should come back later."

"No way," Anne Marie said firmly. "I'm not climbing these stairs again until there's only one of me." She pressed one hand to the small of her back and the other beneath her enormous abdomen. "I'm ten days overdue and living in hell. My feet are swollen, my back aches, and I'm in no condition to be pissed off."

"I'll vouch for that."

They were both startled by Mac's voice behind them. Tulsa wouldn't have projected that caustic voice on this face, worn but good humored, dark eyes deepset, square chin several days unshaven, wavy salt-and-pepper ponytail brushing the broad shoulders of his long buckskin cattleman's coat. Tulsa studied the fringes and intricate beadwork at the yoke, trying to decide if it placed the man in Woodstock or Buffalo Bill's Wild West Show. He leaned against the doorframe, black Stetson in one hand, dilapidated guitar case in the other.

"Gee, Annie, don't grieve for me too long before you get on with your life."

"This isn't what it looks like," she told Tulsa with more weariness than apology.

"It's all yours." Mac settled the hat low over his heavy brow. "Just don't try to fit through the door at the same time."

Tulsa, usually hypersensitive about her weight, didn't get the gist of his barb right away, but Anne Marie bristled. "Should I forward your mail to Beverly's house or straight to hell?"

"All the same. Evening, ladies." Mac tipped his hat, brushed past Anne Marie, and headed down the steps, hefting a bulging lawn-and-leaf bag and the dog-eared guitar case. Tulsa averted her eyes and tried to flatten herself against the wall, struggling to minimize the space she was occupying, but as he squeezed by, there was a horrific moment of entanglement when their guitars clattered together and the whole front of her body was pressed against his back and she inhaled the scent of his long fringed coat. It was still in her head when he disappeared around the corner of the stairwell.

"Where will he go?" Tulsa wondered.

"Who cares?" Anne Marie shrugged, but then rolled her eyes and smiled. "Knowing him, he'll be out back drinking beer when we get down there."

"Oh."

"Ah, geez!" Anne Marie groaned, rummaging through her big pockets. "Please, please, *please* don't tell me I left the stupid key all the way down at—oh. Thank heaven. He left the door open. I guess he's off the shit list."

As they entered the moonlit apartment, Tulsa inhaled the same rich scent: woodsmoke, cinnamon coffee, and the clean air of the night mountains. It was very . . . not unpleasant.

Downstairs, Mac stowed his stuff in the entryway and headed out back. He was never much for parties, but this was no time to turn down free beer.

"Hey, Mac!" called one of three guys nurturing chicken and hamburgers on the stone fireplace, "you still here?"

"No eviction is complete without a couple of free beers, Joey. It's a ceremonial thing you wouldn't know about, being white and so stupid and all."

The guys laughed, and Joey gestured with the sauce-covered spatula. "Hey, Mac, I talked to Dallas about getting an overnight man to replace Bobby, and he said you should come down to the station tomorrow. He's desperate, so who knows. Stranger things have happened in the wild world of broadcasting."

Mac felt a breeze of relief across his brain; Dallas wasn't the only one getting desperate these days.

"Cool," he nodded, "I can think of worse things to do with my evenings than playing Rock'n'roll Radio God."

"Well, actually," Joey said, shifting his feet, "this would be out at the Swamp. You know, on the AM station."

"OK," Mac was unfazed, "Country and Western Radio God. Even better!"

"Yeah," Joey nodded and poked at a sizzling drumstick. "Problem is the money's not quite as good, and you have to work out in the valley at the transmitter . . . and you have to run network all night, so it's pretty boring. And then, of course, there's the Big Dick."

"Ah, Richard the Client-hearted. Is he over there now?"

"Yeah, program director and sales. He wants to get back on the FM, though. Wants to get his butt in my chair in the worst way. Says we oughta chuck the album format and go adult contemporary." Joey shuddered and then sang into the spatula, *"Feee-uh-lings oh-wo-wo feeeeeee-uh-lings . . ."*

"Now in paperback," Mac intoned, *"Radio Politics: When Egos Collide."*

"Yeah, well, be there at eight or my boot's gonna collide with your ass."

"My word as a man," Mac answered, and Joey knew that meant something.

Straying toward the front porch, Mac picked up another beer from an ice-filled garbage can and scaled up over the railing onto the porch.

"MacPeters?" Susan Fowler sat on a rattan loveseat, looking good in her autumn coat and cowboy hat.

"Hey, Sweet Su-ue," Mac sang and sat beside her in the glow of the Christmas lights.

"Hey, Mac." She brushed his arm with her fingertips, the same way you'd test the water with your toes before jumping in the creek. "How ya doin'?"

"Well enough. And you?"

"Can't complain," she smiled.

"I was just heading over to the Joker's for a bit," he said, looking sideways at her from beneath his hat. "Care to join me?"

"Oh, I dunno." Susan raised a Lite beer halfway to her lips, scanning the collective in the yard for any likelier candidates. Nada—but she hadn't been out back yet. "I think I'll take my chances here for a while." She could tell a half-hearted attempt when she heard it, and she wasn't one to compromise her standards. Then again, she wavered, this was Mac, with those brown eyes and that way of his. She'd once described him to a girlfriend as "hung like a pack mule and twice as durable." Susan took out a Virginia Slim and Mac was suitably quick to light it for her, so she offered, "Maybe I'll catch ya there later."

"Later then," Mac nodded, touching the brim of his hat. He ducked past her into the entryway to retrieve his guitar and leaf bag, his entire post-divorce-court estate and not much of a burden.

The Murphy bed had been left open in the third-floor apartment. Tulsa sat down on the lumpy striped mattress and leaned her twelve-string case against the low iron footrail. Anne Marie clicked lights on, illuminating gabled ceilings, narrow wainscoting and a clean hardwood floor, a rocking chair in the middle of a round braided rug, a green-glowing clock radio above the bricked-over fireplace, and bookshelves that flanked and lined two alcoves. The bedroom was the top of a round turret that formed a circular sunroom in each of the apartments below, and its conical plaster ceiling was painted deep blue with stars in constellations. The walls were mostly windows with wide sills and molded glass, rounded to follow the arcing perimeter of the room. Tulsa reached toward them in wonder, looking out over rooftops, through tall pines, and on, seemingly forever, across the wide, moonlit valley to the shadowy mountains.

"So it's cheap, you know, because it's so tiny," Anne Marie echoed from the empty center of the room, "probably not what you're looking, for, but—"

"No, it's perfect," Tulsa answered, creaking up the three narrow steps that wound around an exposed corner pantry to a red and yellow kitchenette. She opened the bathroom door and found black and white checkerboard tile, a pedestal sink, and a long clawfoot tub. "I love it."

"Me too," Anne Marie said. "This was my grandparents' house when I was growing up, and I loved to play up here. Jack thought I was nuts for putting so much work into it, and as it turns out, all we get up here is deadbeats and hippies in transition." Anne Marie caught herself and tagged on, "No offense."

She turned to glare at the rocking chair. It was large and squarish with twisted doweling and round knobs. The grain of the oak was rich and well rubbed and so polished by use, the saddle looked almost warm.

"So," she folded her arms on top of her stomach, "this is what he meant by 'call it even.'" She sat and rocked back, running her hands along the smooth-turned arms. "I remember rocking Colter in this old chair when he was just a little biscuit." She darkened and stood abruptly. "Damn that jerk. Do you think I should keep it? It's sort of a family heirloom."

"Oh." Tulsa wasn't sure how to respond to the rockings and biscuits and heirlooms of people she didn't even know. "I guess that would be up to you."

"Yeah." Anne Marie laid her hands on the back of the chair. "Look, do you mind if I leave it up here for a while? Will you have room for it when you get everything moved in?"

"This *is* everything," Tulsa told her, trying not to sound like a deadbeat hippie in transition.

"What about pillows and sheets and stuff?" Anne Marie wrinkled her forehead, vacillating between her usual tendency to mother the world and a natural unwillingness to lend bed linens to a total stranger.

"I'm covered." But the pun didn't play as well as Tulsa hoped it might.

"OK . . . well . . . oh! First things first. Is this travelers' checks or something?"

"Cash," said Tulsa, embarrassed that she hadn't until that moment thought of getting travelers' checks.

"We accept cash." Anne Marie pushed her hands into the pockets of her skirt as if to warm them up for the money. Tulsa opened her guitar case and took out the twelve-string to reveal a cubby where the neck rested.

"Oh God," Tulsa breathed, "oh . . . "

"Please don't tell me what you're about to tell me," Anne Marie said, sensing a sob story coming on.

"Anne Marie, I had almost two hundred fifty dollars in here—I swear it!—and the only time it was out of my sight was . . . it was . . . "

She reached into the cubby and drew out a pink paper lined with a familiar train-swayed scrawl.

*Anne Marie Dear, Please take good care of this sweet girl. Her young
gentleman will be joining her soon.*

Tulsa crumpled the paper. "She wouldn't."

"Oh, yeah. She would." Anne Marie sounded like she was about to
cry again, and Tulsa was about to join her.

"She left twenty-seven dollars and seventy cents."

"Why does she do this shit to me?" Anne Marie sat down on the
rocker, stroking her huge belly. "Why can't she just be a nice mother?
I'll bet you have a nice mother, don't you?"

"No," Tulsa sat on the brick fireplace ledge, "and, anyway—she's dead."

Anne Marie pressed her hands to her forehead, wondering how
one goes about getting rid of an indigent, unemployed orphan who
hasn't eaten for two days and has the goods on your mother.

"I don't know what to say," Anne Marie shrugged.

"Anne Marie," Tulsa started to plead around the swelling in her
throat, "I don't have anywhere else to go and my guitar here—it's an
Ovation—and I have another one that's worth a lot of money and you
could hang on to them—"

"No. Let's just call this month paid and forget the security," Anne
Marie said wearily. "It's not the first two hundred dollars I've put into
the Regina scholarship fund."

"You're saving my life," Tulsa said.

"You're babysitting," Anne Marie answered, and they both smiled
uncomfortably. "Who are you, anyway?"

"Tulsa. Tulsa Bitters."

"Well . . . c'mon down, Tulsa." Anne Marie got up to leave. "Judg-
ing from the rest of this day, it's going to be a hell of a party."

Mac was at the station on time and listened penitently to Dean
Dallas, General Manager Omnipotent, go on about learning from the
past and no need to dredge all that up.

"What were you calling yourself back then?" Dallas leaned across his
desk in a way that was sort of unsettling and never took his steel-blue eyes
off Mac's brown ones, just in case they betrayed one glint of defiance.

"Gee, that was eight years ago, Mr. Dallas. I really don't recall."

"Peter Michaels," Dallas answered for him.

"Ah."

"Me and the elephants," the GM smiled with all the warmth of an automatic weapon. "We don't forget."

"Would you like me to choose something else in case there are any other pachyderms in the listening audience?"

Dean Dallas offered a cocktail-party chuckle. "That might be for the best, Mac. Now, what did you use at Smooth 105—Michael Patton? And Country 68—Kickin' Mitch Michaels, wasn't it? And Micky 'Pete-man' Peterson at Rockin' Hits 99, and at E-Z 86 AM . . . oh, yes—Albert Camus. That was my personal favorite." Dallas took the gold pen from his desk set and tapped it on the ink blotter in front of him. "You've certainly had quite a career—" three sharp taps—a suspended beat— "haven't you, Mac?" Tap.

You have no idea.

"You know you wouldn't be sitting in that chair right now if I weren't desperate for someone—anyone—with a license to have his face behind that board at eleven o'clock tonight?" Two taps.

"Yes, I know."

There was a brief silence while Mac wondered how much he'd have to grovel to get this job and Dallas wondered how much time it would take to make this guy squirm a little.

"You'll work weeknights eleven to six, Saturdays six to midnight. This is essentially a board op position with virtually no announcing, but when you are on the air, you'll stick to the format without exception and answer to Dick Richards directly. If there's any questionable activity out there—mysterious absences, dead air, late arrivals—I will hear about it, and I will terminate you without delay or remorse, even if I have to cover the shift myself." Mac nodded, not meekly but without blatant defiance. Figuring that was the best he was going to get, Dallas smiled another cool smile. "All right, then. Let's talk money."

That shouldn't take long.

It didn't. Dallas stated his offer, Mac accepted it with some semblance of gratitude, they shook hands and exchanged the standard pleasantries, and then Mac went out to Rina's desk to fill out a W-4 and get a key to the Swamp. She was cheerful and chatty, trying not to let on that she'd heard every word of the grilling he'd received. Mac scribbled on the W-4, wondering what Colter saw in her besides the fact that she'd started Suzuki violin at age three and could now fiddle a bobcat out of a chicken house.

"Oh, did you hear Anne Marie had her baby this morning?" she was asking, all smooth skinned and sunny. Rina always seemed so damn . . . *sunny*.

"No kidding," Mac said. "Party too much for her?"

"Just what the doctor ordered, apparently."

"So what color cigars are we smoking?"

"Bouncing-baby-boy blue!" Rina rattled off the statistics, "Seven twenty-two AM, eight pounds nine ounces, twenty inches long, blue eyes, red hair, Oakley Bozeman, after his great-grandfather and the town where he was conceived."

He couldn't help but smile. The thought of Anne Marie always did to Mac what a summer breeze does to the surface of a wheat field, and when he thought of her like that—strong and beautiful and breeding—

"You're just like Jack," Rina said in her sunny, fair-haired, Eastern European way. "Tough guys love babies. It's a yin/yang thing."

Mac kept smiling.

Lord, Colter, the woman's a complete flake.

"Well?" Joey called as he dashed out to rip the AP wire in the newsroom, and Rina gave a thumbs-up sign.

"Thanks, Joe," Mac said sincerely, adding, "I owe you a beer."

"You owe me a case!" he shot over his shoulder, dodging back into the control room just in time to dive across the console and jam "Bat Out of Hell" into the cart deck.

———

"How 'bout a little Meatloaf for breakfast, baby?" Joey's energized bit clicked on with the clock radio, and Tulsa stretched like an old woman waking up on a park bench. She untangled herself from her makeshift covers and tried to shake the wrinkles out of her jumper. She needed it for job hunting. She'd only ever had one job, and it was in a radio station so Joey would be her first stop.

"Are you kidding?" someone at the party laughed at her when she said she wanted to apply. "Nobody around here has ever had a girl on the air."

Someone else gave her a lead on a night job running a floor scrubber at the Historical Society building.

"—asking for burned-out generic prom themes at eight twenty-eight in the freakin' morning?" Joey mercilessly pursued an embarrassed caller. "'You Light Up My Life'? Can I toss on a little Singing Nun for ya while I'm at it? Ya gotta 'Roll With the Changes,' you early morning animals!" His voice rose like a siren as he rode up the ramp of REO Speedwagon's latest. "Crank this up, babeeeeeee!"

As soon as you are able . . .

Tulsa did crank it up, wondering how Joey could be so wired on so few hours of sleep. His voice was clear, even with the slightly flat quality of the little clock radio. His wit was sharp, and his clean patter surfed between swells of rhythm and music, filling the instrumental intros without stepping on the vocals or allowing a moment of dead air.

"Tight, light, and bright!"

Charles Bitters had uttered the corny epigram, leaning intently forward, holding his tie back from his fettucini alfredo, imparting each word like a pearl of wisdom. "Applies to any format. There are women on the air in most of the major markets these days, and you've got nice, crisp diction so there's no reason you can't work your way up. It's just a matter of perseverance. I only wish I could have started out with the benefit of this sort of entry-level position, but I earned my diploma at the School of Hard Knocks, kid. *Damn—hard—knocks*," her father had repeated, knocking on the table for a percussive accent on each word.

She had to give him credit for effort. For coming at all. In the surrealistic confines of the funeral home, his tall, cool presence did comfort her; his tidy silver hairstyle and matching mustache made her think of Captain Kangaroo, and his lack of pain provided a strange sort of balance. As he escorted her past her mother's coffin and over to the front row of folding chairs, she followed the crease of his sharp black suit, walking close enough to smell the dry-cleaned normality of him. Tulsa realized this was probably the closest thing he'd ever do to walking her down the aisle, and the irony of that exacerbated a sick, giggly impulse she'd been fighting all day. She was still struggling with it that evening as they sat in a corner at the Hungry Peddler, straining to make conversation across the red plaid tablecloth.

"Perhaps I overstepped in arranging this for you, Tulsa, but you're going to need something to fall back on. My attorney will look into the particulars, but your mother's will sounds airtight. Everything will go to this—this friend of hers and some charity for artistic—God knows what." Uncomfortable with the word *lesbian* and unable to come up with a suitable alternative, he kept hoping Tulsa would chime in, but she swirled another forkful of pasta to her mouth, leaving him out there all alone. "Of course, I'd be glad to have you come to Indianapolis, but right now—the timing isn't . . . Did I tell you Shirley's expecting again?"

"No." Tulsa took the last brown roll and dipped it in her thick cheese-and-broccoli soup, scanning for a waitress who might bring another basket. "Is she?"

"Yes. Yes, she is."

"Oh. Congratulations."

"Thank you."

"So . . . you have other kids?"

"Two boys. Tommy's fourteen and Timmy's nine. They're excited about the baby, of course, but it's going to be an adjustment. So to bring a new person into the family just now—especially . . . "

"A stranger."

He sighed and placed his palms on the table. "Tulsa, in all fairness— I never—Look, I regret that we haven't been close. . . . " Tulsa's giggle impulse erupted, but she covered it by coughing into her napkin. "But you're a grown woman now. I can't turn back the hands of time, can I?"

Tulsa did feel some sympathy for her father's predicament. She felt guilty for bothering him, for making him uncomfortable, for existing, a wrinkle in his well-ironed world.

"It's all right, Charles." His name felt like marbles in her mouth, but she would have been more comfortable calling this man "Mr. Bitters" than "Daddy," the way she did in her imaginings. "Jeanne's invited me to stay with her in San Francisco until I finish college. I have a few things I can sell and now your . . . my—this job. I'll be fine."

"Are you sure?" The question was rhetorical, underscored with relief.

Look, Tulsa wanted to say, *you don't know me and I only know you well enough to know that you don't want to know me, so let's just leave it.*

"Sure," she said instead. "Do they have a dessert cart here?"

―――――

Back in the sunlight, Mac shoved the pickup into the sloping street, feeling light as he leaped in and popped the clutch. Dallas had offered more money than he thought he'd have to plead for. Now, Mac calculated, if Bev would just file the damn papers and Lorene would marry that Montana Power idiot, he'd be free of alimony and child support when Colter turned eighteen just ten months from now. Meanwhile, he was going to need a place to live, and only one possibility came to him.

Mac passed through the North Hills and drove for half an hour on Lincoln Road. It all seemed unfamiliar now, and that bothered him a little. This used to be his territory. Now old logging trails had solidified into regular paved roads. Boulders and fir trees came at odds with convenience stores and billboards. Swanky homes sprouted decks and driveways and satellite dishes that riddled the gulches and outcroppings. Thirty miles out, Mac was disoriented enough that he almost missed his turnoff. It didn't help that the gate had fallen down and the tilted "R. MacPeters" mailbox was obscured by creeping, brushy growth.

"Shit," Mac whispered. He knew if the engine died while he was out dragging the gate aside, he'd have a hard time getting it started again. He stepped slowly out of the pickup. It died. *"Shit."*

By the time he got the rusty barbed-wire gate untangled and away, Mac was sweating and his hands were bloody. He spit on them and wiped them on his jeans, trudging up the twin trails of dust that used to be a pebbled drive. The first building he reached was the bunkhouse.

An old saddle of Pa Roy's still perched on the adjoining fence rail. The door stood ajar, but inside things seemed surprisingly dry and solid. Birds had nested in the rafters, and mice had carried away bits and strips of the dirty braided rug, but structurally the one-room cabin was as sound as the day he left it.

I gotta feelin' called the blue-oo-oo-oos
since ma baby said goodbye . . .

He didn't know then that Hank Williams would be dead soon. Or that army recruiters can spot a fake ID a mile away, or that the jungle is so hot, you can't distinguish your own sweat from the humidity hanging in space around you. He only knew that he was making his escape, and it wasn't via the back of the stable. He was sixteen-years-plus-a-day old. So he didn't know he didn't know everything.

. . . I used to love it when she called me
Sugar Da-a-a-addy . . . such a beautiful dream . . .

Satchi made no sound on the step; she was simply there when he spun his guitar like a dance partner. She wore jeans and a pale blue workshirt, her long hair loose except for a narrow side braid bound with a buckskin thong and white feather, and she was beautiful, even more so because of the scars and lines and streaks of gray she carried.

"White Wolf," Pa Roy would have slapped her for calling the boy by his Blackfoot name, "come up to the house. Come get some breakfast."

"No."

"Aren't you hungry?"

"I'll never be that hungry."

"He won't let you go to the army." It was a statement, not a plea, when she added, "He needs you."

"Tough shit. Let him hire somebody to take his crap."

"He says he'll never speak your name again."

The boy shrugged.

"You'll come back."

"I won't," he vowed.

"All things go in circles, White Wolf."

"When he's dead and rotting, I'm gonna sell this place for a fuckin' strip mine and use the money to get as far the fuck away from Montana as I can get."

"Even a dog makes a circle before he lies down."

The boy sighed, having about as much patience for Blackfoot wisdom as Pa Roy did. He put the Alvarez in its case, trying to imagine what he would tell the recruiter about the permission slip. Satchi watched him close and latch the case before she dug into the breast pocket of her workshirt and produced the paper, wrinkled and smudged with black from the woodstove. She smoothed it between her hands and held it out to her grandson, but the boy hesitated.

"He taught me to write, so my hand moves like his," she smiled, enjoying her secret power. "See?"

The boy nodded but still didn't take the paper, knowing that Pa Roy would beat her for signing his name and that, infuriatingly, Satchi wouldn't even try to lie or deny it. Moments passed. She laid it on the bed and extended her arms, a sepia-toned image in the sun-flooded doorway, offering for farewell a poncho she'd made for his birthday.

The thirty-two years between Mac's hands and hers hung inconsequential as cobwebs. Mac reached out in the deserted bunkhouse to accept the poncho, new and white with flying designs of purple, red, and yellow, but a bird suddenly fluttered against the dirty window, the colors shifted beneath his hand, and he recoiled from the image of Satchi's gift bound around the bloodied head of a young girl near Dyen Dau. He uttered something aloud and stumbled back against the wall, bringing starlings from the rafters. The flurry of wings and cries drove him out into the sunlight, where he swore and leaned on a fence rail, searching his pockets for a cigarette.

shit

Just one left and his hands were shaking so, the last precious smoke got bent in half.

fuckin shit

With only two dollars and change in his pocket and no gas in the truck, this would be it till payday. He couldn't afford any decent grass, either, and he would prefer smoking cow chips over that God-awful stuff Sharkey bought in Great Falls. It was a low way to be in. He was half tempted to tap Joey for a couple friendly hits of acid or even ask

Colter to inquire around at school for some hash—he was about that desperate.

Mac lit the crooked cigarette, cherished every inhalation, and allowed the last draw to singe his bottom lip a little before he spit the butt onto the gravel, ground at it with his heel, and headed down the weedy path. The other outbuildings were not in as good condition as the bunkhouse. One yank on the door of the chicken coop and the entire side collapsed. Mac looked up the mountainside to the sagging roof of the great barn and decided it wasn't worth the climb to investigate. Beyond that, the huge stone house dominated the ranch like a sullen monarch, enthroned on a rocky promontory whose only access was a switchback path of flagstones and rotting stumps. The front door of the big house was closed and locked, the thick oval of etched glass still intact, the sitting-room furniture shrouded in silence, dust, and muslin sheets. The stone foundation and porch were still stalwart, but where the back wall met the downsloping hillside, the kitchen steps had been eroded by snowslides and battered by stray livestock. The back door lay flat, partially covering a gaping hole where a cow had come in and crashed through the floor down into the root cellar. Its weight must have been too much for the sagging planks, causing them to give way in a thunder of groaning, mooing, and thrashing, echoed now by the jagged edges and splintered remains of the kitchen floor. The dried carcass in the shallow cellar lent a dark, earthy smell to the silent house.

Mac climbed down to the yard below and, consciously keeping his eyes away from the stable, made his way to the toolshed. There he found a large wheelbarrow, but the wheel was rusted solid and attempts to kick it free only broke the brittle axle in two.

ah shit shit shit!

A crusty pitchfork was the least dilapidated of the toolshed hardware. It was cracked and rough, but it would have to serve. Mac took it over his shoulder and headed back to roust out the starlings. His hand was bleeding again, and the dry afternoon was definitely getting hotter. Pausing at the fence to examine the saddle, he took off his flannel shirt and stepped over the broken boards into the knapweed and wildflowers that had taken over the vegetable garden. Mac waded a few yards in, then stopped and inhaled sharply.

"Sweet Jesus and Maria—I don't believe it." He burst out laughing and started to run. *"Satchi!"*

He bounded over a swale, stumbled, dragged himself up, and kept on running.

"Glory to great Lord Jesus Christ! Satchi, you beautiful redskin goddess, *I love you!*" Rolling and whooping and breathing in the sweet fragrance, Mac fell to the ground and gathered the spiky leaves to him. Some of it was in full flower, ready to be gently picked and lovingly dried. Some of it was still at a stage where it could be pinched back and nurtured into fine sensamilla. There had to be a half acre, he calculated—maybe more!

Originating in the tiny plot Satchi had paced out between the bean blossoms and the tall corn, the cultivation had spread and flourished over the untended years, threading through the sagebrush, climbing uphill to the aspen trees. Mac picked one pliant leaf and tucked it in his cheek to chew while he gathered up armfuls of mature plants.

"Ah, God bless your beautiful soul, Satchi," he breathed, standing in a state of raptus, the mellow scent of his grandmother's abundant bequest filling his heart and head. "I'm home."

3

I t was cold.

Bone-deep, brilliant, blue-white cold like Tulsa had never known. So cold she wouldn't have felt a stone in her hiking boot. So cold her nose went wooden and every bronchiole-igniting breath inhaled ice fire and exhaled clouds that crystallized on the wide brim of her Salvation Army cowboy hat. She tucked her hands under her arms, but her fingers were already stiffened to matchsticks.

"We need a chinook," Colter said as they trudged up Last Chance Gulch on their way home from the library.

"A shnook?" Tulsa felt her Flatlander showing.

"Chinook," Colter nodded, trying to recall how his father explained it. "All the sudden this funky wind blows in over the mountains and it gets to be fifty-five degrees and everybody gets nuts for a few days, wearing shorts and sandals and partying. And then two days later, it's winter again."

But Tulsa still didn't get it, until the following week. As usual, she made her way to the Historical Society building at frigid midnight and sang harmony with the bass thrum of the floor scrubber for six hours, but when she emerged the next morning, braced for cold, she discovered a world gone wondrously sloppy, melting, and miraculously warm. There was an odd sort of carnival atmosphere; it was just a little after six, but people were already out washing cars, sweeping sidewalks, and reading morning papers on the walking mall. These were the same austere early-morning people who populated the austere early-morning streets every day as Tulsa made her way home. But today, they were

41

almost Fellini-esque in Bermudas and bandanas, calling, "Hey there! How 'bout this wind!" and "Looks like we're gettin' some spring goin'."

Down Last Chance Gulch, Tulsa stopped to take her coat off under the statue of the Bullwhacker and checked to make sure the stone Atlas was still balancing his burden despite the steady breeze. She paused at the pawnshop window and Aunt Bonnie's Bookstore, mentally spending her next paycheck.

"Morning, Elsa!" she called, swinging open the screen door of the No Sweat Cafe. "How 'bout this wind!"

"Hey there!" Elsa called back, balancing a tray of Chinook Specials over a booth of hungry hikers. "C'mon in and sit."

"On a day like this? You gotta be kidding!" Tulsa didn't want to tell her she was out of money. "Friday, though." Payday.

"See ya then, sweetie." The *skreeek*-bang of oven doors was followed by the fragrance of quiche and carrot muffins.

Just around the corner at the radio station, Tulsa tapped on the big studio window. Some days Joey would be draped across the console, his head buried in his arms, and Tulsa quickly learned it was better not to bother him when he was like that, but today he waved her to the door and poked his head out.

"Hey, Tul, come in and run the board for a minute while I take a whiz."

"Sure, Joey," she said agreeably, "and let me add that I appreciate your confidence in my ability to execute these responsibilities."

"Oh God, here we go," Joey rolled his eyes. "Tul, I've told you a hundred times they don't want girls on the air here."

"Yes, but you haven't told me why."

"*Because.* That's why. They never had one. It's not gonna happen." Joey went down the hall to the bathroom and Tulsa sat very still, watching the event timer as if it were going to suddenly take off or something.

. . . now that I can dance . . . dance . . . watch me now—uh!

She pushed in a cart with the station jingle, checked Joey's stack, cued up the next album, and waited for the song to count down. She settled the headphones over her ears. "KRNR FM and Tulsa in the morning, here's an arresting selection from the Police."

Raaahx-ann . . .

"It's even more fun with the mike turned on," Joey teased from behind her. She sighed and slid the phones off.

"I think I could be good."

"I think you could too, Tulsa, but people don't like changes. You'd be asking for rations of crap."

"Rina says Missoula has a woman on the air."

"Yeah, and their sales manager is a dyke, too. Big coincidence."

"Then there's Tammy Grimes on CBS, Anna Montana in Bozeman . . . "

"Yeah, yeah," Joey rolled his eyes again, but then he smiled. "You know the Big Dick would shit if I put you on the air." That notion was appealing enough to start Joey rationalizing. "This is 1979. Almost into the big '80s here. Gotta be progressive. Gotta keep up with those major market trends, right?" Tulsa nodded earnestly. "And your voice is pretty mellow."

"I've been told I have very crisp diction."

"And you can be a hoot . . . all those voices you do."

"I've got a license. And I know the music."

"The man would shit neon."

"I'm also a very conscientious employee."

"Neon hammer handles," Joey grinned to himself. "And who's programming around here, him or me?"

"You are, Joey—you! And you're a progressive guy."

"You've done segues, funny little character bits for my show."

"And I worked for a year in Minneapolis. That's a major market."

Joey came back to her for a moment. "What did you do there, anyway?"

"You know," she hedged, "records, weather." Her actual job description included cleaning the studio and reshelving records in alphabetical order, but she had done a winter storm warning once. "I'll do whatever training you want me to do, Joey. No pay. I'll observe, do production. . . . "

"Why am I even considering this?" Joey covered his face with his hands. "Why do you keep pushing this?"

"Why not? Everybody needs to be good at something, Joey, and I know I could get good at this."

"I can't guarantee this is gonna wash with Dallas, Tul."

"But you'll try?"

"You'd be on overnights—the shittiest shift in broadcasting!"

"As opposed to the shittiest shift in *floor scrubbing!* Joey, I wouldn't care what anybody said. I can take it. I'll be on time, I'll work hard." She paused. "Would you say this is nagging, begging, or persistence?"

"All of the above," Joey grumbled, "but I'll see what I can do."

By 8:10, Tulsa was sitting sideways on the porch swing, cracking the lid off her 7-11 coffee and unrolling a newspaper. Colter came out and stretched for his morning jog. Rina dragged Khan and Shasta out for their morning constitutional. Next came Anne Marie, carrying Oakley in a snuggle pack on her chest, pulling Mary Laur by the hand, and shooing the rest of her brood into the Suburban, all in a jumble of kneesocks, backpacks, and lunchboxes. Rambunctious Nick and bookish Emma bickered and bobbed in the rear window, waving when Tulsa called to them to have a good day at school. Jack brought out his workbench and sat tying flies while Tulsa read bits and items from the paper, and eventually everyone passed by again; Rina rushing the dogs back inside and dashing off to work, Colter stumbling up the steps, panting and pretending to be a dying man in the desert: "Water! For God's sake, water!" Sometimes, when Anne Marie got home from taking the kids to school, she invited Tulsa in to sit by the fire and rock the baby and talk about everything in the world, but today they stayed outside on the swing.

"So, how are you liking your first chinook?" Anne Marie asked, tossing a blanket over her shoulder so she could nurse the baby.

"It's amazing," said Tulsa. "Now I know how you survive winters here."

Jack tickled docile, wide-eyed Oakley with the feathery part of a lure before he set the hook in it. "Not much like San Francisco, I take it?"

"No," she said, "or anyplace else I've ever spent the winter."

"Oh?" Anne Marie tried not to sound curious, "Like where?"

"Oh, hither and yon. New York . . . France . . . whatever."

"Tulsa, I can't stand it anymore! What on earth are you doing out here all alone?" Anne Marie's question surprised her because she felt less all alone than ever before. The house was always full of noise, music drifting up the stairs, lively debates heating the front porch. She and Rina drank wine on the porch roof. She and Colter hiked Mount Helena. Anne Marie would knock a few dollars off her rent if she took the kids down to Last Chance to play on the walking mall and get a Coney from the hot dog cart. Sometimes they would knock on her door and beg her to come down for bedtime stories because she had a different voice for every character and never fell asleep in the middle like their mother did. Even Shasta no longer barked when she passed the second-floor landing. Tulsa tried to remember a part of herself that didn't belong here, tried to access some kind of timeline, but Alexandra and Jeanne and Aaron seemed like images from a dream state.

"Actually, I have no idea what I'm doing here, Anne Marie." Tulsa laughed a little. "This just happened to be where I got to."

"Oh." Anne Marie studied Tulsa for a moment, then nodded. "Can you hold the Oak-man for a minute?" she asked, "All this tea—I gotta go see Johnny. Then you should come to Butte with me. Saint Vincent de Paul Bag Day today!"

Anne Marie had introduced Tulsa to the concept of Salvation Army chic. A relentless scrounger, she possessed an almost psychic gift for homing in on that never-even-opened percale sheet set, those perfect rosebud teacups, the embroidered muslin peasant blouse, or the tea-length linen skirt hidden in the jungle of polyester castoffs. Among the treasures that now adorned Tulsa's mantle were two gold-leafed plastic menorahs with screw-in lightbulbs and AA batteries, a kitschy Spanish bullfighter, and a genuine Elvis on velvet.

"Eureka!" Anne Marie cried, yanking free a pair of Lee Rider jeans.

"I don't know . . . those look kind of small."

"No, you should try these." Anne Marie plopped them decisively into the rusty cart. "I don't know how you're doing it, but you look great."

Tulsa knew if she told Anne Marie she was on the Poverty Plan Diet (the one where you can't afford to eat the last three days before each paycheck), Anne Marie would find some kindly way to feed her, and Tulsa couldn't stand that, so she mumbled, "All this walking, I guess," and ducked into the dingy fitting room. She emerged a few minutes later wearing the jeans. "I can't believe it—they do fit!" She checked the size inside the fly. 16 long. The last pair of pleated twill slacks she'd bought at Bay Area Large and Lovely had been a 22.

"Sixteen—that's a *normal* size." Tulsa suddenly felt like crying.

Anne Marie hugged her. "Never question the Bargain Piranha!"

"Not for a minute," Tulsa declared, finding it not so hard to hug back.

"Yeah," Rina agreed when Tulsa pulled the jeans out of the dryer that afternoon, "just the right fade." She shook a load of towels into the washer, and they sat folding, listening to bluegrass music, while Khan and Shasta yawned and stretched and nuzzled their knees.

"All right. Topic du jour," Rina moderated, "First Great Loves."

"Bad topic," Tulsa cringed.

"I smell heartbreak. Spill it!"

"Only Great Love—and not that great."

Rina sat cross-legged and regarded her friend. "You turned your back on civilization because a guy ripped your heart out," she said seriously. "Anne Marie and I have been trying to figure it out for months. Name? Come on. You'll feel better if you just say it."

"Aaron."

"Go on," Rina coaxed, "it'll be cathartic."

"Aaron Proctor Taylor. The Third."

"Oo la la. Sounds rich."

"Well, his parents are."

"And incredibly intelligent and gorgeous?"

"No, they're just your basic middle-aged—"

"Very funny. He's into poetry and literature, I bet?"

"He's a painter . . . and he's really good. Astonishingly good."

"And you think you'll never again experience that particular brand of mind-scattering sex as long as you live."

Tulsa went to the dryer, ostensibly to throw in another softener sheet. When she came back, Rina was nodding wisely. "That's how I felt about my First Great Love. And my second First Great Love. And my fourth . . . "

"Oh, that's comforting."

"You move on, Tulsa. You do. I bet you already have, and you just don't realize it. I was actually sort of married to this one guy, and I thought I'd never be able to breathe again. But now, here's Colter. And I know he's just a kid—his mom had a cat when she found out I was twenty-five—but I love him."

"I know." Tulsa envied the feeling.

"The Colter I love has a very old soul," Rina commented, as if to validate her interest in the Colter who jogged shirtless up Mount Helena every morning. "He had to grow up early, the way his family is. He's an exceptional person—very sensual, intuitive. Of course, the sex is great—but I love the person that he is, and I have such great respect for him as an artist."

Tulsa could almost hear the gentle strokes of Aaron's charcoal and brush, and a lump started forming in her throat.

"Would you believe," Rina confided, sotto voce, glancing over her shoulder to make sure Colter's pottery wheel was still humming upstairs, "I used to have the powerful hots for his *dad?*" They giggled about that a little, and then Rina sipped her tea and asked, "Do you know Colter's dad?"

"No," said Tulsa, "but if he looks anything like Colter, I'd like to."

"Mmmm," Rina shook her head, "he's a whole 'nother story. You won't see him around here; Jack doesn't like him. Maybe I'm confabulating, but I have a feeling Anne Marie and him might have gotten it going at some point."

"Anne Marie and Colter's dad?" Tulsa winced. "I don't believe it."

"Of course, I haven't asked. We mind our own business around here."

"Like hell we do." Joey's slush-covered boots appeared on the wooden stairs. "Hey, Tul, I'm not making any promises," he cracked a can of beer and sat on the bottom step, "but Dallas says you can observe if you want to."

"Good choice," Rina declared, "if he doesn't want to get his ass sued for discrimination."

Tulsa hurried down the hill the next morning after work and stayed for the rest of Joey's shift. Winter resumed its course after the chinook, but Tulsa rode to the station with him every Saturday, arriving with cheeks chapped and hair wild from the Harley wind, staying all day to practice in the production studio, learning to run dubs and cut commercials. She sat in her long, low bathtub every evening, working the handheld showerhead like a mike. "Hello, Helena, I'm Tulsa Bitters, and you're rockin' with KR'n'R FM," she enunciated, mimicking Joey's energetic delivery, enjoying the quality her voice took on with that touch of bathroom reverb.

And so it came to pass that, a few weeks later, when Chunk showed up drunk to his Friday-night shift, Tulsa stood trembling behind Joey at the FM console. Revolving cart racks to the sides, meters, switches, and potentiometers to the front, formed a horseshoe around the operator who perched on a high swivel chair. Tulsa was too nervous to sit.

"Settle down now, Tul," Joey coached. "You OK?"

"I'm OK," Tulsa said unconvincingly.

"I know you are." Joey steered her into position. "Now show me what you're gonna do."

"News outro, hit the logo, hit the music, pot up the mike."

"Right. And then just go for it. Don't forget to pot down the network—they only give you thirty seconds of silence before they start the tone. Take it two hours—just to midnight. That's all you've gotta do."

Joey put the headphones over her ears. Tulsa nodded and turned to brace her unsteady hands on the sliding pots as the door shushed closed and the control board loomed up in front of her like the cockpit of a 747. Tulsa felt her throat close and her chest constrict. She stared at the event timer, struggling to figure out how many minutes she had, and suddenly the newscaster was giving his outro, and Tulsa's trembling index finger was pushing the green button on the logo cart.

Silence.

Frantically, she jammed another logo in and stabbed at the green button.

Nothing.

She jammed a song in the music deck and poked at it.

"Oh, shit . . . "

Tulsa clapped her hand over her mouth, frozen by the sound of her voice standing stark naked in the headphones, clear and audible, even

above the earthquake in her ears. Hammering on the plate-glass window startled her from her cryogenic torpor. Joey was in the hallway,
frantically gesturing and shouting at the soundproof barrier.

"POT IT UP!" He illustrated with a wild cranking motion. "POT
IT UP!"

In a frenzy, Tulsa spread her hands across the board and slid all the
control pots forward, bringing up both tapes and the shrilling network
tone in a cacophonous trio. She ripped them back down and then
rammed them forward and back one at a time till Boston came up.

. . . when I see Marianne walkin' away . . .

Tulsa slapped the microphone switch to the off position, tore the
headphones away from her head, and bolted toward the door, but Joey
was light-brigading in and they collided just outside the horseshoe.

"Oh no you don't!" Joey caught her shoulders and swung her
about. "You get the hell back in there!"

"*Oh, shit!*" Her throbbing heart was almost too much to breathe
around.

"Jesus, Tulsa! What's the matter with you? You just got done showing me what you were supposed to do—why didn't you just do it?"

"I don't know! I just—I didn't hear anything and I just—I just.
Panicked. Oh, God! I've humiliated us both, Joey. I'm sorry!"

"Geez, Tul, get a grip. You potted up your mike instead of the logo,
that's all. It happens, OK? Now when this song runs out—"

"I can't! Didn't you hear—"

"Oh, I heard! You better pray Dallas missed your debut, though.
Not to mention the FCC!" He doubled over laughing, imitating her
falsetto, "*Oh! Shit!*"

"Joey, just let me go home—"

"OK, OK," Joey cleared his throat and composed himself. "Tul,
seriously, it's always different when you try it for real. It's no biggie."

"I thought I could do this. I thought I could, but I can't."

"Tulsa, we do not have time for this."

"I'm sorry, Joey, I'm going home."

"*Fuck that shit, Tulsa!*" It was the first time she'd seen Joey genuinely angry, and it unnerved her even further. "I went out on a limb

here. Half the airstaff is threatening to quit on me if I put you on the air. Dallas is all over my ass—I spent two and a half hours this afternoon convincing that old man you could do this job, and if you don't pan out, I'm up to my eyes in shit. You were so hot to do this—now *do it*, goddammit!" Seeing her look of absolute abashment, he softened somewhat and started coaxing. "You can do this, Tulsa. You can. Just think it through and push the buttons. Just *think!*" Joey pulled her into a hug. "C'mon, Tul . . . you made one mistake. Get over it."

She rested her forehead on his shoulder and began breathing a little more evenly. "Is this what you do for all the guys?"

"No," he said seriously, "so don't make me do it for you."

"OK." Tulsa pulled away and nodded. "OK."

"Just relax. If you don't know what to say, use the cards."

The door shushed closed. She placed the bulky headphones over her ears and swiveled the chair toward the board. Boston was winding down.

. . . away-aaaay-aaaaaaay . . .

Tulsa took a deep breath. She punched the next cart, and Bob Dylan rolled in. Pulling Boston down and potting her mike up at the same time, Tulsa fixed her eyes on the liner card. She heard herself in the headphones, still sounding frightened, but clear and low.

"At ten-fifteen, it's 34 degrees downtown on Helena's historic Last Chance Gulch, and the best rock in the Rockies is right here on 98.9 FM." Dylan came in as if on cue. Tulsa pulled her mike out, and Joey burst through the door.

"And she nails it!" He leaped over the lower side of the horseshoe and embraced her, jubileeing, "She slices, she dices, she—nails—IT!"

"Light, tight, and bright," Tulsa said, still trembling.

"I knew you'd take to the air like a—like a kiwi to fruit salad!"

Tulsa giggled and nodded, allowing the coil of tension across her forehead to slacken just a little.

"C'mere," Joey said, pulling her by the hand, "this is a long song. You have time for a quick break." He led her to his small office beyond the newsroom. On the glass desktop, he'd carefully formed two white lines with a razor blade. "Here," he grinned, rolling a pink sheet from the telephone message pad, "you earned it."

"Oh," Tulsa pulled her hand away, " . . . no thanks." The sight of the neatly arranged cocaine caught her by surprise. She'd actually thought Joey was about to kiss her or something, and she was flustered to realize that that might have been OK—or at least better than sticking a foreign object up her nose.

"It's OK, Tul, I've got plenty."

"No, Joey, really. Thanks, but I don't—um . . . imbibe."

"Oh," he said quietly, "I just thought it might help a little. Sorry."

"No, don't be! I appreciate the thought and I'm not making any value judgments—I just . . . don't." Tulsa was embarrassed to tell him it was the nose thing that bothered her as much as moral scruples.

"That's cool," Joey shrugged and rocked back a little on the heels of his boots. "You better get back."

"Yeah." Tulsa retreated to the hallway.

"Hey, wait a minute! What are you calling yourself?"

"Can't I just use my own name?"

"Do you have an unlisted phone number?"

"Oh." Her heart started churning again.

"Besides, Tulsa is like this town in Louisiana or something, and what the hell is 'Bitters,' you know, it's like *bitter*—like *'yulccch.'*"

"Gee, thanks, Joey. I needed a confidence-builder like that."

"Go segue. I'll think of something."

Tulsa returned to the studio and used the rambling harmonica out ramp on the Dylan song to load some commercials into cart decks.

"'Just Like a Rolling Stone' . . . that's Bob Dylan gathering absolutely no moss on KRNR FM. . . . Music from the Doors coming right after this." Tulsa punched the first commercial and sat rigidly as it ran.

For better broasted chicken—
try batter-broasted chicken at Tony's. . . .

She punched the second one.

This is Judy for the Little Professor Book Center. . . .

Third one.

Friday night, live at the Silver Spur, it's . . .

Last one.

Hey! It's a Prospector Chevy kind of day. . . .

Logo cart.

Rockin' the Rockies . . . K-R-N-aaaaaaarrrrrr!

Thunder rolled in as Tulsa segued to the Doors and Joey entered, grinning. "You're cookin', Tul."

"I think I am, Joey," she answered giddily.

"OK, so air name: Bebe La Babe."

"You're joking."

"OK, Candy Teton. Brandy Teton. Brittany Brandon," Joey kept firing suggestions as Tulsa shook her head. "Tracy Leather . . . Leather Lace . . . Lacey Blaze . . . Blaze Starr . . . Star Blaze . . . "

"These sound like strippers' names, Joey."

"Hey—entertainment professionals, just like you. Umm . . . let's see. Dixie, Trixie . . . Maxi . . . Maxi Sweet! Maxi Night? Maxi Pad . . . " But Tulsa was laughing, holding up her hands. "OK, then," Joey said, incensed, "you suggest something."

"I can't think of anything."

"What's your mom's maiden name?"

"Hermione Gingold."

"Yikes. Well, let's let our fingers do the walking." Joey opened the western Montana directory on the console and started paging through. "Let's see here—George, Graft, Halverson, Hopewood—there you go: Hope Wood. Perfect! 'Hope Wood, wouldn't you?' It's perfect."

"It sounds phony."

"It's supposed to sound phony. Do you think somebody actually named their kid Wolfman Jack?" Joey glanced at the event timer and realized he didn't have time to convince her. "C'mon, Tul, you've got seventy seconds. Close your eyes and point and that's the name you're gonna use." He held the directory out in front of her, and she jammed her index finger in the middle of the page.

"Veteran's Administration Loans," she read, and they both laughed.

"But that could work," Joey persisted, "VA—like Virginia—Loans . . . like a loner—lone star—lone wolf, you know? VA Lones. There you go."

"That sounds stupid."

"You've got twenty seconds, Lones."

"Forget it, Joey!"

"Knock 'em dead, VA! I'll be in my office listening!"

The Doors' storm was dwindling to a drizzle.

"I'll be in here," Tulsa said to the closing door, "broadcasting." She opened the mike and punched up the next cart. "KRNR FM, rock-'n'roll with . . . VA Lones and Led Zeppelin. Time to climb that 'Stairway to Heaven.' . . . "

"*Oh, shit—*"

The voice on the air was choked and frightened and definitely not Chunk.

It was the girl. The girl was on, and she had dead air. Mac's sympathy was only slightly tainted with a bit of mean-spirited amusement. *Lots o' luck, Joe. I hope she's worth it. . . .*

There was a riot of mixed pots, then nothing, then Boston blared forward from the oppressive silence. Joey must have taken over for her. Mac shook his head, rolled the dial over to the country station, and headed east on Canyon Ferry Road, balancing his coffee on a stack of library books in the passenger seat. He figured he'd have time to finish the Heinlein and start the new Asimov after he switched into Larry King.

Out at the Swamp, he paused to adjust the crackly FM monitor as he passed by. " . . . climb that 'Stairway to Heaven.'"

Joey must have talked her through it. Guys at the Swamp were going to be plenty pissed off, too. At least the guys who lived to rock the big time but ended up nursing Dead Fred, the AM board. Mac sat down by the monitor and opened his coffee. The girl's stiff liner card patter betrayed her raw nerves, but the voice itself was low and melodic, and as the night went on, she seemed to get more comfortable.

"CBS Network News of the world at eleven and Mystery Theater with Tammy Grimes happens right here at twelve-oh-seven," and her Tammy Grimes imitation was pretty accurate. "VA Lones here with the best rock in the Rockies on 98.9 FM." She neatly pegged the vocal post at the front of Eric Clapton's "I Shot the Sheriff," dropped in at the end to top-hour ID, and went to the news as slick as could be. She might not be as bad as they all thought.

"Did you hear the bitch?" The evening jock kicked out of the control room and checked the wire, plugged two quarters into the pop machine, and pounded the front of it when his Dr. Pepper didn't hit the chute quickly enough.

"Chunk gets shitfaced and walks out, so Troy moves up to evenings and I should've been next in line to go downtown, but no—Joey calls up this bitch who's been hanging around there. I bet she's blowin' him right now."

Mac shrugged.

"Fuck, man . . . *listen to her!*" The kid cranked the monitor to a painful decibel level. Fleetwood Mac was wringing out the end of "Rhiannon" as the girl goaded, "OK, Stevie, get over it already. . . . VA Lones on 98.9 FM, KRNR . . . Let's take it back to 1971 with clan McCartney—"

We're so sorry . . .

"Ah, that's OK, Paul."

Uncle Albert . . .

"It was Yoko's fault."

We're so sorry if we caused you any pain . . .

Paul dropped back in, obeying her like a trained monkey.

Mac couldn't believe she'd worked a donut on a cold intro. First night, and she works a donut. The AM kid sulkily turned down the monitor.

"The female voice is electronically incompatible," he said. "It's been scientifically proven—chicks don't belong on the air."

"Yeah," Mac said, "you can't argue with scientifical proof."

The kid glared, not quite getting it but suspecting the old guy was making fun of him.

"You've got dead air," Mac added calmly, and as the kid exploded into a cursing, lunging whirl of flying soda fizz, Mac decided he sort of enjoyed doing that. The kid was a smartass, strutting around the local night spots: "Yeah, I'm a dejay." Twenty-one and still living with Mom and Dad in the ol' double-wide. At that age, Mac had been to Korea and back, married Lorene, and moved to Germany. And he never came home to stay until he was shot.

Pa Roy had known he was back in town. Mac saw the old man once at Quality Implements, and the sound of him barking about the price of pitchforks somehow froze Mac behind the tall rack of Big Yank overalls. Pa Roy went on to set another rancher straight on how buffalo infect domestic animals with brucellosis, and then they were talking about the war.

"I don't give a good goddamn what the hippies and Democrats say," the other farmer was grousing, "they shoulda just dropped the goddamn bomb."

"Shoulda minded their own goddam business in the first place," Pa Roy countered.

"All that to piss out at the last minute. Not the way we did it over in the Pacific, that's for damn sure. Cal's boy—he's comin' home, but he ain't got no legs on him. Cal got a letter saying he got 'em blown off."

"Yeah, we got one of them letters."

"Sarah's boy? He hurt bad?"

"Dead." Pa Roy spoke the word like the stroke of an ax.

"Jesus Christ," the other rancher said, "how'd Satchi take it?"

"Ah, she's so bad now she don't know her ass from a hole in the ground."

"First Sarah, now her boy. I'm sorry for ya, Royal. It's a damn shame."

Pa Roy peeled worn bills off the tight roll from his pocket. He moved past the Big Yanks with the pitchfork on his shoulder. Mac saw his grandfather's face under the same old Stetson, deeply lined, tanned like boot leather. He wore the same buckskin greatcoat he'd worn since anyone who knew him could remember. Fringes, beadwork, Satchi's careful stitching and restitching around the yoke.

It smelled like smoke and cinnamon and wind in the night mountains.

======

"So I'm going, '*Pot it up!*' and she's looking like—*whaaaaagh!*" Joey contorted his face, aping Tulsa's panic.

"OK!" She punched his arm. "But I got going once I got going, right?"

"You sure did, hon," Anne Marie hugged her and Jack clapped her on the back. Rina popped the cork from a cheap bottle of cold duck, while Colter stuck stems on the bottoms of plastic champagne glasses. "And Joey, I remember your first night—"

"Shut up, Annie, or I'll get the pictures of you in your maternity swimsuit."

"He's giving this public service announcement," she continued, undaunted, "and he goes, 'The Boulder Singles Club will have their next mating—'"

"'Me first!'" Rina and Jack chimed in on what was evidently a favorite anecdote.

"See," Joey explained over the uproar, "it was supposed to be 'their next *meeting, May* first.'" Tulsa could tell the story still held some sting for him. "I was as scared as you were, Tulsa, and I didn't recover as well. Geez—I was thrashing for months. Seriously, I'm telling you guys, this girl's a natural."

"This *woman*," Rina upbraided him.

"Well now," Jack poured more champagne, "I guess we won't be hearing any more about how shy you are!"

"But it's not me! It's someone who can say things I'd never have the guts to come out with," Tulsa tried to explain. "Nobody can see me, so I can make them see anything I want. So what if I have a figure like Chunk's—my voice is five-foot-six with long blond hair and gigongous gahunnas."

"I should try this," Rina said.

They raised a toast to Tulsa's good fortune and performance, and Tulsa reveled both in the moment and in the luxury of sharing it with friends, lingering, laughing in the entryway until almost three, when Oakley started crying inside and everyone suddenly realized how late it was. Rina and Colter hugged Tulsa and congratulated her again, Joey reminded her that she owed him a beer, and they all went to their private corners of the house.

Upstairs, Tulsa paced, played guitar a little, and paced more, far too wired to go to bed. She lay in the bathtub, replaying every bit, every song, every segue over and over in her head. She thought about her father and wondered if he'd like to know that she was really in broadcasting now, just like him. Wondered if maybe she should even call him up so they could talk radio.

She raided the fridge and did situps but kept circling back to the phone. Jeanne would be relieved to know she had a steady job. Aaron would laugh to hear how she had almost bolted like the Cowardly Lion. He always said how he loved her voice, how it was "smooth as lecithin in a chocolate bar." She went and pulled down the Murphy bed and circled back to the phone. She washed dishes in the kitchen and circled back again. This time she picked it up, dialing the area code and long-distance information. The operator sounded like someone who'd rather be home in bed.

"Minneapolis, please," said Tulsa, "for Taylor . . . Aaron . . . P."

"Do you know what street it's on?"

"Penniwell?" she hazarded, "or somewhere near the UM campus."

"Well, I don't know what's near the campus. I need a street."

"I'm sorry."

"I have an A. R. on Medicine Lake . . . an A. L. on Hennipen . . . A. Proctor—"

"That's it!" Tulsa felt startled. "Aaron Proctor Taylor. The Third."

A computer recording gave Tulsa the number, so she didn't have a chance to explain to the operator that she wasn't really going to call him at three-thirty in the morning just to tell him she wore normal jeans now, walking up and down streets with hills, that she had an interesting job, and that people liked her. That if he heard her on the radio, he'd know what he was missing.

Tulsa dialed the area code and hung up. She picked up again, sat back in the rocker, and listened to the dial tone until it turned to a piercing shrill. She clicked the button down with one finger but held the receiver against her chest. Moments passed. Tulsa's head bobbed forward, and she realized she was falling asleep. Chiding herself for being so stupid, she hung up the phone, undressed, and crawled into bed.

The northern lights were out, turning the predawn all theatrical, and Tulsa had a full view from her round fortress. She didn't even have to sit up. She just lay there, drifting between dreams and the aurora until the dreams became irresistible because Aaron was there. Shaking his head, he took the phone from her cheek and left it shrilling on the floor. He showed her in the phone book where it specifies guidelines for calling people who are no longer interested in you. Tulsa's father was listed there, along with aunts and grandparents she never knew. The name Alexandra Firestein had been crossed out, but Jeanne had penciled her name in parentheses beside it with a languid left-handed stroke. Nannies, acquaintances, rabbis, and English professors had all signed the register, some using red to note specific hours they did not wish to be bothered with her. Tulsa scanned the list for Aaron's name.

"Don't call us, we'll call you," Aaron said. He smoothed her hair away from her face before he faded into the pulsing lights of the studio. Grasping for carts, stabbing at green buttons, Tulsa kept missing them completely or caving them through the front of the brittle machines. Then Joey roared in on his Harley and they beamed on down the white-lined highway.

. . . do ya love me, now that I . . .

Weeks passed before Tulsa could relax enough to sit on the edge of the barstool in the studio. She stood facing the console with her eyes fixed on the event timer, the cart decks, the panel of sliding pots and meters, intimidated, exhilarated, piloting her unseen dirigible. At first she wrote everything down on a yellow legal pad but soon found that if she let go, the music gave birth to the words and the night took its own course. There was no one to please or not, no one to love her or not, only the microphone and wide open atmosphere, limitless beyond the padded pop screen.

The incompatible voice of VA Lones did not go unnoticed. Something different on the generally subliminal plane of radio came out of the background and tripped people up like a crack in the sidewalk. They turned it up. They stood at the counter in the 7-11 for an extra moment. By springtime, VA's patter and catchphrases had infected the talk of local adolescents, and her favorite album cuts started sounding familiar. By the end of summer, Tulsa was thoroughly in love with the job and had even gotten a raise. She got better at doing different voices, and clients started asking for VA Lones on their commercials; that was something Dallas could take to the bank. Joey enjoyed shaking things up a little and was pleased that he no longer had to worry about covering the shift, Anne Marie was happy that apartment 5 finally couched a solid citizen, and Tulsa walked to the station singing every night.

She taped phone bits and ran them on the air, teasing, insulting, wooing whoever was on the other end.

"VA, I'm hungry for some Meatloaf!"

"You got it, little metalhead," and Meatloaf would be there. "High-cholesterol music for those who are no longer satisfied by the emotional tofu of the disco decade . . . "

"Hey, VA, are you as sexy as you sound?"

"Naaa. I'm ugly and my mother dresses me funny. Did you call to make a request, or are you just suffering from the heartbreak of pariah-sis?"

"Well, like, I already called like ten times for the Knack, OK? You know, like, 'Should I Stay or Should I Go.'"

"OK, *like*—you should go. . . . " *Click.* The album pounded in, and VA toughed out the heavy beat. "*Like* I say he goes and *like* he goes, peaceniks." She had a way of talking with the rhythm, making herself part of the music. "It's my show, Sharona. Get the Knack!"

. . . ma-ma-ma-mah-eeey Sharona . . .

VA Lones could get away with stuff like that. VA Lones was hot. Tulsa grew immune to the men and boys who called to ask what was

she wearing or would she meet them at Casino Jack's. They were pre-
dictable enough that she soon had six or seven automatic comebacks,
a few of which could even be used on the air. Adolescents pulling
pranks, women telling her it was about time there was a woman on the
air, people of all sorts telling her that girls didn't belong on the radio
or that they didn't like her opinion on one thing or another; the
phone stayed alive until almost two-thirty every morning. The invita-
tions Tulsa politely refused. The requests she hunted for. The compli-
ments she took with a large grain of salt, and the "rations of crap" she
ignored, just like Joey told her to. Tulsa stoically endured the chilly
jock meetings, pretending she didn't get the rude jokes, refusing to be
baited into political arguments, and avoiding conflicts of any kind. Her
coworkers eventually tired of the Freeze Out VA campaign; one night,
Troy actually stood around to shoot the bull during the first ten minutes of Mystery Theater.

The backstage dusk of the night radio station was her domain,
where she was free to sing harmony to the music and talk to herself,
practicing bits out loud before she ran them up the on-air flagpole, but
she was glad to hear Joey's Harley roar up the street every morning.
She waved to him through the hall window as he headed for the little
office with the glass-topped desk. She tried not to think about what he
was doing in there. They'd never spoken about the white lines again,
and Tulsa felt stupid for not figuring out sooner the source of his electric energy and oppressive periods of silence. It was none of her business.

. . . so on and so on . . . shooby dooby dooby . . .

Joey whirled through the studio, pulling his music, parodying Sly
and the Family Stone, trying to crack Tulsa up while she was doing the
weather, tearing down the hall at five minutes till, spilling coffee and
trailing teletype copy.

"Hey, VA? High school basketball tournament scores," he called,
rifling the garbage can in the newsroom. "I need 'em."

"I don't have them," Tulsa said. "I changed the paper in the teletype a while ago, so it was off for a bit."

"Shit. Get 'em for me, please? I'm gonna be busy in my office for a
few minutes. Just call the Swamp, OK?"

Tulsa ran her finger down the posted directory until she came to the number. While she waited for an answer, she couldn't help giggling at the derogatory things written by the names of various people on the personnel list. She stopped smiling when she noticed that whatever had been written next to her name was blotted out with black china marker.

"KRNR AM, Peter MacMurphy." The sleepy voice jarred her attention back to the matter at hand.

"Oh, hi. Um, Peter, do you have the high school tournament scores?"

"Ah, is this the famous VA Lones?"

"Well," Tulsa couldn't tell if he was being mean-sarcastic or just teasing, "it's the VA Lones part, anyway . . . sort of."

"Just a minute," he yawned, "I'll get the scores."

Tulsa waited for a minute or two but had to set the phone down to do the weather, punch up her last song, and do her final bit for the morning. She picked it up when she was through and heard him in the distance doing weather. Then music was playing, but she couldn't tell if he'd picked her up again or not.

"Peter?" she prompted.

"It's Mac."

"Sorry. I had to set you down for a minute."

"Not to worry. So. Sounds like you've got a handle on things over there."

"Thanks," was her automatic response now.

"I caught that first night—"

"Oh, no. The airshift that will live in infamy."

"Hey," Mac laughed, "I've listened time to time. I'm impressed."

"Thank you. I appreciate that." Tulsa shifted the phone to her other ear, wanting to redirect the conversation. "So you're my AM counterpart?"

"Well, I babysit Larry King, which pretty well runs itself."

"I don't know why everybody whines about working at the Swamp. Who wouldn't rather be a button monkey instead of actually working for—" The moment Tulsa realized what she was saying, she naturally started babbling. "I mean—you know—not that anybody thinks that—"

"It's OK," Mac said, so gently that Tulsa suddenly and uncomfortably felt as if he were a real person. She silently blessed him for moving quickly and casually on to a new subject. "Actually, I enjoy the excuse to plunder my local library by day and drink the blood of my latest victims by night."

"Anne Rice?"

"Yes!" Mac was pleasantly surprised. "And I'm always pleased to make the acquaintance of a fellow philobiblist. How are you on Tolkien?"

"*The Hobbit* and all the ring stuff, but *Silmarillion* was like slogging through a marsh."

"Stephen King?"

"No thanks!" Tulsa was emphatic. "In fact, I generally don't do scary books. Or movies. Godzilla is about as far as I go."

"You've got to be kidding."

"Hey, I have a theory about Godzilla. . . . "

Mac was just responding that this he had to hear when Joey pushed past the door and pointed to the clock above the console. The news was almost over.

"Share your theories over a beer," he groused, "I need my scores."

Tulsa nodded and made room for him behind the board. "Mac—I need those scores. Joey's got his undies in a bundle."

"Hey, Mac," Joey took the phone from Tulsa's hand, "you tryin' to move in on my girl?" He guffawed at whatever it was Mac said in response. "Five-six, long blond hair, gigongous gahunnas."

"Joey," Tulsa nudged him.

"No, just my neighbor . . . Forget it, man, she's too young for you. Anyway, I think she's lesbo."

"*Joey!*" she hissed, not sure why her face was suddenly burning.

"Oh, man, that's pathetic. You're a lonely, lonely guy, aren't you, Macmeister." He laughed some more. "OK, scores, man, I'm in a hurry here."

Gathering her notebook and *Rolling Stone Encyclopedia of Rock and Roll*, Tulsa left without waving to Joey, but he was intently copying down the scores and sparring with Mac and waved without knowing he was being ignored. She stopped in at the No Sweat, but nobody felt like talking that morning. The sun was up and out of the haze as she made her way up the hill. Anne Marie was on the porch clapping mud off Mary Laur's pastel blue sneakers.

"Morning, Tulsa!" She waved and motioned her in. "Want some tea?" Tulsa shook her head. "Why so glum?"

"I don't know. . . . I just hate VA Lones sometimes."

"What do you mean?" Anne Marie brushed the last of the mud crumbs from between the tracks on the bottom of the shoe. "You are VA Lones."

"No, I'm not! She's my evil twin. Now nobody wants to know *me*."

"Tulsa, you're the first person I've ever met who's jealous of herself." Anne Marie went in with the shoes, and Colter came out in his heavy sweats, stretching for his morning run.

"Hey, Tul, I got that stuff in the mail."

"That's good," she answered absently.

"Problem is—they say I can't take the GED test until I'm eighteen."

Tulsa looked up at him in surprise. "You aren't eighteen?"

"Not for a couple months."

"Aren't you supposed to be worrying your parents or playing basketball or going to the hop or something?"

"I'm not real big on the 'supposed to' thing. My parents are basically cool, but . . . " He placed his palms on the doorframe and pressed, flexing, extending. "I'm better off here. Long story, as they say."

"Hmm," she sighed. "Well, let's keep studying anyway."

He nodded and squinted toward the rising sun. "Rina and I are taking the kids to see *Bambi* tonight at Second Story Cinema." He bent to tie his sneaker, adding, "We could use another grownup. You know how it is with the Gang of Four."

"Sure. That would be fun."

"OK. Well, see ya later then."

"See ya," Tulsa called, but he was already off the porch, jogging up the street toward the Mount Helena trailhead.

"See ya," she said again and went in.

―――――――

Mac waited a couple days, looking for a reason to call VA, but nothing obvious presented itself. He was annoyed with himself for thinking about it, with all the work he had to do.

The place was shaping up fairly well, all things considered. The walls were lined as high as he could reach with bookshelves made of stacked-up bricks and boards. The fireplace looked less crumbled with the woodstove installed in it, and Mac finally worked up enough nerve to go in and take Pa Roy's Regulator clock from the front room. The bunkhouse was cold, even with the woodstove from the big house kitchen, so Mac invested in a small kerosene unit, but he hated the way it ate up the oxygen in the room and he worried about it being near the refinishing chemicals he was using on the old table and chairs. He finally had the outbuildings at a point where he could start thinking about animals, chickens and a few sheep for starters. He planted his first year of alfalfa and had already started seedlings and mapped out a plan for the garden—an eclectic patchwork of vegetables, legumes, and marijuana.

Plenty to think about without VA Lones on the brain, but somehow, every time he hit a commercial break, her voice cropped up in one form or another—everything from a sultry Russian spy to Captain Bob's spokeschicken. The other FM jocks, who had at least come around to tolerating her presence, were always promo-ing her show just so they could toss in some clever innuendo or other. "Wouldn't you love to spend the night with VA Lones?" It bothered Mac. Or maybe she bothered him. He felt like he'd heard the first seven notes of an octave and that last one was hanging out there just beyond earshot.

After the chicken bit, Mac came in with his midnight weather and brought up the network. The private line was blinking. Dick Richards liked to call and catch people napping, so Mac figured he'd better answer it.

"KRNR AM," he said with little enthusiasm.

"So, do you want to hear my Godzilla theory or not?"

Mac sat bolt up straight, accidently kicked his coffee, and dropped his cigarette in it as he lunged to catch the cup before it went over. It took him a moment to realize he should be saying something.

"Mac? Are you there?"

"Hi." He shook his hand to throw off the scalding coffee. "Aren't you supposed to be inspiring the rock and roll fantasies of our local youth?"

"Mystery Theater's on."

"Well, you little button monkey, you."

"Mac, I'm sorry about that."

She sounded so uncharacteristically timid, Mac wanted to tell her he'd been thinking about her, that he was glad she called.

"Not to worry," he said instead, "tell me about Godzilla."

"Well," she began in a tone that made him lean back and put his feet up again, "it's about empowerment. Here's a culture that's just been bombed to smithereens, defeated, stripped of the dignity around which their lives revolve. Enter Godzilla, a seemingly invincible enemy. He gives them something to conquer, vanquish, destroy! He's a cinematic messiah, sacrificing himself to empower them. And they loved him for it. He became a good guy in the later films, you know. It's because we all need dragons to slay. It's the reason poets want to suffer and old people want to talk about their perforated spleen or tell you how terrible it was growing up poor and rural. Validation comes from facing a seemingly invincible enemy. Think about it—Ulysses, Beowolf, *Gone with the Wind*—*Bambi*, for Pete's sake . . . "

Drifting between what she was saying and the pure blue-violet sound of her voice, Mac made a mental note not to tell her that he grew up poor and rural, though his spleen was intact, as far as he knew.

"Are you still there?" She sounded unsure again.

"Mmm-hmm. Just mulling."

"Oh."

"So how did you come to this startling revelation?"

"Just mulling."

There was a brief silence.

"Ever seen a bull snake?" Mac asked.

"No," she said. "Why? Do you have one there?"

"Not unless you count Dick Richards." Mac liked the sound of her laughter—like the creek when it trips on a riffle. "I saw one under my truck this evening."

"Really?"

"Seven feet or more."

"Did you kill it?"

"Why would I do that?"

"You saw no reason to kill a seven-foot snake? What if it bit a little child or ate a—a cat or something?"

"I hate cats," Mac replied, "and I'm not that keen on little children either."

"Oh," she said.

"Bull snakes keep the rattlers down. And if I let him grow till fall, he might get big enough to make a new cover for my guitar case."

"Terribly clever of him," VA quipped. "So how did you like *Interview with the Vampire?*"

"Well," Mac considered how to put it, "I couldn't stop thinking about the tree that gave its life."

"You're kidding!" she cried, sounding so disappointed that Mac wished he'd lied. "I thought it was brilliant, and I don't even like scary books!"

"Well, you're safe with that one."

"Oh, I get it—she's exploring the psychosexual ramifications of being a vampire and you're saying, 'Ya call dis art?'" VA did her Butchie the Trucker dialect. "'C'mon, lady! Rip somebody's head off!'"

"I calls 'em as I sees 'em, kid."

"Oh, Mac. The disillusionment. I thought you were a 'fellow philo-biblist.' I even looked that up in the dictionary," and to prove it, she added, "It means book lover."

"Yeah. I saw it on one of those word-of-the-day calendars."

"So . . . " she reached, "you play guitar, huh?"

"Yeah."

"Me too."

"Yeah? Maybe sometime—"

"So how long have you been working out at the Swamp?" she interrupted.

Mac lit another cigarette. He didn't like dancing around this way but had the good sense to give her the elbow room. He'd already decided that if, in addition to that voice, VA Lones had the attributes to attract Joey's attention, she'd be worth the trouble. Between plugging in commercial carts and pausing for weather, the conversation meandered on to the best pawnshops in town, trees in backyards of houses they grew up in, Dante's seven levels of Hell, the book he was reading, the book she was reading, and whether or not a degree in the liberal arts has any marketable value.

"Where did you go to school?" Mac asked her.

"School o' Hard Knocks, man. Damn. Hard. Knocks." VA knocked on her console, and Mac laughed. "Let's see, I majored in English at Minneapolis, switched to art history at Berkeley, and then dropped out. How about you?"

"Got about halfway through an English lit degree at Carroll right here in tropical Hell-enough. I'm not sure what I expected to do with it. Not this."

"Now you're going to tell me you don't like radio either?"

"Would you like to hear my theory about radio?"

"I'm sure it's blasphemy, but go ahead."

"I think Theater and Music got drunk and laid down together one night, and the brain-damaged bastard offspring of that union was raised to a state of perpetual adolescence by a pack of used-car salesmen. That's Radio."

"Oh, Mac," she was only laughing a little, "really?"

"I'm not into it the way you are, VA." Mac was amused that she sounded so disappointed. "It's a job you're supposed to either get really good at or outgrow. These days, I mostly concentrate on my ranch, anyway."

"You have a ranch?"

"Well, technically, my grandfather has a ranch, but he's been in an old folks' home for about eight years. So I will eventually have a ranch—if the petrified old fart ever kicks off."

"So sentimental," she chided.

"He's not a real sentimental cowboy." Hearing the finality in his voice, Tulsa didn't feel free to ask further. "You don't sound like you're from Berkeley," Mac headed her off. "Doesn't that make you a Valley girl?"

"I grew up in San Francisco, mainly, but I lived in Peoria when I was real little. Then New York, New Haven . . . and France. Cape Cod for summers. Mexico sometimes. And Minneapolis."

"Was your father in the service?"

"I wouldn't know," she replied sharply. "Why do people always ask that?"

"Because they're idiots." Mac hoped it sounded like an apology.

"How 'bout you?" she asked.

"I'm not an idiot."

"I mean, where are you from?" A giggle rippled through the question; he liked it a little more each time she did that, he decided.

"I was born and raised just north of town. Never left Montana till I was sixteen. And I never met anyone who was born in Peoria."

"You still haven't. I was born in Tulsa, Oklahoma. Hence the name."

"How do you get Virginia Lones out of—?"

"I'm not Virginia Lones!"

"Oh, no—of course not." Mac hesitated for a moment, wondering if she wanted to be asked. "Who are you?"

"I just told you." A little more of her soft laughter spiraled through the phone line. "Tulsa. Are you really Mac?"

"MacPeters, not MacMurphy. Chalk that one up to His GM-in-ence. I guess he had a dog by that name at some point. A mangy one he didn't like."

"Hey, I know a MacPeters. Colter MacPeters? Do you know him?"

"Not nearly as well as I'd like to." Mac consciously weighed it and decided to add, "He's my son."

"Oh." Her questions hung almost tangibly in the air.

Mac cleared his throat. "Guess we all have our myriad identities, don't we."

"Ooo, Mac," VA's Brooklyn bimbo voice let them laugh again, "how meta-fizzy-cal!" but then she said sincerely, "I like Colter. I like him a lot."

"Me too. He's a good kid."

"Yeah. I'm helping him study for his GED."

"His—you are?" Mac said, unpleasantly surprised and a little jealous; Colter hadn't mentioned dropping out of school, and he never asked Mac for help with anything. "That's very generous of you."

"Not at all. In exchange, he's making me matching cups and plates and these great wine goblets. I just have random Salvation Army stuff right now."

"Nothin' wrong with ol' Sally Anne," Mac said philosophically, "but Colter's stuff is special. He was born in Japan." Mac needed to reassure himself that he was privy to a few things about Colter that weren't common knowledge.

"Yes, I know," Tulsa said. There was a little silence before she gently added, "He said his father was in the service."

"Yeah." Mac dug for a cigarette. "So, what in the name of Casey Kasem made you call yourself VA Lones?"

"Joey got it out of the yellow pages." Tulsa gladly went back to the safer topic. "Veteran's Administration Loans." Mac seemed to get a particular kick out of that. "At first, I felt weird about the whole air-name thing, but now I'm glad. I don't want to be VA Lones all day. It's too much work. If people thought that was me, they'd expect me to be—I don't know—funny or interesting or something. I like being the last one in disguise at the Mardi Gras."

"That's an unusual attitude for a jock," Mac said. "They usually do more broadcasting in the bars than they do on the air."

"And I hate being called a jock!" Tulsa lamented. "A jock is something guys put over their genitals." She quickly added, "I'll thank you not to touch that."

"Not with a vaccinated cattle prod," Mac shot back. "But in this business, you've gotta be careful where you leave such attractive openings."

"And there's another one! You see what happens?"

"It's tomfoolery like this that gets people hurt, missy." It felt good to spar with her.

"Before this conversation gets any worse, I think I'll make a graceful exit. I'm already into my newsbreak, anyway."

"VA—" Mac started.

"Tulsa. For real people, I'm Tulsa." Her tone was warm enough to feel for a moment. "But only for another ninety seconds! I gotta go, Mac." She was VA again, but before she hung up, she added, "Talk to you later?"

"Yeah."

It was half question, half casual; Mac wasn't sure if it meant to call or be called, but he recognized it didn't matter. They'd connect one way or another.

With the resoundingly empty receiver still against his face, he realized how the full, real quality of her voice had filled his head, how he could feel it in his brain stem, sinuses, and jaw. He finally put his finger on the reason why VA Lones was riding around in everybody's car, sitting at everybody's kitchen table, reclining unseen in bedrooms and bathrooms and the intimate confines of stereo headphones: something about her voice. Something unpolished, easy, and welcoming. Mellow and low, without being forced or throaty, it was clean and clear as cold water and moved with the same tumbling presence. There were no demands in it, no expectations. Just an open-ended octave that left Mac hanging on for one more.

4

The private line lit up at 12:10, just as Tulsa brought up the pot on CBS Mystery Theater. She'd come to anticipate the moment the way you look forward to Sunday or dessert or your favorite comic strip each day.

"This is VA Lones."

"''Tis a beauteous evening calm and free.'"

"Wow, onto the classics tonight," she teased him. "What's the matter, library out of Clive Barker?"

"Well, if you can't get your money's worth, at least—"

"—you get your Wordsworth," Tulsa chimed in. "Boo hiss. But I'll overlook it. This time." Tulsa stretched the coiled phone cord and settled back in her chair. "OK, Mac—I've been saving this for you all day—"

"Oh, boy."

"What did the zen master say to the hot dog vendor?"

"I'm baffled, VA," Mac said, like a good vaudeville straight man. "What *did* the zen master say to the hot dog vendor?"

"'Make me one with everything!'"

Mac rewarded her with a generous hoot. "You're improving."

"All these months of hanging out with you, I guess."

"I guess," Mac said, and cleared his throat, trying to sound off hand. "So . . . Colter told me he passed his test."

"Yes!" Tulsa sprang forward from her chair. "I'm so proud of him, Mac! He really worked hard for this."

"I know. And you did too. I want to thank you for that, Tulsa. He wouldn't have done it without you."

"Oh, of course he would."

"Bullshit," Mac cut in. "Now, can't you just say 'you're welcome' without a bunch of self-deprecating horsecrap?"

"You're welcome without a bunch of self-deprecating horsecrap."

"Better," he nodded. "So, when do we celebrate? Seems like this calls for pomp and circumstance of some sort."

"Well, actually," Tulsa answered uncomfortably, "umm . . . Lorene—Colter's mom . . . "

"Yes, I know."

"We just—at the house—at Anne Marie's—they just had a . . . a small kind of . . . get-together kind of . . . thing."

"Ah-huh."

"I'm sorry, Mac."

"Not to worry," he said, and Tulsa heard the hitch of his lighter. "I guess she's used to covering all the bases."

"Yeah, I guess."

"So . . . " He inhaled deeply and the chairs creaked on both ends of the line as they leaned back, preparing to talk for the customary hour until Tulsa's airshift started gaining momentum and Mac retreated with his latest library find into the automated comfort of the Larry King Show.

"Do you have a window?" Tulsa asked when it was almost time to hang up.

"Nope. This place is like a crypt."

"Then you should go look out the door," she told him. "It's snowing."

"Ah," Mac smiled and closed his eyes so he could see it. "It's gonna be a good year, Tulsa. Lots of moisture."

"It's really coming down now," Tulsa went on, "piling up on the boulevard all down the Gulch, all heavy and quiet . . . you can see it falling across the streetlights, making that big halo—is it light or shadow? I can't decide."

Mac turned toward her words, and he could almost feel the sound on his face, fleeting, cool, and soothing. He drifted with the way she brought the image billowing out of the immense night sky like a tranquil white parachute settling over his dark studio.

"It feels like the sky is falling."

"Mmm-hmm," he willed her to go on, and she did.

"Like we're the people inside a glass snow globe, angels or Elvis . . . Mr. and Mrs. Santa . . . living in all this quiet commotion. . . . "

"That's why you have to shake things up once in a while."

"Mac," she asked, "are you too hip to believe in Heaven?"

He didn't answer, and she fell silent until a long, involuntary sigh fogged the wide glass window, reminding her which side she was living on.

"Are you still there?" she asked.

"I'm always here," Mac said, and there was another silence.

"'Tis a beauteous evening,'" she finally said.

"'Calm and free.'"

"You know what you are, Mac?" Tulsa confided from the safe distance of her dimly lit studio. "You're my kindred spirit."

"Is that anything like a blood brother?"

"Well, yeah," she considered it and added, "only more sanitary."

Mac laughed a little but didn't reply.

"Well," she said, "I really should go."

"Thanks again for helping Colter."

"Oh, c'mon, we just—" She felt an ursine rumble from the other end of the line. *"You're welcome."*

"Much better. I owe you a beer."

"Yeah."

"Yup."

"OK . . . well. Hey, don't forget to look at the snow, OK?"

"Right."

"OK . . . well . . . I guess I'd better get to it."

"Talk to ya later, VA."

"Yeah."

Tulsa set the phone down and stared at it for a bit, then turned to the board. As she wove through the night, it felt different somehow. Beyond the snow and space and stars, beyond the microphone, the air had a texture now, a comfortable voice, a name.

The snow was melting when morning came. Tulsa walked home, leaving squelching sounds and pooling footprints through the clean, quiet streets. As the sunrise stretched up the mountainside behind the house, she sat on the porch swing listening to the trickling, thawing sounds that came up in proportion with the warm morning wind.

The chinook breeze brought a gentle illusion of spring that persisted for three days. It teased and played with people, singing a siren's
song; it coaxed them to ride their bicycles down the hill to see them
wipe out on the slushy corner, enticed them to wear shorts to ridicule
their chilly, chapped knees. There was an unspoken urgency, an understanding that this moment of delight came at the dear price of another punishing dose of Montana winter. Colter had warned her a year
ago that everyone gets a little bit nuts when the chinook winds blow.
And Joey was a little bit nuts to begin with.

The third day of the chinook, Tulsa waited for him on the swing.
The mailman came and whistled away. Jack finished tying a batch of
flies and went out fishing. Anne Marie sprayed the porch floor and
washed the downstairs windows. Rina came home for lunch and went
back to the station, and still no Joey. A little after noon, Colter came
out with pottery smuck on his jeans and sat down beside her.

"Past your bedtime, isn't it, Tulsa?"

"Yes," she answered flatly.

"Don't wreck yourself over it. He'll show up."

Just looking at the steps convinced Tulsa she was too tired to climb.

"Colter, did you know Joey is . . . " She stopped, in search of the
best possible phrasing.

"Joey's . . . what?" Colter prompted, and started guessing when she
didn't respond. "Are you guys sleeping together or something?"

"Of course not!"

"Then what?" Colter sounded impatient.

"Just that he—he has a habit—"

"He's a toot fiend."

"Don't make it sound like that!"

"Well, how should I make it sound, Tul?" Colter looked perplexed,
and to his horror, she started crying. He stood, holding up his smucky
hands, not knowing if he should hug her and get her all messy. "Geez.
Cut it out now, OK? C'mon . . . " He opted to put his arms around her,
and she didn't seem to mind the smudge of gray slime on her shirt. "It's
not like this is the first time anyone went on a bender. Some people
just need to blow off steam once in a while. You can't let it get to you.
You'll go nuts if you let yourself think there's something you can do
about it."

"When he didn't show up this morning, I didn't know what to do. I called everywhere I could think of. But at seven o'clock, Dallas came in and there was nothing I could say, Colter. What was I supposed to say? He got Dick Richards to cover the shift. He's going to fire him."

"He won't," Colter said with certainty, "I don't know how he does it, but Joey can jolly that old man around just about anything. Rina says it's 'cause clients love him. Always want him at live remotes and on their ads and stuff, and that counts for a lot of money. Last time he did this, they tracked him down in Spokane, partying with another jock and these women they picked up in Chawelah. The guy he was with got fired, but Joey actually ended up getting a raise. They'll bust him down to some crummy shift and let someone else be PD for a while, and eventually he'll be back on Dallas's sunny side. You'll see. Just mind your own business. Get some sleep and get up and go to work and let Joey take care of himself. He's a big boy."

"Yeah, I guess." She sounded neither comforted nor convinced but went in and climbed the stairs, past Joey's barren apartment, up to her own.

Tulsa slept with the windows open, listening in her sleep for the roar of the Harley. She awoke cold and headachy before the clock radio popped off and sat in the clawfoot tub, staring at the soap swirls. Hanging her head upside down over the heat register to dry her hair intensified the dull pressure behind her eyes. She pulled on jeans with a big tie-dyed shirt, climbed into her Irish wool sweater, and trudged down the hill toward Last Chance Gulch. She passed the Serendipity Apartments, where Joey sometimes stayed with a particular girl, but there was no light in her window and no Harley in the parking lot.

Troy waved from the half light of the studio as Tulsa fumbled for her front-door key. She jiggled the door open and felt a flood of relief.

"You juvenile delinquent!" Tulsa strode toward the light in the little office beyond the newsroom. "Where have you been?"

"Excuse me?" Dick Richards looked up from Joey's glass-topped desk.

"Oh. Sorry—I thought . . . Where's Joey?" Tulsa hated how meek it sounded.

"Not here," Dick smiled and made a game show gesture toward a stack of cardboard file boxes in the corner, "but thank you for playing."

No comeback came. Tulsa knew through the grapevine what Dick thought of her, and now he was about to discover his harsh judgments were true: she really was a fat, ugly bull-dyke who had no business being in radio.

"I guess you're 'Vee-Aay' Lones." The name suddenly sounded too stupid for modern civilization. "We didn't really get a chance to talk this morning. I'm Dick Richards."

"Nice to meet you," she mumbled, accepting the sales meeting handshake.

"I'm anxious to talk with you about your show, VA." He gestured to a chair, and she sat. "I really enjoy that refreshing sense of humor of yours."

"Thank you." Tulsa felt herself staring, disarmed by his pleasant tone.

"However, now that the novelty of a female announcer is wearing thin, I'm looking forward to finding ways we can work together to turn our weaknesses into real strengths."

"Oh. Great."

Dick laid a color-coded format clock on the desk along with a stack of cards and some articles photocopied from *Radio and Records*.

"We're implementing a more mature format—adult contemporary music, liners geared to reinforcing audience retention, better information as far as news and weather—obviously, credibility presents a challenge here."

"Credibility?"

"But I think we can solve that by having the evening announcer cart up state and local news for your show. You'll intro and outro him and then do the weather where people can accept a lighter touch."

"Well, I put a lot of prep time into making that state and local news an important part of my show. I build a lot of bits around current events and local politics and offbeat things that come down the wire."

"Oh, I recognize and applaud the effort, VA, but I have to tell you—we've caught some flack about your commentary."

"That just proves people are listening."

"An interesting theory," he smiled, as if he were taking a child by the hand. "But I really feel more of a 'hostess' approach will preserve both continuity and a pleasant, accessible tone."

"I see."

"One less thing for you to worry about." He patted her hand. "In fact, we're going to tighten up the playlist and subscribe to a show prep service."

"I'd rather do my own prep."

"Well, consultants have determined—"

"Most of what I play is requests. Taped phone-bit requests."

"VA, I don't intend to argue programming with someone who's barely gotten her feet wet in the business."

"I've learned a lot in the last year—"

"Well, evidently you haven't learned to take constructive criticism."

"—and I've worked very hard to compensate for people's attitudes—" Tulsa struggled to find some solid ground, but he held up his hand.

"VA, VA, we're both professionals here, so I hope I can be frank."

"Too late. You're already Dick," Tulsa blurted, almost against her own will.

"Look," less than amused, Dick leaned forward with his hands spread on the desktop, "I don't know what you did for Joey that got you this job—" Tulsa felt his eyes on her vacant sweater. "—but I'm not interested in any." It sounded like he'd practiced the speech. "Nor am I interested in your smartass, stream-of-consciousness style of so-called announcing. Bottom line: anyone who isn't able to adhere to the new format will find herself out in the Swamp plugging carts into Larry King. Do we have an understanding?"

Tulsa nodded, stood, and stepped back from the doorway, feeling herself crumbling behind her mask.

"Have a good show." He extended his foot to close the door on her startled expression.

Tulsa's stomach constricted, and the muscles around her lungs ached. She hated the Big Dick for making her feel this way. She hated Joey for being such an irresponsible jerk. But most of all, she hated herself for not telling them both to go to hell. VA Lones wouldn't take crap like that from anybody. VA Lones didn't care what anybody was or wasn't interested in and always had a quick comeback trippingly on her tongue. VA Lones . . . *does not exist*, she reminded herself.

At midnight, Troy beat a hasty retreat, leaving her alone with Mystery Theater and Dick's presence hanging heavily in the air. She

stared at the private line, waiting for 12:10, and when the light
blinked made a grab for it.

"Mac!"

Nothing. Dick had picked up in the office, blocking Tulsa from
the line.

Hang up, Mac. Please, just hang up without saying anything.

The square button stared like a cyclops, then blinked on hold.

"Phone call, VA," Dick crackled across the intercom. "It sounds
personal. Let's not have any more personal calls during airshifts."

Tulsa picked up but somehow couldn't find the voice to speak.

"Tulsa?" Mac sounded concerned. "Tul-saaaa . . . talk to me."

"Do you know where he is?"

"Yes."

"Is he OK?"

"Almost."

"Would you please tell me what is going on?"

"Just relax. I ran into him at the Joker's. He'd been partying since
the weekend, started acting like a yutz, and somebody cleaned his
clock for him, that's all. He'll be in tomorrow morning, and you can
count the stitches on his head."

"He doesn't have to bother coming in," Tulsa hissed. "He doesn't
have a job, Mac. Dick Richards is cleaning out his office right now."

"Tulsa, relax—station politics work themselves out. Give it a few
days. Joey'll land on his feet like he always does." It annoyed her that
he was laughing. "One time, he and I ended up in Chawelah with
these—"

"Yes, I heard. He got his job back and now all the reindeer love
him."

"He'll go down in history."

"According to what I hear, he *is* history."

"Joey's good, and Dallas knows that. He's not going to find anyone
as good as Joey for a long while. He gets more than his money's worth
out of Joey, and for that he's willing to put up with the occasional out-
break of bottle flu. Besides, he's got a strange kind of fatherly affection
for the guy. They've been through a lot together in the last ten years."

"But what if he finds out about the—" she whispered the word—
"cocaine?"

"Tulsa, he knows. He's not a moron."

"Oh! But I am?"

"I didn't say that," Mac cut in curtly. "Look, darlin', people are gonna do what they damn well feel like doing. You don't have anything to say about it."

"What he's doing is self-destructing. Isn't anybody going to say anything about that?"

"Just leave it, Tulsa. What Joey does is Joey's business."

"What's the matter with you? How can you even call yourself his friend? He got you that job. He got me this job. We owe him, Mac. We owe him better than a lousy beer!"

Mac took a long, deep draw on his cigarette. "Joey's a big boy," he said in a way that evidenced the taut set of his jaw. "He can take care of himself."

"You're the second person to tell me that today."

"Then why don't you listen?" He used his horse-gentling voice.

"I've gotta go," Tulsa said abruptly.

"Are you OK on this?" The way he asked made her believe it truly mattered to him, but she didn't want to feel OK on this. She didn't want Mac to make it go away with his soothing tone and even temper. "Tulsa?"

"Fine."

"You need to know that Joey's not the one to worry about here. Richards was against hiring you in the first place, and as it turns out, you're the best thing Joey's done in a long time; that doesn't help."

"I don't need any help."

"No," he said, "I know you don't. You can handle it. Just ride it out. No matter what they do, just swallow the medicine and ride it out. It's just politics. It won't last. It doesn't mean anything."

"Well, not to you, I guess," Tulsa said flatly.

"Tulsa, why don't I swing by there in the morning—"

"Don't bother."

"C'mon. We'll just get some breakfast."

"I said I've gotta go," Tulsa repeated and hung up. She jumped when she saw Dick standing outside the window. He held up his wrist and tapped his watch and mouthed, "No more calls."

Tulsa nodded and turned away, pretending to pull some carts. Her head was throbbing. The request lines rang all night, and she let them, making the motions of an airshift but not really doing anything. She plugged in Troy's news without commenting on it and played songs she hated without ridiculing them: just time, temperature, "this is," "that was."

For a while, she'd forgotten what she was hiding behind the translucent microphone, but the moment his eyes moved from her fly-away hair to her pear-shaped torso, Dick had known she was nothing to be reckoned with. She wasn't what boys in high school called "dating material." She lacked what her mother called "a spark of divine fire." Brave or beautiful; one or the other would have satisfied Tulsa, but she knew she was neither.

She spoke to no one on her way up the hill in the morning, hoping the expression spackled to her face would warn them off like the slicing beam of a lighthouse. She climbed the stairs to her apartment and slid down the inside of the closed door. Her ear to the hardwood floor, she descended into a hollow pod of sound; Colter's pottery wheel, Oakley's plaintive wail, the rush of blood through her own head. She slipped through a crack in the brittle shell into a sleepstate where a growing gray mass of uneasiness waited. Drawing out of the distance, thundering footsteps could be felt. Thudding. Closer. Imminent.

And now, a screech like metal twisting through a guardrail, like heads being split and stitched, clocks being cleaned and formats being followed.

godzilla

———————

The jock meeting at the Swamp took on the mood of an impromptu celebration. Nobody cared much for Dick Richards, and with a morning man on the way out, everyone but Mac expected to move up a shift. After a rousing chorus of "Ding Dong the Dick is Dead" came discussion over who would be the new PD, and everyone but Mac voiced an opinion on why they were uniquely qualified. It ended up being Troy. He was coming over from the FM, and Danny Dukes, the evening kid, whose real name was Walter Wetzenski, was being shuffled over there, much to his jubilation. Mac shuddered at the thought of that kid in the studio with VA, and as if that thought brought her into the room, the discussion turned to the person most likely to be the next to go.

"I give 'er two weeks with the Dick. He says he's gonna blow her out faster than she can shake her little ass."

"Yeah, and remember what he did to that fag from Billings."

"Brrr," they recalled that effective freeze-out with loathing and admiration.

"He was screwed before he sat down."

"He wished!" And they laughed.

"I don't know how she lasted this long anyway—she sucks!"

"That's how she lasted!" More laughter.

"No shit. Everybody knows she licked her way into the job."

"Well, she must give it pretty good 'cause she's a dog."

"No shit?"

"We're talkin' Towser, man." Barking and howling, followed by more laughter.

"I didn't think ol' Joey was that hard up."

"No way is she gonna last—unless she's fucking Dallas too."

The general assembly was amused by the idea of that and continued in the theme, speculating on the possible locations and circumstances of such a liaison and then, tiring of that, cracked open another round of beers and resumed debating who would get her job. Mac sat quietly, relieved to hear that Tulsa would not be promoted to evenings. A self-indulgent part of him wanted her to be held back solely for the sake of that one hour every night he had come to look forward to. Her voice had made its way through the wires into his bloodstream, and the last several Sundays—those being his days off, and hers as well— he found himself sitting on a rocky ledge above the bunkhouse, missing her at midnight, toking his pipe, mulling things they'd said, and waiting for one-ten, when the feeling passed enough for him to go in and read again.

"Mac!" someone called from the hallway newsroom. The whiff of beer and potato chips, blending in the smoky haze with reams of paper and teletype ink, smelled like poker night at a UPI office. "Get your ass in here and have a beer!"

Mac went out and sociably took one and then went back and unsociably closed himself in the control room with Larry King. He didn't like all these bodies in his night space; it made him jumpy, and he re-mained uneasy even after the meeting moved to a bar in town. Weari-ness combined with the beer made it tough to stay awake until nine the next morning. Nonetheless, having promised Berryl that he would clean up Joey's mess if she and Yak would drop the charges against him, he stood outside the Joker's Wild until she drove up in her old Ford half-ton and jangled her keys in the lock.

"You look like hell," she commented matter-of-factly.

"I feel like hell."

"I hope your buddy's planning to come back here and do some ex-plaining to Yak this afternoon. He's gonna have to pony up for that window, not to mention three stools and all those glasses. And his tab. And if he's got any decency, he'll pay Ben Sharkey's tab too. Picking on poor old Ben that way. Couldn't stand up to someone half fit to fight him. Honest to God, I never seen such behavior from a three-year-old."

"I didn't know you served three-year-olds in here, Bee."

"Sure we do." Berryl was riding a real high horse this morning. "On toast with gravy." She started up again, but when she discovered no-body was arguing, the fun went out of it. She drew a beer for Mac, who wordlessly took a trash can over and began picking up pieces of what used to be a stained-glass window. Berryl started sweeping behind the bar. Every once in a while, she came across a shard of glass or a blood-stained napkin and held it high between thumb and forefinger before dropping it into the garbage can. Each new ort gave her fresh reason to shake her head and sigh sanctimoniously at Mac. He went out back, found a sheet of plywood, and, while the early drinkers drifted in, used it to replace the cardboard Yak had slapped up the night before. A few people commented on the fight, but nobody in this crowd really knew Joey that well or cared about the implications of his latest adventure. None of it caused a ripple ten feet outside the station walls.

Ben Sharkey drifted in and sat beside him.

"How is it, Mac?" he grunted, easing his stiff, gangly frame onto a barstool.

"It is," sighed Mac. "How are you doing, Shark?"

"Been better."

"Did you find your tooth?"

"Yeah. Damn thing fell right into my shirt pocket."

"Well, that's good anyway."

"Yeah."

Berryl brought Ben a beer and assured him it was on the house. She even smiled and put a corky coaster under it while pointedly ignoring Mac's empty glass. She was distracted from snubbing him when the phone rang. It was Yak, evidently, and she was evidently not too sweet on what he had to say.

"The hell you say . . . no! I mean it. You're not going fishing and leaving me here to—I don't give a good goddamn how they're rising! I don't care if they're in a goddamn feeding frenzy! You get your butt over here and help me with this mess. . . . That's for the liability insurance? Yakov, I asked . . . Yes, I know, Yak, but we can't even legally open till we get . . . well, yeah . . . and those tap handles." Mollified by whatever it was Yak told her then, she added, "OK, see ya in a few."

She clapped the phone back on the wall and strutted away in her too-tight jeans. Mac and Sharkey stared, caught between sneaking respect for her and deep sympathy for Yak. Mac took the cigarettes from his shirt pocket and offered one to Ben.

"Shark-man, if I ever let a woman paper-train me like that, do me a favor and put a bullet in my skull."

Sharkey *fr-frmphed* and accepted the cigarette.

"I'll be back," Mac said, dismounting from the barstool.

"I'll be here," Ben said, pulling at his beer.

"So will I," Berryl threatened from down the bar, "and so will Yak!"

"I'll talk to Joey. I said I'd talk to him, Bee, and I will."

"Well, you can tell him I'm adding two bottles of Jack Daniels and a peppermint schnapps to that list!" Berryl called. "I just seen the cracks in 'em!"

Mac went out to his truck and raised the back window of the capper. Inside, Joey was still soundly out, and Mac was annoyed to see that he had wet himself on the North Face sleeping bag. He clapped the window down, opened the driver's-side door, and started pushing. When he leaped in to pop the clutch, he barked his shin on the bottom of the door and almost didn't get the engine started. This was not a good day.

Mac drove out toward the hills and stopped on the first healthy in-
cline. He could hear Joey groaning in the back, and he'd been on
enough high-country weekends to recognize that ominous tenor.

"Not in there, you don't!" He bolted to the back of the truck and,
in one swift motion, dropped the tailgate and hauled Joey out by his
boots. Dumping him unceremoniously to the gravel shoulder of the
road, Mac grabbed the back of Joey's leather jacket and rolled him up
on hands and knees, supporting him by his heaving midsection.

"Oh, man—oh—shit . . . " Joey was gasping. His streaming blond
hair was matted with mud, blood, and vomit. One eye was swollen
shut, and the stitches above his ear were bleeding again, stained white
dressing dangling by a tattered strip of surgical tape.

"Take it easy, bro," Mac said, thinking of the times Sharkey had
done the same for him. "You ain't lucky enough to die of it," as Ben
used to say.

"Lemme alone," Joey blurted. Leaning against the truck, Mac let
him stumble a few yards down the road and watched him fall.

"C'mon back, Joe," he called patiently.

"Fuck you. . . . "

Mac sighed and started after him. "C'mon, Joe. Get in the truck."

"I said lemme alone, asshole!" The voice was hardly recognizable,
but the syllables were slightly less slurred. "I got someplace I gotta be."

"Don't make me chase you, Joey." Mac was getting mad. "Just get
in the goddamn truck."

"Fuck off, man!" He fell onto his knees again. "Hey . . . where's my
bike?" His voice panicked as if he'd awakened to find himself castrated.

"Impounded."

"Owwww . . . " Joey put his hand to his throbbing head, slowly realizing that it did belong to him after all. "Oww—shit, man . . . *shit!*
I'm bleeding here . . . I'm hurt!" His yowling fell to a whimper. "Shit,
man. I'm *damaged!*"

"Relax, Joe, you just pulled some of your stitches."

Joey squinted and shuffled back toward the truck, genuinely
touched.

"You took me to get stitches?" He sat heavily on the tailgate. "Hey,
thanks, Macaroni Man. I love you, man, and I mean that. I owe you a
beer."

"Get in the truck, Joe. You've got errands to run."

"Fuckin' right, I do! I'm gonna kill the asshole who busted my head open!"

"Actually, Joe," Mac couldn't help smirking a little, "that was Bee Maclusky. And I assured her you'd be in today to apologize profusely and pay for all that stuff you broke before she laid you out."

"Fuck," Joey said weakly and slumped into the front seat. "I wanna go home. I need something to eat. I need some blow."

"Here," Mac said, offering a small tin box out of his buckskin coat.

"Oh, man, you're savin' my life, Mac." Joey took a joint and a wooden match from the tin but couldn't seem to combine the two in the necessary effort. Mac took the joint and lit it, pulling the flame deep into the tightly rolled paper.

"That's it," he tried to speak without exhaling, "no toot." He handed the joint to Joey and breathed out. "Just a little homegrown, strictly for medicinal purposes."

As the truck rolled forward and lurched to life, Joey inhaled the joint in just a few long draws, letting the last one burn his fingers a little. Then he leaned his head against the window and smiled.

"Mac, you're nothin' but an old hippie, you know that? Just an old grass-tokin', fringe-coated, peace-lovin'—"

Mac pulled onto the shoulder again. "Everybody out."

"What are we doing?" Joey wished he hadn't asked as soon as he saw the creek tumbling alongside the road. His lopsided grin faded. "No fuckin' way, man—forget it! It's fuckin' cold out!"

"You reek, Joe. I've passed roadkill that smells better than you."

He strode around the front bumper and pulled the passenger door open.

"No way, Mac . . . *Maaaaaac NOOOO!*" But it was too late. Mac slung Joey over his shoulder and slid down the snowy embankment, digging in his heels and letting forward momentum chuck his burden neatly into the icy water. Joey howled and brayed, ducking and struggling in the swift, thigh-high current until he found his feet and climbed out.

"These are my *leathers*, you jackass! My fuckin' *leathers!*" Joey yelled hoarsely. "These are gonna cost you!"

By the time Joey had peeled off the black jacket, pants, and T-shirt, Mac was back from the truck with the North Face bag. He tossed it at Joey along with that morning's *Great Falls Tribune*. Joey used the paper to dry off and wrapped the sleeping bag around himself.

"Sheesh . . . something peed on this sleeping bag," he grumbled.

"I know. It's gonna cost you."

Joey started laughing. "You're not gonna believe where I've been in the last twenty-four hours. . . . "

"Make that seventy-two hours," Mac said, "and I've probably got a better idea than you do."

"Whoa, man . . . shit. I gotta call the station and tell 'em I'm sick."

"Like this is news to them?"

"Whoa . . . shit."

"It's not going to be so easy this time, Joey. People who were depending on you are pissed righteously off."

"So who died and made you Jiminy Cricket?"

"When you didn't show up yesterday morning, VA took it pretty hard."

"VA?" Joey was confused for a moment. "This is about VA now?"

"You put her in a weird position."

"Yeah, I think you're the one who wants to put her in the weird position, man," Joey snorted in amusement.

"I've never even met the girl." Mac was angry now, guessing that, in light of the last two days, he probably wouldn't. "And I'm not the one who went out and got fucked up and left her to catch all the shit! Do you have any idea what's going on over there?"

"I don't give a rat's ass what's going on over there. I'm quitting."

"Gee, where have I heard this before?"

"I'm serious this time." Joey made a finite gesture. "I'm through."

"What makes you think you have a choice?" Mac asked.

"Aw, fuck, man." Joey rapped his head against the window. It hurt so much, he did it again, only harder. "Fuck me. . . . "

"No, thanks," Mac said, turning up Benton Street, "trying to cut down."

———

It started, as she knew it would, within a day or two of Joey's disappearance. There was a jock meeting to go over the new format, and

even those who were finally beginning to laugh and talk with her before Joey left now avoided her eyes. If she spoke, someone spoke over
her. If she persisted, her comments were followed by a weighty silence,
and then Dick would roll his eyes slightly and say, "Well—getting back
to business . . . " She kept thinking about what Mac told her; she swallowed the medicine, but as spring came on, it was starting to form hard
lumps in her throat and stomach.

She arrived at the station every evening to find the studio closed
and hung heavy with cigarette smoke. Everyone but Tulsa had moved
up a shift, and Troy was now doing morning drive out at the Swamp.
The new evening guy who came over from the AM to fill the open
shift answered Tulsa's attempts at conversation with monosyllables.
Mornings were even worse. Instead of the Harley roaring up at five,
Dick Richards's pale blue Pinto station wagon putted into the parking
lot and every fiber of Tulsa's being went tense. Each morning, he
handed her a yellow legal sheet of notes he had taken while shaving,
eating breakfast, and driving to work.

"Dear Mizz Lones," it always began, "Nobody really cares that Bob
Dylan's real name is Zimmerman," or "Please try to tone down the annoyingly high pitch of your voice," or "Don't say it's 'about' time for
the news. It's either time or it isn't."

Her already heavy production load doubled. Tulsa would drag open
the file drawer labeled "VA LONES" to find the usual voicework orders assigned her by the copywriter, compounded with endless dubs,
tags, and other dirty work originally assigned to someone else, the
name crossed out and written beneath it, "VA, Need by 6 AM." Sometimes the same work would come back to her the next night with no
explanation other than "VA, You need to do over."

This particular night, Tulsa dragged open her file drawer and saw the
healthy pile of dubs before she even noticed that the neatly typed "VA
LONES" label had been replaced with one that simply said, "CUNT."

Tulsa stared at it for a long while before she peeled it off and crumpled the sticky yellow label in one hand, squeezing almost hard enough
to milk the venom from it. She swung her arm over in the exaggerated
motion of a crane boom and mechanically fanned her fingers open one
by one until the wad dropped into the trash basket. There was no satisfaction in it, though; the label was already branded across her forehead,

in her heart. She slid the drawer closed and started sorting through the orders. Toward the top was a "Dear Mizz Lones" note.

"Dear Mizz Lones, In an effort to conserve costs, we'll be handling some of our own domestic duties. Since you have a free hour at the top of your shift, you've been assigned to clean the lavatory and kitchen areas."

It occurred to her that she might cry or throw something or just storm out and leave Dick in a lurch to cover her shift. But she suddenly felt too tired for any of that. Tulsa pulled her sweater over her head. It was early yet, a full two hours before midnight. She could still get back in time to get it all done. She went out the back door and started down the block. There was a bar down on Last Chance Gulch, where music and people noises were always spilling out into the street. Outside, the Bullwhacker statue cracked his whip overhead to keep the exiting patrons in line, and large dogs waited without even being tied for their masters to amble out into the cool evening. Sifting through the stained-glass windows, even the arguments sounded inviting and alive, especially to someone who had never set foot in a place such as that.

Tulsa's mother was a teetotaler and a bit of a hermit. She and Tulsa went to foreign films and art galleries or, in the last years, stayed home to read and play guitars or just sit perfectly still while Jeanne sketched portraits of them. Aaron was more the coffee house type. He frequented civilized receptions at the Performing Arts Center and establishments furnished with overstuffed divans, not wooden booths, and tables for chess, not pool.

Tulsa pulled open the door of the Joker's Wild Saloon and inhaled the scent of beer, sweat, fried something-or-other, and pine spray. The woman behind the bar sported an enormous beehive and the same kind of fringed-yoke shirt in which Dale Evans used to yodel her way across the backlot prairies.

Happy trails to you.

In a corner above the crowded little dance floor, two big speakers blasted Western swing from either side of a buffalo's head.

. . . across the alley from the Alamo . . .

Glass-eyed goats and elk stared down from the walls, and disembodied antlers racked guns, pool cues, and cowboy hats. Glistening fish were frozen midleap above each booth, and the table tops were de-coupaged with yellowed newspaper clippings, old postcards, and sepia-toned pictures of cowboys and Indians. The mirror behind the bar was taped with outhouse cartoons and signs that said things like "In God we trust, all others pay cash" and "Guns Don't Kill People. I Do." Dwarfing the cash register was an enormous animal head. Beneath the shaggy trophy was a plaque engraved "Yak's Yak," and beneath the shiny plaque stood Joey.

His bruised and mottled cheekbone and eye were in the sickening yellow-green stage of healing. Absorbed in conversation with a man who was almost as large and shaggy as the beast on the wall, Joey seemed appropriately intimidated. Tulsa watched him take the mop thrust at him by the enormous fellow. They continued their deep dis-cussion, Joey shrinking back from the big man's gestures toward a sec-tion of stained-glass window that had been replaced by a large piece of plywood.

"Shut the door!" someone yelled, jarring Tulsa from contemplating whether to run to Joey and hug his battered remains or stride up and kick him in the pants. She stepped back from the threshold, letting the door close in front of her.

Alexandra Firestein: "Indecision is, in itself, a decision . . . isn't it?"

Tulsa headed back toward the station.

"VA!" Joey's voice behind her only made her walk faster. "Tulsa, wait!"

"Don't even bother apologizing, you little maggot!" Tulsa wheeled on him. "And don't come knocking on my door anymore, either!"

"Why should I apologize to you?" He was still holding the mop, and Tulsa could smell that he'd been drinking. "I only wanted to tell you that I've been listening to your show the last few weeks—"

"I'm thrilled."

"—and you suck."

"Oh, well, fuck you very much."

"I mean it, VA, you really suck. You're trashing everything we built up."

"*We* built up?" Tulsa cringed at the annoyingly high pitch of her voice. "The only thing you built up is your mucus membranes."

"You know what I mean."

"Yes," Tulsa said sweetly, "and you know what this means." She gracefully extended her middle finger in Joey's direction, then continued her stride toward the station. When she looked back over her shoulder, he was already opening the stained-glass door of the bar.

She wandered on the mall a bit and sat on a stone bench outside the Rialto until her backside grew numb and her cheeks stung and her feet ached from the cold. Then, guessing by the moon that it was late, she headed up the street again. When she reached the full plate-glass window that faced the street, Tulsa leaned against a lightpost and watched the studio from the shadows. Dim illumination filtered through curling cigarette smoke. Dick was standing beneath the track lights with one elbow propped on the top of the console, shooting the breeze with the evening guy. They laughed, and the evening guy made an odd series of gestures.

Something cold trickled down Tulsa's spine.

Dick moved toward the door, and Tulsa, without knowing why, scrambled off the curb and crouched in the shadows between two parked cars until he cleared the entryway and putted away in the pale blue Pinto.

Jamming her key into the front door, hands trembling, Tulsa made a direct path to the production studio and grabbed the trash basket. The yellow label was gone. Tulsa swore and, like a frustrated child, struck her forehead hard with a closed fist. She looked at the pile of production and swore again. Only thirty-five minutes before midnight.

She began sorting the stack into two smaller mounds. By 11:55, she had hastily finished two recording projects in the first pile, adding music beds and slapdash sound effects where they were called for on the tidy production orders. She initialed each one with a pink highlighter, signifying mission accomplished. More than an hour's worth of dubs would have to wait until morning.

The new evening guy did his top-hour ID, switched into Mystery Theater, and left without a word. At 12:10, the private line blinked in the half light of the studio, but Tulsa ignored the flashing beacon. Mac had called every night the first week. As soon as she heard his voice, Tulsa pushed the hold button and didn't release it until after three. She wasn't above wanting him to eat his heart out a little bit and took a small, mean satisfaction in the persistent blink. She spent little time indulging her odd mix of feelings the first night he didn't call. But now, here he was. Phoning her up for a bunch of phony, faky, why-don't-I-swing-by-there-and-pick-you-up-for-breakfast bullshit.

Pulling her music and mentally lambasting Mac, Joey, and the world, Tulsa let it flash for a full ten minutes while she prepared the precise combination of scathing remarks.

We both KNOW what you want. Don't waste your time thinking you'll get it from me. We both know what YOU want. Don't waste your time thinking . . .

But just as she laid a cool hand on the receiver, the blinking stopped.

oh, poop.

And then lit up again.

HA! OK . . . webothnowhtuwntdon'twastyrtimethnkny'llgtitfrmme. . . .

Tulsa picked up the phone and said acidly, "We both know what you want—"

"First of all, I want this phone answered promptly and professionally." The slicing edge in Dick Richards's voice cut Tulsa's legs from under her. He went on for a few minutes about business phone etiquette, enjoying the way he'd caught her volunteering another item to his yellow legal pad. "I also expect you to be in the production studio a full hour before your shift."

"I'll get it done during Mystery Theater. Because I have absolutely no intention of using that time to clean any—"

"Well, after tonight, that won't be a factor." He paused for effect. "Mr. Dallas and I would like to meet with you in his office this morning at eight."

Tulsa's heart bottomed out. "Fine," she said with resignation.

"Eight o'clock. Meanwhile, I want this phone answered properly."

She replaced the receiver and took a deep breath. It didn't matter now. The scaly green heel was about to descend on her broadcasting career. But instead of the anticipated anger or sadness, Tulsa felt the burden of the past weeks dissolve in an almost euphoric flood of relief. The fissures of her brain expanded to admit a cool breeze of sound and illumination. Her heart felt carbonated inside her chest. She spun the barstool around and jumped off, the sudden rush of heady energy so real it made her run to the bathroom. After that, she returned to the production studio, studied the unfinished pile of dubs for a moment, and took up a red felt-tip.

"FORGET IT," she printed carefully on the first one and jotted "TAKE OFF" neatly on the next. Then "GUESS AGAIN" on the third order and "NOT IN THIS LIFETIME" on another. Growing bolder, she came up with "LIFE MUST BE ROUGH WITH A PIANO TIED TO YOUR ASS" and finally, the irresistible "FUCK YOU TO SASKATOON."

She piled the orders into Joey's box, which was freshly relabeled for Dick Richards. That tidy label inspired her. She took a pink sheet from the telephone message pad, rolled it into the typewriter, and pecked out "THE BIG DICK." After taping it in place, she snapped the light off and ran to the control room.

She went to the contraband album closet and began flipping through a shelf labeled: DO NOT PLAY. NO LONGER FORMAT APPROVED, using the remaining minutes of Mystery Theater to select her favorites and check a few references in the *Rolling Stone Encyclopedia.* By the time the one o'clock newsbreak was ending, Tulsa had removed the masking-tape barrier and a sign reading "CARTS ONLY" from the turntable bay. She cued up Phil Collins's *Face Value* album and hit the start button, gently holding the edge of the disc to keep it from wow-ing on the start. She realized how much she had missed doing that.

Network outcue, pot up and hit logo cart, pot up record. Mike in. Release.

"Fear not, gentle folk of the mountains," Phil's eerie intro pulsed in beneath her blue-violet voice in the headphones. "Weeping endureth for a night but joy cometh in the morning. VA will walk with you through the witching hours, into the fuchsia dawn . . . so come unto the place where I wait, spinning threads of music to weave the night's all-empowering cloak . . . to shroud those who would be invisible . . . embrace those who lie alone and comfort those who fear infinity. Parting will bring such sweet sorrow, so rock and roll, kiddos, till it be morrow. . . . "

She rode it right to the vocal, physically feeling the light and shadow of her voice weaving through the minor key of the music.

. . . I can feel it coming in the air tonight . . . I know . . .

"Philip, my sweet . . . I've been waiting . . . "

. . . I've been waiting for this moment all my life . . . Oh, Lord . . .

Tulsa pulled back from the post, where heavy drums drove the music sweeping up. The phone lines came to life before she even had a chance to load the Otari deck for taped bits and requests.

Flushed and free-falling, VA Lones sailed her airship into the night.

———

Mac looked up from *The Dead Zone* and strained to hear the FM monitor in the hallway. He could have sworn he heard a phone bit. Something about "life is a casaba melon." He dropped his feet from the console and went to the doorway.

" . . . so what'll it be, my little pumpernickel?"

"We're partyin' with ya, VA!" Raucous agreement chorused from the background. "How 'bout some 'Wooly Bully'?"

"You got it." She hit the cart and Sam the Sham slammed in.

Uno! Dos! One—two—tres—quatro!

VA cut back in and used the bounding instrumental intro for a trampoline.

"Success is counted sweetest by those who ne'er succeed. . . . Come, Samuel, my Sham-you-will fulfill my sorest need!"

. . . 'ow-day Joe 'ow-day . . .

Mac immediately knew what was happening. He started for the phone but heard Larry King's outro and dove back into his own studio just in time to hit the spot set. She was at it again when he came out.

"How come you've been playing all that boring crap lately, VA?"

"I was being a contemporary adult . . . or a temporary adult . . . or something."

"Oh," the caller said, not getting it. "Well, can we get some Bad Company on?"

"I've got 'Rock'n'roll Fantasy' burning a hole in my turntable even as we speak, turtle ears."

"Cool! Keep crankin', VA!"

"Yes, my moonlit ones, call upon VA and confide your rock and roll fantasies. . . . " Bad Company careened up beneath her, and Tulsa rode up the ramp on a Harley of her own. "'Come, ye most careful layers of T-squares . . . explain to me the mystic wild parabola of love. . . . '"

"*Archibald Ruttledge?*" Mac slapped the top of the monitor and whooped out loud. Archibald Ruttledge over Bad Company? *Nobody* read Archibald Ruttledge. That one was for him and he knew it, just as surely as if she'd dialed the Swamp's unlisted number and whispered it in his ear.

Mac abandoned both Stephen and Larry King altogether, dragging a chair out by the FM monitor in the hallway. Her voice was so ripe, her patter so inviting, each song took a new meaning and even the monitor itself seemed rounder, smoother, and more electric. By 3:30, the temptation to dial the private line overcame his irritation at her recent childish behavior. The midnight conversations meant something to him—though he wasn't sure what—and he disliked the fact of that almost as much as the idea that he couldn't speak freely to her without incurring some sort of tantrum. The office line rang seven or eight times before she picked it up.

"Good evening," she chirped, "you've reached the downtown studio office complex of KRNR FM Radio, a division of Ick-arus Broadcasting Incorporated. This is Mizz Lones, and *how* may I help you?"

"Archibald Ruttledge," Mac said. He didn't want to apologize or be appeased; only to let her know the message had been received. "I told you I'm always out there."

"Oh, Mac—I was hoping you were," she said in earnest, not even trying to conceal anything from him. "So. Long time, no . . . not see."

"Who are you calling a Nazi?"

The familiar laughter rippled like clear water through the coiled phone cord. "Mac, I want to tell you—oh, shoot. Hang on a minute." He heard cussing and clattering carts in the distance. "Mac?"

"I'm here."

"I'm incredibly busy. Would you believe the phones are still ringing?"

"Oh, yes. I believe it."

"I have to go. I'm sorry."

"It's OK. I'll call you tomorrow."

"I won't be here," she said, and Mac heard the first lilt of weariness to shadow her voice that night.

"Ah, don't do it, Tulsa. Just ride it out, darlin'. You can ride it out."

"I tried, Mac. It's a done deal." Then she took a deep breath and added, "But I was hoping we would still—I mean—could I call you there?"

"Tulsa—"

. . . once I made love to a girl and she tickled my ear with cornsilk . . .

"Tulsa, why don't I come by there after—"

"Crap!" she shrieked, and Mac turned his ear away from the rude shock of being hastily dropped on her console. He could hear her in the distance.

"*Yes!* Hello! Crisis programming alert! OK . . . just a moment of silent prayer, dedicated to my all-too-brief career in broadcasting. Thank you for joining in, brothers and sisters, and now say 'Amen' . . . 'Ah-women' . . . ah, nuts."

. . . devil with a blue dress blue dress blue dress . . .

"Rats." She was back on the phone. "Dead air. And just inches from a clean getaway."

"VA, you can fight this."

"No, I can't, Mac. Really. I've gotta go . . . but, really—it's OK."

"Tulsa—" he started, but she was gone. He sat, the receiver melded to his hand, his hand poised halfway between his grizzled cheek and the body of the telephone, but there was thumping on the back door before he could fully consider the pros and cons of calling her back to ask a question he wasn't sure he wanted answered.

"What do you want?" he called through the steel fire door. Distinctly hearing the sound of someone retching on the other side, Mac dropped his head forward against the wall. He tried to calculate the number of times he'd used the phrase "I owe you one" minus the number of nights Joey had come thumping on the fire door lately. The result was beginning to come up less than even. Mac swung the door open and waited while Joey recovered enough to stand upright.

"'Morning," Joey grinned. "Can I get a ride back to town with you?"

"Sure," said Mac.

"How 'bout a little of that ol' homegrown?" Joey looked so sheepish and stupid, Mac wanted to shake him. But to do that, he would have had to touch him, and Joey was revolting.

"Tackle box," Mac said grudgingly and held the door long enough to watch Joey shamble safely into the back of the truck. Still grinning, he waved and pulled the capper down behind him.

ya aint no kind of man if you cant hold a little whiskey

Pa Roy's philosophies were always clear cut and seldom generous toward the man who showed himself vulnerable in one way or another. He enjoyed a good three-day bender as much as the next cowboy, but there was a certain decorum that needed to be maintained.

When his grandson crawled out of Ben Sharkey's Ford the night before his sixteenth birthday, Pa Roy dragged the boy across the front porch and made him sit at the kitchen table, miserable and vomiting. Mac could vaguely remember Satchi pressing a cool cloth to his face, holding a basin in front of him, and his next recollection was of being slapped awake.

" . . . think yer a real cowboy, huh . . . ready to drink like a man?"

Satchi started to say something, but Pa Roy barked and she went away without making another sound. He pushed his own glass across the table and filled it, emptying the bottle. The boy tried to get up, to stumble to his room, but the thunder in his head and the force of Pa Roy's hand kept him in his chair.

" . . . can't even hold a little whiskey . . . easy-ass city boy . . . sorry as that piss-poor city boy . . . did it to yer mother . . . "

The boy sat, woozy and indifferent, having heard it all before. He had no rage left.

" . . . ignorant half-breed whore . . . "

He had long ago spent it, riding horses hard, pitching hay, or waling on the Alvarez. And anyway, he told himself, he would be gone soon. Pa Roy had promised to sign permission for him to join the army as soon as he could split and rick a cord of wood in one day. The next day, he did it.

He started just after sunrise. Ben Sharkey sat on a fence rail for a while, hung over but unfailingly cheerful, watching his best friend flail at log after log, commenting on what a dumb-ass way it was to have to spend your sixteenth birthday and alluding to a wild night in the offing. By midmorning the boy hit his stride and developed a method that minimized the number of strokes to each piece of timber. Satchi brought out a jar of ginger water, some bread, and pemmican at noon, but he wouldn't sit beside her for even a few minutes. He paused only long enough to pull off his flannel shirt and drink the whole jar of water in one draft. She had torn strips from an old sheet, and he let her wrap them around his blistering hands before he took up the splitting maul and continued hacking. She came back in the dry heat of the afternoon but stood away, noiselessly, knowing he wouldn't want her to hear the sounds he made as the maul tore into his soul along with the heart of the tree. The sun was just touching the far rim of the mountains when the boy stumbled up the steps to the kitchen, sweating and sunburned. He reached a swollen fist into the pocket of his jeans and gingerly pulled out the paper with thumb and forefinger so as not to stain it with his bloodied hands.

"Sign it," he rasped, victorious; still breathing hard and hoarse, he dropped the form on the table.

"What about yer chores, boy? You still got horses to tend."

Pa Roy's head was bent over his supper. There was a glass of whiskey next to his plate, as always, and the tumbler was already half empty.

"Sign it," the boy repeated, his voice cracked, proud and pleading.

Pa Roy grunted and chuckled without looking up.

"Now yer ready fer a drink." He pushed the whiskey tumbler toward his grandson, and the boy took a long draw on it without flinching. Satchi stared into the fire, rocking back and forth a little, humming softly. Moments passed. Pa Roy scraped his chair back, put one boot on the edge of the table, and started rolling a Durham cigarette. "You ain't goin' nowhere, boy. Yer just beginnin' to be some use around here."

There was another moment of heavy silence, and then the boy hurled the tumbler past his grandfather's head. Crystal and amber caught the firelight and exploded against the wall, showering the floor

with whiskey and glass. Pa Roy bolted to his feet and, as a matter of re-
flex, his grandson covered his face, but the old rancher was laughing.

"Think you can take me now? Do ya, boy? *Do ya?* C'mon! You give
it a try, boy—I'll lay you out colder than a goddam wedge."

Pa Roy's whiskey-thickened laughter followed the boy out into the
evening air as he ran down the road, cursing, slashing his raw hands
through the night air, striking at invisible foes. Ben Sharkey was waiting at the end of the road with a half keg of beer and two older girls
from town.

"Happy Birthday," they rowdied, but the song faded as he drew
closer.

"What the fuck?" Ben was in no mood to have his best-laid plans
go awry. "Where the hell is your shirt, Tarzan?"

The boy scuffed his feet on the gravel and said nothing. Surprise
and disappointment were undisguised in the face of the girl meant for
him.

"Phew! You need a bath," she said in annoyance.

She raised a cigarette to her full, apple-colored lips, and Sharkey
instantly sprang forward to provide a light. The flame illuminated her
large eyes and pouting mouth. She wore a pastel sundress, clean, crisp,
and rustling with crinolines, her shoulders white as milk in the moonlight. Painfully conscious of his filthy jeans and the sweat-streaked
sawdust film on his body, the boy writhed inwardly. He desperately
turned toward Ben, and inspiration flashed across Ben's face.

"HOT POT!" he cried, and the girls squealed with delight as he
swung them into the truck, and that was how they all ended up in the
creek, their clothes fluttering in the evening breeze.

Sulfurous vapor hung above the hot spring, unbearable to the boy,
so scorched were his back and shoulders. He lingered in the cool shal-
lows, sitting on a flat rock, letting himself slip under for long moments
at a time. The girl waded over to him and dipped frigid water over his
sunburned neck. Shivering and giggling, she led him to the horse blankets spread beside the bank. She tossed one around him and, stepping
to the Western swing on the radio, twirled under his arm so the
scratchy brown fabric surrounded her as well. She willowed back
against his chest, held his hands in front of her, kissed the torn and
blistered palms, slid them down her throat to her breasts. She guided

them in a circular motion, then pressed them down over her ribcage and abdomen, standing on one foot like an ibis in order to part her legs.

The boy was suddenly and acutely aware of every aching muscle in his body, his arms quivering with fatigue, his torso burning with sunscorch and excitement. The indescribable softness of her cheek soothed his cracked lips. Droplets glistened across her skin, cool as new snow on his dry tongue.

She made a small sound as he crumpled forward, pulling her to the ground; a songbird sound, almost. A sweet sound.

5

"FM 98.9, KRNR with Blue Oyster Cult; 'Don't Fear the Reaper.' I know I don't, my friends, and he's bearing down on me in an ice-blue Pinto station wagon even as we speak. . . . Give me some walking music, Mr. Zimmerman." Tulsa hit the Bob Dylan cart and let the intro establish for a moment before going into her final bit. "I'm on my way down the hill . . . just like the proverbial rolling stone. . . . Coming your way after the news—it's the president of the phallic fraternity, the premature ejaculation poster child, the Big Dick himself, Mr. Richard Richards, and more power to him . . . but not to worry," she threw in some Walt Whitman for Mac, "'I announce natural persons to arise, I announce uncompromising liberty and equality,'" and then finished, "That's it for VA Lones . . . shalom, my friends.'"

It's a long song, almost seven minutes. Tulsa had time to return all the albums to the no-no closet and clear away her notes and time figures. She reeled off the tape of phone bits, erased it with the bulking magnet, and brought in the news with a straightforward ID at the top of the hour.

"You're listening to KRNR FM, Helena, Montana. It's six o'clock." Tulsa dragged the headphones back from her ears, shook her hair loose from a ponytail catch, and tried to yawn some oxygen to her brain. She was exhausted. Her stomach was growling on empty, but her head was clear, her heart light.

Dick was standing outside the control room window with his expensive headphones in one hand and the red-lettered production orders in the other. Tulsa was surprised to see him smiling and nodding.

It'll be a long time before someone that good comes along. . . . One time they tracked him down in Spokane and he actually got a raise. . . .

She pushed through the soundproof door and nodded. "Morning, Dick."

"I finally figured it out at about quarter to six," he said. "I'm driving over, going 'What the hell?' and then I come in and I see these." He held up the orders. Tulsa swallowed and reminded herself she was no longer intimidated by him. "You thought he was going to can your ass." The way he was giggling made Tulsa nervous. "He was going to bump you up to evenings! Even though I tried to tell him. He was planning to give you a raise! But you thought he was going to can your ass . . . so . . . you . . . " He was laughing so hard now he could barely speak. "You punched your own ticket, Lones. You screwed yourself."

Tulsa's mind was numb. She went to the production studio to gather her things as best she could with her hands shaking so.

Dick followed her, waving the orders. "He's going to come in and find these on his desk along with a full report of every snotty remark . . . every time you broke format . . . all that phone crap. And this!" He clenched the pink slip she taped over his production bin. He followed her to the front door, frustrated that she wouldn't make any additionally incriminating remarks in her own defense. "You be here at eight, Mizz Lones! If you want your final paycheck—you be here!" The front door banged closed behind her, but it couldn't completely mute the sound of his laughter.

The sidewalk rolled and pitched beneath her feet. By the time she reached the No Sweat, Tulsa could feel the muscles in her face working independently of her will to stay calm. She barely made it into the bathroom before crumbling completely. She locked the swinging stall door and climbed up to sit on the old-fashioned water box, rocking back and forth, reeling off a large mass of paper to muffle her sobs. The door creaked open, and she could see Elsa's Birkenstocks beneath the half wall.

"Are you OK, Tulsa?"

Tulsa clamped her hand tight over her mouth, but the Birkenstocks showed no sign of taking their owner back to the kitchen.

"Tulsa?"

Oh, crap . . . she knows I'm in here. Probably wants to hug me or something.

"If you feel like talking about it, c'mon back. I just took the carrot muffins out of the oven." Elsa's tone was easygoing as her boyish haircut, casual enough that Tulsa risked uncovering her mouth to blurt, "OK."

The door closed, and Tulsa heard Elsa, Liz, and Betsy clanging and stirring in the kitchen across the hall. She relaxed a little and used a portion of the toilet paper mass to blow her nose.

"It's cathartic in a symbolic way," her mother told her. "All this negative stuff builds and builds and then you cry and your body says 'blow it out!' That's what it says." She held the bouquet of Kleenex under the nose of her chubby fifteen-year-old. "C'mon. Blow. Like the north wind." She had begun using that line when her daughter was a toddler, and it still seemed to amuse one or both of them. "It'll be all right. Jeannie says you can stay here as long as you want and—who knows? With me out of the way, you might be able to get to know your father. Jeanne's going to send him a telegram and tell him to come for you. And I'm sure he will. He's basically a good person, Tulsa, and it's me he was afraid of, not you. You'll be all right, Guppy," she said. "You will, you know."

No, I don't know! I don't know what I'm supposed to do! I don't know where I'm supposed to go! I don't know if anyone else will ever love me.

"Yes," Tulsa blurted around the dampened Kleenex wad, "but Mom . . . "

"Hmm?" There was something about her mother's voice that could make her feel physically cradled. "What is it, baby girl?"

"Mom, please, can't you try a little more chemo? Please! Just *try?*" Tulsa inhaled raggedly. She was struggling to talk without wailing, without bawling like a newborn calf. She was trying to be cool and well ironed like her linen-clad mother, but she found it impossible to speak without gasping after every word. "Mom—I'm—*scared*—!"

"Oh—my baby—so am I!" She pulled Tulsa close. "So am I . . . " She was crying too, but the way they do in movies, tears softly spilling, voice husky but evenly flowing and still beautiful. "But I'm eager in a way. I don't want to linger and make it even harder for you and Jeannie. I'm so tired of struggling. I want to know the answers. And I've had such a wonderful time. You and Jeannie . . . the books and the tours. This isn't a tragedy, Guppy, I've had a full life. I've had love."

Laughter rippled through her tears. "Are there any other clichés I should be tossing around?"

"Maybe that you'll miss me." Her mother's arms around her made it possible for her to speak without flying apart.

"Oh, little Guppy," her mother whispered, "more than anything."

———

Mac came out of the Swamp at six and tapped on the back of the capper.

"Joey?" There was a low moan from within. "Joe, you want me to drop you at your place or Patty's?" Mac was prepared to envy him in either case. When there was no answer, he lifted the back window. "Joe, you can't stay in there. Now, c'mon—your place or Patty's?"

Joey slid down to the tailgate and dropped it so he could climb out and pee against the corner of the transmitter building.

"Not Patty's," he croaked, fumbling himself back behind his zipper. "She's not liking me too well right now."

"Go figure," Mac said, knowing the sarcasm would be lost on him. "Get on in and I'll take you home, then."

"No, I gotta go to work."

"Joey, remember? You don't work there anymore."

"No," Joey spread his fingers and dragged his greasy hair back from his eyes. "At the No Sweat. I'm supposed to be there at seven."

"Really?" Mac said distastefully. "You look kind of scummy to be in the food service industry."

"I'm just washing dishes."

They pushed the truck onto the downsloping drive and ran forward with it, Joey moaning at every step. After they leaped in, he rested his head against the gun rack behind the seat.

"Aren't you ever gonna get this thing fixed, for crissake?"

"Still gets me there," said Mac philosophically.

They drove on in silence for a bit, each on his own private frequency.

"Talked to Tulsa this morning," Mac said, turning onto the main road.

"Peachy."

"She's in trouble."

"I know," Joey said, "but she can take care of herself."

"Yeah." Mac hoped he was right and was uneasy to hear the pro-tective tone in his own voice.

"God, she's so funny sometimes," Joey laughed even though it hurt. "We were getting off on her at Chooch's last night . . . she was cookin'. Yup," he added with satisfaction, "I gave her a talking to before her shift. Guess it must have got her over whatever she had up her butt."

"Actually, I think it's whatever's up your nose that started all this." Mac wasn't sure why he felt like defending her. "I'm beginning to won-der myself if you've got a handle on it."

"Fuck you, man. You're a great one to be talking."

"Smoking a little homegrown isn't quite the same as snorting your whole paycheck every week."

"Yeah, well, you keep tellin' yourself that, bro."

"You're outa control, Joe. Trust me on this, if you don't lay off, you're gonna hurt yourself."

"Jesus P. Christ, Mac!" Joey put his hands to the sides of his head. "Just shut up, will ya? Where have you been the last ten years? I party. I've been partying since you've known me, and I'm gonna party till the day—aw . . . just shut up. I feel like my fuckin' head's gonna fall off."

They drove on in silence. Pulling up in front of the No Sweat, Mac couldn't resist lurching to a stop.

Joey groaned and opened his eyes. "God, I don't wanna do this."

"Have a nice day, Joe." Mac clapped him on the shoulder. "I hope you enjoy your new career."

"Yeah, and I hope your dick falls off."

"'Better to have loved and lost than never to have—'"

Joey slammed the door and headed into the cafe.

———

"So then she goes—'Up next is the pre . . . the premature ejacula-tion poster boy . . . '" Elsa was laughing too hard to continue, and Betsy was getting impatient. Tulsa could hear them through the air vent as they bantered and baked in the kitchen. "She goes—she goes . . . oh, geez . . . "

"She goes what? Spit it out! I hate it when you do that. Liz, make her stop doing that." Betsy rattled something heavy into the oven and slammed the door. "Who cares about VA Lones, anyway? She's turned into a total drone."

"No, you should have been here while we were baking this morning," Elsa giggled. "It was like the old VA."

"Face it, Els; she knuckled under to the good ol' boys. She probably works for half what Dick Richards does, sucks him off, and shines his desk with Lemon Fresh Pledge while she's at it."

"Betsy," Elsa cried, "how can you say that!"

"No way," Liz threw in, "because if Joey hired her, you can bet she's blond and has big tits and just oozes around getting treated like a goddess. But she got the job and she is good, Bets. You have to give her that."

"She's a feminist pioneer in her own little way," Elsa maintained.

"Yeah, right." Betsy fed something into a grinder. "Candace asked her to speak at a coalition meeting and she said she doesn't know anything about feminist issues! Said she'd never even *heard* of Alexandra Firestein!"

"Well, maybe she doesn't do politics. Does that have to be part of everybody's job description all the time? Liz, pass me that paprika."

"You know what that says to me?" Liz asserted. "Lesbophobia. Here's somebody who has your basic Brady Bunch family back in Acorn, Wisconsin, and she's terrified that if she ever met a real live dyke—"

"Can I please have that paprika?"

"There's more than enough paprika in there, Elsa—"

"Elsa! Don't! It doesn't need that much paprika."

"You can hardly taste it! Why even bother calling it paprikash?"

"Is Tulsa still bawling in there?" Liz asked.

"*Shhhh!*" Betsy hissed, and their voices fell sotto. A minute or two later, the bathroom door creaked open, and Tulsa saw the Birkenstocks again.

"Croissants are out," Elsa said solicitously.

Tulsa forced a deep breath, stepped down, and unlatched the door.

"'Morning," Elsa said. Ostensibly at the mirror doing something with her close-cropped hair, she stepped aside so Tulsa could reach the sink.

"Hi," Tulsa said and rinsed her hands and wrists.

"Croissants are out," Elsa repeated, "quiche in five minutes."

"So I hear." Their eyes met in the mirror. "Elsa, do you know why I pass by here every morning?"

"Gotta be the continental cuisine," she smiled. "You're headed home from work, aren't you?" Tulsa nodded, and, suspecting it might have something to do with her swollen eyes, Elsa asked, "You work up at the Historical Society building, right?"

"I used to." Tulsa leaned in to splash cold water over her puffy face. "But now I'm VA Lones."

"No shit. Are you really?"

"Yeah," Tulsa shrugged, "but I'm getting fired today."

"*No shit! Are you really?*" Elsa's sympathetic expression gave way to something between morbid curiosity and scientific interest. "So that's what all that Dick thing was about this morning? And then—but why didn't you ever say anything—or Joey? I can't believe he didn't tell me. I can't believe I didn't recognize your voice."

"Well, I asked him not to," Tulsa started to explain, "and with the audio-processing—"

"So this is what you look like! Where are you from? Are you gay?" Her voice dropped down. "Or are you sleeping with Joey? I mean, did you—of course you didn't—did you?"

"No! I didn't, I don't, and I'm not going to!" Tulsa was disappointed that, when it came right down to it, even Elsa assumed there was only one way for a woman to be a pioneer in her own little way. "And there's no big political agenda, either. I needed a job, he needed somebody, and—much to everyone's surprise—I turned out to be good at it. Or maybe Joey was just trying to stir up trouble. It doesn't matter now, anyway. But Elsa, I want you to know that I'm not . . . from Wisconsin."

"Oh. You heard all that. Oh, geez! Betsy's gonna freak! We gotta tell her!" Not giving Tulsa a chance to resist, Elsa dragged her out of the bathroom and through the swinging shutter-doors to the kitchen, calling, "You guys! Betsy, you're gonna freak! Liz! Liz, guess what?" They looked up from their dough-kneading and table-cleaning, tough to impress at this hour of the morning. Elsa held up her hands and announced, "V—A—*Lones!*" punctuating each syllable with a tap on Tulsa's head. They stared for a moment and then burst into a chorus of surprise, amusement, and assertions of having known it all along.

"Please," Tulsa touched Elsa's elbow, "don't tell anyone else, OK? This is all ending sort of inauspiciously."

"But—you're V—A—*Lones!*" Elsa tapped her head again.

"She sure was last night." Joey was leaning on the inside of the doorframe. He looked like complete and utter hell with his greasy hair and dirty T-shirt. Even from across the room, his eyes were visibly bloodshot.

"What are you doing here?" Tulsa hoped he was too insensitive to notice she'd been crying.

"Reporting for duty," Joey said humorlessly.

"Joey's washing dishes for us till he gets back on his feet," Elsa explained brightly, not caring that Joey was visibly humiliated. She looked at her watch. "You've got a little time, though. Not much to do yet. Want some tea?"

"Coffee!" he pleaded. "Coffee and aspirin. Lots of aspirin."

"I was speaking to our customer, Joey."

"Red Zinger, please." Tulsa couldn't help laughing.

Joey slid into a high-backed booth across from her. He was all pathetic and rumpled in a warm, puppy sort of way. Tulsa briefly wondered if maybe he had planned to kiss her *after* she snorted the cocaine that night. Then she flashed on the thousand or so times in the last month she'd taken Joey's name in vain, cursing him, his dog, his dipsy blond Barbie doll girlfriends and the ship they all came in on, and the soft thoughts evaporated.

"Get it together, Jeeves." Elsa set down the Red Zinger along with Joey's coffee and the aspirin bottle. "I need you in about ten minutes."

He nodded, though it obviously pained him. Sliding his back to the wall, he put his feet up and began telling Tulsa about the previous night's party adventure without remorse or chagrin.

"You were the life of the extravaganza, Tul. We had you cranked. We were so hammered—gettin' into all that headbanger stuff you're comin' out with, so then Sledge is wanting to call you up only the line's busy—can't get through and he's getting all pissed off. . . . " Joey went on, providing sound effects, demonstrating facial expressions of various people, but never coming to any real point except to say, "You were all over it, VA! Way out there."

"That's gratifying," Tulsa nodded. "Eight incoherent bikers agree. I'm 'all over it.'"

"'Course, I guess I can take a little credit."

"Credit for—?"

"For motivating you. Setting you straight last night."

"Oh, yeah," she blazed, "Dallas is going to can me in less than ninety minutes and you can claim most of the credit for that! If you could have kept your runny little nose clean, we'd both be happily employed right now!"

"Hey, I don't get paid to fuckin' babysit you!" With one hand, Joey jabbed his spoon at her for emphasis. With the other, he pressed his temple as if being angry and holding his head up at the same time were more than he could handle. "I'm not responsible for your crummy little career any more than—"

"Joey! What are you doing to her?" Elsa passed by and smacked his arm with the flat side of a serving tray. "You've got five minutes."

Joey glared after her and then slumped back down in the booth.

"What makes you think you're getting fired, anyway?"

While he rested his forehead on the cool tabletop, Tulsa began with the morning he failed to show up and ended with Dick Richards's laughter following her down the street. Joey grunted acknowledgment at various intervals and, in the end, was laughing, until Elsa called to him that there were dishes in the sink. Joey rolled his head sideways and crawled out of the booth with a whispered exit line to Tulsa. "I can't fuckin' believe I'm taking orders from someone who was my groupie less than six weeks ago."

"I heard that." Elsa came over with Tulsa's breakfast. "Now I'm Tulsa's groupie." She set down the Mountain Sun Special. "On the house, VA!"

It was almost seven. Tulsa's mind was reeling with possible scenarios and explanations, ranging from an inoperable brain tumor to split-personality disorder. She rehearsed different tones and expressions in her mind—penitent, pathetic, defiant—but it all led to the single possible conclusion: Dallas would see right through anything she said; she would be summarily dismissed and never work in broadcasting again. The best she could hope for was to maintain eye contact in an attempt to escape with her severance pay and a shred of dignity.

Joey came back at quarter after. He wiped his hands on his white apron and sat down. Elsa had loaned him a clean T-shirt and made him go into the back room and wash up before he started work. He seemed to feel a little better.

"Well, at least you got some job experience," he offered. "You can apply at the other stations in town." Tulsa was wishing he would just go away, but Joey persisted. "And you and I are buds again, right? And you and Mac are buds again. He was happy about that."

"That's nice."

"Nice?" Joey leered. "You think it's nice to tie some poor guy's pecker in a knot?"

"Oh, I did not. We're just friends. We just talk."

"About what?"

Tulsa tried to think what seemed so important all those nights.

"Books," she said, "politics, religion, ranching. Whatever."

"Whoa . . . stimulating. No wonder he's not getting any."

"Yes, well, I guess we can't all be as electrifying as you and your beer-swilling biker pals, Joey. Maybe us drones are so easily amused, we don't have to be anesthetized in order to have a conversation."

"Et tu, VA?" Joey frowned. "This is my second Moral Majority temperance lecture today, and I haven't had fuckin' breakfast yet." He got up and trudged back to the kitchen, leaving Tulsa to shuffle her blueberry yogurt granola from one side of the bowl to the other.

Seven-twenty.

Other customers came and ordered and talked back and forth. Tulsa saw many of them almost every day, but she realized she could call only a few of them by name. She didn't really know them, nor they her. A feeling she had almost forgotten washed over her like a tidal pool, bringing with it the flotsam of insecurity and plain weariness. Tulsa closed her eyes, willing herself to be calm, searching through the debris for some kind of comfort.

i'm always out there

Seven-thirty-five.

———————

The women working inside the No Sweat waved to Mac, and he wished he had the money for a Western omelette or even just a cup of coffee. He hadn't even been into the Joker's Wild since the weekend. Yak and Berryl were a little less indulgent about his tab since Joey busted up the place (though Mac had yet to figure how that was his fault).

Materials for repairs on the ranch had taken up the lion's share of every paycheck since Colter's long-awaited birthday. Mac had put a new floor and support beams on the front porch, fixed the roof, and was building a shower outside the warm outer surface of the stone fireplace; the water trough out in the yard had started feeling pretty cold along about January. The gate was mended, the underbrush cut back from the road. Mac was even thinking about replacing the fence so he could put a horse out there. Mr. Chadwick, his neighbor to the north, had offered him a reasonably good mare for less than two hundred bucks. Mac wanted that horse so bad he could practically feel her underneath him.

But the stable . . .

It loomed in his dreams: the sagging roof sheltering a blackness deeper than the cold, trickling well. Pa Roy's voice. The searing razor strop. Starlings rising in a shrill tornado. Scarlet stains that smattered the weathered walls like wildflowers.

Mac shook off the images and dug into his shirt pocket for a cigarette. Going out behind that stable was something he couldn't quite bring himself to do yet.

"Whole thing's rotting," he told Mr. Chadwick. "I'll need to build a new one before I can take on a horse."

"Well," Chadwick said, his leathery hand on Mac's shoulder, "I for one would be damn glad to see you get things back to business over there. It's always good to have neighbors."

Chadwick was an old man, a contemporary of Pa Roy and Satchi and Mac's mother. He spoke about those days with such clear memories and unclouded practicality that Mac wanted to avoid the rancher and his white-haired wife, who came over offering cookies and a cold beer when he was out working on the gate near their mailbox one day. They knew. They had witnessed it all.

"Roy was talking with me and Mother about buying the rest of the place, don't you know," Chadwick told him.

"No, I didn't know." Mac was disturbed to hear it.

"Yeah, we were working on an agreement to that effect when he had his stroke and then—well, one thing and another. We figured it might go up for taxes or something down the line and we'd take it then."

"Well, that's not gonna happen, Mr. Chadwick," Mac said.

"I guess he didn't figure on you comin' back," Chadwick said, tucking a chew of tobacco inside his cheek. "Just didn't figure you'd end up back out here after all this time."

"Guess not." Mac offered no explanation, and Chadwick didn't press for one. That would have overstepped the bounds of what's neighborly. Without bringing up ancient history, he answered Mac's questions about what happened to Satchi and loaned him a horse so they could ride up to the place where she was buried. He didn't talk about the way Roy lived after she was gone. Chadwick figured there was no point to it; he was a utilitarian man by nature, a good rancher and a thrifty citizen.

"This is as far as I go, son," Chadwick reined up his Morgan and pointed up the hill. "Just over that rise is where we laid Satchi. You might remember from when your ma passed."

"Not really," Mac admitted, and he didn't go forward.

"You can bring Hally on back to the barn later."

Mac didn't answer, and the horse beneath him shuffled her feet as if she sensed his hesitation.

"'Course on the other hand," Chadwick said, squinting into a hazy sky, "looks like we might get rain this afternoon. Maybe another day would be best."

"Yeah, maybe that would be best," Mac said, relaxing his grip on the saddle horn. They turned their horses down the hill and rode back without speaking.

No point talking about it now, old Chadwick figured. No point now.

―――――――――

At seven-fifty, Tulsa reluctantly got up to leave the comfort of the cafe and face her gloomy fate. "I'll be back for a job application," she told Elsa at the cash register. "Well . . . 'into the valley of death rode the six hundred. . . . '"

Elsa patted the back of her hand against her chin in a "buck up" gesture and then raised two fingers. "Shalom, my friend."

Slightly braced by that small kindness, Tulsa made her way up Last Chance Gulch. There was a fifteen-minute newsbreak at the top of the eight o'clock hour, and Dick was just slipping into it with a smooth ID when Tulsa passed the window. He was practically salivating with sweet anticipation by the time they reached the door of Dean Dallas's office. Dallas was on the phone but gestured them in, and they sat uncomfortably, waiting for him to hang up. In front of him on his tidy desk was the stack of production orders and a manila file folder labeled TULSA (VA Lones) BITTERS. It was fat with letters, and Tulsa's W-4 form was paperclipped to the front.

Fine, Big Brother, keep a file on me. I hope you didn't miss the time I got my period and stained a Greyhound bus seat . . . lied to mom about wearing a padded bra . . . pretended to recognize the Impressionist painter Aaron was talking about. . . .

Every complaint, every offense. It would all be trotted out before her now in some Kafka kangaroo court.

Dallas smoothed his tidy white mustache as he brusquely wound up his conversation and then folded his hands in front of him.

"We have a problem." His tone was paternal.

No shit, Sherlock.

"We've had this problem for a while," he said, leaning forward across the desk, "but now it's getting in the way of business. We need to take care of it, and we need to take care of it today. This morning."

then do it already just do it . . . he's gonna do it

"VA, my two teenage boys are great fans of yours. Just this morning, they were raving about how great you are, so I turned on my radio just in time to hear you call Mr. Richards—your program director and immediate superior—an extremely vulgar nickname. Then you proceeded to extend the entendre into an entire medley of vulgar remarks."

Tulsa concentrated on keeping her face frozen in an uncaring expression, but she could feel the result was more pinched than defiant.

"Then," Dallas continued, "I arrived at the office to find these—" he held up the production orders—"and this." The pink "Big Dick" label. "Now, I'd like to hear something in the way of an explanation."

Tulsa's halting delivery reflected each bruising heartbeat. "All I can tell you, Mr. Dallas . . . "

No kidding! There's our hidden camera right over there!

" . . . is that, in the last several weeks . . . " She drew a deep breath and concentrated on the tone her mother reserved for the most fractious press conferences and panel discussions. " . . . I have been shunned at best and, at worst, actively harassed. It was cold from the start, but I knew there was some controversy about bringing a woman into the airstaff and I assumed that it would pass if I proved myself competent and conscientious. After a year or so, it did get better, but since Joey's—departure, it's gotten worse. Worse even than it was at the beginning."

"Yes," Dallas was surprised at her unemotional discourse. "There was some controversy, but it seemed like a progressive thing to do, and progressive is good. However—" His eyes went to the unfortunate "Saskatoon" order.

"*However,*" Dick jumped in, "I think our basic situation here is a personality conflict between Miss Lones and virtually everyone she comes in contact with. This isn't a political issue, it's a personal attitude problem."

"Attitude," Dallas said quietly. "Attitudes are important."

"Now," Dick continued, "these production orders, for example—"

"Were assigned to someone else," Tulsa interrupted, "and then dumped on me in addition to my usual production load, which is . . . "

really running the best thing Joey's done

" . . . formidable. Since so many clients specifically request my voice."

Dallas looked to Dick, who offered a highlighted photocopy of a page from the employee policy handbook along with a smooth explanation of why it's sometimes necessary for the overnight announcer to pick up a little slack on busy days. Dallas looked to Tulsa.

oh crap

"Mr. Dallas . . . "

I'm with the CIA and am unable to discuss the nature of my mission. . . .

" . . . if Mr. Richards can produce a single order indicating that any previous overnight announcer has been expected to do other people's production—"

"Well," Dallas brushed the idea aside and looked at his watch. "We don't have time for that, and it's rather immaterial, anyway. I think I have a clear picture of the situation at this juncture—"

"No!" Tulsa surprised herself more than anyone else in the room. "No, I don't think you do, Mr. Dallas."

"I beg your pardon, VA?"

"I don't think you have a clear picture of the moral and legal ramifications of what's been going on here." Her Firestein kicked in, and she was off. "Is it acceptable practice, according to the employee handbook, to ostracize and persecute one member of the airstaff? Is it a prerequisite for the job of announcing that one's genitals be shaped like a microphone? Has any male announcer at this station ever been asked to clean the bathroom or the kitchen or make coffee for the sales staff? I cannot accept that you could possibly have a clear picture of this situation and reach the conclusion that you've obviously reached. If you do have a clear understanding of it, how can you allow the situation to continue as if—"

"I said I think I do," he interrupted curtly.

shut up! shut up! just swallow the medicine! he sees you!

"And I'm glad we all agree that this situation cannot continue."

Tulsa half expected Dallas to push a button that would swing away a trapdoor, dropping her into a bottomless pit. His words became slurry and distant, like the backwards message on a Beatles album.

" . . . despite your little tirade . . . that in the last twelve hours alone . . . "

mom

" . . . more than sufficient cause to terminate your employment . . . "

daddy?

"... ample evidence of VA's inability to get along with ..." Dick chimed in, righteously indignant, "... not a team player ... structure of a real format ..."

The GM opened the manila file folder, and Tulsa realized he was holding up the crumpled yellow paper that had been taped to her production bin. There was a weighty silence, and Tulsa felt the word branding into her forehead as though the file contained a report on Aaron's top bunk and how she didn't even make him beg.

"This whole matter truly saddens me," the GM said.

smartass stream-of-consciousness cunt punched your own ticket

Tulsa and her immediate superior both sat forward in their chairs and began speaking at once, but Dallas raised his hand.

"Please," he smiled diplomatically, "I think we can agree there's been regrettable behavior from all parties involved. And further agree that it cannot and will not continue." Each word was audibly underlined.

"Mr. Dallas," Dick sputtered, "you can't force people to like someone they just—can't relate to."

"They don't have to like her, Dick. They don't have to like her, look at her, take her to the prom, or include her in the tiddlywinks tournament, but they do have to work with her as long as she's employed at this radio station. Perhaps," Dallas suggested, "a positive example would facilitate relations or at least curtail the exchange of obscenities to the point where the station is no longer vulnerable to discrimination lawsuits and FCC fines."

vulnerable to discrimination

"Only one four-letter word in radio, you know: SELL." Dallas smiled again. "Now, Dick, didn't we decide that VA is ready for a better time slot?"

"Well, not exactly. I said—"

"And did I mention to you that Walt Bloyer approached me at the Rotary last week, saying he'd like VA to be the official voice of Bloyer Chevrolet?"

... official ... Rotary?

"Now, that's a big account, and I like to keep my big accounts happy—not to mention my teenage boys." Dallas actually chuckled.

Boys? Accounts? Am I fired yet?

"So we're going to move Miss Lones to the evening shift, as we discussed."

not fired not fired I'm not fired!

"And just trash the format?" Dick complained. "Blow off listeners and alienate the rest of the airstaff?"

Dallas motioned to the file. "It's apparent from our last survey numbers, she's not blowing off listeners. Quite the opposite. And the format won't be a problem for you, Dick. I've decided to let Troy take a shot at programming and move you into sales full time. AM sales dropped by a disturbing percentage last quarter, and we really need someone with your aggressive skills on the street."

dick gone—me here

suck—fired, good—not fired

Confused as to whether this was good news or bad, Dick started to say something else about all his highlighted sheets and notes, but Dallas glanced pointedly at his watch.

"I wish we had time to explore some of that, Dick, but I don't want to interfere with your air work." More of the smile. "Troy can slide into the morning spot next week, we'll go to the Overland for a strategy lunch, and you'll be off!" He stood, shook Dick's hand, and walked him to the door, clapping him on the back, "Congratulations!" before shuffling him effectively out.

Tulsa sat, stunned, in the midst of the one scenario she hadn't imagined.

He was on my side.

A gray-pinstriped Godzilla, returning in later episodes to defeat Megalon, Mothra, and the Tokyo Smog Monster!

"You'll move to evenings Monday, VA," Dallas said, consulting his desk calendar. "Live remotes at Bloyer run every other Saturday through the summer."

live re—

"Live . . . in person?" Tulsa felt a stab of panic. "I can't do that."

Dallas glanced up, unsure if she was joking. "The intern from the engineering staff will do all the setup. You'll be paid at an hourly rate in addition to your usual salary, but I'm sure you understand why I'm going to hold off on the pay increase I was prepared to offer you."

"It's not the money, Mr. Dallas," Tulsa tried to assure him. "I just—I don't think I can talk with people . . . looking at me."

"Don't be ridiculous."

"Really, thank you, but I'd rather just stay where I am."

"VA, don't push your luck here," Dallas cut in, and Tulsa noticed for the first time how his eyes were pale gray as hailstones. "You're hanging on by a thread here and for that, you can put Walt Bloyer at the top of your Christmas list. I was not very amused by any of this." He gestured to the orders and Dick's legal pad. "I don't appreciate having my Saturday taken up with sandbox squabblings. Troy will be returning Monday as FM program director, we will reinstitute the album-oriented format, and you will be the embodiment of cooperation and company loyalty from this point on. Be as progressive as you like, but keep in mind that the truly creative have no need of vulgarity. Radio is a business, Ms. Lones; not a game, not an art form—a business. The listeners you deliver are the commodity I sell. You put people off, I have no product and you have no job. And if you have a problem with your production load, you bring it politely and professionally to the attention of the station continuity director."

Tulsa nodded. "Yes, sir."

"Have we covered this subject to your satisfaction?"

"Yes, sir," Tulsa nodded again.

"Do you have any questions?"

Tulsa shook her head. "No, sir."

"Then why don't you go home and get some sleep." Dallas sounded only slightly softer at the edges. With an air of dismissal, he took some paperwork from his briefcase and didn't even look up to add, "Please consult the handbook regarding company dress code for live remotes before you go to Bloyer's."

Tulsa stood shakily. "Mr. Dallas?" He looked up sharply from his appointment book. "I was just wondering . . . about Joey? Since you're going to need someone on overnights—I realize this isn't really any of my business—"

"That's right, it isn't." The GM went back to his book.

"But if you could maybe just talk to him—"

"Ms. Lones," Dallas impatiently held up the crumpled yellow paper.

———

"And he said, 'Where do you think I got this?'"

Mac sat with his cowboy boots on the console, listening to Tulsa replay the whole incident like Mean Gene Okerland laying out the gory details of a Saturday Night All-Star Wrestling brawl.

"So I just sort of slunk from the room and mumbled something lame like 'have a nice day' or something like that—Anyway, I felt like a complete idiot, but very happy, and I went home and got the first decent sleep I've had in weeks. This has all been so weird and awful. And I've been so weird and awful. Mac, I'm sorry."

"Not to worry," Mac told her. "How does Joey feel about overnights?"

"Not great. He's covering tonight, but before he starts full time, he has to go for this six-week detoxification thing at a hospital in Billings."

Mac didn't want to get started on that subject. "The midnight hour is going to be pretty lonesome around here. I don't suppose Joey has read much Camus." He missed her already.

"Well," Tulsa laughed, "you probably aren't built like most of his luscious little phone pals, either."

"True enough."

"Mac . . . if you wanted to . . . I mean, you could call anyway. I could—you know—I wouldn't mind waiting around after my shift."

"OK." He was doing that gentle thing again. "OK, I will."

"Do you think you'll still listen sometimes?"

"Always." Mac gathered his resolve and cleared his throat. "Well, VA, it seems like we should celebrate." She didn't say anything, so Mac looked for another opening. He wasn't going to let her avoid another obvious "so why don't we . . . " lead in. "It's Saturday night," Mac forged ahead. "We both get off at midnight. We're both used to staying up till dawn. . . . "

"Mac—"

"You said you wanted to hear the coyotes sometime, and this would be a perfect night to do it. Waxing gibbous. We could howl at the moon."

"I'm sort of tired tonight, though."

"Just coffee then." Silence. "C'mon, Tulsa, how long are we gonna keep tap dancing around this?"

"Mac, did you ever wonder what I look like?"

"Why would I wonder that?" He tried not to sound impatient.

"Curiosity."

"If I were that curious, I'd drive by the studio." He had, but the blinds were closed. "Did you ever wonder what *I* look like?"

"I asked Joey and he said you're the spittin' image of that dirty old man from Rowan and Martin's *Laugh-In*."

"Well, that's Joey. Generous to a fault."

"But Colter says you're a regular Prince Valiant."

"Darlin', I really don't see what—"

"Mac, guys ask me out all the time because they hear me on the radio and they think I'm something I'm not."

"And you never go because you think they're something they're not."

"All I'm saying," Tulsa sounded irritated, "is that if you're expecting—"

"I'm expecting coffee," Mac gently overrode her, "but hoping for coyotes."

More silence.

"How 'bout it?"

"Really, Mac, I've got production so . . . I'll talk to you next week, OK?"

She left him alone with the phone, and he knocked his forehead with the handset. He was just telling her earlier about the elk on the hillside above the bunkhouse every morning, how last Sunday, by moving no more abruptly than the sun-drawn shadows, he was able to approach one animal and, after the better part of the morning, got the curious bull to take a sweat-salty red bandana right out of his hand. He was just between contemplating the irony and concluding that Tulsa would not like being equated with a bull elk when the phone blinked.

"I don't have a car," she said.

"Not to worry, I'll pick you up." Mac tried to lower the timbre of his voice and wondered why it wanted to form an owl's nest just above his Adam's apple.

"This is weird," Tulsa said dryly.

"Is it?"

"We've never even met, but I realized this morning you're the only person around here who really knows me. I missed you, Mac."

"Thank you for that, Tulsa," Mac said, and he meant it. "I missed you too."

"That's why I don't want to wreck it."

"Good God, Tulsa, to hear you talk, I'm already envisioning some kind of gargoyle. I'll be pleasantly surprised if you're three degrees shy of Quasimodo!" He was glad to hear her laughing again. "I've already seen everything I need to see. You read books, you love to laugh, you care about people. . . . "

. . . you have a voice I would willingly drown in.

"Stop! All that's left is 'nice personality'—then I'll know you really are prepared for the worst."

"I'm prepared to go for a drive, Tulsa. Let's not get ahead of ourselves. This isn't about—" Mac hated being so unable to choose his words with her. "Let's just go see what the coyotes have to say about it."

6

ulsa recognized the coat but didn't know from where. It was the style of cowboy coat she'd grown accustomed to seeing since she came to Montana, but this one was different; you could tell by the wear of it that it hadn't come from Capital Sports and Western. It looked like it belonged in a museum or a John Wayne movie, not at the plate-glass front door of Icarus Broadcasting, Inc.

"Love your coat," she said as they stared at each other, each acutely feeling their own real and imagined shortcomings.

"Thank you." Mac was nervous and acting sort of odd and courtly. "It belonged to my grandfather. Very warm . . . good coat."

Tulsa nodded.

"Yup . . . very good coat." Mac was struggling to think of a way to politely motivate her toward the door before Joey came in and started making asinine remarks. "Do you have one? A coat? It's likely to be pretty cool up there."

"Well . . . this." Tulsa held up the bulky Irish fishermen's sweater, thinking she should warn him how fat she was going to look in it. "It's pretty warm."

"Ah. Irish wool."

"Yes. Irish. I got it . . . in Ireland."

"What a coincidence."

"It's very bulky . . . the sweater, that is. Mmm-hmmm . . . 'cause, you know, I have noticed that the nights are colder out here. In the mountains, I mean. I've noticed it's really . . . you know—colder."

"Yup." Mac glanced down at her feet. Sure enough, she was wearing flats. Those hiking boots couldn't be adding more than a half inch to her height. An inch, maybe. Beverly (or was it Vivian?) had given him an expensive pair of Tony Lama's for their one and only Christmas together, but even with the two-inch heels, the brim of his hat barely met Tulsa's eye level.

"Are you sure we haven't met somewhere before?" Tulsa asked, hating how cliché it sounded. "Because I'm sure I remember seeing that coat somewhere."

Mac panicked a little.

Oh, shit, I slept with her and was too hammered to remember. . . . I hate it when that happens. . . .

But he was fairly certain he would have remembered this girl. She was taller than just about any female he knew; a full six feet, he was guessing. She had at least two or three inches on him, anyway. And that wild auburn hair, pronounced nose and jaw, her soft hazel eyes. She was different, handsome enough that Mac was sure he wouldn't have forgotten her.

"Were you at Joey's Christmas party?" Tulsa asked, and they both started reaching.

"I managed to miss that one. Do you get into the Joker's Wild very often?"

"Only once, actually—just briefly."

"Oh . . . well," Mac was relieved. "Guess it's just one of those coats."

"Yes. Well . . . sssoooo . . . " Tulsa pretended to adjust levels and potentiometers in order to avoid his disquieting brown eyes. She tried to make herself more diminutive, leaning back against the console with her feet wide apart, calculating she must be towering at least four or five inches over him.

"Take it downtown, kids," Joey groused, backing into the studio, balancing a stack of carts in one hand, coffee cup in the other. "I've got an airshift to do."

"I'll see you in the morning, Joey." Tulsa wasn't looking forward to his leaving. She gave him what hug she could around the carts and coffee.

"Yeah, see ya." Joey wasn't looking forward to his leaving either and shrugged away from her.

"The amazing Joseph Penopscott," Mac commented out on the sidewalk, "from dishwasher to disc jockey in the space of one afternoon."

"He's kind of upset about going to Billings," said Tulsa absently. She was still studying the coat, searching for it in a confabulation of images and recollections. Mac opened the passenger door of the pickup at the precise moment the engine died. He cursed himself for optimistically parallel parking in a spot that would need to be steered out of.

"Oops," Tulsa said at the truck's final shudder.

Mac swore softly and then said, "Tulsa, I have a potentially painful revelation to make here."

Assuming it had something to do with her, she drew back, steeling herself for the lame excuse he was about to blurt in order to dump her.

"The truck has to have a push start," Mac said, opting against trying to come up with some entertaining way to put it. "Could you just hop in and steer while I give it a shove?" Then, misinterpreting her expression, he guessed she wasn't understanding the "push start" concept and hastened to add, "Not to worry, it's old reliable once it gets going."

"Actually," Tulsa responded, "I have a bit of a painful revelation for you too—I mean, besides the way I look."

"I thought we declared a moratorium on the self-deprecating remarks."

"OK," she said, "it's just that—I don't actually have a Montana driver's license yet, so—you know . . . I probably shouldn't drive."

"Mere technicality," Mac said, moving to the back of the truck. "Just pop the clutch when I tell you."

"Or—any driver's license, actually," Tulsa tagged after him, "I mean—a current one, so . . . I'd really rather not."

"Well, darlin', it's just for a minute—just down the hill." He gestured to the slope, a little annoyed that she was making him beg.

"Mac, I don't know how to drive! OK?" she finally came to it, more than a little annoyed that he had to have a tree fall on him. "See—I can't drive because . . . I really can't drive." She giggled nervously. It wasn't the laugh that Mac loved tickling her for on the phone. It was forced, high and tight.

"I see." Mac knew they were both coming to the same uncomfortable conclusion. "Well, then."

"I don't mind pushing." She was being straightforward, he knew, and not patronizing, but that almost made it worse. "Really, I don't mind."

"No, I'll get Joey—"

"Mac, that's silly. I'm about a foot taller than he is—or you too, for that matter—and probably outweigh you both by a bushel of rocks. You think I don't know I'm built like the proverbial brick shithouse? I don't expect to be treated like some delicate little flower of the north-land so just . . . shut up and drive, OK?"

Seeing nothing else for it, Mac nodded and got in, and Tulsa went to the back of the pickup and heaved it out into the street, which, blessedly enough, had a pretty healthy downgrade. *Thank God for small favors*, Mac said harshly to himself as the truck picked up and rolled forward. He popped the clutch and slammed on the brakes, throwing open her door, and Tulsa dove in singing, "I feel pretty . . . oh, so pretty . . . " and then in her best rancher drawl said, "Yeah, there's sumpthin' 'bout a woman who can push a half-ton Ford . . . mmm-hmmm!"

Mac wasn't laughing. They drove for a while in silence, each try-ing to connect the other to that comfortable night voice they knew.

Off to an inauspicious start, Mac observed dryly, wondering how many levels of hell he had set out to explore this evening. He was be-ginning to notice an old familiar weight on the back of his neck when he heard her clear, rippled laughter. It started low; he felt it resonat-ing just behind his own ribs. It came up the back of his shoulder like the foam on a cold beer and, without the distillation of electronics, it was tantamount to having a kitten in your nightshirt.

Before he could catch it, he let loose the throaty blast that made people turn and look at him in movie theaters. That contagious hoot left Tulsa practically hysterical, and soon they were both open and breathing and tremendously relieved.

"This day sure didn't turn out the way I thought it would," she said. "I'm still employed, I push-started a truck, and now I'm boonie-romping out to visit wild dogs in a stone quarry."

They were already a couple miles out of town and winding upward through Grizzly Gulch into the National Forest. Mac reached over to pull Tulsa's seatbelt across her, and she inhaled the scent of his buck-skin coat. There was suddenly something about the way his ponytail brushed his shoulder, the way the lines crinkled at the corners of his deepset eyes and etched around his mouth in evidence of how much

he liked to laugh. And that coat. Fringes and beadwork like Woodstock or Buffalo Bill . . . dogeared guitar case, lawn-and-leaf bag—it all
came together with the scent of the night mountains in the image of
an angry man at the top of Anne Marie's stairs.

"*You?*"

"What?" Mac grinned at her, innocent, unsuspecting.

"I know who you are! You're that—that—You were arguing with
Anne Marie. And you made a rude remark . . . *about my weight!*"

Mac's brain reeled back through the ten thousand or so arguments
he'd had with Anne Marie over the last twenty years, desperately trying to place Tulsa's face amidst one of them.

"I mean *rude!*" The angrier she got, the more her voice took on an
almost feline quality. "How could you make a crummy, insulting, rude
remark like that to a total stranger?"

better than insulting my friends?

"Tulsa," Mac resisted the comeback in the interest of unruffling
her feathers, "I don't know what you're talking about. I've never
even—"

"She kicked you out of the upstairs apartment and I moved in and
you were—you said—something about—about me not fitting through
the door!"

"No . . . " The scene played itself like a bad slide show in Mac's
head. "That wasn't you—" He tried to remember her face, but all that
came back to him was the two of them standing there: Anne Marie
pregnant as a barn and this other girl, not significantly smaller. But
that girl was not Tulsa.

Not VA!

"But that couldn't have been—you were so—"

"BEEF-O! A cow! Go ahead and say it."

"That's not what I was going to say! You were just—"

"Fat! I was fat. I was *gigantically* fat."

"Well . . . OK, but you've certainly . . . " Mac had absolutely no
idea where to go with this. "Now, you're really . . . very . . . "

"*Fat!* I'm still fat, and I'm certainly making no apologies about it to
you!"

"Tulsa, you are not fat," Mac argued, though he knew that was
about as pointless as a rubber crutch.

"That's what you've been thinking since the minute you saw me tonight, isn't it? 'Lord! What roundup did this heifer stray from?'"

"Don't be ridiculous. It doesn't make a damn—"

"VA Lones: she puts the broad in broadcasting."

"Cut it out, Tulsa—"

"But at least when you have car trouble, it's convenient to be out with a *hulking androgynous barn!*"

"Stop it!" he barked, and the tone shut her down long enough for several deep breaths. "Jesus. How could you even say something like that about yourself? Now, listen," Mac gentled his voice, "I'm sorry that happened. It was a weird time for me and it wasn't you—" But she shook her head.

"Just go back," she said quietly.

"No."

"*Yes!*"

"Forget it." Mac's eyes never left the winding mountain road. "I'm not going to let you manufacture some excuse to sabotage this."

"'This?' This what?"

"Well, I guess that's what we're here to find out."

"Oh! Now we're finding out things, are we? What happened to all that be-as-you-feel 'coffee and coyotes' crap, *darrrrrlin'*," she mimicked him with an exaggerated drawl and then, narrowing her eyes, threatened, "Don't you even think of doing something weird like—like making a pass at me or something!" It sounded odd; she'd never used the phrase "make a pass" in context with herself.

"OK. I'm cool." Mac's tone was calm, but he skidded the truck into a gravel-spitting Y-turn. "Let's go back. But don't you even try to whine and complain that I wasn't interested in you or didn't try to know you or whatever the hell it is you think everybody else is getting and you're not. If there's one thing even wider than your ass, Tulsa, it's this line of crap about how—*shit!*"

Tulsa was so intent on coming back with the mean artillery that she didn't see the deer leap from the shadows into the glare of Mac's headlights. He slammed on the brakes, fighting for control of the fishtailing truck, but the pickup struck the animal with a sickening thud and spun a complete 180 before wrenching to a halt on the steeply angled shoulder.

"*Jesus*," Mac breathed in the immense silence that fell. "Shit."

He placed his hands on top of the steering wheel and briefly rested his forehead there. Tulsa sat wide-eyed, arms taut, gripping the dashboard. After a moment, Mac opened his door and stepped out into the dark, leaving his buckskin coat on the front seat. He came around to the passenger side and opened the door.

"Are you all right?"

Tulsa nodded without looking at him or letting go of the dashboard.

"Good," he said, and unfastened her seatbelt. "Get the flashlight from the toolbox. Get out on the other side. There's quite a little drop-off here."

She felt for the light, turned it on, and clapped it against her hand to shake the connection to life. They didn't have to shine it on the thrashing animal to know that it was still living, but the flickering light revealed frightening glimpses of exposed muscle and bone.

"Sweet Jesus and Maria . . . " Mac uttered, already on his way back to the truck to get a rifle from the gun rack. He loaded it with two shells and returned to the struggling deer.

"Mac," Tulsa ventured, "please, let's just go down and call somebody. . . . "

"There, girl," Mac was saying softly, "It's all right, pretty beauty." He stroked the deer's nose, then stood and, still speaking low and gentle, pumped the shells into her head. Tulsa flinched and made an involuntary sound with each report. Mac checked the rifle and used a rag to wipe off the barrel before hanging it back on the rack. Slinging the seat forward, he came up with a large Bowie knife and rope and started rolling up the sleeves of his flannel shirt.

"Mac—please . . . "

"Just hold the light, darlin'." He used the same gentle tone he had used on the doe. Tulsa said nothing more, but Mac noticed how the flashlight trembled while he gutted and cleaned the deer. It was well after two by the time he tossed the rope over a branch and hoisted the carcass up into a tree.

"I'll pick it up later," he said without expression. "Looks like a lot of meat can be salvaged and at least part of the hide." Wiping the knife on the weeds, Mac resheathed it and tossed it back behind the seat. He kept a gallon of water in the capper for the temperamental radiator, and he used that to clean his arms and face. He slumped wearily against the open door for a minute before leaning in to open the glove compartment and bring out the silver snuffbox. After tapping some marijuana into a little pipe Satchi had carved from sarvisberry wood, he inhaled deeply and held it, looking at Tulsa over the glowing bowl. She stood by the bloody bumper, clutching the flashlight and shivering visibly.

"C'mere," Mac said, but she didn't, so he went around to her. "All right. C'mon now . . . " He pulled her bulky sweater from the cab and laid it across her shoulders. He tried to pull her toward him, but she was rigid. "OK, darlin'," he kept saying as he rubbed her ice-cold hands briskly between his own. "OK, that was a little rough." He offered her the pipe. Tulsa took it and drew deeply. The sensation was that of molten lava flowing into her lungs, and she immediately began choking and gasping. Mac thumped hard on her back. "Put your head forward, darlin'. That's it . . . head down."

When she could breathe again, she croaked, "I don't smoke."

"No kidding," he almost smiled.

"Not good for my throat."

He offered her a canteen instead, warning, "That's whiskey."

"Oh . . . whiskey hates me." Tulsa held it away from herself for a moment, braced, and took a long draw. She winced, took another healthy swig, and handed it back to Mac, wiping her mouth with the back of her hand. "Thanks."

When the pipe was empty, Mac crossed the narrow road and peered down the rocky slope. "Whew," he whistled. "Good thing we landed on the uphill side."

Tulsa didn't respond, so he came back and surveyed the damage to the grill and bumper and suggested they should try to get the truck going. Since they were pointed uphill again, they both pushed with open doors, jumping in the moment there was a spark. It took four tries before the pickup finally sputtered to a reluctant start.

"I guess we got turned around," Mac said. Tulsa nodded but couldn't find her voice just yet. "You OK?" Mac asked after a bit.

"I cannot believe you did that," she said. "Is that even legal?"

"I was responsible for it, Tulsa. Leaving it to suffer and die would be pointless." Mac suspected she knew all this already but needed to be reassured she wasn't accessory to some horrific mutilation-murder. "It would stink and bring bears up to the road and waste a healthy animal."

"Oh, well, thank you, Marlin Perkins."

After that, she didn't speak for a long time.

"You OK?" Mac asked again, straining in the dark cab to see if she so much as nodded. He reached below the 8-track for the Patsy Cline tape he'd searched out and bought, and Tulsa flinched when the back of his hand grazed her calf. Things were not panning out quite the way he'd imagined, Mac was inwardly mourning. He punched up the Patsy Cline tape, looking for a logging road so he could turn back toward town.

. . . I go out walkin' after midnight . . .

It was way too loud, still calibrated to blast Hank Jr., but when Mac reached down to adjust the volume, Tulsa reached over and brushed his hand with her fingertips. The gesture was tentative, but her touch was strong and almost unbearably pleasant. He could still feel it all the way up his arm, even after her hands were back folded in her lap.

It was so dark at the quarry, the stratified backdrop of black and midnight blue was more a cool pressure than an image on the eyes. They sat on a ledge, waiting for the coyotes to emerge and watching the moon and stars travel across ragged openings in the cloudscape. Mac struck a match and held it to the little pipe. He inhaled deeply and held it, then offered the pipe to Tulsa. When she shook her head, her hair shifted on her shoulders, the copper in it catching the orange glow from the bowl. He breathed out and looked away.

"Is that one?" Tulsa whispered, pointing to the far ridge, which was momentarily visible in the teasing moonlight. Before Mac could answer, the coyote stretched a long, melodic howl across the quarry.

"Oh!" Tulsa said softly and settled her back against the stone wall behind them. Mac caught a breath of patchouli and jammed his hands in his pockets to keep himself from reaching for her. He leaned his

head back and sent up a long howl. Tulsa giggled uncomfortably, but
when the coyote extended another bell-shaped cry in answer, she
looked at Mac in amazement.

Mac folded his arms and leaned back, feeling a little more sure of
himself.

thanks, dog

"I'm glad I came," Tulsa said when the arcing song faded.

"Yeah. Me too." He offered her the whiskey and she took a noisy
swig.

"Was it wonderful growing up out here?"

"No."

"Tell me."

"No."

"Why not?" she persisted. "Didn't you have a happy childhood?"

"No," said Mac, and, hoping to divert her attention, asked, "Did you?"

"Yes," Tulsa answered without hesitation, and he could hear her
relishing it. "I lived in this wonderful world of books. Narnia, Oz,
Wonderland, and anywhere Dr. Doolittle could take me. Laura Ingalls
Wilder and—oh! Lucy Maud Montgomery: *Anne of Green Gables.*
Anne was my best friend. She was more real to me than the tutors or
babysitters—I didn't really know any other children. We traveled a lot.
We saw Stonehenge and that huge David—you know, that Michelangelo one. I'd go with Mom while she lectured at colleges and political
things, or we'd go to bookstores and I'd read and she'd sign books all
afternoon and then we'd go out at night to the ballet or the symphony
or just looking at the lights."

"I take it she was a writer."

"Very astute."

"What was her name?"

"Firestein." It was the first time in two years Tulsa had spoken the
name, but the lump in her throat faded after a moment, and she
thought that must mean she was getting over it. "Alexandra Firestein."

Mac searched his memory for the name. *Alexandra Firestein.*
Alexandra—

"Firestein?" he exclaimed. "As in *Catalysts?*"

"And *Greetings from the Fissure of Rolando* and *Bodies, Brains, and
Other Myths* . . . "

"And *Belladonna*—" Mac stopped, but Tulsa finished the title.

"*The Lesbian's Cookbook.*" Tulsa was incredulous. "You read that?"

"Well, no—but, naturally, I've heard of her. And I did read the *Life* magazine thing when she died. 'Alexandra Firestein,'" he recalled, "'Genetrix of the Femilitant Movement.'" He shook his head, trying to encompass it. "Your mother was—*the Tupperware Lady?*"

"Don't call her that!" Tulsa exclaimed defensively. "She hated people calling her that! She wasn't a Tupperware Lady and she didn't 'emasculate' anyone or 'seduce' anyone or anything else they said about her. And I can't believe you actually know that stuff, anyway."

"Well, the philosophy is pretty much crap, but her poetry was incredible! Her passion and command of the language—" Mac's mind caught up with his mouth. "Well, I didn't mean 'crap,' of course, just—"

"Yes you did!" Tulsa cried in amusement. "You did too! And you're not the only one who thought so. My mom was widely . . . misunderstood."

"It was controversial stuff for the early '60s."

"My mother wrote what she believed. She refused to be a hypocrite."

"No kidding."

"And I respect that, but . . . " Tulsa smiled a little and shook her head. "Her worst nightmare was that I would fall in love with some poor schmoe and have five kids. She made me think there was something evil about that, something pathetic or pulverizing or something. By the time I passed the five-eleven, two-hundred-pound mark, she was in hog heaven. Not a lot of boys are into the large-sensible-jumper look. Of course, she took the view that guys never asked me out because they were intimidated by my superior intellect." Tulsa picked up a stone and dropped it back and forth between her hands. "Ultimately, she was pretty disappointed in me. Just before she died, she cut me out of her will."

"Why?"

Tulsa spread her hands in front of her and shrugged.

"Aren't you just a little bit angry about that?"

"No. It doesn't bother me," Tulsa said, trying to mean it.

"Geez, I'd have been pissed as a newt."

Tulsa shrugged again.

"And this is your definition of a happy childhood?" Mac said suspiciously.

"Well, OK—the adolescent part wasn't so great." Tulsa's tone changed. "Mom got sick and we moved to Minnesota so she could go to Mayo for chemotherapy, but then—she wouldn't take any more. So we went home. After she died, I stayed with her partner, Jeanne, and . . . I met . . . a guy—Aaron . . . he was one of Jeannie's students. He liked me to sit for him because I could just sit there—quiet, you know? Still. And he made me feel like I was . . . I mean—I'm not, but . . . in those paintings—I was beautiful or . . . something."

Mac felt it getting crowded and passed her the canteen again.

"But obviously," Tulsa swigged, sighed, and used a stick to scratch a design in the dirt, "that didn't work out. But I found this travel brochure when I was looking through Mom's stuff, and so I'm here." She helped herself to the last of the whiskey. "And I'm sitting on a big old rock and it's so cold my butt's asleep."

"Now in paperback," Mac said, "the VA Lones Story."

"No," she corrected him, "that's the Tulsa Bitters Story. VA doesn't hang out in rock quarries. She drives a '62 Mustang convertible, her blond hair shining in the sun, her legs willowy, nicely waxed, her breasts full, yet perky."

Mac smiled until she prodded him with the stick.

"C'mon . . . your turn. Tell all."

"No," he said, but compromised, "not just now."

The coyote was back, closer this time, and his nightsong justified a comfortable silence, moments, minutes, maybe an hour or more. Mac was not certain if the migrating morning stars were shifting out of design or merely marking time that passed more rapidly than was natural. His lungs were so full of air, he could feel them pressing out against his ribs each time he inhaled Tulsa's scent of patchouli and Lemon Zinger tea.

"Tulsa?" She was looking away to the coyotes on the ridge, so close it made his arms ache. "This might constitute a pass . . . but would it be all right if I kiss you?"

Mac wasn't sure she heard; wasn't completely sure he'd actually spoken the words out loud, until he sensed the movement of her hand along the sandstone ledge. Their fingertips met and they raised their palms, each reading the other to get a sense of where to go, to shift into alignment, to come together.

Tulsa was unprepared for the absolute comfort of his mouth. There was no intrusive tongue, no impatient moan, only an astonishing solace she had no recollection of needing until that moment. When he drew back and touched his forehead to hers, she was terrified that he only wanted her for that suspended second or two, but then he returned, and kept returning, offering her that wanting like a gift, nourishing her with it like milk.

He did nothing more than kiss her for a long time, fully on her mouth, lightly at her temple, nose, and neck, straying across her collarbone, filling her head with the cinnamon coffee scent from the stairwell. He spoke softly to her about her voice and the dark and the deep blue music as the coyotes sang and the moon moved closer to the rocky rim.

His hand drifted inside the Irish wool sweater, but Tulsa tensed.

"OK," he withdrew unhurriedly, not apologizing, still keeping her close. "I'm not assuming anything."

"I know. I'm just sort of . . . self-conscious there."

"Hmm," Mac smiled against her cheek, "yet perky."

She laughed and relaxed into him and he held her that way until her own exploring gave him leave to wander again. He swept the Irish wool up over her head, tie-dyed T-shirt with it, and laid his buckskin coat around her shoulders so she wouldn't feel the cold sandstone beneath her back.

Tulsa consciously tried to slow her pulse, not exactly sure what she was supposed to do to accommodate him. He stretched out over her but braced himself on his forearms, unwilling to give her his weight, creating more shelter than burden. His body was different this way. Tulsa pressed her hands down across his broad back, discovering sinew and strength she wouldn't have guessed were there when she first saw him. Mac exhaled and allowed himself to settle just a bit. She shifted her hips to nestle him and they lay, listening.

"Brrr," Mac finally said. "Strangely erotic or just plain damn cold?"

"The classic Apollonian-Dionysian conflict."

"It's up to you," he told her.

"You're the one whose backside is out there. I'm actually pretty cozy."

"I told you it's a very good coat." Mac nuzzled his way inside the collar and down behind the fringed yoke.

"Mm-hmm . . . " she concurred, "so . . . what do you think?"

"I think it's time to find out what sort of frontiersman I really am."

A bold one, Tulsa told him a little while later, as the sun rolled up the far side of the ridge. Bold and brave.

———————

It was no easy chore hauling Pa Roy's brass bed down to the bunkhouse, but Mac had done it with a little help from Sharkey. After pulling out the plank-and-chain bunks, they went up to the big house to see if the old bed was still good. Mac swapped a set of tire chains for a clean mattress at the secondhand store and spent three January afternoons sanding and polishing the heavy head and foot boards.

The bed was spread with a white Indian blanket whose flying patterns of plum, gold, and red made Tulsa the center of a burning star. As Mac moved over her in the overcast midmorning light, arrows of color seemed to shift and kaleidoscope outward from her auburn hair. She was laughing for plain gladness, reminding him what a joy these things could be sometimes.

"Mac, will you tell me something?"

"What?"

"Are you always this . . . indulgent? Or have you been finessing me?"

"I've been finessing you," he said honestly.

"Oh. Well—" She rolled up on top of him. "Don't stop."

"OK." His mustache tickled her when he smiled.

"I can't figure out . . . " She stroked his face, searching for something, " . . . what it is that you want from me."

"I want you to tell me."

"Tell you what?"

"Just tell." His hands roved upward from her waist.

"I don't know what you want me to say." Tulsa felt inhibited suddenly, but Mac wasn't having any of it.

"Oh, you know, you brat," he growled behind her ear, "don't even try to tell me you don't know. It's right there," he touched her, "on the tip of your tongue," and kissed her, "I can taste it," he lightly bit her bottom lip, her chin, sing-songing, "Tulsa-my-girl . . . talk to me. . . . "

"I don't want to."

"Liar."

She shook her head, grasping to guide him so he would just get on with it already, but he rolled her under him again and drew back out of her reaching.

"C'mon, Mac," she whispered, "would you just . . . "

"What?" he whispered back, and " . . . just what?" he kept coaxing as he singed a path from her shoulder to her hip. He crouched back and swept wide arcs with his mouth, inhaling and nuzzling from one knee to the other, then rooting and nipping his way back again, settling at the center. Tulsa didn't even recognize the sound that brought out of her, more like bird or branch than human voice. She reached for something to hold on to, but Mac kept her there, brought all her blood and reason down to a specific inner place where it concentrated for as long as she could stop breathing and then pulsed, dissolved, dispersed to the surface of her body. She tried to arch away from it and clamped her hands over her mouth to stifle the embarrassing alto sounds that caught across her throat.

"Don't do that!" Mac raised up and trapped her wrists above her head. *"Don't stop it . . . let it come. . . . "*

" *. . . I can't. . . . * "

"You can! I want to hear you. . . . "

He drew her knee to her chest, knowing and stroking her, but still not allowing her to take him in. Tulsa tried to think beyond the rushing in her ears and the intimate taste of herself on his mouth, tried to come up with some words other than the single expression that blocked out everything intelligent.

" *. . . be—with me . . . inside me. . . . * "

" *. . . no . . . no euphemisms . . . you speak the truth to me. . . . * " His voice came from deep in his chest, no more teasing than his iron grip on her wrists. *"Tell me!"*

She told him. She whimpered it once first, but then bucked beneath him and told him out loud. The raw words in the context of her mouth struck through Mac with the force and effect of a splitting maul. He lunged down and forward, lunged again, and let himself fall into the compulsive rhythm. The brass bedrails creaked and hammered an increasing cadence against the wall. Tulsa sank back into a confusion of equal and opposite reactions—joinings, juxtapositions, harmonizings. She tried to say the simple syllable of his name, but he inhaled the voice from her mouth. She tried to tell him again, but Mac was beyond the place where he could speak his own language. The moon, the morning, the rhythm brought his low groan up into a bell-shaped bray.

He collapsed on top of her, chuffing like a grizzly bear, conscious of every quaking muscle in his body. He tasted salt sweat at her temple, but before he could find enough voice to ask her if she was all right, Tulsa covered his face with her hands and pulled his mouth back to hers. She wanted to keep on and he tried for a while to kiss, to talk, but the weight of his own body became unbearable and Mac fell asleep, tangled up with her in sheets and blankets.

Tulsa lay awake, running her fingers back from Mac's forehead, studying the gray hair shot through the black. Steady rain fell on the warped glass window behind the comfortable sound and scent of him as his body became warm and relaxed and his breathing deepened to a rumble. Pine boughs creaked and tossed outside on the hill, but inside the bunkhouse was large and silent.

Muted daylight filtered around the edges of a wide plank door to reveal a single room with stone chimney, wooden floor, and beamed ceiling. In addition to the bed, Mac had scavenged an antique chifforobe and a small round table with three straight-backed chairs. A plain wooden rocker faced the fireplace where the woodstove had been installed, and in the kitchen corner stood an old propane-powered icebox, a tall pie safe, and a wooden dry sink. Mostly there were books: stacked on the table, piled up on the clean-swept floor, and shelved on rough-hewn boards clear up to the ceiling along every available wall. Tulsa could smell the dry paperbacks and crumbling leather-bounds along with the coffee on the stove and the wind outside. A Regulator clock ticked above the mantel and borne on the tempered swing of its pendulum, Tulsa eventually dozed, distantly aware that she was dreaming of toy cows on a glass shelf . . . her mother's footsteps in the hall . . . walls of white . . . swaying train . . . all on a long and pleasant journey.

She faced the board in the control room, her skin luminous with its pale green energy. Lowering her mouth to the microphone, she inhaled, dragged deeply, licking in a long draw of electric energy. She held it for a suspended moment, then exhaled spirals of light and sound. She tried to stir away from the image when she saw Aaron on the far side of the window, but her body was paralyzed with sleep, and just as her hand met the glass, he was lost in falling shadows and coyote songs and the tempered rhythm of the Regulator clock.

Tulsa opened her eyes, afraid she'd spoken Aaron's name out loud, but Mac was focused on the Louis L'Amour paperback he held up to the propane lamp. His other arm rested around Tulsa's shoulder, his wrist lazily grazing back and forth across her bosom.

"Hi," he said without looking away from his book, and gently rolled her nipple between his thumb and index finger.

Embarrassed, Tulsa stirred and pulled the blankets up to cover her chest. "Let me know if you find anything there."

Mac's answer was to drop the novel and tell her to "just shut up, you." He wasn't buying into any of that and there was no use denying it, anyway; the girl was flat as a door. But her nipples were hard and sweet as Christmas candy, and Mac told her that as he kissed and searched and circled at them. Tulsa curved toward him, twining her long, smooth legs with his stocky, weathered ones.

"Lord," he told her, "it's been a long time since I felt like this."

"Like what—exhausted?"

"That too."

"I've wondered," she confessed.

"Hmmm." They were lying close now, face to face, but he avoided her eyes and concentrated on gleaning pine needles and bits of yellow grass from her hair. "Well, I used to be married. Used to see different women from time to time. Can't quite remember why."

"Well," Tulsa touched him, "this is probably as good a reason as any."

"Yup," he smiled, and they drifted together for a while, enjoying the private sounds of the rusty bedsprings, the mountains, and each other.

"Hey, Mac . . . "

"Hmmm . . . " He liked taking words from her tongue the way a bee takes pollen from a day lily.

"I have to go to the bathroom."

His growly chuckle warmed her neck. "I don't think you're going to like it," he cautioned. "I tried to wake you up before the rain started."

"No . . . "

"Looks like it's clearing off already, though."

"Mac, tell me there is a bathroom in your house."

"There is a bathroom *near* my house." He added the disclaimer, "You should have gone at the gas station."

"I did! But that was at seven o'clock this morning and now it's— what time is it, anyway?"

"Time for you to go hiking."

"Oh, funny." Tulsa muffled his amusement with a goosedown pillow. "Will you at least walk with me?"

"Hey, you're the one whose backside is out there," Mac said from beneath the pillow. "I'm actually kind of cozy."

Tulsa retaliated by throwing the covers off him on her way out of the warm bed into the chilly room. "Well, I need a flashlight or something."

"No, a little light only makes the rest seem darker." Mac pulled on his jeans and tossed her a clean flannel shirt from the chifforobe. "Moon's almost full, anyway."

"Yeah." Tulsa tried to swallow her uncertainty as she stepped out into the disorienting drizzle.

The arid mountain accepted the sporadic showers, giving back a loamy smell of ozone and wet pines. The parched dirt drank so deeply, there was no trace of mud in the yard, but up the hill the stubborn rocks stayed slippery. Even with Mac's solid arm at her waist, Tulsa felt cold and wobbly as they made their way up the footpath to the outhouse. He pulled the door open and took a box of wooden matches from the lintel.

"See? All the comforts of home," he said, lighting a citronella candle in a wall sconce. As Tulsa peered past the chipped porcelain seat into the gaping pit below, Mac set the matches back and stepped out. "I'm gonna go down and put a fire in. Then I can fix some—"

"If you say venison, I'm leaving."

"—coffee." He started to scuff off down the path.

"Mac!" Tulsa wanted to ask him not to leave her there alone, but when he turned back, she was too embarrassed. "Could you get my purse out of the truck? There's a toothbrush in it."

"You carry an extra toothbrush," he smiled, "but you don't have a diaphragm?"

"You carry condoms," Tulsa took umbrage, "but you don't have a bathroom?"

"Sounds revealing in either case." Mac let the spring-hinged door slap shut, leaving Tulsa in the gloom.

"Mac?"

"Yeah," he echoed from the other side of the rickety wooden slats.

"I do have a diaphragm."

"Oh." He came close to the door. "Well, OK, darlin'—that's . . . fine."

"I just didn't expect to need it, you know?"

"I know, Tulsa." There was a pause. "Are you sure you're gonna be OK if I go down and make some coffee?"

She debated for a moment and then lied, "Sure." But as his boot-steps crunched away down the weedy pebble path, Tulsa felt the out-house shrinking, disappearing into the measureless face of the mountainside. All around the tiny structure, tall pines hushed and soared. The creek tumbled far off and nightbirds called. But the sounds that had lulled and moved her while she was safe and warm in the brass bed now obscured the labored breathing of a psycho killer. The darkness itself, somehow domesticated by Mac's presence, now swelled to mask terrifying anomies of the wilderness: a silver-tipped grizzly, fangs dripping and gleaming in the moonlight; a razor-clawed bobcat poised on the roof, sinewy haunches stanced for ambush. The toilet hole gaped gloomy and bottomless, scritching and slithering with exoskeletons and leeches teeming upward from the unspeakable, pungent blackness. Tulsa stood with her back against the door, her chest rising and falling, her bladder so full it radiated a painful stitch just inside her hipbone. Ruffling her hair to shake out the spiders undoubtedly spinning down from overhead, she tried to estimate how much time had passed, convinced that he was at that very moment driving up the road as fast as he could go. There was a thump on the door and she let slip a mousy scream before she realized it was Mac.

"You OK in there?"

"Umm . . . sort of . . . "

Mac knew by her high, tight pitch and his own vivid childhood memories that the after-dark privy could be dank and menacing territory.

"Tulsa," he cajoled, "I promise there are no giant rats in there."

rats?

"Snakes got 'em all."

"You slug."

"OK, I'm kidding, Tulsa. . . . Tulsa?" He tapped on the door again. "C'mon, darlin', I've been using this thing since the day I was out of diapers and I never have yet been bit on the butt. Not by a snake, anyway." She didn't answer. "I'll let you check me for scars."

"I'm sorry, Mac," Tulsa peeked sheepishly around the edge of the door, "I think I need to go home."

"Well, of course, that's up to you, but it's a good thirty minutes to the nearest public restroom." She made a shrill sound between her clenched teeth and clapped the door shut again. Mac heard rustling and some squeaky cussing, followed by the telltale echo of a long, steady stream falling far below. There was more rustling and Tulsa emerged, head high and hands out in front of her.

"Soap and water. Immediately."

Mac bowed and motioned toward the pump out in front of the bunkhouse. He had already filled the trough, adding a soup kettle of hot water from the stove, and left a towel on the fencepost. "You go on down," he told her. "I gotta see a man about a Russian racehorse and then I'm gonna smoke for a bit."

Tulsa shivered down the slope and splashed a little in the water. Her neck and body were whisker burned and sticky with dried sweat, and she was sore and damp between her legs. The icy water on her face was not as painful as she thought it might be, so she took off the flannel shirt, kicked off her shoes, and shucked out of her jeans. Gritting her teeth against the cold, Tulsa held her hair up over her head and stepped into the trough, trying not to scream too loudly. She washed quickly and leaped back out, dashing to the porch to dry herself. From there, she watched Mac sitting up the hill on a boulder, toking his pipe in the light of the moon. It bothered her. He wasn't, according to all those health class films, the way drug addicts are supposed to be: greasy haired, strung out, amoral party animals. Mac's house was clean and austere and he was the most quiet person she'd ever known. Cowboys tended to be blustery, radio guys were mostly egomaniacs, and the literary types, just plain obnoxious, but Mac defied all those categories, sitting calm and solid as the grass and granite hillside.

By the time he came back, Tulsa had gone in, seeking the warmth of the woodstove. She was sitting in the rocking chair, cradling his guitar, stroking the slender neck and singing a Patsy Cline song the easy way a person does when she's mellow and satisfied and thinks she's alone. Outside the window, Mac could hear her, textured, low, and bluesy. He leaned his forehead against the door.

. . . crazy for tryin', crazy for cryin',
and I'm crazy for lovin' you . . .

She finished the song and went back to meandering on the strings.
You're too old for this, cowboy

His body ached down to the bone, every muscle and joint telling him he could never keep up with a young girl who wanted so much so well. When he tromped noisily on the porch boards and rattled the door open, Tulsa turned from the firelight and smiled. He stood behind her, resting his hands on her shoulders as she wandered and riffed.

"Tulsa," he said, "I won't tell you I've never been in love before, but only one other woman has played my Alvarez."

"Tell me."

Mac sat cross-legged at her feet, gazing into the fire.

"My mother," he began, "had jet-black hair and a golden voice."

―――――

From the first time Royal MacPeters had the Blackfoot girl in the fragrant hayloft, she loved him. His was the only human touch she'd ever felt. The stone big house Royal's father built before he died was the only home she'd ever known, and the thought of leaving there was worse than any punishment Royal could mete out to her when it became apparent that she was carrying his child. The white doctor wouldn't come for her, so Roy obeyed her calm instructions, looped a rope around the brass headboard, tied a knot in a whiskey-soaked rag, laid the blade of his Bowie knife in boiling water, and, when it was over, placed the baby, messy and squalling, on the bed beside her. The great stone house, grayed and settled with time, seemed to shift and breathe with a new sort of sound and daylight. Satchi secretly called her daughter White Feather, but in front of Royal, who didn't go in for Indian ways, the baby's name was Sarah Emily MacPeters, after his mother.

Satchi was pregnant again by summer, but that baby boy emerged feet first, blue and lifeless, the cord wrapped tightly around his neck. The following year another boy was stillborn, and Satchi did not conceive again, making Royal's shame and disappointment complete. Instead of strong, tall sons, Royal worked the ranch with cowhands hired seasonally for branding, calving, and driving the Herefords from grasslands to market. They lived in a one-room cabin down the hill from the stone house and didn't become overly friendly with Roy, who was gruff and demanding and quick to fire them and fight them. Sarah refused to say which of them got her pregnant the summer she turned sixteen. Royal beat her, hoping she would either speak the man's name or miscarry the child, but she kept silent and gave birth to a son in the spring of 1934, and no amount of intimidation could dissuade her from naming him Michael White Wolf MacPeters.

That year was a bad one for Royal. The summer was scorching and arid and the winter dragged on through April, with long, agonizing cold snaps that trapped them inside for days on end. Impossible drought and the failure of his winter wheat forced him to sell off most of his cattle and more than five thousand acres. He worked the remaining sixty-five hundred with just the Indian woman and her daughter and one or two transient hands until his grandson was old enough to help. At three, the boy collected eggs and fed chickens. At five, he began mucking out stalls in the stable and watering the horses, pigs, and sheep. By the time he was nine, he was splitting wood, digging fencepost holes, and shooting and riding well enough to go hunting with Pa Roy.

Royal liked to eat his supper in silence and spent evenings sitting at the table, drinking whiskey from a large glass tumbler, staring at the fire or pacing on the front porch. His smoldering temper was quick to blaze out, and though his grandson remembered a deep, rolling laughter now and again, Pa Roy's moods were generally black. Sarah was wise enough to keep the boy away from him. They would walk to the creek and fish for brown trout or climb up to the timberline and look down across the ever more populated valley.

After dark, they sat in her room and she played guitar. Her voice was low and sweet as jam. She and the boy would listen to the radio late into the night, copying down words to all the songs on the Grand Ol' Opry: Jimmy Rodgers, Roy Acuff, Patsy Montana. They would figure out the guitar chords, singing in harmony. Where the Alvarez came from, Sarah's son didn't remember, but she told the boy that his father, Hank Williams, had given it to her as a promise gift and that someday, he would come back in his Cadillac, beat the crap out of Pa Roy, and take the rest of them to live in Nashville, Tennessee, and they would be famous singers on the Grand Ol' Opry, that's what.

Sarah always laughed like a child and loved to bait and devil her father, even when she caught hell; getting whipped or locked out of the house for the night. She would sing a song he'd forbidden, walk along the high fence rail in front of the stable, throw rocks at the chickens. She would talk Blackfoot in front of him and refuse to answer to her white name, but at the same time, she wriggled away when Satchi tried to braid her waist-long black hair, and one day came back from town with it bobbed just below her shoulders and bleached a brittle orange-blond, the color and consistency of dry straw.

Shortly after that, Pa Roy caught her kissing a town man who had come to buy a pony from them. He punched out the town man, whipped Sarah until the strop drew blood, and then used his long knife to cut off the rest of her hair at the nape of her neck. That night, as the Grand Ol' Opry scratched over the radio and Satchi pressed a yarrow and wildflower poultice on her back, Sarah took the boy's hand and pulled him onto her bed, curling up close behind him. She barely spoke except to ask him what he wanted for his birthday tomorrow. Hank, the boy tried to tell her—he just wanted Hank to come, but he could barely speak for fighting the burning in his throat. She put the Alvarez away in her chifforobe behind one pretty yellow dress and four plain flannel shirts and locked the door.

The next morning, the boy awoke to the sound of Satchi keening.

They buried his mother in a meadow a little way from Royal's father, mother, and sisters and the tiny babies who never even had names. Royal and the boy piled rocks all around the grave for a border while Satchi and the neighbors rode back to the house and all the women brought out food. After supper, Pa Roy sat staring at his whiskey and Satchi smoked her pipe and rocked in front of the fireplace. People sat about awkwardly until Mrs. Chadwick offered to take the boy back to their place. Mr. Chadwick even offered to pay Pa Roy for the work he would do, but Pa Roy said they would be shorthanded now and the boy would have his mother's chores too, and then everyone left. The next day, he helped the boy whitewash the back of the stable, sullenly pointing out places where the viscous paint failed to efface the seeping red stains. It was done now, he said, and nobody would speak Sarah's name in his house again.

Years passed, and Pa Roy's moods descended deeper. He beat the boy for coming home late from school, for not finishing his chores to strict satisfaction, but most often for things that fell into ambiguous realms of "lip" and "bullshit" and "Indian talk." He mounted a broken wagon wheel on the back wall of the stable and the boy would stand, feet apart, arms wide, gripping the spokes, silently cursing the old man with every stroke of the razor strop.

When they went hunting up into the mountains, they stirred beans on the fire and Pa Roy drank cinnamon coffee and told his grandson about bullsnakes and mountains and weather, about having women and training horses and about the life he could have had if he had only married a girl from town. He told of how he was an only son with seven sisters, born in a log cabin that burned to the ground when he was twelve. Royal's mother and two of the sisters were killed in the fire, and his father took the other girls to a boarding house in Winston and, as soon as it was spring, put them on a train to Pennsylvania. Then, along with Roy, who was of necessity a man now, the patriarch of the MacPeters clan set to rebuilding. They erected a large barn on the blackened cabin site and lived in it with the livestock while they laid the foundation and front porch for the great stone house up on the hill. Royal's father was determined it should have an expansive sleeping loft for grandchildren and an airy sitting room for the girls and their suitors. He kept speaking of how the family would come together again next fall . . . next spring . . . surely by next year Christmas. But Royal turned eighteen and it was still just the two of them, so they hired a young Blackfoot girl to keep house, and from the first time he had her in the fragrant hayloft, Royal loved her.

In the night mountains, Pa Roy wanted to be a patriarch, and the boy desperately needed a father. But after three days or so, they would ride back home, dragging a pallet of venison and skins, and Pa Roy would sit at the table drinking whiskey after supper and the boy would hide from him, reading books in the lamplit barn or slipping down the road to meet his best friend, Ben Sharkey, who always managed to beg, borrow, or steal beer and cigarettes for them to take down by the creek. Ben was almost two years older, wild-eyed and smart. They slashed their palms and pressed them together, dreaming of how they'd one day get the hell out of God-forsaken Montana. When Ben was old enough to join the army without his parents' permission, he stood beside his blood brother, who swore to the recruiter that he was seventeen too, and this was indeed his father's signature on the crumpled permission slip.

It was in the army that everyone began calling him Mac. His twenty-year hitch began when he was barely sixteen. He served both in Korea and in Vietnam, where he was shot in the back by a frightened young private just ten days before he was to get out and go home. Between tours, he was stationed in Kentucky, Wisconsin, and Kokomo, Indiana; each time with a different wife. He married Lorene O'Donnel twice in Montana and once in Japan, but she was a Helena girl and pretty much stayed there, with or without him. He got himself shipped overseas every chance he got, but even when he was forced by marriage or divorce to spend time in Montana, Mac felt about as far from the old place as a man could travel.

By the time he retired from the military and came back home for good, Colter hardly knew him, Ben was in the VA psych ward, Satchi had suffered a stroke that left her simple-minded, and the ranch was down to a hundred sixty acres. He never went there, though Satchi sang and rocked in his dreams, spinning dreamcatcher's tales of Spoo-pii the turtle and Piye the Feather Woman who brought the pipe as a gift from Api-stoh-toh-ki, the Creator. He longed to ask her things and tell her things and touch her. He kept resolving to go Saturday, next Sunday, as soon as it warms up a little. . . .

One day, Mac returned home to find a large Bowie knife stuck in his front door. Below the familiar curve of the pearl-inlaid handle hung the buckskin coat and a long black braid. Satchi had gone to make peace with her ancestors, and passed away with her was Mac's last chance to do the same.

———

Tulsa didn't speak until Mac was through. As she listened, she played softly on the Alvarez, got up to bring him coffee every so often, and eventually stretched out beside him in front of the fire where he sat cross-legged and didn't move for the two hours it took him to tell as much as he was ready to have her know. When he finished, there was silence for a while, and then he seemed to return to the same place she existed, and Tulsa felt it was all right to sidle over against his back, her arms and legs around his middle.

"Now in paperback: The White Wolf MacPeters Story."

Mac relaxed against her and they sat that way for a bit until he became aware of her soft kisses growing more insistent at the back of his neck. "Lord, you brat kid, are you trying to kill me?"

"Oh, c'mon . . . " She pressed her hands down, across his chest and stomach to his lap. "What kind of frontiersman are you?"

"Tired and hungry, darlin'. Really." Mac suddenly felt confined within the bunkhouse walls, stifled by Tulsa's constricting embrace. He'd already compromised his usual comfort level by bringing her here in the first place. He didn't know what he was thinking—letting her sleep here all day, telling her all that about old things that were none of her business.

"We should head into town," he told her, trying to keep his voice even.

"Later." Tulsa shifted to face him, too wrapped up in things to realize that he wanted her to go. She kissed his mouth and pushed his shoulders back to the floor, tugging at his shirt tails, nuzzling her way down to the front of his jeans.

"Really . . . no more, Tulsa . . . "

"Would it make you nervous to know," she spoke without looking up from his silver belt buckle, "I haven't actually done this part before?"

"Then don't, babe. You don't have to—"

"See, I made the mistake of explaining my mother's philosophy on this to Aaron and after that, he just . . . well, you can imagine." She concentrated on the buckle, trying to figure it out.

"Tulsa, c'mon . . . " Mac tried to grasp her shoulders, thinking he'd damn well better get this girl gone right now, before he wanted any worse to have her stay. She won her battle with the buckle. Every instinct told him to recoil, but his body had already gone ahead without him. The longer she kept on, the further she drew him away from himself and each little eternity she paused, to change her position or catch her breath, hardened the knot of panic inside him. Along with the paralyzing possibility that she might stop, Mac felt certain dread and knowledge that if she continued, she would take something from him and swallow it forever, ingesting him so deeply he would never withdraw himself whole.

"*Tulsa!*" he strangled, "*Jesus God—you gotta stop. . . .* "

But whether she heard him or not, Tulsa persisted. She continued the relentless exploring, listening, moving on instinct, until Mac finally caved in, his fists clenched against the involuntary movement of his hips. She tongued him clean like a mother bear and drew the back of her hand across her mouth, resting her cheek against the warm fur of his belly, smiling at the rise and fall of his labored breathing.

"Jesus, Tulsa . . . Sweet Jesus and Maria . . . "

"Shhh," she kissed and calmed him, "you see? It's all right. I've read *Fear of Flying*. And *Delta of Venus*."

Mac lifted a wave of auburn hair that had fallen across her face.

"Lord," he groaned, letting his head thunk back on the wooden floorboards, "I love a woman who reads."

7

T ulsa crept into the entryway Monday morning at ten and almost made it to the first landing before Anne Marie's hiss snaked up and caught her like a lasso. *"Tulsa!"*

"Morning," she mumbled, not looking but knowing there was no escape.

"Tulsa, get down here!"

"Actually, I'm really tired, Anne Marie."

"Would you just—*gt dn hr!*" Anne Marie gestured emphatically with her hand and some sort of clench-jawed verbalization. Tulsa backed down the stairs and through the French doors.

"Please," Anne Marie pointed to the street where Mac was just pulling away. *"Please!* Tell me that was not who I think it was."

"Anne Marie—"

"Are you insane, Tulsa? Are you *crazy?"*

Tulsa folded her arms across her stomach and realized that it was whisker burned, too. She dropped onto the long peach-colored sofa and smiled. There was not a thing Anne Marie could say—

"First off," Anne Marie said anyway, "he's married."

"Separated over two years, divorce in the works."

"OK, how about the fact that he's about fifty years old?" She ticked negatives on her fingers. "He could be your grandfather!"

"Forty-seven. So father, maybe—great uncle, max. And I'm very niece to my Great Uncle Max," Tulsa delivered with Groucho brow action and invisible cigar.

"Tul, you don't know anything about him," Anne Marie was almost pleading.

"What happened to all that wonderful minding our own business around here?" Tulsa sighed. "I'm a big girl, Anne Marie. I can take care of myself."

Anne Marie sat beside her friend. "I know, Tul, but all that aside— there's something you better know." She looked so strained, so concerned and motherly, Tulsa wished she could say what Anne Marie wanted to hear.

"What?" she said instead. "That you slept with him at some point in ancient history?"

Anne Marie's mouth dropped.

"That bastard!" she screamed in a whisper, *"He told you about that?"*

"Nope," said Tulsa, taking devious delight, "you just did." Over Anne Marie's angry sputtering, she added, "And I really don't care to know the details."

They both knew that was a lie, but Anne Marie visibly calmed herself and swallowed hard. "All right. Let's just drop it. But Tulsa, last night—"

"Last night was none of your business, Anne Marie. And now, I'm going up to bed." She kicked her feet down from the coffee table and spun toward the door. "Don't do this to me. Please! I haven't felt this happy in a long, long time. I'm entitled to enjoy it a little."

"OK—fine, but last night—"

"No!" Tulsa held her hands over her ears.

"Tulsa, listen to me!"

"I don't want to hear it! You're the one who doesn't know him. And you don't know me, either, so just shut up and *mind your own business!"*

Tulsa was halfway out the door when Anne Marie seized her hand.

"OK. Have it your way." She was sounding suspiciously cheerful all of a sudden. "C'mon back down if you need to borrow some tea or something."

"And mind your own damn tea, too," Tulsa snapped. She stomped up the stairs, leaning over the banister to flip open her mailbox and take out two sales circulars and a single postcard. Irritated and fatigued, she headed up the first flight. (Hennesy's had Lee Riders on sale.) Anne Marie just had to be everybody's mother. (Twenty-five percent off.) Or maybe she was jealous. (Capital Sports and Western.) Or upset about Joey leaving. (Big boot roundup.) Tulsa felt a twinge of guilt when she realized she hadn't been there to say goodbye to him. ("The Twin Cities Welcome You"; Saint Paul's Scenic Skyline.) She misstepped and caught herself, trying to blame her racing pulse on the steep pitch of the stairway.

My Hippolyte . . .
no

Having a miserable
not happening

time. Wish you were
joey's idea of a joke

here. Please
him and colter or

come home. I
anne marie?

love you.

Tulsa stared at the postcard, straining the words through a mesh of vessels that were emptying the blood from her head. She turned it over. Turned it over again. There was no postage on it. She assimilated this information, comprehended the implications, but was still some-how unprepared when she looked up and saw Aaron sitting there on his suitcase. His corn-colored hair was longer than it used to be, his angular face softened and matured by the red-gold shadow of a beard and mustache. And now he was standing, still long in the legs and broad in the shoulders but not so lanky and boyish as he used to be. His seastone eyes were as clear and magnetic as she remembered, and "Hello, Tussles," he said, just as sweet as a daydream.

Her mouth felt like novocaine aftermath, her lips hardly able to form words, but after a weighty moment, it seemed like she ought to say something.

"Umm . . . how long have you been sitting here?"

"A while. I flew in last night, but I missed you."

" . . . oh . . . "

He extended his hand to help her up the stairs, and warm memories coursed upward from the back of her knees to the nape of her neck.

"Your neighbors told me you work nights," he said.

"Yes! That's right!" His smile was enough to make Tulsa start stammering excuses and denials. "I work nights and . . . in the morning—I get home. So—here I am . . . just . . . getting home. From work." She fumbled to unlock her door. He reached past her and Tulsa breathed deeply. Linen, tweed, and clean hair.

"They seem like quite the eclectic group."

"Oh yeah," she said weakly, "they're really . . . quite . . . mm-hmm."

"Colter was showing me his studio. He's doing some interesting work."

"Yes! Isn't he. Colter. Very . . . very interesting guy."

"Oh," Aaron hesitated. "Is he?"

"No! No . . . no, no. I just meant . . . you know—his work."

Aaron smiled again and stepped toward her, but she sidestepped.

"*Tea!* I'll just run down and borrow some." She bolted for the door.

"No, don't bother," he called after her, "Tussles, really . . . "

"Be right back," she called, bright as saccharine. Desperately, penitently taking back everything she had just thought about her, Tulsa clung to the banister all the way down to the first floor where Anne Marie posed, holding the door open, looking at her watch.

"Five . . . four . . . three . . . two . . . Ah, revenge is sweet."

Pressing her temples to keep her head from flying off, Tulsa dodged into the kitchen, pacing and squeaking, *"oh god oh god oh god!"*

Her eyes met Anne Marie's and they burst out laughing, but after a minute, Tulsa sounded like she was getting a little hysterical.

"This *cannot* be happening!"

"OK, Tul," Anne Marie said, taking her by the elbow, "get a hold of yourself. This is just a guy. Just a guy you used to know." She tried to decide if Tulsa was laughing or crying and determined that she was doing both.

"You know that isn't true! You've been listening to me whine for the last year about how I can't get over him and he's so wonderful and so beautiful and—Oh! *Isn't he beautiful, Anne Marie?*"

"He's beautiful, Tul."

"Anne Marie, this is my punishment. He's going to smell it on me. He's going to know just by looking at me—*just look at me!*" She raised her shirt to show her whisker-burned stomach and chest, then started pacing again. "I go my whole life attracting *nobody*—I wait two years— *nothing*—I do it with somebody else and WHAM! Oh, shit . . . Anne Marie, what am I going to tell Mac? I don't care what you say, he *is*—" she made a gesture with one fist to her heart, though she wasn't sure what that meant, "and he does—because otherwise . . . oh, shit, Anne Marie, I'm a slut. A *slut!* And I did it outside! I used an outhouse. And condoms. And I helped kill an animal. Cut its head off. *Ate it!*"

They stared at each other in horror and then burst out laughing again.

"Drink this." Anne Marie put a glass in her hand. Tulsa downed the strong dry sack and felt somewhat better, once she was through gagging. "OK now," Anne Marie rubbed Tulsa's shoulders like she was sending Rocky Balboa into the last round, "you don't owe anybody any explanations, but you've gotta go back up there."

"No, I can't. I can't." Tulsa sat down and covered her face with her hands. "I have to leave town, cut my hair, or kill myself."

Anne Marie sat beside her. "Shall I get the scissors?"

"Only if you're out of razor blades."

"All right, c'mere." Anne Marie dragged her into the bathroom, raked a brush through her hair, and hastily twisted three notches of braid into it. "Take this." She pressed a box of Cranberry Cove teabags into Tulsa's hand. "And this." She hugged her tight, then stepped back. Tulsa saw something in her furrowed brow.

"What? What?"

"You do smell like you've been doing it."

"*Nnnnnnnnaaaagh!*"

"Not to worry! Not to worry!" Anne Marie dragged her back into the bathroom. "Baby powder or rose hip talc?"

Tulsa pointed to the rose hip cannister, lifted her shirt and held out the waist of her jeans while Anne Marie battered her with the powder puff.

"OK. Now pull your sweater on. There. You're perfect." She steered Tulsa to the door and gave her a slight push. "He's lucky if you even look at him twice. *He's* lucky. And you can worry about Mac later. If there's one thing he understands, it's eat 'n' run, honey. He's no stranger to the one-night stand."

"Do you really think that's all he was doing?" Tulsa held on to Anne Marie, not sure which answer would be worse.

"Oh, sweetie . . . go upstairs. This is what you've been wanting! I know the timing turned out a little awkward, but," she put her hands on Tulsa's shoulders, holding her at arm's length, "love is about every day, not just the weekends. Love is about bread and butter, Tul. Mac is about—"

if you say venison i'm leaving

"God, I don't know—beer and beef jerky. There's a guy upstairs you could make a life with. Don't mess that up for some . . . don't mess it up for anything."

Tulsa nodded, knowing Anne Marie was right but wishing she could have avoided the phrase "eat 'n' run." She started up the stairs, but the cold and exertion of the weekend quickly caught up with her. Her legs felt stiff and trembly. She pulled Mac's flannel shirt out from her chest and tucked her nose inside the collar. It smelled like woodsmoke and Mac's body. Behind the chalky rose hips, her own body still smelled like sex and panic. Tulsa leaned against the wall. No matter how tightly she shut her eyes, tears squeezed out. Her throat was blocked by a painful lump she couldn't seem to swallow. Hugging the tea to her chest, she struggled to make herself breathe, but the lack of sleep combined with the farcical impossibility of it all crushed her into the corner of the landing. She felt herself freezing, falling, being pulled into some sort of vacuum, and had just begun to slide down the wainscoting when she felt Aaron's arms around her. Kissing her wet cheeks and aching throat, he kept telling her that he was here, that everything was all right because he was here now.

"I love you, Tussles. . . . I still do. . . . Please say you still love me. . . . Do you?" he kept saying between and around kisses and Tulsa kept answering, "Yes, but—"

"But nothing."

don't stop it let it come

"Nothing else matters." He drew her up to the apartment, kicked the door closed, and frantically pulled her sweater over her head.

"Wait," Tulsa said feebly. "Please, Aaron . . . "

"Yes." It was an old private joke between them. "You please Aaron—immensely." He dropped the Irish wool on the floor behind her.

"Aaron, *don't!*" she said more firmly. "Seriously—*stop it!*" She clenched her arms against her sides to block his hands from moving under Mac's shirt.

"What's wrong?" He looked disappointed and surprised; in two years together, she had never once turned him down.

"I'm sorry," Tulsa tried to regulate her voice, "I'm really tired and grungy and I just need to sit in the bathtub for a little while, OK?"

"Oh. Sure. Of course."

Tulsa retreated to the bathroom, thinking how hellish she must look to him without makeup, without styling spritz, without a thick padded bra under expensive preppy clothes. Someone who looked like she did at this moment must be nuts turning down someone like him.

"Look—just make yourself at home, OK?" She opened the bathroom door a crack, threw the box of teabags out, and slammed it again, as if she were feeding beef to a Bengal tiger. She turned the water on hard and hot and sat on the toilet seat, afraid to take off her clothes because she felt herself disintegrating inside them. She pulled the drain chain so the running water would continue to cover her meeping sobs without overrunning the tub, but by the time it refilled, she'd settled somewhat and let herself sink into the steam. Her mind gradually ceased racing, and a desolate calm slowed her pulse. Tulsa took a deep ragged breath and started giggling again. She couldn't stop. This whole stupid entanglement was so—

A week ago, she and Mac would have laughed about it. She would have related the tale to him like a Molière farce, complete with *Psycho* violins and the *aaaack! sproing-ng-ng* sound effect of her face falling right off the front of her head when she saw Aaron at the top of the stairs.

"Tussles?" Aaron called solicitously. "Here's your tea." Without waiting for an answer, he opened the door and stepped across the checkered floor with two cups on saucers. Tulsa thrashed her knees up to her chest to hide herself, wishing she had either bubble bath or the willpower to tell him to get out. His eyes were blue and unwavering, and he didn't bother to pretend he wasn't looking at her.

"I like your place." Aaron sat up on the toilet tank, feet on the seat, elbows on his knees, nonchalant, sipping his tea. "It's very quaint."

Tulsa mumbled something into her teacup.

"So . . . how have you been?" he asked.

" . . . ok . . . " Tulsa searched for VA Lones, but her own small voice emerged.

"Several people have been extremely concerned about you."

"Oh." Tulsa hoped he could tell she didn't want to hear about it.

He could tell but continued anyway. "Jeanne and I were frantic that whole first year, imagining all sorts of things about how you might have joined a cult or gotten involved with some serial killer or something." She gave him such a look, he decided to change the subject. "Anyway, I'm just glad you're all right."

"Yeah."

"Are you back in school?"

She shook her head.

"I finished my master's at Minneapolis last year." He waited a moment before adding, "Then I got in at Delacroix."

"*Oh, Aaron!*" Tulsa leaned forward to grasp his hand. "I'm glad! I know that meant everything to you."

"Actually, I sort of burned out on the idea after—everything." He blew across the rim of his cup. "But Jeanne thinks it's important for me to go."

"Aww. Tough life of the protégé," Tulsa teased. "I hear Paris is positively punishing this time of year."

There was a silence, and then Aaron cleared his throat. "So you're just . . . "

"I have a job."

"That's great. The real-life thing. Grit and all that."

"Oh, it gets gritty all right."

"What do you do?" he asked. When Tulsa started giggling again, Aaron looked at her, confused but smiling, wanting to understand and laugh with her.

"Actually," Tulsa said, "I'm . . . I'm a disc jockey."

"You're kidding."

"Would you rather I joined the cult?"

"No—but you're so . . . I just couldn't quite picture it."

"Of course you can't picture it, darlin'—it's radio!"

Tulsa meant to make an expansive gesture, but her teacup tipped on its saucer and spilled on Aaron's shirt sleeve, and her giggle impulse erupted with a loud snort. Pulling away from the scalding Cranberry Cove, Aaron dumped his own cup onto the front of his pants, and then Tulsa couldn't stop laughing.

"God, you're in a bizarre mood today." He shook his head and set the cups in the sink, but being soaked gave him an excuse to pull off his shirt and his gray twill pants, and then he was stepping into the long lion's-foot tub with her and the room suddenly seemed very heavy with steam.

Tulsa shrank back into the corner, wondering why she hadn't converted to Catholicism and become a nun or leaped off a speeding train when she had the chance. She knew that if she got out, he would see her, but if she stayed in, he would touch her. She pulled herself in like a turtle, knees tucked under her chin, arms closed around them. "Aaron—"

"You look so . . . amazing. . . . "

"Aaron, I can't do this right now."

"What's wrong?" He pulled her foot toward him and stroked a slippery bar of soap across the bottom. "Still feeling grungy?"

"Yes. Very."

He slid the soap around her ankle and up her calf to the back of her knee. He sponged and kissed her face and body, ladled water over her hair and massaged shampoo through it, saying how much he liked it long. When she sank underwater to rinse, tossing her head like a mermaid, Aaron pulled her hips down toward his, lifting her feet apart and up, onto the rounded ceramic lip of the tub, and Tulsa couldn't push him away—not after all the nights and mornings she had cried for him. Aaron's erection slid inside her, cool compared to the hot water, smooth and slender compared to

mac

Tulsa jerked away and upward so abruptly, she struck her head on the faucet, sloshing water onto the floor as she scrambled to get out.

"I'm sorry . . . I'm sorry," she and Aaron both kept saying at the same time but for different reasons. Tulsa threw open the linen closet and grabbed for the largest towel, holding it in front of her with trembling hands.

"Here." She handed him a towel, crying again, partly because her head hurt so bad.

"I'm sorry, honey," he said again. "Too soon—I know. I'm an idiot."

"*Please!* Just—here." Tulsa thrust the towel at him, averting her eyes from the obvious focal point.

"Don't be angry at me for wanting you." He slid a warm, wet hand down from her elbow and took the towel. "But it's OK. I can wait." Without hiding or behaving like a stranger, he dried his long fair legs and lean body while Tulsa stared at the floor and tried to breathe normally. "Whatever you need."

Tulsa wasn't sure what he was trying to say or wanting her to say in response, so she simply said, "Thank you. Now, could you please . . . ?"

Aaron nodded and gathered up his clothes, kissing her cheek and apologizing again as he left the bathroom. Tulsa was suddenly too tired to hold up her soaked and throbbing head. She wrapped the towel around herself and lay down on the tile by the radiator, pushing the dial just enough to kick it on.

what'll I do mom what'll I do

Aaron was here and that should be all that mattered. For a long time, she'd been telling herself this would make everything all right.

"I'll make it be all right," she had told him, trying not to let it sound like begging. "Just tell me what you want me to do."

He shook his head miserably, gathering his books and records from her shelf. "I just need to be by myself for a while so I can tune into what I'm feeling about all this. Then—I don't know. Maybe someday we'll be able to get past all this anger."

"What? What does all that even mean?" She spread her hands open at her sides. "*This* is some day, Aaron—it's *this* day—*today!* The only day I can think about, because I love you and I can't just—*not!*" More fighting and crying, and then he was gone, but she kept telling herself, *someday* . . . She had imagined, planned, nurtured it a million different ways. Now it was here, and she was screwing it up.

She closed her eyes, trying to block out images of the bunkhouse, the brass bed, the Alvarez. On the rocky outer rim of her consciousness, coyotes sat, silently waiting for the moon to rise. Something inside her turned. The baby was growing, reaching, extending its hands out through her skin into the sunlight. She wanted to give it to Aaron as a gift, wrapped in her body, ribboned with her auburn hair. But he disappeared into the fog that falls in the mountains at night, moving so quietly she had to work her way up the hill, touching and reading the braille face of every tree. Now the baby was tearing her open that it might come away. She looked down to see blood flowing out of her, swirling red onto a sheet of white morning haze. She wanted Aaron to see all that she had done for his sake. She stepped into the trough to cleanse herself for him, but suddenly she was beneath the frozen water, watching him pass by on the other side of the solid surface. It rippled into a kaleidoscope of plum, blue, and black, and then, mercifully, enveloping darkness fell.

———

"Well, don't you look like the cat who swallowed the canary," Berryl said.

A little while after he dropped Tulsa off at the house, Mac was comfortably saddled up on a barstool at the Joker's Wild.

"Hey, Mac, how is it?" Yak was playing the jovial bartender. "What have you been up to this weekend?"

"Oh . . . split a couple cords of wood," Mac said for his own amusement, but Ben Sharkey was sitting just down the bar, and it didn't get past him. He *fr-frmphed* and brought his beer over, reaching out a ratchety hand to nudge Mac's shirt pocket. Mac proffered the pack of Camels, but they both noticed there was only one left.

"It's yours, Shark-man," he shrugged. Ben took it, looking expectantly at Mac over the flame of a Cricket lighter, but Mac wasn't talking, so they just leaned their flannel elbows on the bar and sipped from their heavy glass mugs, and Ben watched his old friend looking satisfied and foolish; a man who'd been laid like the Last Iron Mile. Mac drank only one beer and a shot of Jack and actually paid for them before he left.

"This must be serious," Berryl called after him.

Hopping into the rolling truck, he found the Patsy Cline tape still in the deck and turned it up loud as if he were a kid cruising. He was

tempted to turn back up Benton and knock on her door, but he knew
she needed to sleep, and he needed to get back to the ranch and do a
few things. He had decided to take on a couple of horses so he could
teach Tulsa to ride (she'd be a natural, Mac figured, with those mile-
long legs of hers), but that meant putting in some serious fence work
and finally facing the stable—either to repair it or tear it down. It also
meant haggling with old man Chadwick over the docile white mare for
Tulsa and, he hoped, something more spirited for himself. He pulled
onto the Chadwicks' access road instead of going to his own gate.
That's another thing, he decided then and there. The old gate had to
go. Mac wanted one like the Chadwicks', with a hewn log arch and a
hanging sign. It would say "White Feather Ranch" instead of the plain
"R. MacPeters" that was scrawled on the mailbox now.

When Mac pulled up to the yard, Mrs. Chadwick was hanging out
her wash and her husband was driving off on a John Deere tractor
mower.

"Hello!" she called, and Mac waved. She invited him in and
brought out cookies as if he were still the ten-year-old they hired for
odd jobs. "Well, this is such a lovely surprise. I was just saying to Dad
that we should look in on you down there."

Mrs. Chadwick was the kind of woman ranchers are supposed to
marry. She was sturdy now and could have been called strapping when
she was younger. She could do a man's work when she had to but was
always a wife. She had borne several children and mother-henned
them well, but not so much that they were eager to leave when they
grew up. The Chadwicks' two youngest sons were majoring in agricul-
ture in Bozeman and would be coming back to run the place someday.
Pictures of them and the other children and grandchildren were scat-
tered over the walls in every room of the house, and the long kitchen
table echoed with the din of all the breakfasts and suppers they had
gathered around. When Mac was a boy, Mrs. Chadwick had always
made him stay for those huge, hearty ranch suppers with everyone
talking and laughing at once. It was how he knew such things were
possible.

"I'm hoping to buy a couple horses from you folks," Mac told her.
"And I want to ask you about Pa Roy. See, I've decided to get the
ranch going again, but I can't borrow money against it or even find out

if the taxes have been paid until I get power of attorney. So I need to find out where he is."

"Well, of course, Dad's in charge of the horses, dear, but for Roy—" Mrs. Chadwick wrinkled her forehead into the same expression she would get years ago when she saw blue-green bruises on the boy's face or angry red welts on his sunburned back. "How long has it been since you've seen him?"

"Quite a while."

"He isn't well, dear," she said. "He had a stroke and now they're saying Alzheimer's."

"Where is he, Mrs. Chadwick? I just need to know."

"I'm not sure how it is he came to be over there, but Dad and I have been up to see him a few times." She went to the cupboard for a pen and paper and wrote out the name and address of a place in Townsend. She brought it back to Mac along with another oatmeal cookie. "We talked about buying the rest of the land, you know. We already have most of it, Michael. Nobody knew if you were ever coming home."

"I know," Mac said uncomfortably, "but I am home, and what's left is mine. I'm working it. I earned it," he added, meeting her kindly blue eyes, and she nodded. "I don't have anything else to give my son."

"I'll mention to Dad about the horses."

"I could pay half now, but I'd have to sign a note for the rest—just until next month when I finish with the stable."

"We trust you, Michael." She laid her hand on his shoulder, and, given the way she smelled like fresh laundry and oatmeal cookies, Mac would have leaned into the plump front of her old-fashioned apron if he'd had a little less pride. Instead he got up abruptly, thanked her for the cookies, and surprised them both by kissing her on the cheek before heading hastily out the door.

Late-afternoon sun prismed through the warped glass windows at the bunkhouse. The bedding was still rumpled and the pillow sighed a breath of patchouli when Mac laid his head down. The scent reminded him of how Tulsa burrowed into the curve of his arm when she was sleeping, how she reacted when he kissed the smooth inside of her knee, how she arched and climaxed and explored, concentrating so fiercely he had to laugh at her. And it reminded him of how much his body ached. Mac pulled off his boots and didn't wake up until well after dark. He barely made it to the Swamp on time for his airshift. He never got much production, which suited him fine, so he settled right down to drink his coffee and smoke a cigarette and wait for midnight. He was looking forward to listening to her tonight. When he had mentioned it to her that morning—that he liked being with her out there in the ether, she giggled at the corny sentiment. Until he heard her on the FM monitor, he'd forgotten that Tulsa was now on the evening shift.

"Come on!" VA Lones razzed a caller about their unsuccessful bid in the Gino's Pizza Pop Quiz contest. "What kind of instant-gratification, TV-addicted, brain-dead product of modern education—it's William Shakespeare, for Pete's sake! Geez! I guess I should've asked you the name of George Jetson's dog."

"Astro!" the caller chimed in. "Hey, I oughta get something for that!"

"Yeah, you ought to get something all right—hey, it's past your bedtime, anyway, ya little wart. Better luck next time, OK?"

"Will you go out with me, VA?"

"What are you, *meshuggener?*" She cut up in a voice she called the Yiddish Boompa. "I'm old enough to be your grandma, ya little matzo ball!" Then she was VA again as Clapton's double driving guitars came in. "No pizza for that loser, but it's been a slice! Derek and the Dominos will dance you up to CBS news at the top of the hour with a little *Laaaaaay-laaaaa.* I'm VA Lones—nighty-night, my little Pop Tarts . . . shalom, friends."

She timed out the last of the bit with the rhythm of the ramp and passed it to Clapton, slick as you please, but Mac was having trouble connecting the cold monitor with the warm reality of Tulsa. He gave her a minute to get out of the control room and dialed the office number.

"Yes," she picked up almost instantly, "this is VA Lones."

"No it isn't," Mac teased. When she didn't respond, he felt something bearing down on him like a pair of headlights. "Do I get anything for knowing it was William Shakespeare?" There was another empty moment before they both spoke at once. "Tulsa, I want you to know that—"

"Mac, I have to talk to you—"

They both stopped for a beat or two, and then Mac said, "Go ahead, darlin'. I'm listening."

"Aaron is here."

"Is he?"

"Mac, before you say anything, I want you to know . . . "

a natural, she would have been

" . . . if I had any way of knowing . . . never would have . . . "

those mile-long legs of hers

" . . . a friend that meant more to me than . . . "

yup . . . way too old for this, cowboy

" . . . so I need to know if you were just . . . or if this . . . "

. . . and I'm crazy for lov-

"Mac?" He was startled to realize she'd stopped talking and was expecting some sort of response. "Are you still there?"

i'm always out there

"Please say something."

"It's cool," he said without even taking the cigarette out of his mouth.

He jammed a dead line button, and the connection was broken.

———

Outside the studio, Aaron waited for Tulsa in a little red rental car. He could see her on the other side of the plate-glass window, talking on the phone. After a few minutes, she laid her arm against the wall and just stood there, the handset pressed to her chest.

"Was that Jeannie?" he asked when she finally came out.

"What?"

"Jeanne. On the phone just now."

"What—were you sitting out here watching me?" Tulsa glared.

"Well, no—I just—" Aaron could get past the way she looked, but she was in a dark mood and he hated that. "I promised her you'd call, that's all." He started the engine and headed down the hill. "Hungry? Maybe we could sample some of the finer local cuisine or go hear some jazz or something."

"You're not in New York, Aaron," Tulsa said defensively. "I don't think you'll find the selection of vegetarian jazz establishments very stimulating on a Monday at midnight."

"What about that place—"

"Bar food and fast food. That's all there is after ten." She knew he'd rather starve than eat anything that came wrapped in paper.

"OK, well, how about if we go home and fix something?"

"If you say venison, I'm leaving." Tulsa started laughing again. She'd been doing it all day, making some bizarre remark and then sailing off into paroxysms. It was really beginning to irk him.

"Well, let's go get a glass of wine, then. I'm sensing the need for a calming influence here."

Tulsa responded positively to that suggestion, realizing that the home Aaron expected to go to was hers.

"Thanks a lot, God, for suddenly deciding to answer all my prayers."

"What?"

"Nothing," Tulsa snapped, pointing to the streetlight. "Turn left up there."

Aaron pulled into a parking space in front of O'Toole's, looking doubtfully at the bawdy atmosphere spilling out onto the sidewalk. Tulsa started to get out, but he reached across and pulled her door closed.

"Wait." He dropped his hand to her knee. "We have to talk for a minute. Now, I'm sorry that you're upset about this afternoon. I was an idiot. I was pushing. But I apologized. That's all I can do."

"It's not that." Tulsa desperately wanted to be out of the car, to be walking home, up her own dark streets to her own quiet rhythm. There was no breathing room in this stupid little car.

"Then what is the matter?" Aaron persisted. "I assumed you'd be happy to see me."

"Well," Tulsa said primly, "I might have been happier with a little advance notice. Anyone from Dear Abby to Genghis Khan knows you don't just show up out of the blue, expecting somebody to drop everything. Including their pants."

"I didn't expect—" He checked himself and started over with a less adversarial tone. "Would it interest you to know that Jeanne's been going wild searching for you the last two years? Do you know how hard it is to locate someone who has no driver's license, no credit cards, no bank accounts? She finally found you through a private investigator—for which she laid out a bloody fortune."

"Then why isn't she here?" Tulsa didn't really want to know.

"She's afraid to even call you. She's afraid to set you off again."

"So she laid out a bloody fortune for you too?"

"I wanted to come because I thought you might want me to. And because I wanted to. But Mom and Dad thought it was a mistake, and they weren't being very supportive, so—she helped me out, yes."

"Oh, yeah. Dear Mommy and Daddy." There was an awkward silence and then Tulsa added, "Maybe you should have listened to them."

"I don't understand how you could just take off and abandon people who care about you."

"Well, that is particularly ironic coming from you, Aaron," Tulsa flared. "After you blew me off with that lame 'I need my space' crap."

"And what's your excuse for doing this to Jeanne?"

"Jeanne was married to my mother, not me."

"She was a parent to you practically your whole life."

"She was in pain every time she looked at me!"

"So you couldn't even let us know where you were going?"

"I didn't *know* where I was going! I didn't *care* where I was going. And you didn't care either. Don't bother pretending you did. I was just a big mistake you made. Your parents were absolutely right."

"You weren't the mistake, Tulsa. What happened was just . . . an accident."

"*Shut up!*" Tulsa would have been screaming if her teeth were not so tightly clenched. "I told you not ever to speak about it! *Ever!*"

"We *need* to speak about it, Tulsa. It could have ruined our lives. To go ahead with it would have been ridiculous."

"Don't tell me you were concerned for one second about ruining my life. All you wanted was to get off and not be bothered."

"You know that's not true!" Aaron pressed the heels of his hands against the steering wheel. "And if you weren't so self-absorbed, you'd see that it hurt me just as much as it hurt you."

"Oh, horseshit! *Horseshit! HORSE—SHIT!*" Tulsa cried, striking her fists on her thighs. "You self-inflated overeducated pedantic pontificating goddamn asshole *liar!*" She was crying now and shook off his attempts to touch her. "How would you know how much it hurt me?"

"Because I love you—"

"You love to *fuck* me," she stated, using the word in context for only the second time in her life. "That's what you love. But you didn't want to accept any responsibility for the consequences."

"That's not true! I gave you the money and—"

"Your *parents* put up the money!" Tulsa scoffed. "Your eternal *parents!*"

"And I told you I would be there for you! I said I wanted to go with you."

"You *said?* 'I just can't do this right now' was what you said. And then you convinced me that I couldn't go on by myself, and I've learned in the last two years that I could have. And sometimes I wish to God I had, because now I have nothing. I only did it because I thought it was the only way we'd stay together, and then you dumped me anyway! It was all for nothing!"

"Tulsa, even you couldn't be that simplistic." He was doing the long-suffering act that infuriated and humiliated her. "Love does not conquer all. You were nineteen years old, for God's sake—I was barely twenty-one! You know as well as I do that it just wasn't feasible. Neither one of us had a job, an education, any kind of future or stability. Neither one of us was capable of being a parent three years ago."

"Don't you ever say that I was incapable," she lashed out.

"And don't you ever say that I didn't love you!" he lashed back. "I did love you, and I still love you. And I think you still love me too, or this wouldn't be so hard. But we can get past this, Tulsa. I came out here because I believe that."

"Well, then you did make a mistake." Tulsa's voice came from a cold, hollow space just inside her ribs.

"My mistake was thinking I'd find the same person I knew in San Francisco. I don't even recognize you! You used to be so quiet and round and soft. Now—you smell like a Chinese opium den, your hair is—and this whole '60s fashion statement . . . I mean—you look fine, Tulsa. If you wanted to lose weight—if that was a problem for you, then—great. And this—natural thing or whatever . . . that's all OK with me. I don't care if you don't want to put yourself together every day or bow to the oppression of underwear or whatever your mother's big hangup was, but . . . that's not the point—the point is . . . that . . . it's . . . "

Tulsa let him squirm in that mess for a few minutes before sarcastically cutting in, "You loved me for my mind, remember?"

"Yeah, I remember." Aaron sounded defeated. "I remember that I saw you from the second floor of the gallery . . . reading in the courtyard with your feet up on that Fortenais sculpture . . . and I ran faster than I've ever run in my life to get down there before you left. I remember that we talked about Keats and Milton and Kafka and it made me feel like my brain was on fire. I kept looking at your eyes and wanting to—learn you . . . save you on paper and keep you in my head. I sat there praying that someday you'd let me . . . that you'd let me see you. And I remember that you were so scared of making love, even though you tried to make me think you knew what was happening, I could feel you trembling." His voice held an unbearable quaver, and Tulsa bit her lip hard. "I remember how much you wanted to please me . . . and how much you did please me and how, even while I was inside you, we talked about music and art and things that really matter. I remember how you listened to me and how you loved my work. And how you loved me. That's what I remember." He nodded, and that slight motion slid a tear down his cheek. "I'm sorry I let you down, Tulsa—Jesus, I'm so sorry! But I never thought you'd disappear like that. I didn't know how much that would hurt."

Tulsa shifted in the awkward confines of the front seat, trying to somehow gather him over to her, to bring their bodies together, to go back.

―――――

Alexandra Firestein: "It is imperative that I be true to the person I am destined to be . . . "

"I don't want you to think I'm accommodating him or something," Tulsa assured Anne Marie, "because I'm not."

"Of course not. Hand me the eyeliner there."

"I mean, I'm not going to change who I am just to please a guy."

"Certainly not. Blusher, please."

" . . . *else my life becomes a lie and all that I touch is diminished.*"

"I'm still true to the person I am destined to be," Tulsa said. "This is just for the Bloyer thing."

"Absolutely," Anne Marie agreed. "Tulsa, you don't have to sell it to me! If I had an adorable ar*teest* in my apartment, I'd be working at it a lot harder than you are. And I'd be a lot happier, too. There." She held up the compact mirror to show Tulsa her handiwork. "You're gorgeous."

"Thanks, Anne Marie."

The porch swing drifted back and forth in the morning air as Anne Marie collected articles from her lap into her cosmetics bag.

"Did you talk to Mac yet?"

"Briefly," Tulsa cringed. "He says he's cool."

"Can't say I'm surprised." Anne Marie started snapping greenbeans from a basket into a large aluminum bowl. "Sex has brought about the death of many a good friendship."

"I feel like such a sleaze."

"Oh, don't be so hard on yourself. And don't worry about Mac. Frankly, he's probably breathing a sigh of relief."

"Maybe." Tulsa almost wanted it to be true for his sake. "Does he really strike you as that kind of person?"

"Yes." Anne Marie emphasized by snapping two beans at once. "I've known Mac since I was sixteen. I went to high school with his ex, and we used to double. 'Lorene and Mac and Annie and Jack.' They got married and moved away. She came back a year later by herself and they were on again, off again till Colter was about twelve. Anyway, the summer before we got married, I took Jack over to the VA hospital in Great Falls for that thing with his knee. And while I was waiting for him—well, Mac was there and Jack had helped him over in Vietnam and Lorene was my best friend so . . . I was just—I was just trying to be nice and . . . we got to talking and . . . he really knows how to talk."

Greenbeans were suddenly everywhere, and the tin bowl clattered like a fire alarm on the porch boards.

"Oh, damn!" Anne Marie dropped to her knees and started gathering the beans. Tulsa dropped down to help, but Anne Marie grasped her hand. "Please, don't let Jack know I told you. The subject is absolutely closed as far as he's concerned. I only want you to know, Tulsa, because Mac is . . . he's just—Mac. Living out there like some hermit, no electricity or plumbing . . . and this radio gig—where he sits alone in the dark all night—it's the only job he's managed to hold on to since the army. And then he was—you know . . . there—in the hospital."

"I know. He got shot in the back."

"Tulsa, he was in the psych ward. And not for the last time, either. When Jack found him, he had totally lost it. After he got out, he was drinking and doing a lot of drugs. Even straight, he was certifiably nuts. Lorene wouldn't take him back after that. She told him he couldn't come around Colter anymore, and then he was picked up out in the rock quarry one morning, practically dead, half frozen, wearing nothing but warpaint. He'd been dropping acid and eating peyote up on the ridge and he—fell . . . or something."

If Tulsa could have run away, she would have, but there were still beans on the porch floor and Anne Marie still gripped her hand.

"All right," she admitted, pulling away, "maybe I don't know him as well as I thought I did."

"Tulsa, there's just something about Mac that makes women want to hold him. I've never known him to leave a party alone. And I don't know what it is—those brown eyes—the way he can make things sound like poetry when you know it's plain craziness! But ask any one of several ex-wives or dozens of former employers how good he is at keeping commitments. Ask Colter."

"Anne Marie, I can't talk about this anymore."

"I'm not saying you're not special, Tul, but—" Anne Marie paused and took a different approach. "You're always saying that someday you want what Jack and I have; home, family, the long term. Well, you're not going to get that with Mac. And he knows it. He's unstable, he's a pothead—"

"Anne Marie, please! I don't want to talk about him anymore! I don't want to think about him anymore! The last few days have been so weird; I feel like dancing for joy one minute and throwing myself in a rendering vat the next. I just don't want to think about him anymore, OK?"

When Aaron came out, his hair still wet from the shower, they were snapping beans in silence. He leaned down and kissed Tulsa's cheek.

"Let's go get some breakfast," he said.

"Do you guys have plans for the weekend?" Anne Marie asked. "Jack and me were taking the kids to Virginia City, and we thought you might want to go."

Tulsa started to say something about the Bloyer remotes, but Aaron was already answering, "Thanks, Anne Marie, but I think we're going to stay in. We've got to figure out when we're leaving and start going through all that junk my Bohemian lass has managed to collect. I've never seen a home furnished entirely with knickknacks, paperbacks, and incredibly ugly lamps."

Anne Marie saw the look on Tulsa's face and quickly got up to leave with a bit too cheerful explanations over her shoulder about laundry, baby, etcetera.

Tulsa waited until the door latched behind her.

"Aaron, I have a job. Do you understand what that means?"

"Well—sure . . . "

"I can't just pack up and leave."

"Can we discuss it over breakfast?" Aaron pulled her up to a hug, and Tulsa nodded. "Do we have to go to the No Sweat again?" Another nod. "The food is fine, but I don't usually like to think about *sweat* while I'm eating. And those women are so militant. I'm surprised cowboy balls and penis fricassee aren't on the menu. Geez, it's like hanging out with—"

"Actually, why don't you go ahead without me, Aaron," Tulsa interrupted. "That way, you can go where you want and . . . I haven't had a chance to pick up my guitar since you got here—I wouldn't mind a little time alone."

"Oh, come on, Tussles," Aaron sighed. "I wasn't saying anything about your mother. I was just commenting."

"I know. I'm just not hungry."

"I don't believe it," Aaron teased, pulling her close again. "You seemed to be working up a healthy appetite earlier." He tipped her chin up and asked, "Did you call Jeanne?" Tulsa didn't answer. "Honey, you can't keep putting this off. She's not angry. She respects your privacy. But she said she had something important to discuss with you."

"She wants me to go back to San Francisco."

"Yes. And so do I. Because we both love you, Tulsa." Aaron kissed her and then added, "The least you can do is call her."

"Aaron, please, just leave it alone. It's none of your business."

"All right," he said, getting her up from the swing, "come. Breakfast, an errand or two, and then—who knows? I might let you seduce me again."

When they walked into the No Sweat, Aaron waved to Colter, who was across the room drinking coffee. Colter waved them over to join him, and Tulsa realized too late that sitting across from him inside the tall-backed booth was Mac. He seemed amused to see Tulsa cringing as Colter pulled up an extra chair.

"Hey, Aaron! Come and meet my dad. Dad—Aaron, Tulsa's friend from back East," he was saying enthusiastically. "You oughta see the work this guy is doing, Dad—he's a regular El Greco. He did this cool stuff on those trapezoid pots I made, and I can't wait to get them over to the Archie Bray, man—they're gonna go crazy." As an afterthought, Colter added, "Aaron—this is my dad."

"Indeed," Aaron nodded respectfully and addressed Mac in a way that made him feel old. "It's a pleasure to meet you, Mr. MacPeters. Colter tells me you're an accomplished musician."

"Indeed," Mac said.

"I'd love to hear you play sometime. I'm developing a new appreciation for country and western. It's like the Grandma Moses of music, you know? Pure, broad, colloquial—"

"Waaaall, by cracky, it gives us sumpthin' to do betweenst shovelin' shit and gittin' snowed in with the anee-mules," Mac drawled, and Aaron looked at him curiously.

"Aaron's got a fresco internship, Dad," Colter was going on, hardly able to imagine such a wonderful thing. "He's going to Paris."

"So what's he doing here?" Mac muttered.

"Looking at the mountains," Aaron said. "I finally get the Russell Chatham thing. This is beautiful country. We'll have to get back for a visit sometime."

"Will we?" Mac said, raising one eyebrow at Tulsa.

"I wish we didn't have to leave so soon," Aaron went on, "but it might not be too late to get Tulsa into school yet this semester."

"Actually," Tulsa tried to find her voice, "I don't know if—"

"What about VA Lones?" Mac asked.

"Well, I haven't really decided—" Tulsa tried again.

"Oh, I think someone with a mind like Tulsa's can find a larger purpose than spinning the latest John Cougar tunes."

"True," Mac agreed. "Beats the shit out of being a button monkey, though."

Tulsa's face burned, but Aaron wasn't listening.

"I wonder if anyone's interested in taking our order," he said impatiently.

"Sometimes you have to go over there," Colter motioned toward the large kitchen window, through which the women could be seen and heard, talking and laughing and drinking tea. "C'mon, I need some more coffee, anyway."

"Oh, let me get it," Tulsa tried to object, but they were already up and gone, leaving her at the table, trying to avoid making eye contact with Mac.

"Hello," he said. She could feel his gaze through the unfamiliar layer of makeup on her face.

"Hi."

"So what's your major this time, Buffy?"

"I haven't even decided if I'm going back, OK?" Tulsa straightened in her half of the booth. "And I haven't given notice at the station, either, so you can tell your ol' Swamp buddies to keep their greasy little eyeballs off my airshift!" Mac's smile at that seemed encouraging, so Tulsa searched her brain for some sort of pleasantry. "So . . . how *is* the Swamp these days?"

"Still there."

"I thought you'd be home in bed by this time of morning."

"Yeah, well . . . " Mac stretched his legs beneath the booth and propped his feet on the wooden bench, close enough that the side of one boot touched her leg. "Some people don't move quite as fast as some others." He reminded himself that she deserved that and worse, but the expression on her face made it difficult to hold the set of his jaw.

"Mac, I said I was sorry. I didn't plan this. I didn't know."

"Apparently you don't know your ass from a doormat, either." He poured sugar in his coffee and stirred it with a butter knife, even though there was a spoon right in front of him. "I wish I'd known you were so easy to boss around."

"Nobody's bossing me around, Mac." Now she was getting mad. "And nobody's going to make me feel guilty, either, sitting there like the walking wounded. If anything, you're the one who's getting a great deal here."

"Oh?" Mac leaned forward to a this-I've-got-to-hear posture. "And just how do you figure that?"

"Well," Tulsa shrugged, "it's not like you intended to . . . follow up."

"Follow up?" Mac orally dissected each word.

"You know exactly what I mean. It's not like you were going to call me up Monday night and say 'Grow old along with me, the best is yet to be'!"

"No," he admitted.

"In fact, it's safe to say that from the start of this big buddy-ol'-pal thing, you figured you'd take me out some day and do exactly what you did—"

"What we did."

"—and then go merrily on your way. Do you deny that?"

"No."

"Oh." Tulsa drew back and looked away. "Right—I knew that. So . . . fine. OK. A good time was had by all."

"Yeah."

"And no additional hassle is necessary. Aaron made it simple for you."

"What a guy."

"What are we talking about?" Colter was back at the table, and Aaron was right behind him.

"Godzilla," Mac said.

"Oh, great!" Aaron rolled his eyes and set a cup of tea in front of Tulsa. "Don't tell me you got her going on that!"

Mac waited for a comeback, but it didn't come. He shifted his boots off the seat so Colter could sit down and took advantage of the momentum to get up.

"Well, on to Lincoln Road," he said. "Pleasure to have met you, Señor El Greco. Be seeing you, Colt." Mac settled his hat down close to his eyes and nodded. "VA."

When Mac left the No Sweat Cafe, it was sunny and just beginning to warm up from the cool mountain night. He tossed the buckskin coat in the back of the truck before pushing out onto Last Chance Gulch. The air in town felt too hazy to breathe, and Mac was headed out on an errand anyway. On the way to Townsend, he pulled off the road near the old Dodge Brothers' Boarding House, now a stonework shell standing alone on the state-owned antelope range just this side of Winston. He remembered Pa Roy telling how they had taken the women there after the fire. Images and voices lined the gravel path across the railroad tracks as Mac poked around, stepping through fallen walls and over the debris of days gone by.

Testing the wooden staircase and finding it sound, he went up to the second floor and sat in a corner to smoke some homegrown. The stone window ledge offered a panoramic view of the Scratch Gravel Hills, and Mac sat for a long time breathing it in. He watched a single antelope as it grazed in the yellow prairie grass. It lifted its head and perked its slender ears forward. A train was coming. The antelope bounded away in long, graceful surges.

When he finally felt ready, Mac went back to the truck and headed toward Townsend. At the outskirts of town, he referred to the address Mrs. Chadwick had written out for him. The home was only a few blocks away, and just before he reached the door, Mac decided to go back for the buckskin coat. The day was really too warm for it now, but he wondered if Pa Roy would recognize him without it. Mac threw it over his shoulder and entered into the cool, sterile smell of the building. Mrs. Chadwick had written the room number on the paper, so Mac would have passed the front desk without stopping had the woman there not called out to him.

"Michael?" she trilled. "Why, Michael MacPeters!"

"Well, hi there," said Mac, trying to sound like he recognized her, but she could tell he was faking it.

"Maureen," she prompted, and when he didn't respond, added, "Maureen Fay Lester? Only it's Maureen Farrel now."

"Oh, of course," Mac tried to sound a little more convincing. "Well. Good to see you again." He had a sinking feeling from the way she was looking at him that he must have been with her in some long-ago Buick or back porch or haymow. Her hair must have been less severely sculpted back then and her lips not quite so shiny a coral pink. She put her hands on her ample hips and looked at him wistfully and then with a tinge of irritation.

"Well, anyway. We're here for Grampa?" She used that solicitous inflection that only sounds plausible when you're seriously sick or hurt.

"Yes," Mac said. Yes. He was here for Pa Roy. But he suddenly felt unsteady when she beckoned him to follow her down the hall. She opened an olive-green door, and Mac was taken aback by the smell of foot powder, cigars, and bodily fluids. He saw typed labels on the door, and the lower one said "Royal MacPeters," but somehow Mac couldn't seem to decipher the name or connect it with Pa Roy. He stepped back, thinking that this was the wrong room, that it was all a bad idea to begin with, or perhaps even, in the back of his mind, that Pa Roy would be lying inside dead, festering. But when Maureen Fay Lester, now Maureen Farrel, smiled and gestured for him to go in, there was no honorable way for Mac to run. He stepped past her and the door shushed closed, sealing him into the stifling airlock.

The man on the first bed was asleep, mouth open and hands contorted at his side. Mac knew only by the family pictures above his bed that he was not Pa Roy. There was a white curtain on a ceiling track between the two beds, and a drift of smoke was curling up from behind it. Mac forced himself to approach, his heart hammering. His hand was shaky when he reached out to ease the curtain aside.

"Pa Roy?" The boy's voice came out of Mac's throat in a hoarse whisper. There was no answer. On the wall above the bed a beaten brown Stetson was hanging. There was also a photograph of Pa Roy and his father at a bucking-horse sale in 1906. Beneath that, a tooled leather frame held a picture of Mac's mother, sitting perfectly still on the back of a black pony. When he saw it, Mac inhaled sharply and choked on the rank air.

"Git the hell outa here. You ain' 'lowed in this room." The old man was sitting in the corner, birdlike face toward the window, stained fingers curled around a cigar. He was wearing a red plaid shirt and brown workpants, just as he'd worn every day the boy had ever seen him, but his barrel chest was sunken and his once strong arms and legs lay wizened and bony beneath the flannel and denim. His hair was wispy and colorless as glass fibers, and a stippled beard shaded his hollow cheek. When he squinted at Mac, the whitish, watery look to his gray-blue eyes made Mac wonder if he was blind.

"Git the hell out!" The grumble evolved to a croaking shout.

"Pa Roy—"

"Git the hell outa here, you . . . you ain't 'lowed in here . . . I ain't hirin' no goddam Indians. . . . "

Mac knelt in front of his grandfather and spoke soothingly to him, showing him the buckskin coat and telling him how tall and strong Colter had grown to be. The old man's raspy breathing increased and his watery eyes narrowed.

"You got that propane tank full, boy? Goddammit, I'm sick of tellin' you." His voice was thick and crumbly. "I'm goin' out to look at them horses, and I'll whip yer ass if they ain't mucked out proper."

"Yes, sir," Mac spoke softly, resting down on his haunches beside the chair.

"And don't give me none of yer smart lip."

"No, sir."

Smoke from the acrid cigar swirled in the sunlight between them.

"Git yer chores, boy. You ain't goin' nowhere till them chores are done."

"Yes, sir. But Pa Roy, there's something you gotta do." Mac steadied himself on the nightstand and sat up on the bed.

"Git the hell offa there! Don't you dirty up my bed!" Pa Roy croaked. Whether he was trying to strike Mac or merely wave him away from the bed was unclear; in any case, he only succeeded in tossing his cigar across the room. "Shit. Boy! Go git that goddam thing."

Mac picked it up and brushed dirt and lint away from the end Pa Roy had been biting. The old man was shaking so, he couldn't get a grip on the cigar until Mac closed his own firm hand over his grandfather's gnarled one and slid the stogey between his fingers.

"What're you doin' in here, boy?" He was hunched down in the chair again. "You oughta be out tendin' to them horses."

"I want to, Pa Roy. I want to take care of everything. But I need you to sign a paper that lets me do it. I've got to own the land or I can't pay the taxes on it or borrow money against it. Understand? I can't do the chores, Pa Roy. I can't do anything until you sign this paper." Mac took the lawyer's envelope from his pocket and spread the contents on a tray attached to the arm of the chair. Pa Roy looked into his eyes for a long moment and then nodded slowly. Mac smiled tentatively. Pa Roy nodded again and ground the hot end of the cigar against the power of attorney document.

"I ain't signin' nothin'. You ain't goin' nowhere, boy."

Mac dropped his head forward and rubbed his hands over his face. Taking a box of wooden matches from his coat pocket, he relit Pa Roy's cigar. The old man sat mumbling and smoking, sometimes aware of Mac's presence and other times seeming to watch his own silent movie of horses and women and burning timbers. For the first time in his life, Mac looked at his grandfather without feeling afraid.

i'm the strong one now old man

" . . . just never you mind goin' nowhere, boy . . . never you mind. . . . "

"You're too late, old man," Mac spoke quietly so as not to rile him again. "I'm gone. Sarah's gone, and Satchi's gone. Thirty years are gone, and pretty soon, old man, you're gonna be gone too."

"You . . . " The old man looked at him, suddenly calm and lucid. "You come runnin' back, eh, boy? What the hell d'you want here? It ain't fuckin' Christmas, is it?"

Mac shook his head.

"You got whiskey?"

Mac nodded. He took the small flask from his coat and helped the old man steady it enough to get a good swallow.

"Yeah," Pa Roy nodded appreciatively, "I'll do that again."

Mac steadied the flask again and then used his sleeve to wipe the side of his grandfather's atrophied mouth. The old man grunted and struggled forward in his chair.

"Help me take a hike up the hill, boy. I can't take a shit in that goddam tin plate they keep bringin' in here. . . . I can't take a shit with that bitch standin' there smilin'. . . . "

"OK, Pa Roy, I'll help you," Mac laid his hand on the old man's shoulder, "but first, you help me. I want my ranch, old man. I earned it. I need it! And one way or another, I'm gonna have it, so you may as well sign the goddamn—"

"You ain't got no ranch, boy," Pa Roy coughed through a brittle laugh. "Bauers owns the grazing land. Chadwick owns the land yer grandma's buried in. Gillotti owns the timberland . . . owns it all. . . . "

"I know, Pa Roy," Mac coaxed, "but what's left—one hundred sixty acres and the big house and the outbuildings—that belongs to me—me and my son. But I need you to sign this paper so I can work it, Pa Roy. So they don't come in and take it for taxes."

"What're you doin' in here givin' me yer goddam lip when there's horses out hungry in the stable? I'll whip yer ass, boy! I'll whip yer ass bloody . . . you go fill that propane tank out back o' the bunkhouse before them no-good fuckers get back or they'll have a piece outta ya, too."

"Pa Roy, please . . . "

"Just you git to yer chores, boy . . . never you mind . . . you hear?"

"Yes, sir," Mac said quietly. He sat back on his haunches again, watching the smoke trace the current of the air. Then he rose, took the tooled leather frame from the wall, and slid it into the wide side pocket of his buckskin coat.

"Take it, boy. . . . " Pa Roy wasn't even looking in Mac's direction. "She was a redskin whore, and yer a little red bastard. You went off tryin' to be a white man just like the sonofabitch she killed herself over."

Mac took the brown Stetson, too. He put it on and worked it a little, but he couldn't seem to get it caved in right and comfortable around the braid behind his neck, so he tossed it back on the bed and settled his own black one down close to his eyes.

Pa Roy pointed the cigar at him. "You ain't goin' nowhere, boy."

"Yes, sir," Mac said quietly.

He stepped around the curtain, opened the door, and strode down the hallway, headed for outside air.

8

V A LONES suCkS (of K

Beneath mismatched newsprint letters was a grainy photograph of the outside of the radio station. In the foreground, a magazine picture of a smiling hunter was pasted so that the barrel of his upraised shotgun pointed to the auburn head of the shadowy figure in the studio window. Tulsa turned the paper over and looked inside the envelope again.

"I'm not having a good day," she decided out loud, and made a mental note to lay off the NRA bits for a while.

"Welcome to the glamorous world of showbiz," Joey would have said. "Don't let it get to ya, VA." Tulsa missed him.

She crept to the darkened production studio and picked up the phone, holding it in her lap a long moment before dialing the Swamp number. An unfamiliar voice answered.

"Is Mac around?" asked Tulsa, trying not to sound like VA.

"Nope."

"Where is he?"

"I dunno. Called in sick, I guess. Who's this?"

Tulsa hung up and crept back to the control room to retrieve her bag and big Irish sweater. Just beyond the wide plate-glass window, Aaron waited in the little red rental car, tapping and drumming on the steering wheel, listening either to the radio or to the intricate symphonies of his own mind.

———————

Mac and Colter sat facing each other in a wooden booth at Bert 'n' Ernie's. Colter didn't like the dead-animal decor at the Joker's Wild, but he didn't want his father to drink alone, not the way he was tonight. They hadn't spoken for several minutes, and Colter was beginning to feel uneasy.

"So . . . how was he?" he asked, hoping it didn't sound as stupid as he thought it did.

"Well," Mac laughed grimly, "probably better than me at this point."

"Why can't you just let it go, Dad? Just move on, you know?"

"It's mine, Colter." Mac was serious enough to scare his son a little. "He owes it to me. I'm not going to let him crawl off the face of this planet and take everything with him. Not after all—"

"Dad, just relax," Colter tried to use a tone of voice on him that Mac recognized from his own horse-breaking days. "It's not worth it."

Mac lowered his eyes and took a long pull on his beer. He contemplated telling Colter about things, but there seemed to be no point. Colter was raised in a world where, if anything, too many people loved him. Lorene, her parents—Anne Marie had always doted on him, and when Mac was with him, he felt so guilty about being gone that he let the kid get away with murder. He doubted the boy had ever been spanked, much less—whatever.

"It concerns you too, Colt," he said, taking a different tack. "You know, if I don't have it, neither do you, and it might not be so bad to live rent free in a great big ol' stone house. All the studio space you could want. We could build you a kiln, and we'd have income from boarding horses so you could concentrate on your sculptures instead of pumping gas."

Colter glanced up in surprise. "How did you know about that?"

"This is a painfully small town, Colt," Mac reminded him. "You couldn't piss in the brickyard without my finding out about it. Anyway, there's no shame in honest work."

"Yeah, minimum wage on graveyard shift. Big achievement." Colter sighed. "Mom's bummed about it, even though I keep telling her it's just till I sell some of my work. She's still on me to take that Montana Power job Ron lined up—or go to the Vo-Tech for diesel mechanics or something, but . . . " Colter shrugged, shook his head, and looked to his father, not expecting guidance but hoping for understanding.

"You have to do what you're put on this earth to do, Colt." Mac reached across the table and laid a solid hand on Colter's forearm. "You have to. If you can't, you incinerate from the soul outward."

Colter studied his father, wondering for the first time what it was that he might have wanted to do with his own life at some point in the past.

"But Dad, what if she's right? What if I can't make a living at it?"

"Then you'll have the ranch."

Mac studied his son, feeling only slightly guilty for making a real estate pitch out of the first father-son talk they'd shared in a while. He sat back and watched Colter reevaluate his stand on the MacPeters estate.

"Well," Colter hedged, "what can we do about it?"

"Hell if I know." Mac shook his head. "Have him declared incompetent, maybe. Or just wait and see if he kacks it. Couldn't be much longer—Christ, you can practically see right through him. Meanwhile, I'll try to put some more money together so I can go back and tell the lawyer it wasn't as clear cut as he thought it was going to be." Out of the corner of his eye, Mac saw Tulsa and her golden-haired boyfriend sliding into a booth near the door, and he added, "Things seldom are."

Colter followed his father's glance and waved to Aaron, who waved back but looked less than enthusiastic. "Dad? You and Tulsa—"

"Mind your own business, Colt."

"Are we talking about—"

"We're *not* talking," Mac tried to interject.

"Was it like one of those circumstances-beyond-our-control things," Colter persisted, "or were you thinking you and her . . . "

"You know damn well what I was thinking—and it's none of your goddamn business." He got up and went to the bar for another beer. When he came back, Colter was looking miserable, and Mac hated that. "C'mon, Colt, don't get bent out of shape."

"I don't mean it to hurt you, Dad," Colter said earnestly, "but if you really care anything about Tulsa, leave her alone. Don't mess with her."

It did hurt him, knowing that Colter viewed him as someone from whom people needed to be protected, but he nodded, not knowing how else to respond.

"Aaron really loves her—wants to marry her. It's not just a party to him."

"Trust me, Colt," Mac tipped his glass and drained his beer, "being married to that girl would be no party."

"Dad—"

Mac held his hand up, wanting to remind the boy who was the father around here, but not quite sure how that would be accomplished, he decided to go for another beer instead. He could see from the bar that Aaron was not enjoying himself. Tulsa was scarfing an extra-large post of onion rings and swilling wine like a Hungarian chef. "Slow down, darlin'," he said under his breath, "you're gonna hurt yourself."

She was laughing, loud and brassy. She took off her Irish wool sweater, and her face was flushed rose in contrast to her pale hands and white peasant blouse. She looked up and caught Mac staring at her. He dodged back into the booth, but the next minute she was shaking Aaron's hold from her elbow, coming toward Mac and Colter.

"Mac! Would you please set this boy straight?" she slurred. "Pizza Pop Quiz! Who wrote the story about the guy turning into a giant cockroach? It was Camus! *Cah-mooooo*. And this boy is trying to tell me it was *Kafka!*"

Mac studied her expression and determined that she knew damn well it was Kafka.

"Why don't we go home and look it up?" Aaron suggested calmly.

"Not to worry! Mac here almost got half a degree in English literature."

"I apologize, you guys." Aaron looked embarrassed. "C'mon, honey, I think Colter and his father are trying to talk."

"Colter wants me to stay, don't you, Colter?" She giggled and skootched in next to him, hanging on his arm as he shrank back from her sloppy embrace. "Because Colter is my best friend. Did you know that? I love you, Colty, and I really mean it. You are the only truly decent man I've ever met. *Theeee—onleee—one-uh,*" she italicized, directing pointed glances at Mac and Aaron in turn. "And you're such an adorable hunk." She bit her bottom lip and sighed heavily. "I love you as a person, Colty. And I respect you as an artist."

"OK," Aaron said with flagging good humor, "let's get you home to bed."

"Oh, I know you want to get me home to bed, Hank Aaron." Tulsa snorted indignantly. "Home to Minion-apolis Missus-enota. *But—*" she leaned forward and poked her finger into his chest for emphasis, "I'm not going anywhere, pal. *I'm* gonna stay right here all by my*self,* and I can *do* it, my friend, because *I* am *Veeee—Aaaay—fucking—LONES!*"

"Why don't I get you some tea, Tulsa?" Colter tugged her back to her seat, and Mac, who wasn't even trying to hide his amusement, recognized that horse-breaking tone again. "Here you go, Tul, c'mon— Lemon Zinger?" Colter coaxed. "Or do you want some Red? Would you like that?"

"Oh, yeah," Tulsa looked blearily across the table at Mac, dropping to the purple timbre that had half the adolescent boys in town up late at night, licking the syllables like all-day lollipops, "I like red." Mac cleared his throat and Tulsa started giggling, shrill and loud.

"Tulsa, we are going now," Aaron bit off each word and took her hand.

"Oh, just—*sit-sit-sit-sit-sit,*" she waved him down with a defensive air. "I'm sorry, OK? I apologize. That's all I can do." She wrapped her arms around him. "You're an adorable hunk too."

"We should start our own calendar," Colter said, setting her off laughing again and eventually, after another round of Saint Pauly Girl beers, even Aaron was beginning to recoup a bit of his festive spirit.

"So, Mr. MacPeters," he said, "am I right? Was it Kafka?"

"Yup. It was Kafka. *The Metamorphosis;* the crawling Gregor Samsa." Mac looked at Tulsa and shrugged. "Sorry, darlin'. He wins the panda bear."

"Well," she drawled, "fuck me dry and call me Dusty."

"Nice talk, honey," Aaron chided. "You eat with that mouth?"

"Sure," she punctuated the innuendo with a dainty belch, "but you'd have to buy me dinner first."

"*Tulsa!*" he hissed. "Good Lord."

"Speaking of which—Excuse me! Excuse me!" she flagged a passing waitress. "We need a Nacho El Grande platter. Supreme. Lots of guacamole, please. And another round. And some fried veggies. And onion rings. And another round. Oh, I know!" She brightened and clapped her hands together with a little squeal of delight. "We'll run a tab!" Lolling across the table, she dug Aaron's wallet from his jacket, deftly whipping out a MasterCard and laying it ceremoniously on the table. "Drink up, gentlemen. Courtesy of my associate and his financier, Jeanne Petit Compton."

"Jeanne Petit Compton . . . the artist?" Colter asked, wide-eyed. "You *know* her?"

"She's Tulsa's dad," Aaron supplied, and Colter looked even more confused when Tulsa blurted "fuck you" in lieu of an actual retort. Aaron deliberately relaxed his jaw and then reached for her hand. "I would have figured you for a mellow, introspective drunk. Promise me you're not going to start a brawl."

"Well, if she does," Colter asserted, "I wanna be on her team!"

They all laughed at that, letting some of the tension drift out of the circle, and then the nachos came and the conversation moved on to music and Whitman and Wordsworth ("'Tis a beauteous evening, calm and free,'" Mac and Tulsa said, accidentally together) and a wide range of other topics upon which Tulsa was finding it increasingly difficult to focus.

"Yeah," Mac commented at some point, "those people who say you can't do much with a liberal arts education just don't hang out in the right bars."

"You OK, Tul?" Colter asked.

"Oh. Yeah. Fine." She laid her head on the table beside the remains of the Nachos El Grande. "Just feeling a little spinny."

" . . . and the psychologist says, 'Ah, pianist envy!'" Aaron got a good one in and Tulsa was vaguely pleased that the others rewarded him with a big laugh.

" . . . rock'n'rollers with chemical abuse problems . . . "

Tulsa realized she'd faded out for a moment.

"Umm . . . you guys?" she said feebly.

"I never had any problem abusing chemicals," Mac quipped.

"Excuse me . . . gentlemen," Tulsa tried to interrupt.

Laughter.

"*Gentlemen!*" Tulsa gathered her dignity. "I beg your pardon. But I'm going to throw up now."

More laughter.

"I think she means it, fellas," Mac said quietly.

Colter bolted out of the booth, bruising his hip on the armrest. Dragging Tulsa to her feet, Aaron steered her with some difficulty toward the hallway where two doors were labeled "Squaws" and "Braves." He watched her disappear through the red "Squaws" door and then came back and sat down.

"I should have taken her home," he said, "but the way she's been today—frankly, I wasn't in a big hurry to be alone with her."

"Hmmm," Mac calmly regarded the boy, "guess you're not as smart as you think you are."

"What?" Aaron smiled and then faded, wanting to be in on the joke until he realized it was on him. They focused on their drinks. In the silence, Mac could practically hear the gears turning in Aaron's brain, processing the wildly improbable scenario.

"You have to understand," Aaron said, to himself as much as anyone, "Tulsa has had a very difficult time since her mother's death. She's confused right now. She doesn't know what she wants—"

"Oh, she knows exactly what she wants," Mac said. "It's just not necessarily the same thing you want."

More heavy silence. Colter hoped she would come back and they could all leave before his father said anything else out of whiskey or just plain orneriness, but Aaron had had enough to drink that he was feeling a little ornery himself.

"Yeah?" He focused his steady, ocean-colored gaze on Mac. "And just what the hell do you know about what she wants, Cochise?"

"Well, Aryan, I don't see where that's any of your fucking business." Mac left Colter and Aaron staring after him as he strode down the hallway and pushed through the black "Braves" door.

When he emerged, he saw that Tulsa was still missing from the booth. He nudged the red door open slightly and spoke her name. No answer. He tried to push the door a little farther but found it blocked. Mac put his back into it and created enough of a gap to squeeze through. Tulsa was slumped against the other side, her head on her knees. Sliding down beside her, he stretched his legs out on the tile floor and laid his hand on the back of her neck.

"Rough night."

She nodded without lifting her head.

"You need water, darlin', it's the dehydration that really does it to you." Mac rubbed her shoulders. "Did you get any supper besides all those munchies?"

She shook her head and groaned a little at the sensation that induced.

"Do you think you could eat—"

"*No!*" she moaned.

"I wasn't even going to say venison." Mac didn't hear an actual laugh, but he felt her shoulders lurch a little in response. "C'mon, let's get you cleaned up."

He dragged her to her feet and helped her perch up on the edge of the counter while he sponged her face and neck with wet paper towels, tugging her chin down so he could wipe the corners of her mouth.

"Why do people like getting drunk, Mac?" She was starting to clear up a bit. "This isn't fun. This is horrible. I feel like I'm gonna die. . . . "

"Hmm. And you're afraid you might not." Mac understood all too well. He cupped his hand to dip cool water from the faucet to her lips and then let her rest her head on his shoulder, her arms around his neck. He stroked her hair, rubbing gently behind her ears.

"Why are you doing that?" Tulsa mumbled into his flannel collar.

be still white wolf it will take the fever from the brain

"Because right now you smell just like an Irish setter I used to have."

She still couldn't laugh but found the strength to kick his shins before she wrapped her legs around and linked her feet behind his knees. Mac couldn't help it, pulled close like that; a week of longing and frustration began to manifest between his body and hers. When she recognized it, Tulsa felt distantly pleased, and she let herself rest against the warm pulse.

"Hmm," Mac said.

"Don't even think it."

"That's just hydraulics, darlin'—it's not a voluntary muscle."

"Neither is this." Tulsa placed his hand over her heart, lifting her head for a moment but finding it far too unsteadying. Mac resumed stroking behind her ears, speaking low and comforting things into her hair.

"Hey, Mac?"

"Hmmm."

"You're in the ladies' room."

"I'm a ladies' man." He felt her smile slightly against his neck. More hydraulics. Mac stepped back and tried to help her balance herself. "Let's go get that young sheik of yours to take you home and tuck you in."

She whimpered when her feet hit the hard floor, but she nodded, dragged her sweater down from the half wall of the stall, and reached for the door.

"Mac?"

"I'm here."

"Do you want to shoot me?"

"*What?*"

"Because if you do, this would be a good time to do it." Tulsa slid to the floor again. "Gut me. Clean me. Hang me out to dry."

"Now, c'mon, darlin' . . . you're getting sloppy here."

"I'm a waste of a healthy animal," she moaned.

Mac tried to pull her up, but she wasn't cooperating. She was a big girl and he wasn't at all sure he would be able to carry her if it came to that.

"C'mon, kid, let's go. . . . "

"I'm not going," she said.

"Oh, sure you are."

"No." Tulsa looked up at him earnestly. "Mac, don't make me go back in there. Let's go for a drive. We'll go out to the quarry. We'll howl at the moon . . . we'll just—talk. OK, Mac? Please?" Her voice caught on his name, but she wasn't quite crying.

"No, Tulsa." Mac mustered his resolve and shook his head to physically remove the notion. "I'm not gonna help you hide from that boy."

even if the yellow-haired twerp deserves to be taken down a notch or two . . .

"I stink." She turned her face to the wall. "I'll bring bears up to the road."

"C'mon, darlin', help me out a little here." Mac pulled her sweater over her head and worked her arms into the sleeves. "We've both had a hell of a day, so let's just pack it in, OK?"

even if this is one of those ripe Golden Delicious apples of opportunity that so rarely fall from the tree of life . . .

"Mac." Her eyes were dry and focused and way toward the green side of hazel. "Please."

Mac eased the door open a crack and looked out to make sure no one was in the hallway, then seized her elbow.

"If you throw up in my truck . . . " he threatened.

Flattening their bodies against the wall, they scuttled down the hall through the kitchen door labeled "Employees Only." Mac nodded to the surprised cooking staff, dragging Tulsa out through the fire door into the brisk night breeze of the alley and around the block to get back to the truck. The fresh air did Tulsa some good; she was giggling and dun-dundle-un-dun-dunning the James Bond 007 theme but stopped abruptly.

"Wait!" She grabbed Mac's arm. "I left my purse at the table."

"Colter will take care of it."

"No, I need it, Mac."

"Tulsa, for God's sake—"

"I've got my period."

"Ah." Mac nodded but then made a definitive gesture toward the truck. "OK—no problem. We'll stop at the store."

At the 7-11, he stacked a box of tampons on the counter along with two large coffees, some Alka-Seltzer, and a gallon of spring water. When he came back out, she was asleep.

———

The almost-morning sky expanded over the ranch like a Charlie Russell painting. The sun wasn't quite up to the level of the far hills yet, so it was still fairly dark and morning stars still domed the silent mountain. Striated clouds washed cinnamon, rose, and azure across the horizon, and it was all damn picturesque from Mac's point of view, though he was beginning to feel stiff and achy, wedged as he was in the fork of a tree up the hill from the outhouse.

He wondered how much longer Colter and Aaron were going to sit there on the back of the little red car. They'd been talking there by the bunkhouse since just after three. Now they were stretching, watching the sunrise. Mac shifted his weight in the tree and longingly eyed the outhouse below, feeling all those beers with every beat of his pulse. He was about to swing down and tell the two of them to just beat it when Aaron rubbed his hands over his face, kicked the splitting stump, and savagely pitched a rock in the direction of the bunkhouse.

Mac felt an unexpected shot of sympathy for the kid. He was a lot like Colter in many ways, and Mac hated the idea of a girl wrecking Colter the way Tulsa was doing this boy. He sighed guiltily and remained cramped in the tree until the red car roared up the drive and out of sight. He stopped at the outhouse on his way up to the logging road where the truck was parked with Tulsa in the back, still soundly out and showing no signs of life.

"After five o'clock, darlin'. Rise and shine." Mac opened the capper, dropped the tailgate, and dragged her out by her feet. Tulsa sat up without groaning or whining, but she didn't look good. Mac handed her the water jug and told her, "Drink. As much as you can."

They drove in silence down and around the steep hill to the bunkhouse. Tulsa went up to the privy while Mac put a fire in the woodstove so he could cook some breakfast. By the time she had pumped water into the trough and bathed and dried and dressed, he was setting venison steaks and poached eggs on the table along with hot coffee, toast, and Mrs. Chadwick's bullberry jam.

"You cut your hair," he observed when she came in.

"Yeah." She forked her fingers through her soggy mane, still shivering from the cold water.

"Feel like eating?"

"Depends on what you're serving," Tulsa said suspiciously.

"Think of it as generic protein critter." Mac held her chair out for her and laid a red checkered napkin across her lap. She looked a little pale, but, he was surprised to observe, her eyes were clear and sharp and she didn't seem to be hung over much at all. She ravenously put away a bigger breakfast than Mac would have made for himself and drained more than half the water jug. "'Ah, the natural equanimity of youth!'"

"*Candide,*" she said.

"You win the panda bear." Mac nodded and poured more coffee. They sat for a bit, the Regulator clock ticking and the teakettle whistling soft and steady.

"You've been doing a lot of work around here," Tulsa commented.

"Oh, yeah."

"You planted flowers."

"Yup." Mac looked at her, trying to guess if she was making small talk or actually interested. "Would you like to take the nickel tour?"

"Yeah," Tulsa nodded hearteningly. "But I'll have to owe you the nickel."

Mac smiled. "I'm cool."

They walked between long, straight rows, and Mac proudly pointed out the finer aspects of his vegetable garden, including the aesthetic line of impatiens all the way around the perimeter. They came to the small cornfield beyond that, and Mac led Tulsa into the thigh-high stalks. She pushed through several rows and found they surrounded a smaller field of spiky plants.

"What's this?" she wondered aloud.

"This would be cannabis sativa," Mac said. "The corn keeps it from being visible to the road."

"Ingenious," Tulsa said uncomfortably.

"I don't trust that stuff you buy." He bent down and absently dragged a few weeds from between the neat rows. "You just never know."

"No . . . I suppose not."

"C'mon." Mac took her hand again. "I'll show you a special project I've been working on."

Behind the bunkhouse Mac had built a small lean-to and covered it with shingles. Shaded by pines and bolstered by the bunkhouse wall, it was cool inside, and a musty smell aired out when he pulled the door open. Rows of jars were shelved on planks, some with plain soil, some laced with a fine network of white roots, and some with puffy white tops peeking through.

"Mushrooms," Tulsa observed.

"Psilocybin mushrooms," Mac clarified.

Tulsa didn't know what that meant, but he seemed so pleased with the accomplishment, she felt obliged to say, "Oh . . . wow."

Mac laughed. "I keep forgetting how young you were in the '60s."

"Oh—you mean *mushroom* mushrooms?"

Mac nodded.

"Hallucinogenic mushrooms?"

Mac nodded again, and he was grinning. "The hard part is obtaining the spores. Then you culture them in bulgur wheat or barley and then case that in sterilized potting soil. Pretty fascinating, and actually very simple."

"Sure," said Tulsa, "I'm surprised they never featured it in *Foxfire*." Noting Mac's quizzical expression, she added, "Sorry, I keep forgetting how old you were in the '70s."

They walked for a while and ended up sitting on a ridge above the big house. It was Mac's favorite place to survey his kingdom, and he liked the feeling of Tulsa sitting there beside him. "So," he was winding up a lengthy explanation about how many dollars per acre a ranch had to yield each year, "since I can't support enough cattle to really make a go of it, my idea is to generate more of a specialty product."

Tulsa looked at him, wide-eyed.

"Buffalo!"

"Oh," she laughed, relieved, "I thought you meant . . . the other stuff."

"No! No . . . that's not for sale, that's just for—" He couldn't come up with a word. "Does it bother you?"

"What?"

"The other stuff."

"Mac," Tulsa sounded slightly irritated, mostly because she didn't know how to answer, "I was raised with this image of people who smoke pot. It's just not something nice people do. Not *openly* anyway."

"Thank you, Emily Post: Arbiter Elegantiarum."

"And acid and peyote and all that . . . I don't know—it's just scary."

"True," he nodded, "but less scary than real life sometimes. I guess that's why they're so popular. Besides, this isn't like Joey. These are natural. Clean, homegrown, and natural. For Pete's sake, my grandmother's the one who—"

"You're rationalizing."

"And you're making judgments without any frame of reference," Mac said curtly. "Tell me drugs are immoral, Tulsa, tell me they're illegal, tell me they cause car accidents, cancer, and male-pattern baldness, but don't tell me they're 'scary.' I have no respect for 'scary'—particularly from someone who can't perform a fundamental task like driving a car." Mac stretched his legs and folded his arms across his chest. "War is 'scary,' Tulsa—poverty—violence. Republicans. *Life* is 'scary.' Drugs are a vacation."

They sat for a while, saying nothing.

"So . . . just raw?" Tulsa finally asked. "You just eat them?"

"Some people put them on pizza and things. I usually just eat them."

"And then . . . "

"I journey. Just like you secretly wish you could."

"Oh," Tulsa huffed, "like you know all about my secret wishes."

"You wish you could reach through the looking glass. And you could, if you weren't so busy hiding under the nice clean covers." Tulsa tried to look away, but Mac drew the side of his hand across her cheek and turned her eyes back to his. "You say you want a home, a family—but you're sitting here instead of heading back East with a decent, educated young man who wants to marry you." He shook his head. "You know that's not what you're hungry for. You know you're not gonna get full by eating or drinking or having a man inside you, not even by pretending to be VA Lones. . . . But the longer you fake it, the harder it is to tell somebody the truth."

"Stop it, Mac." Tulsa swallowed a ragged breath.

"You lie to that boy, Tulsa, and you're an expert in the art of self-deception, but I know you."

"You do not know anything about me—"

"I was listening." His face was very close to hers. "I heard you."

"I was just . . . I didn't—that wasn't me!"

"Oh, yeah," his voice was softened by an unsettling smile, "that was you. It was the single most honest moment of your life. The one and only time you cut through all your bullshit and told the truth, plain and simple."

"*Stop it, Mac!*"

"But you don't tell that boy the truth, do you, Tulsa? You're pretending, and he doesn't even know." His voice fell lower until it was little more than whispering. "Does he even know, Tulsa? That you're faking it?"

"No."

Tulsa broke away from her reflection at the dark center of his eyes, got up, and bolted down the hill. Anne Marie was right, she decided.

. . . he really knows how to talk . . .

Mac watched her while she paced and scuffed around the bunkhouse yard a while and finally sat down on the splitting stump. Then he followed her down.

"Ready to go?" he asked cheerfully, but she didn't answer, so he went inside, collected the dishes from the table, and brought them out by the pump to wash.

"Can I try one?" Tulsa kicked at the woodchips around the stump.

"Tulsa, I wasn't daring you." Mac shook his head. "Trust me, dar-lin', a couple buttons of peyote ain't gonna give you anything you don't already have."

"I understand," she nodded, looking at him expectantly.

"And they can give you diarrhea like you don't even want to know." Tulsa shrugged, but Mac shook his head again. "I'm serious, Tulsa."

"So am I."

"Well, you think about it for a few days." Mac picked up the split-ting maul and balanced a log on the stump. "If you're still interested, we'll talk about it."

"Would you go with me?" she asked. "On a journey?"

"Nope." Mac shook his head and swung the heavy maul, cleanly parting the log with a practiced downstroke. "Not while I'm babysit-ting." He knew before the halves hit the ground that it was the wrong thing to say.

"Babysitting?" Tulsa drew back and started sputtering. *"Babysitting?"*

"Ah, geez." Mac propped the maul against the stump. "That's not what I meant. I'm just saying I want to make sure—ah, shit." Mac gave up trying to explain and dug into his pocket for his keys. Tulsa was al-ready striding toward the truck, quacking on, but he had neither en-ergy nor desire to argue with her. He was wondering what the water would be like over by Toston Dam today. They both slammed their doors.

"All right already!" he shouted over her. She paused for a breath, and he seized the opportunity to ask hopefully, "OK. Wanna go fishing?"

Wrong.

"*What?* You haven't been listening to a word I said!" Mac shuddered at the sound of that familiar phrase, and she was off again, taking that voice of hers higher and tighter till the mellow burgundy cast of it was all but lost. " . . . enough to know one when you see one AND—" she finished with the big guns, "you read *stupid books!*"

"Hey, now, you leave your mother outta this."

"*Aagh!*" That got her. Her eyes went very wide and then very narrow. "I'm not surprised my mother's writing is *over your head.*"

Mac ground the starter, hoping against hope.

"You and your H. P. Lovecraft. How can you consume that pultaceous crap and pretend to call yourself literate?"

"Well," Mac bristled, pumping the gas pedal, "it keeps me occupied while you're busy sucking up to pretentious, Ivy League bedfellows."

"Someone who reads real literature while you sop your brains in *The Breasty Bimbos of Outer Space.*"

"I'm not going to get sucked into this," Mac muttered, still grinding away to no avail.

"*Killer Tits on Planet Yok-Yok?* Yeah, some meaty subtext there."

"Elitist."

"Escapist!"

"*Pedagogue.*"

"POTHEAD!"

"OK," Mac said through gritted teeth, "that's fine. I'm cool." He got out, strode like a rooster around the front of the truck, and yanked open the passenger door, catching Tulsa firmly by the arm.

"Oh, real manly!" She was startled when he dragged her out of the pickup, but not intimidated enough to lose her sarcastic edge. "I suppose this is where you kiss me hard and make me like it."

"No, this is where you haul your ass out here and push the fucking truck!"

"Push your own fucking truck!" She slammed the door, and the rearview mirror toinked off the windshield onto the front seat.

"Look what you did, for Christ's sake!" Mac roared. "You—you damaged the goddamn vehicle!"

"Oh—" Tulsa opened her mouth to apologize but started laughing despite herself. It was the blue-burgundy laugh that Mac had been missing. He felt his body relax all in one breath. He even toyed briefly with the idea of kissing her hard and making her like it, but not sure he'd like it very much himself at the moment, he went back to the woodpile instead. He propped up another log, split it open with a clean downsweep, split each half again, and tossed the quarters into a box by the bunkhouse door.

Damage a man's vehicle . . .

"Mac?" Tulsa meandered over, trying to quell her giggle impulse. "Mac, I'm sorry. I'll fix it. I'll pay for it." He kept splitting and she came up behind him. "I'll ride around with you and hold it up."

"No thanks."

"C'mon . . . really—I'll pay for it."

"Never mind," Mac sighed, "it always does that."

Tulsa gestured toward the splitting maul. "Can I try?"

"Sure." Mac handed her the maul and stepped back. "Easy . . . careful now. Make it a smooth—*not so high! NOT SO HIGH!*"

The heavy maul pulled her arms back over her head, twisting her wrist and thumping her painfully on the tailbone before she let it drop onto Mac's foot.

"*Aaaagh . . . goddamnsonofafkn*—" Mac held out his hand to ward her off. "Get away from me, you! You're a one-woman path of destruction!" They limped and cussed and laughed at each other for another minute, and then Tulsa picked up the maul again and Mac stood behind her, his hands over hers, guiding her through the first couple swings until she found a rhythm.

"Oh, I'm a lumberjack and I'm OK," she sang, swacking at the logs, giving a victory whoop every time one fell in halves, and when Mac came out from putting away the breakfast dishes, he was pleasantly surprised to find the woodbox full. He let her feed the chickens and then set her to weeding the tomatoes while he hauled rocks down the hill in the new wheelbarrow so they could make a border for the herb garden by the bunkhouse porch. After lunch, they started on the corral, tearing

down and hauling away the last of the old fence, measuring and marking corners for a new one.

"Guess you never read *Tom Sawyer*," Mac ribbed as he watched her
go to it with the posthole digger.

"Yeah, I was wondering when we'd get around to whitewashing
the—" Tulsa bit her tongue and glanced at Mac, but he had his back to
her.

"You getting hungry for supper?" he asked.

"Yes," she said truthfully, "but I should think about getting home."

Mac was quiet. Tulsa leaned one arm on the digger and rested her
head in the curve of her elbow. She had never in her life felt so deep
down tired, and it felt good. It felt right to stand there in the growing
shadow of the mountain, sweating and breathing, surveying a good
day's work, dirty and dog tired and hungry for supper.

"Why don't you stay?" Mac said without turning to her. "I was
thinking about making some mushroom soup."

He made her eat venison, too, Tulsa remembered later. For the
protein, he said. And he kept filling her water glass. Then it was dark
and they were singing and singing; she harmonized and Mac played the
Alvarez.

Time passed out of proportion and he was patting her cheeks vig-
orously, brushing her hair back from her face. "*Tulsa* . . . c'mon back
now, darlin'."

She had just seen something incredibly large moving across the
clouds.

"Mac . . . what was that?" she whispered in awe.

"It's OK. You went away for a little while, but you're OK." He
didn't understand, and that was painful to her. "Hey . . . what's this
now . . . shhhh . . . "

Tulsa realized she was crying, and when she didn't know why or
how to control it, she began to sob, struggling with the tangled liga-
ments that tethered her living soul to the inside of her chest. Mac held
her hard, pinning her arms at her sides and stroking her face.

"Just let it go, darlin', it's just overflow. That's all . . . you're still here . . . I'm still here. . . . " Mac cradled her cheek in his hand and his voice traveled to her ear, through muscle and bone and the intricate synaptic network. Palms pressed against the passenger-door window, Tulsa tried to tell Mac as they coursed up the mountain how the glass rippled beneath her hands, warping to the rhythm of passing trees. Her voice was lost in the rushing of the pines, but Mac nodded, and she knew his brown eyes had drawn thoughts from inside her mind, photo-synthesizing them into words. The Doors swam through the radio to the moon, speaking in neon tongues, and the music coiled around her like an electric eel. Tulsa grappled with unbearable overperception. " . . . *mmmmm . . . mac . . .* "

"Almost there," Mac smiled and nodded, his presence expanding out and upward as though he were on an enormous movie screen.

She reached toward the music, but Mac caught her hand before it came to the flames. He threw dead wood and sage into the fire and a plume of sparks exploded, soared, sang. Tulsa lay in the astounding embrace of the earth, rocks rearing up beneath her back, hurling her forward through shifting space.

high ridge   fire music

moon rhythm   cliff song

Mac separated her auburn hair, made a braid at the side of her head, and bound a feather at the end with a piece of brown grass. Tying her shirt around her waist, he brought his hand across the inside of her thigh, collecting the rivulet of blood, smearing it across her forehead. He dipped two fingers deep into the palette of red and stroked wide bands down from the bridge of her nose, arcing across each cheek, dipped inside her again and underscored his own eyes that shone in the dark like volcanic glass. Using a blackened sage root coaxed from the fire, he marked their chests and forearms.

blood joining   prayer mark

fire spirit   sage song

Tulsa heard the rush of his silhouette moving across the boulders. They stood on opposite sides of the fire, each shadow shadowing the other, crossing without touching, revolving without a sense of substance.

dance drum   wind music

mountain rhythm   moon song

Sarah and Satchi and Alexandra Firestein pounded hollow burning logs with the brittle bones of elk and of their enemies, each pulse bringing up a shower of sparks. Tulsa reached and turned, dancing to the cadence of rock upon fire, dancing with them their ancient dance, chanting and extending the pure voice of woman through the strain of flying cliff and burning sky. She watched the song emanate from inside herself, stroked it with her tongue as it painted upward from her throat in blue-white harmony with the aurora.

wolf brother   mountain spirit

fire mother   wind song

Mac and Tulsa lay before the fire, forming an arrowhead, their skulls touching at the apex. They raised heavy hands toward the full face of the setting moon, joining, shadowing until the last of their energy dissipated and the last of the darkness fell away.

blood joining

sage smoke

gray dawn

peace

9

The stars on Tulsa's round ceiling were spinning out of orbit when she woke up alone in the Murphy bed. Shuffling toward the bathroom, she saw Aaron stretched out on her tatami mat and red reading pillows. With a halo of golden hair curling out from his pure-featured face, he looked sensual and serene as a Botticelli angel.

Tulsa sat in the bathroom for a while, feeling queasy and intensely thirsty. Her stomach convulsed with gas and that diarrhea Mac had warned her about. She slumped sideways, resting her forehead on the cool porcelain wall tiles, no real thoughts forming, only a confusing montage of images that left her an observer in her own mind.

"Aaron! They're down here!" She could remember Colter calling. "Oh, God—she's hurt . . . she's bleeding. . . . " Aaron's reply was unintelligible, but his anguish was clear. "Go back to the truck and get a blanket. Tulsa?" Colter was closer now. "Can you hear me, Tul?"

"She's OK." That was Mac, sounding far away and groggy.

"What did you do to her, you poisonous sonofabitch?" Colter. She would not have thought he was capable of such rage.

"She's menstruating. That's all it is."

"You twisted bastard!"

"Just calm down, Colter—"

"Christ, I hate you!"

Tulsa opened her eyes a slit, just long enough to see Colter swing wildly at his father. Mac seemed more annoyed than hurt when the clenched fist caught him in the mouth.

"Ouch! Goddammit!" they chorused in what could have been comical unison. "Shit!" There was a blessed moment of quiet as Mac rubbed his jaw and Colter sucked on his knuckles, and then Mac said, "Get some water from the truck."

"Fuck y—"

"*I said GO, boy.*"

It was a voice Tulsa did not recognize. She closed her eyes, hoping to escape, but the flat stone floor blocked her from sinking back into the glowing center of the mountain. Aaron lifted her head to his lap, brushing tangled hair from her eyes.

"Honey? Tulsa? Please, be all right . . . Jesus please . . . please let her be all right . . . " He covered her with something warm, and she gradually became cognizant of the sharp rocks beneath her, the biting early morning air, and the fact that she was naked except for the stained shirt tied around her waist. She was overtaken by such uncontrollable trembling, she could barely feel Aaron's hands attempting to rub some blood flow back into her arms. "Tulsa? Please, wake up." He dabbed at her face with the blanket. "God, Tulsa, what have you done?"

" . . . don't . . . touch me . . . " Her voice felt thick and foreign in her inflamed throat. " . . . just leave me alone. . . . "

"Here—c'mon, honey, hold on to me. Can you sit up?"

" . . . no . . . just . . . please . . . just go away. . . . "

"Jesus. You're half frozen. We need to get you home, Tulsa, c'mon."

Tulsa let him prop her upright against a rock. Colter was making his way back down the hill with the water jug, and Mac was sitting on the ground, bare legs and bruised feet sticking out from his buckskin coat. His face was still smeared with her blood and black soot and his hair was loose, falling feral over his shoulders. He smiled at her just slightly, and she just slightly nodded.

So now you know.

Yes.

"Can you drink something, Tul?" Colter held the jug to her lips.

"Oh my God . . . look at her pupils. . . . " Aaron reeled toward Mac. "What the hell are you on?"

"I'm not on anything."

"What is *she* on?"

"Her own." Mac pulled his jeans on and picked up his boots.

Aaron stared him down, ice cold and calm. "I hope the sheriff appreciates your sense of humor."

"She's not under the influence of a controlled substance."

Colter understood, educated by his mother crying on the phone at Gramma's house, his father rationalizing from a traction rig in the VA hospital.

"It's mushrooms," he told Aaron. "He probably has them growing somewhere."

Aaron came back to Tulsa and kicked an empty whiskey bottle away from her leg. "Are you hurt?" She shook her head as best she could. "Do you think you can walk?" She nodded. "Where are your clothes?"

A blank stare was all she could offer, but Mac cleared his throat and gestured toward the smoldering heap of burned branches and sagebrush. Tulsa turned her head from Aaron's agonized expression. He covered his face with his hands for a moment, then strode over and hauled her to her feet, wrapping the blanket around her, and the odd company made its way up to the road. Tulsa had a difficult time without any shoes, but Aaron was unsympathetic as soon as he discovered she was basically all right. They reached Mac's pickup and the red sports car parked just behind it.

As Mac opened the truck's passenger door, Tulsa reached out of the blanket and put her hand on his. "Mac—"

"Tulsa," Aaron said sharply, "get in the car."

"I have to go."

"If you think that's best," Mac nodded, closing the door and tossing his boots through the window onto the front seat.

Tulsa flashed for a second on the way she'd seen her face reflected with the firelight at the dark center of his eyes, and she suddenly felt angry and cheated. This was—broken somehow; that he wasn't closing his arms around her, begging her to stay with him, fighting for her, even taking the decision out of her hands completely by demanding that she return to the bunkhouse and lie beside him under the patterned blankets—just to rest, to sleep and release this overwhelming weariness. But Mac was already walking away, and she was left standing in the road, blue lips slightly parted, each shallow breath clouding the air in front of her.

"Need a ride, Colter?" Mac asked carefully.

Colter's eyes came up to Mac's, but he was too choked to say what was in his heart. He swallowed and cleared his closing throat enough to ask, "*Why?*"

Mac shook his head and pulled open the driver's-side door. He released the brake and began pushing, padding alongside, bare feet running raw on the gravel. He jumped in and the engine sparked to life, leaving Colter in a wake of dust devils. As his father disappeared down the road, he leaned forward, hands on his knees, and cried.

Tulsa remembered nothing else until she awoke, bathed and wearing a nightshirt, under her own familiar stars.

She opened her eyes when Aaron tapped on the bathroom door.

"Come out of there, Tulsa."

"Why?"

"Because I need to use the bathroom." When he came out, he laid his clothes over the rocking chair and sat on the edge of the bed. "I called Jeanne."

oh, lord . . .

"She's extremely concerned, and with good reason."

"Aaron, what do you want me to say? *I'm sorry!* Sorry and sore and completely humiliated, OK?"

Aaron shrugged and lay down on the bed, his back to her. Tulsa tried to snuggle, spoon-style behind him, but he shook her off.

"Don't hang on me."

She faced the other way, leaving an unfamiliar gap between their backs, listening for a change in his breathing.

"So what's the deal with you and Cochise?"

She scrunched closer to the edge of the mattress. "I think you know."

"Yeah." Aaron breathed in as if he had more to say but instead wrangled his pillow so he could lie on his stomach.

"Guess that serial killer's looking better all the time, huh?"

Aaron didn't respond to her attempt. Tulsa simply wanted coffee and breakfast—just that—more than she'd ever wanted anything.

"If it was Colter or somebody—at least that I could understand—but this guy? God! Tulsa, he's weird! And he's *old!*" Aaron spoke the word like a Klansman speaks a racial epithet. "What could you possibly see in that sleazy old . . . hippie?"

"He just . . . " Tulsa tried to find one thing in a snowglobe of images and ideas, trying to rationalize for herself as well as for him. "He tells me things."

"What could that reprobate tell anybody?"

"That bull snakes keep the rattlers down. It's the dehydration does it to you. And a little light makes the rest seem darker. . . . "

There was a stony silence.

"Why didn't you tell me, Tulsa?" Pain was true and evident in Aaron's voice, and Tulsa would have said or given anything to change it.

"I'll tell you now," she promised. "I'll tell you the truth." She caped the covers out behind her so the sheet billowed up and resettled over their heads in a cool white tent. She climbed on top of him, straddling his legs and stymieing his attempt to draw his knees up and brush her hands away.

"I feel like I don't know you anymore, Tulsa. I don't understand you."

"Then *don't* understand me!" She brought her fists down on her thighs. "Just *ff*—" She stopped herself. Aaron would want something more aesthetic. She finished the phrase, "—*find* me."

"I'm trying, Tulsa, but you keep running away."

She shifted forward, ready, waiting for Aaron to give himself up to her. She swayed there, suspended, arcing low over him like a thunderhead until he threw off the stifling covers and allowed himself to slide inside her. He held her hips in his hands and set a pace until she halted and hushed him, palms flat on his chest, lifting herself up. When he was still, she began to rock, her respiration tearing more and more ragged and then turning to sobs. He tried to comfort her at first, but the simple friction eventually drove him past the protocol of caring, past anger, past remembering in whom or what he was immersed; all these things fell away, forgotten, weightless on the plateau where he anticipated, and then advanced, and then released. When he clenched and shuddered beneath her, Tulsa realized he had gone on alone, and, frantically, she rocked faster, but her own panic kept her from coming to the forgetting place; the harder she rode him, the harder she cried.

he doesn't love you jesus loves you

She was one of those people who were always on the news, crying and crawling for the television cameras. Tulsa pulled her raincoat around her and tried to continue across the parking lot, but the woman in wire-rim glasses would not be left behind.

says he loves you but   love a murderer   lose your immortal soul for nothing   for nothing   only jesus   forgive   sins of   holy spirit

Her voice climbed through painful registers of pitch and volume in an effort to rise above the bullhorns of two policemen who prevented her from climbing the clinic steps alongside Tulsa.

your immortal soul for nothing   no murderer hath eternal life   thou shalt not mother   doing to your   baby

A man shoved a placard forward.

look at   look   a mommy shalt not   doing   kill your baby

A tiny figure, mangled, dismembered, covered with blood and endothelial tissue. A little boy on the man's shoulders held the blown-up photo of the fetus's severed head, thin-lidded eyes protruding, gory amphibian mouth agape.

look what you   shalt not   doing to your   murder the children

Tulsa put her hand to the side of her face, shielding her eyes, but the man kept shouting and the little boy kept looking at her soulfully.

baby's   holocaust   blood on your hands   into the death chamber

"You shouldn't have tried to come here today, miss." A policeman steadied Tulsa with a hand beneath her elbow, but she could barely hear him above the chanting. " . . . busing people in from . . . calling it Operation . . . "

shalt not   mother   kill babies   cold blood

Grasping, bellowing, begging, they were lying across the pavement, crawling toward the clinic steps, relentless as termites.

christ died for   whore   sins   shalt not   baby doesn't have to

"Back of the yellow line! Escort! People, you are to stay back of the yellow police tape! This is private property!" the policeman was shouting. "I need an escort over here!"

murderer just kill   made a mistake but   cold blood   sins forgiven   not too late to rescue   shalt not   child   from the butchers

"OK, c'mon!" A young woman with a baseball cap huddled Tulsa behind the spines of a wide yellow umbrella and pushed her through the crowd up to the doorway. From the top of the steps, it looked just like TV: a flat, faceless mass, their chanting muted by some sort of self-defensive volume control in Tulsa's head, but the woman in the wire-rims reached through the screen and seized the sleeve of Tulsa's raincoat.

It was as if a glass wall shattered. Voices flooded forward, faces took shape, eyes crawled over her like fire ants. They stripped away an inner curtain, witnessed her most private acts. They observed what she and Aaron did in the upper bunk and the gallery stairwell. They would write to Jeanne. They would call Charles Bitters. They would tell God, and God would tell Tulsa's mother.

"Get off her!" The yellow-umbrella girl tried to place her body between Tulsa and the shrilling of the woman. "Get back, dammit!"

"Please miss, let me help you! Jesus, please, don't let her kill her baby!"

She pressed something small, soft, and ripe into Tulsa's hand and the sight of the bloody fetus ripped her voice from her chest in a broad, raw scream as the escort forcibly dragged her inside the door and the policeman draped the wire-rim woman, reaching and weeping, over his shoulder.

"Maaa-maaaaa!" Tulsa couldn't tell if the mournful cry came from her throat or her womb or the disembodied head on the grisly placard. "*Mama! Mommmmmmmmmmm . . .*"

"Shhhh, honey, stop! It's a mouse!" A nurse shook Tulsa's shoulders to make her listen. "Shhhhh . . . look, sweetie, see? It's just a little mouse baby."

shaltnotkillthoushaltnotkillshaltnotkillthoushaltnotkillthou

The chanting penetrated the doors and windows of the waiting room. Wrapped in a white blanket, rocking and shivering, Tulsa disintegrated into sobs.

"Shhh . . . honey, stop it now . . . stop. . . . "

Aaron hushed and comforted, stroking her back until her crying subsided and she sat up, raising her arms to lift her damp hair off her neck. He felt an almost physical pain when he looked at her sitting astride him, backdropped by windows full of hazy dawn. Her eyes were shut tight and she was trying to be silent, though her mouth trembled and she made a small sound with each movement.

"I can't take this, Tulsa," Aaron said hoarsely, "I have to leave. Today. I'm sorry, but I have to."

She nodded.

"Please—" he gripped her wrists—"come with me."

"What for?" Tulsa bowed her head to his chest.

"I don't know, Tulsa. For this . . . " He reached further inside her. "And to talk and . . . and—I don't know. Jeanne says you can move back in with her for now and later . . . someday when we get past all this—"

"Then *what?*" She pushed against him with wide open hands. "What do you want? Tell me what you want and I'll do it! I'll make it be all right. Just don't let it all be for nothing, Aaron—" She was sobbing again. "Not all for nothing."

"Shhh." He drew her down to him. "Honey, stop this . . . stop it. . . . "

"*I can't!*" Tulsa pulled away. "Don't you understand? I wish I could stop it, but I can't! It's in my dreams at night!"

"What?" Aaron sat up, taking hold of her hands. "What is?"

"The baby . . . " She shook her head, trying to free herself. "The baby on the poster . . . torn apart and thrown away. And all those people screaming and grabbing and *looking* at me! I felt like I was—it felt like—" Tulsa choked, almost gagged on the unspeakable truth, "like *rape!*"

"Oh, God . . . Tulsa . . . " Aaron tried to hold her hard enough to prevent the past. "Why didn't you wait for me?"

"Why didn't you marry me?"

"The same reason you won't marry me now! It has nothing to do with the baby. We did what we had to do."

"*We* did nothing. *I* did it." She pounded a closed fist against her stomach. "I'm the one who's left to live with it."

"That was your choice, not mine," Aaron strained to keep the anger out of his voice, "and if you think I don't live every day with that—"

"With what? You weren't even there," she dismissed him.

"And *that's* what *I'm* left to live with! I begged you to wait, goddamm it, I pleaded with you! I wanted to be there with you, but you took that away from me. *I begged you, Tulsa!* But you never gave me the chance to be—*anything* for you." Aaron pushed her back so he could face her, and he was furious. "What was I supposed to do? I was in fucking Paris, Tulsa! It took Jeanne a year and a half to get those people at Delacroix to *talk* to me, but I blew the interview off and I got on the next plane home—just to have you tell me that it was too late—that you went right out and fucking did it—just to be a perverse *bitch*—just to twist a knife in my gut! You trashed five years of my life! Everything I worked for! I could have had that internship, Tulsa, I could have been in Paris *three years ago!*"

"Or you could have had me, Aaron." Tulsa pulled the sheet up in front of her. "I honestly thought you'd ride up like Barbarosa on Deutschland's darkest day—all you had to do was say we could have a life together—a family—and you still could have done anything you wanted to do. I never would have held you back."

"Who are you trying to kid?" he derided. "How was I supposed to support this happy little family, huh? What did you expect me to do?"

"Nothing. I had no right to expect anything from you. That's something you made perfectly clear."

"That is such bullshit!" There were tears of rage and hurt in his eyes. "I only wanted you to wait three damn days!"

"You wanted me to shut up and spread my legs and get rid of it!"

"Oh, Jesus, Tulsa," he turned his face away, "you know that's not true."

"Because then you'd be free to walk away while I was still bleeding—" The satisfaction she got out of slashing him eclipsed any interest in truth. "Just go on and be Mommy and Daddy's perfect artistic golden boy—"

"You walked away, Tulsa! *You* did! You tore me apart, and you did it on purpose, and you're doing it again *right now!*" he accused. "Only this time, *I'm* leaving, Tulsa. I'm never screwing away another opportunity for you."

"*I'm* the only opportunity you ever screwed away. I should have never let you touch me. I should have listened to my mother—"

"Your mother never even knew me!"

"Oh, she knew you all right. She knew that all men are selfish, stupid, spiritually vacant pigs who only know how to take and enslave and run away!"

"You don't believe that crap! I *loved* you, for Christ's sake!"

"For *your* sake! For *you!* Everything was always for you."

"If blaming me is the only way you can stand it, Tulsa, then blame me. But it was for your own life as well as mine."

"I would have sacrificed myself! I would have been a good mother."

"Oh, bullshit. You *have* sacrificed yourself because you don't know what a good mother is." Tulsa struck out at him, but he caught her hand. "She's the one who dumped you, Tulsa, not me! She took her money and her fame and her political agenda and she flat fucking dumped you!"

"She was beautiful and strong—*alone*—and I could have been like her if I hadn't listened to you, you rotten bastard!"

"*Stop it!*" Aaron seized her arms. "Can't you get it through your head? Can't you understand that reality isn't always what you tell it to be? That you don't live in a book where you can just write yourself a happy ending? Accepting a thing isn't the same as liking it, Tulsa. Sometimes you hate it. Sometimes it breaks your heart. But you accept it and you do what you have to do and you get on with your life because *that's* what *is*."

"You ruined my life. *That's* what *is*."

"How? By telling you the truth? I told you the truth, Tulsa. I said I couldn't do it because *I couldn't do it!*"

"You could have, if you loved me. I would have done anything you asked."

"All I ever asked was that you grow up and lay claim to your own life just like—just like you're doing now." Aaron was as startled by the realization as Tulsa. "But now—I hate it." They sat for a moment, just breathing, seeing.

"Why?"

"Because," Aaron shook his head, trying to understand it himself, "I want the same sweet lover I knew . . . and now you're so—this just isn't you."

"Yes it is, Aaron."

"No. No, it isn't," he shook his head. "You're upset and you're confused, and I understand why now."

"No, Aaron—"

"It was harder on you than I realized. . . . But now we can talk about—the experience. And we can work through all this and you'll see—just . . . please . . . " he took her face in his hands, kissing her mouth and cheeks and eyes, "*please*, come home with me. We can get past all this if you'll just come home."

When Tulsa finally spoke, it was fine and small as a gypsy moth.

"I am home."

Aaron placed his hand on the back of Tulsa's neck and leaned toward her until their foreheads touched. He stroked her hair, speaking softly of the arrangements and particulars of his leaving, and then they were quiet.

"Aaron?" Any more than a whisper would have separated them.

"What is it, Hippolyte?"

"Thank you for coming."

He smiled at the old private joke, but his voice was hoarse and obstructed when he tried to answer. "My pleasure."

The attic warmed with light as the sun moved above the trees and fully into the framework of the windows. People were beginning to stir downstairs. Abstract sounds drifted up through the stairwell; some shaped like children's voices, some the color of dishes and things—but in the small round room, there was no sound except morning.

———————

Aaron drove away in the rented red sports car, and Tulsa lay for a long while on the front porch swing. The calm that came over her was such that she didn't even feel herself falling asleep. She was vaguely aware of the slats of the swing beneath her face and body and of the breeze that rocked her ever so slightly. The chains creaked and the tall pine trees whispered. Tulsa could feel the mountains bearing upward beneath the house, the resonating of Earth on its axis. There was a floating sensation and then the feeling that her hair was drifting down over her face, that it was growing, floating out further with each sway of the swing. Her mother sat beside her, running her fingers through it, smoothing it away from her forehead like she always did when her little guppy was feverish or had been crying. Tulsa had so dearly ached for that soothing ritual during the days, nights, and years after her mother died that now, returning to the surface of the dream, she tried to hold her mother there beside her, to pretend that she and Anne Shirley were still virgins and that Aaron was only just now running toward her across the gallery courtyard. But her spirit drifted upward, alone through the vacuum and into a translucent white tent. The sound of boots on the porch steps brought her to a place just behind her closed eyelids. She was aware of a shadow between her and the noonday sun.

"Mac?" He was reaching out to her.

"Hey, sleepyhead, got a package for ya."

Tulsa sat up, her head heavy and her neck stiff. It took her a moment to comprehend that it was the mailman standing before her, his hands outstretched, extending a rectangular package.

"Certified. Need you to sign right here. . . . " He set down the package and extended a clipboard and pen.

"OK," she said in the additional moment it took her to command her own hands to spell out her name. "I can't think who'd be sending me—" Tulsa recognized Jeanne's lefthanded slant across the face of the brown paper. It was a book; she could tell by its solid, familiar feel in her hands. "Thanks, Ed."

He whistled into the entryway, put letters into the tin boxes, and whistled back down the porch steps, wishing Tulsa a good day. Anne Marie came out to check her mail and saw Tulsa on the swing, head bowed, staring at the package.

"Hey, Tul."

"Hi."

"You OK?"

"Oh, yeah." Tulsa appreciated that Anne Marie said no more about the weekend; only indicating that she knew and was open to talk, if needed.

"Whadya get?" Anne Marie sat next to her and sorted through her own pile of bills and letters.

"I don't know yet." Tulsa wasn't sure if she wanted to know.

"Well, open it!" Anne Marie urged. "Do you need a knife or something?" Tulsa shook her head and tugged at one end of the wrapping. She stripped the paper back and uttered a nonverbal sound. The dust jacket was a pale spring green with fuchsia and blue lettering. "*Sweet Epiphanies,*" Anne Marie read over her shoulder, "*The Life and Art of Alexandra Firestein*—yikes! You're into the Tupperware Lady, huh? Tul? Tulsa?"

Tulsa couldn't answer. She was gulping and bawling against the palm of one hand, pressing the book to her chest with the other, astounded to discover such sediment from her days of dry silence at the hospital, the funeral, the crematorium; a condensed mass of pure sorrow, still intact just behind her heart, waiting all this time for the muscle to pull slightly aside so it could pour out.

"Mom," she sobbed like a little girl lost in K-Mart, "I want my mom!"

"Well, good grief . . . " Anne Marie set her letters aside and circled her arms around Tulsa, shushing her, trying to understand what the matter was. "Is this from your mom, Tul?"

"This *is* my mom."

"Who is?" Random bits of other conversations suddenly fell together. "Alexandra Firestein is . . . was . . . Tulsa, now, calm down . . . geez, honey . . . " Anne Marie gave up trying to comfort her long enough to go in and pour a cup of tea. She brought it out and Tulsa took it with unsteady hands, fighting for deep, jagged breaths and trying to speak around the barrier in her throat.

"I want my mom—I need her now. God, why didn't she stay with me?"

Anne Marie was at a loss. She tried to set the book aside, but Tulsa gripped it so tightly, it had to be included in the hug.

"And she—wu-husn't the—Tu-hupperware Lady!" Tulsa gulped.

"No . . . no, of course not."

"She was ju-hust at one stupid pa-harty."

"Sure . . . OK . . . c'mon now, let's take a look and see what it's about, shall we?" Tulsa recognized the upward inflection from the bag of mommy tactics Anne Marie used on Oakley but allowed her to tug the book far enough from her body to trace the words "Compiled and Edited by Jeanne Petit Compton?"

"They were . . . together," Tulsa said. "When I was little, Mom and I moved to San Francisco because Jeanne's gallery was there, and then when—later, Jeanne moved to Minnesota with us so Mom could be by Mayo Clinic. She handled things for Mom. And then she took care of me."

"Sounds like a family."

Tulsa nodded.

"Are you and Aaron still fighting?"

"No. He's gone," Tulsa said miserably. "He went home."

"Oh, no . . . oh, Tul . . . "

"It's OK."

"He's probably just mad about the weekend. He'll be back."

"No."

"Oh, Tul. So—what does this mean . . . with Mac?"

"Nothing."

"Damn him, anyway. When I see that irresponsible jerk—"

"It wasn't Mac, Anne Marie. He was just there."

"Oh, sweetie. What a weekend." Anne Marie put her arm around Tulsa and they let themselves swing gently in the mountain breeze, saying nothing until Oakley burst onto the porch, banging the wooden tail of a stick horse on the floor behind him. When he saw that Tulsa had been crying, he climbed up and patted her on the cheek.

"Oh, sweetie, whatsa matto?" His crooning tone of concern was an echo of his mother's and, recognizing it, both Tulsa and Anne Marie laughed. They pulled him into a hug sandwich and rocked that way until Oakley got restless and started begging Anne Marie for a banana.

"Go ahead," Tulsa told her, "I'm OK."

She gathered the torn paper and took her book inside.

————

It is true that I met Alexandra at a Tupperware party, Jeanne wrote in "A Foreword to the Diaries."

I was a frustrated artist. I wanted to paint but was sent to business college by my parents, who wanted the best for me and feared I might not attract a good husband. I let them send me, let them believe that it was I who could not attract men. I'd known for a long time there was something unnatural inside me, a mortal sin that would keep me from being any man's wife. So I let them send me. A position with a large corporation took me from my native Georgia to Tulsa, Oklahoma. I was as successful as a woman could be in the business world of the 1950s, and I never went to Tupperware parties. I was at Evelyn's that day only because she was a neighbor who once looked after my cat while I was away on business. I felt obligated. But "No, my sweet epiphany," Alexandra maintained until the day she died, "it was God and heaven and destiny."

It was the summer of 1957. She was wearing a neat poplin shirt dress, a dusky rose, and satin pumps dyed to match. Her hair was pulled back into a tidy chignon. We all wore Lucille Ball's ice-blue eyeshadow in those days, and it looked particularly horrendous above Alexandra's soft hazel eyes.

"This is Mrs. Ann Bitters, our new sales trainee," bubbled Charlotte, the plastic pitchwoman. "I'll let her demonstrate some of the features of our new Freshness Plus line, and then we'll have coffee and take orders while Evelyn treats us to some of her scrumptious huckleberry gems and nut tasses!" And the ladies all smiled and cooed politely. Alexandra stood, cleared her throat, and began her well-rehearsed speech about cooking ahead and family picnics and grinding your own baby food and how to burp the seal to lock in flavor.

"I have a little daughter myself," she said and sounded genuine for the first time. "And I want only the best for her. Only the very . . . freshest. Only I can't give her . . . I want so much for her. . . . "

She faltered, and Charlotte offered a pale green bowl, oddly shaded by a purple substance within. "This is the huckleberry compote you'll be enjoying in Evelyn's gems and thumbprint cookies, and, as you can see, she's made up an enormous batch and stored it in a Super Fresh Double Quart so she can dip out just what her family needs and pop the rest right back in the freezer!"

"Yes," the trainee echoed vaguely, "just what the family needs."

"Evelyn put up this batch of compote last summer, and right this minute she could pop it right back into the freezer for another six to eight . . . Why—Ann, dear? Are you all right?"

The young trainee was giggling uncontrollably, and the honesty of it was infectious. Soon we were all laughing without the foggiest idea why.

"Just *pop* it in the freezer!" Alexandra bubbled. "*Pop* it in there and shove it clear to the back. You can keep it frozen in there for—oh, Lord, I don't even know! You should live so long!" And we all sailed off laughing again. "You just keep it there. Cold. Sealed up tight. Out of sight. It'll still be there, frozen like a warlock's heart long after you've begun to rot."

All the ladies sat silent, eyes wide, hands frozen in their laps.

"It will remain after you have faded . . . and died . . . *putrefied.*"

"Oh my," someone said, "I think she's having some sort of breakdown!"

I was stricken mute by the emerald clarity of her gaze. It held me, suspended me above myself in such a way that I could only hang there in the air, leaning forward slightly from the dizzying precipice of the floral sofa.

"Oh!" she gasped, "you are all so beautiful—so radiant at this moment! Do you see? Each one of you is shining bright as an angel!"

"Charlotte!" Evelyn hissed. "Do something! Call someone!" But the rest of us sat transfixed, suddenly seeing that divine aura, or desperately wanting to.

"Why do we seal it all away? We allow only what is needed by others. Our best ideas, our deepest desires lie frozen while we struggle to keep that lid locked down airtight. We don't want anything inside to breathe or grow, it terrifies us so! Oh, please don't, my beautiful, angelic darlings! Don't you do it!" She peeled back the lid from the pale green bowl, dipped one trembling finger, and touched it to the tip of her tongue. "Oh, Evelyn! It's heaven!" Eyes closed by intensity and elation, she slowly dipped two fingers, then her whole hand, tasting it with a profound sensuality, lapping at the palm, darting and sucking at her glistening wrist and thumb. *"Heaven!"*

"It's . . . my mother's recipe," Evelyn said uncertainly.

Alexandra dropped to her knees and set the bowl before us on the glass-topped coffee table, reverently as if it were the Host upon the altar. Plunging both hands into the compote, she anointed her face, neck, and breasts in a sanctifying ritual, baptizing herself with sweetness. She held her hands forward, imploring, offering the holy communion, blessing and beseeching each of us in turn to taste, but we were too stunned to move. There was a long silence. Then suddenly a young woman from across the street (I never knew her name, but I had been watching with fascination as she grew more and more pregnant that summer) eased herself forward from her folding chair. She knelt on the floor, took Alexandra's hand, and raised it to her lips.

"It is good," she said softly. She turned to the other ladies, who drew back in horror and shook their heads, but I fell to my knees before Alexandra, pressed her palms to my face, and, for the first time in my life, kissed the lips of another human being. Oh, the sweet huckleberry sacrament of that kiss! It absolved me of my inner evil, made straight the unnatural order of my self. In Alexandra's emerald eyes, I saw myself reflected, bright as an angel.

"Well," Charlotte said, clipped and tense, "perhaps this would be a good time for coffee."

I quit my job the next day. I moved to San Francisco and took a loft apartment where I began painting, reveling in my art, embracing the strength gained from starvation, and finally, after a few years, coming to some success, for I was still a good businesswoman, you know. In autumn 1961, I was offered a show at a gallery in New York, and while I was there, I went to hear a lecture by an emerging controversial author. The moment she stepped to the podium, I was stricken anew by that emerald intensity.

"My name is Alexandra Firestein," she said. "I have been called a 'femilitant,' a threat to the young women who read my poems, a pestilence on this God-fearing nation. But, in truth, all I am is a woman who has learned to love as God intended me to love, a mother who desires for her daughter the freedom and acceptance I never found. I write in celebration of that love and in search of that acceptance." She opened the book and read.

> "There is a beauty in you I shall not find elsewhere,
> My sweet epiphany . . . "

Her voice penetrated the auditorium like a solitary silver lamp, and I listened, every bit as transfixed as I had been that pentecostal day on the floral sofa. She painted legends, made parables, spoke her poetry like a clear, warm liquid.

> "Now comes the light and leaden time,
> This parallax, ascension, graceful decline . . . "

I stood with the throng to applaud her at the end and waited to get her signature on my copy of *Belladonna*, but by the time I came to the front of the line, I could scarcely speak, my heart was throbbing so.

"Ms. Firestein," I stammered, "I'm sure you don't remember me—" But she cried out and, toppling her chair in the process, sprang to her feet to embrace me. We held each other, kissed, wept, laughed.

And *"heaven,"* we whispered again and again, there, that day and for the fourteen years of quiet mornings, tangled nights, and open-windowed afternoons that came thereafter. *"Yes . . . heaven."*

With fall coming on, evening fell quick and cold, but there were no coyotes on the moonless quarry rim. Maybe it was too breezy up top. Maybe they were off raiding someone's campsite or garbage cans. Mac sat with his legs over the ledge, puffing on a pipe of homegrown. The crop had come up nicely, shielded by the fortress of corn which was now eye level and heavy with golden ears.

He squeezed for the Sunday paper rolled up in the wide side pocket of his buckskin coat. Still there. Mac wasn't generally much of a pack-rat, but he thought he'd keep this one. There was an article about the growing trend of bison husbandry in North America and a story about Edward Abbey, one of his favorite authors. On the same "Books" page, there was a sidebar detailing the top ten books on the *New York Times* best seller list, and the name Alexandra Firestein leaped out from behind a respectable number four. Back on page 3 in section D were the obituaries.

"ROYAL MACPETERS: LINCOLN AREA RANCHER." It listed him as being 103 years old, a fact Mac wouldn't have known but recognized as noteworthy. "Member of various taxpayers' and ranchers' groups, including the Beef Council and the Lincoln Agricultural League, which lobbied successfully to halt a program reintroducing wild wolves into the Crazy Mountains and surrounding ecosystems," it continued. "Preceded in death by his common-law wife and one daughter. Survived by one grandson, Mitchel W. MacPeters, and a great-grandson, Colter O. MacPeters." All in all, an eventful Sunday newspaper, but Mac changed his mind and poked the fire with it, letting the orange flames lick the rolled edges black and then blossom yellow. He held it till it singed his fingers, then tossed it onto the burning sticks.

The nursing home called the Chadwicks, apparently. One of the Chadwick boys was listed as having made arrangements for services. Old Chadwick took it on himself, though, to drive over and rap on the bunkhouse door early Saturday morning. Mac answered the door with a book in his hand. He listened, nodded, closed the door. Chadwick didn't expect anything different, and he figured he'd wait a little before bringing up the matter of the land.

Sunday afternoon, Mac put off driving up Benton until he heard VA Lones on the air, doing a hyped-up car sale remote from somewhere or other. He pulled up out front, waiting to shut off the engine until she handed it back to the studio and the kid there kicked into Tom Petty and the Heartbreakers. Out on the porch swing, Jack rocked with Oakley and Mary Laur, reading to them from an oversize book with animal caricatures on the cover.

"Hey, Mac!" Mary Laur remembered him singing in the evenings when he lived upstairs. "Where's your guitar?"

"Hey, Pickles. Where's your nose?"

They both smiled when she put her tiny fist to her face and then held up her hand with the thumb peeking out between her fingers.

"Here it is!"

"Better put it in your pocket."

"Will you give me a horsey ride?"

"Naa, darlin', horsey broke a leg and had to be shot."

Her expression fell, and Jack cleared his throat. "Tulsa's not here, Mac. She's working."

"I know." Mac didn't like how Jack was eyeing him, like the bouncer in a cowboy bar. "I'm here to see my son."

Jack nodded toward the door and went back to the animal book.

"*Who Says Whoo*," Mac would read, "'There's a grumpy old bear in the woods. What does he say?'" And Colter would supply a ferocious growl. That was the gist of the game, but Mac would try to stump him. "What does a *platypus* say?" Colter would come up with something and try to stump him back.

"What does aaaaaa . . . *warthog* say?" And his daddy would snort and snuffle under the little red sweatshirt, tickling Colt's tummy with his whiskers. The boy's hair was curly, maple-syrup brown, and so soft Mac had to kiss the top of his head every once in a while.

"What does a *mommy* say?" Colter quizzed him.

Mac studied Lorene dozing on the couch. "A mommy says 'I love you.'" He looked back to his little Colt. "What does . . . what does a daddy say?"

"A daddy saaaays . . . " The child wrinkled his forehead a moment, puzzling on it, then brightly answered, "He says 'See ya later!'"

Mac knocked on Colter's door and waited for a bit. When Colter finally answered, his hands were thick with grayish slop and his face was set in an unfamiliar expression.

"Hey, Colt."

"What do you want?"

"I want to talk to you."

"Well, I'm not interested in talking to you."

"I'm sorry you feel that way, son. Nonetheless . . . " There was a strained silence. Mac hooked his thumbs in his pockets and rocked back on the heels of his cowboy boots.

"*What?*" Colter leaned against his doorway and sighed impatiently. "What do you want? She isn't here."

"I know!" Mac wished to God the boy hadn't grown up to be so much taller than he. "It's you I'm here for. C'mon, Colt . . . it's been almost three months now. How long are you going to take on over this thing?"

"This *thing?*" Colter's eyes were clear and almost as dark as Mac's. "I don't know, Dad, but maybe *this* thing combined with all the other things—maybe it's just not worth it."

"Worth what?" Colter said nothing, so eventually Mac decided to press on. "I suppose you saw the paper this morning."

"Yeah," Colt replied bitterly, "congratulations."

Mac let that go by. "I was wondering if you'd help me take him up and bury him. Chadwick says we can borrow horses. He and some other neighbors are going up, but Colt, these guys are all about eight days older than God. I could really use your help."

"Yeah," Colter looked away for the first time since he opened the door. "You could really use . . . "

"C'mon, Colt. He was your great-grandfather. Son, you and I are all that's left of this family."

"Oh," Colter actually laughed, "don't lay this on me like it's some big moral obligation! I never even laid eyes on this guy, and I've heard how he was, Dad! You think I don't know anything? Mom told me he made you be—like you are. That's all that keeps me from hating your fucking guts."

"Well, that's plain bullshit, Colt—nobody makes anybody be like anything."

"Then why do you do this shit, Dad? Look what you did to Tulsa! You just couldn't stay off her. You screwed up her whole life. Aaron dumped her because of you."

"Well, I guess I should have asked who had clear title to her," Mac flared, "but I thought she was an adult who could go out and get looped if she damn well pleased." He shoved his hands in his pockets. "I care about her too, Colt. A lot. And I would have had her home, squeaky clean and safe as houses, by lunchtime if you two had just stayed the hell out of it and—goddamm it, I told you before, what goes on between me and that girl is none of your goddamn business!"

"OK, then how about Mom?" Colter folded his arms across his chest despite the pottery mess on his hands. "Would you be interested to know she got married last weekend?"

"Not to that Montana Power weasel!"

"Hey, Ron saved her life, as far as I'm concerned. She's finally with someone who treats her like a human being. Someone who made her forget about you."

"Oh, no. She can fuck Biff Kilowatt till her eyes turn green—she'll never forget we had a life together."

"So that gave you the right to tear her up over and over again?"

"She threw me out that last time, Colter! I didn't want to go! I loved her. I loved you. I still do!"

"Gee whiz, Pop, it's swell being one of these people you love so much," Colter said, "but frankly, I'd feel a lot safer on your shit list!"

"Then keep talkin', boy!" Mac seized Colter by his sweatshirt and yanked him forward. "You just *keep on talkin,'* 'cause you're closer to my shit list than you'd like to think!" He shook him, just once but hard. "And while we're at it—you may have a couple inches on me but you're still an easy-ass little city boy, and if you ever try to pop me one again, I'll lay you out colder than a fuckin' wedge!" Mac released his hold with a forceful backhand motion that slammed Colter against the wall. "Now, are you gonna trot yer ass up there and help me bury that old fart or not?"

"Go to hell."

Colter slammed the door and Mac slammed his fist against it, wheeling to stride down the porch steps, past somber-faced Jack and wide-eyed Mary Laur. When evening came, he went up to the quarry to smoke and sit and look at the northern lights. Mac wasn't one for making apologies. He figured he'd give Colter a couple weeks before he tried to approach him again, but Tuesday, when Mac got to Chadwick's, Colter was there. They saddled their horses in silence, much to Mac's relief, and rode up into the hills with four or five other ranchers from Lincoln and thereabouts. They buried Pa Roy beside Satchi and Mac's mother. This part of the land actually belonged to Chadwick now, but he was a good neighbor and knew that Roy would have done the same for him.

Being the young pups of the group, Mac and Colter did most of the digging, hacking their way through weeds and roots and pulling enough big rocks out of the hole to shore up a wooden cross. They stood, drenched in sweat, and watched the old men use long ropes to lower the plain pine box into the ground. Mac tried not to breathe so hard while one of the Chadwick boys who had grown up to be a United Methodist minister said a few words. Then each of the ranchers said a little about how hard Pa Roy worked and how his place used to be a real nice spread back then, and then they mentioned times when he and Satchi had done neighborly things; helping them out when they were stove up or giving them rides to town and what not. Mr. Cledginocci commented on that beautiful daughter they had, and they all agreed it was a tragic accident, a real shame.

Then they all stood about uncomfortably till Mac told the others, including Colter, that they should head down before the trail got dark, promising to return Chadwick's horse to him later that evening. When he was through filling in the hole, Mac used the remainder of the rocks to frame the fresh grave so it would look like the others. He took a jar of ginger water out of his saddlebag and drank it while he watched the evening sun shining rays of Buddha through distant thunderclouds, all gold and silver and purple at once. He tamped some homegrown into his pipe and decided that this was a spectacular view up here. He thought he just might borrow enough against the hundred sixty acres to buy this section back from Chadwick. Mac decided to talk to him about it. That and the horse he would be needing.

Only one, he reminded himself, now that it seemed Tulsa wouldn't be riding with him. Months had passed since they'd seen each other. They hadn't even spoken on the phone, but he couldn't resist listening to her on the radio. She whispered through all his dreams lately, lying there with that wild auburn hair spread out or sitting in the rocker, stroking the slender neck of the Alvarez. However, Mac reminded himself, there was no time to mourn all the long and lazy lovemaking they would have done. She belonged with a young man who could give her a home in town and children around a supper table. If not Aaron Proctor Taylor the Third, then some other boy just as foolish and as lucky. She should have that, he magnanimously decided, even if she didn't even know yet that she wanted it.

For him, there was the ranch now, and as he rode down, surveying the abandoned big house and rundown outbuildings below, he knew he had his work cut out. Mac hoped he could get Colter to help him. The boy was getting to be a fine carpenter, and Mac enjoyed the vision of the two of them, working side by side, sweating and drinking beers and clapping each other on the shoulder when they stepped back to peruse the job well done. Mac nodded, thinking maybe he should get two horses from Chadwick after all.

He didn't realize how stiff and sore he was from the day of riding and digging till he dismounted at the end of Chadwick's drive. Passing beneath the glow from the kitchen windows, Mac could hear the din of a late supper inside. The family reconverged on the ranch house every weekend, and some of the older grandchildren had stayed all summer. Mac smiled when he heard Colter's laughter among the noise as he led the Morgan into the barn. He pumped water first so the animal could drink while he dragged the saddle down, slung it over a railing with the others, and hung the bridle and reins on big square-headed nails above it. He was just beginning to brush the nettles and dust from the Morgan's withers when Chadwick came through the double doors with his eleven-year-old grandson.

"Hey there," he said, and Mac said, "Hey."

Chadwick offered him a can of beer. "Yer doin' the boy's job there. C'mon up to the house. Mom's got supper waiting."

"No," Mac shook his head. "I rode him. I'll put him up."

Chadwick nodded and set the beer up on the side rail, leaving Mac to curry the horse with the boy watching.

"You gonna muck out too?" the boy asked.

"I'll muck this one after I finish brushing him down," Mac answered. "Then I'll give you a hand with the others—but only if you're really working."

The boy was visibly pleased by his good fortune and jumped down from the railing to grab a pitchfork. "Can I have a drink of your beer?"

"Don't push your luck."

The boy shrugged and grinned and started dragging the pitchfork through the hay in the neighboring stall.

"How come you got that braid?" he asked. "You an Indian or something?"

"Or something." Mac picked an apple from a bushel basket, took one bite, and fed the rest to the horse.

"Your grampa died, huh?" The boy wasn't asking a question but informing Mac that he knew grownups' business.

"Yup," Mac acknowledged.

They worked a while in silence and then the boy piped, "He sure was old."

"Yup."

"More than a century," the boy told him and then added, by way of explanation, "That's a hundred years."

"No kidding," Mac smiled.

"Gramma made me go with her to take him some Christmas cookies last year." The boy climbed up and leaned over the top of the stall.

"Oh?" Mac paused, resting his elbow on his pitchfork.

"Yeah. He sure was old."

"Yup."

"Scary, kind of."

"Yeah . . . kind of."

The boy disappeared behind the side of the stall again. Mac could hear him working and talking to the horses, and it made him wonder what Colter would be like if he'd been raised on the ranch instead of in town.

"My grampa ain't scary." The boy was two stalls down now.

"Nope," Mac called back. "He's a damn good neighbor."

They worked together, talking sometimes, sometimes just working, till all the stalls were clean and Mac had taken a good look at every horse in the barn. He was inspecting the teeth on a Morgan named Jim Bridger when he heard Chadwick's voice over his shoulder. "Mom tells me you're lookin' for a horse."

"That I am, Mr. Chadwick. I'm gonna need at least one now that I'll be working the ranch again."

"Well," Chadwick shifted his weight and scuffed one boot on the barn floor, "I guess we need to discuss on that a bit."

"How's that?" Mac didn't like the look in the old rancher's eyes.

"He left it to me, Mac."

aint goin nowhere boy you aint goin nowhere

"No, that's not possible. My lawyer said if he was to die without a will—"

"There was a paper on file at the bank. Roy left the house, the buildings, and the last hundred and sixty acres to Mom and me. C'mon in, Mac." Chadwick tried to take Mac's arm. "We'll see what we can come up with."

But Mac stepped back, still trying to comprehend what his neighbor was telling him. "That sonofabitch . . . "

"Now, Mac, that ain't no way to—"

"That sucking son of a blue blazing bitch!"

Chadwick stepped back, not because of Mac's initial fury but because the next moment, he was roaring with laughter; whooping like a wild man and hardly able to stay on his feet. Chadwick's grandson came running at the sound of Mac's contagious hoot, but the look on his grandfather's face told him not to join in. Mac was leaning on the saddle rack, holding his sides and sincerely trying to stop. "Oh, shit . . . that blackhearted old fuck . . . "

"Watch yer language in front of the boy," said Chadwick, placing his hand on his grandson's shoulder, and the realization that some grandfathers actually said such unimaginable things stabbed into Mac's heart like a pearl-handled Bowie knife. "Now, Mac, listen—we could work out a lease—"

"No—I'll buy it back from you, Mr. Chadwick," Mac was serious again, though he was still breathing jaggedly. "I've got a job. I can get another one. . . . "

"Son, I'd give it to ya without a second thought, but I had to pay some back taxes to keep the state from taking it right off. More than twenty-six thousand. Plus penalties. Mom and I can't just swallow that."

"No . . . no, of course not, but . . . " Mac's brain was reaching for any possible solution, but nothing was coming to him.

"C'mon in and get some supper now." Chadwick tried to guide him toward the door again, but Mac leaned forward with his hands on his knees.

"He's still doing it," Mac said quietly, and Chadwick knew exactly what he was talking about. "It'll never change. That sonofabitch is stronger than by-God Death itself."

"Son, we can work this out, now . . . you just c'mon in and sit."

"*Twenty-six thousand? Plus penalties?*" Mac's sharp, bitter laugh had only irony in it. "I can't even keep up with my fucking bar tab. How is it that you think we're going to *work this out?*"

"Let's go get a drink, son. We'll discuss it over some supper—"

But Mac was already headed for his truck. He was whooping again in a way that made Chadwick's grown daughters come to the front

window to shake their heads and cluck with concern, placing protective arms on Colter's shoulders as his father drove away.

When Mac reached the gate, he got out to open it, then circled
around to the back of his truck to get a crowbar instead. The dry wood
splintered without much effort, but Mac couldn't stop until he'd
bashed the gate to sticks and litter, then turned on the mailbox
marked "R. MacPeters," hammering it to the ground for good measure.
He leaped back into the driver's seat, gunned the engine just in time to
keep it from dying, drove back and forth over the debris a few times,
and rammed up the drive. He swerved off the beaten path and, in a
riot of splintering slats and ripe vegetables, took out the garden fence
before the balding tires mired in the tilled-soft soil. Mac twisted the
wheel and rocked the wallowing pickup back and forth till it clutched
enough solid ground to drag itself forward. Mowing through the careful rows, he left behind a ragged quilt of broken plants and posts and
then smashed through the fence on the other side, steering into the
cornfield. He leaned hard to counter the centrifugal force of the circling vehicle as graceful stalks beat at the windshield, battering a
machine-gun patter, flying all directions. Slashing leaves gave way to
open sky and the truck bounded up into the yard, obliterating part of
the front porch on the bunkhouse before Mac could haul it sideways and
lurch to a stop over thirty feet away. The momentary rush and clatter of
settling boards and birds' wings and disturbed evening air fell away into
a silence, swift, cool, and profound as Loch Ness. Mac crept out of the
truck, aware that all the destruction he could wreak would never leave
so much as a ripple on the surface of the vast mountain night.

Plunging his head into the trough, he shattered the liquid image of
a full-faced moon that lay on top of the water. He held himself under
till his lungs ached and then brought his head up, flinging his hair
back in a silver arc, shaking like a coyote and howling from the chill.

Mac heaved the wooden cover off the well and kicked through the
pine needles till he uncovered a piece of twine that disappeared into
the cool depths. Hauling up on it, he drew out a Ziploc bag of grayish
peyote buttons. He ate from the bag, resealed it, opened it again, ate
again, and then dropped it back down into the darkness, where it made
a distant plopping echo. Mac dragged the cover back over the mouth
of the well. Needing to rinse the grayish taste and unpleasant consis-

tency from his mouth, he went into the bunkhouse for some whiskey, and by the time the full fifth was down to one or two swallows, Mac's stomach was beginning to feel oppressed and ill.

He started up the hill toward the outhouse, but halfway there, the land began to buck and pitch beneath him, trying to cast him off. He lay face down and clung to it, wrestling it by its scrubby buffalo grass topnotch. His clothes were choking him, clinging to him like the stench of animal blood, like the leeches in the jungle swamps, like the villagers who were afraid for G.I. Joe to leave. He gave them his food, his water, his whiskey, grass, and speed, and still they clung to him, beseeching him in a language no more intelligible than that of the wasps and daffodils. He struggled to crawl uphill, but they were reaching out of the rocky soil with small, vise-grip hands, voices that dwindled to a whine and then disappeared into the sucking and thrumming of helicopter blades.

Mac heard before he actually saw the young girl. The lieutenant had her under his arm—she was that light; just balsa bone and gossamer flesh—carrying her toward an abandoned hut. The high, thin sound she made was unbearable, so reedy it was almost a whistle, something akin to a metal file ratcheting across the taut strings of a violin.

"Mac!" Ben Sharkey ran toward Mac with the smooth-faced private, machine-gun fire sending up small tufts of dirt behind their pounding feet. "What are you fuckin' crazy, man? GO! GO! GO!" They ran several yards and then dove down to the ground. "Mac! Get back here, ya shithead!" Ben threw a rock and it glanced off the side of Mac's helmet. Someone was coming on the other side of the hut, and inside he could see the lieutenant on top of the girl.

"Get off her, you asshole!" Mac's voice was all but obliterated by the sharp blasts and the girl's piercing shrieks. "I said GET OFF!"

Gunfire. Splinters flew from the flimsy structure. Sharkey yelling. Helicopters. Mac leveled his weapon toward the lieutenant's head.

"Get—the fuck—OFF."

The girl's luminous black eyes connected with his at the same moment the young private's bullet struck him in the back. The impact slammed his body forward, and he heard the dull, distant discharge of his own rifle. He watched the bullet travel through the heavy, humid air, through the lieutenant's neck and into the girl's smooth forehead.

There was a moist little sound—*psssahh*—and a breeze through her hair as part of her china-doll face simply disappeared.

Mac crawled to her, dragged the lieutenant's body aside. He pulled off his poncho and tried to cover her wide eyes. He stroked her blood-soaked black hair and cradled her until Jack burst in and found him there, rocking and weeping.

"Ah, shit . . . HEY, WE GOT THREE IN HERE," Jack bellowed over the thrumming. "ONE'S ALIVE."

Satchi wrapped him in a blanket, poulticed him with color and song.

" . . . *brave souls and soldiers* . . . *let va take you into the night with* . . . "

Her voice was unbearably close to his ear.

" . . . *to cbs news* . . . *top of the hour* . . . *shalom friends* . . . "

Like a long needle, it injected her secrets into his brain tissue.

" . . . *peace* . . . "

tulsatchi tulsarah tulsacid

He stroked the face of the radio and gently closed it inside the blazing woodstove. From beneath the burners, Mac could still hear Sarah harmonizing with Hank.

. . . no matter how I struggle an' strive . . . never git outa this world alive . . .

The moonlit stable stood before him. A whiskey bottle shattered against the boards and swirled like paisley. Quail and starlings screeched and fluttered. The whiskey whitewash pulsed blue-violet and then red again, scrawling in amber the unpronounceable names of the nameless: his father and father's father, unknown bastard sons of his own, men and boys he'd killed in Korea and Vietnam, forgotten whores and virgins with whom he'd lain down. The shotgun was cool and solid in his hands while the rest of reality peeled off in multicolored layers, exposing naked skin, then raw muscle, and finally dry white bone.

aint goin nowhere boy be sitting here a certain caliber do they don't follow up on cant just swallow you aint goin nowhere cochise beat yer red ass bloody

The wagon wheel was still there, though parts of it had long since rotted away, and the whole thing appeared to be spinning as Mac steadied himself. He could see red rope burns glowing on the spokes that pointed to two and ten o'clock. He lifted the shotgun. Cool and solid. One spoke shattered, and the wheel sagged, groaning. Mac staggered a little at the backfire, feeling his skull splintering with the wooden slats of the stable wall, but he aimed and fired again.

The bullet traveled toward its mark on the other side of time, and Mac flew forward with it, free and unafraid, until Pa Roy's voice, searing as a well-seasoned strop, caught him like razor wire.

propane tank boy that propane

10

Did you know the old man's dog is dead?
Only family the geezer had
so now he eats Alpo all by himself
with a million other old hungry-eyed men.
He marries a bag lady in my script
and she buys him a brand new collie pup.
But I've called for makeup fourteen times
and I've still got circles under my eyes.
         from *Greetings from the Fissure of Rolando*

T ulsa had read a book a day, almost without exception, from the
year she turned five, but now there was enough autumn in the
air to make her pull an afghan around her as she sat on the
front porch swing, and she was still working her way through her
mother's memoirs. Tulsa would have devoured the book had it been
written by anyone else, but she couldn't bear to live out the story in
just a few days, to reduce her mother's animated existence to those or-
derly blocks of marching text, especially knowing she would eventually
reach the end.

The book wanted to give way somewhere close to the middle at a
chapter headed "Baby's Patent Leather Shoes." Jeanne had marked
that page with an envelope. Tulsa took it out and sniffed it, examining
the way the lefthanded script curved around her name. Even though
the envelope was beginning to be dogeared, it still smelled like Shali-
mar. Tulsa had resisted opening it or reading the chapter it marked.

After all these months of carefully practiced separation, she didn't want to feel loved and babied, sweetly manipulated back into the embrace of a family that no longer existed. She knew she was Jeanne's only way of holding on to Alexandra; she was the lingering ache that kicks up in a once broken bone, the itchy red scar that proves you weren't just whining—it really did hurt that bad.

"How's it goin', Tul?" She jumped when she heard Joey's voice. "Have you still got your nose in that dykes-from-hell thing? C'mon, give it a rest." Joey tugged on the afghan. "Let's go for a ride and get some breakfast. It's been a while, you know?"

"Yeah, it has." Tulsa took the envelope from the dustcover to mark her place. "But where's Mindy today?" she asked, chirping the name like she was speaking of a Pekingese.

"Ol' Mindy started calling in too many requests." Joey swung his leg over the seat and jumped on the starter.

"Hey, Tulsa!" He raised his visor and stuck out his tongue. "What's this?"

"What?"

"A lesbian with a hard-on."

Tulsa whacked the back of his helmet with her book and climbed on, hooking two fingers through his belt loop. He was in a better mood these days and seemed to be on a pretty even keel. Dallas made him work like a navvy most of the weekend, and Joey knew better than to come to the station in anything but his natural state of functioning, unfamiliar as that felt at first. He had little time for partying and, back at the bottom of the Icarus Broadcasting pay scale, little money for nonessentials.

At the No Sweat, Joey scored a newspaper that someone had left in a neighboring booth and started doing his Dear Abby thing, reading the letter in a falsetto whine and answering with a tight-jawed Midwestern twang.

"'Dear Confushed in Coo-kah-mon-gahhh, You are shimply too shcrewed up for your own liver. . . . '"

"Oh, God! Joey! Let me see!" She tore the paper out of his hands and spread it in front of her over the top of teacups and leftover hashbrowns.

BLAST INJURES RANCHER, RESULTS IN DRUG CHARGES
It was the big house she recognized in the hazy photo; the
bunkhouse lay in unidentifiable ashes, the mountain itself obscured by
billowing black smoke.

" . . . explosion late Wednesday night . . . " Tulsa scanned, trying
to make sense of disjointed phrases. " . . . blah, blah, blah . . . left
Michael Wolfgang MacPeters . . . " She looked up at Joey and in unison they said, *"Wolfgang?"* Joey laughed nervously, and Tulsa shook her
head. " . . . um . . . critical condition at Saint Peter's . . . *shit* . . . suffered internal injuries, second- and third-degree burns over sixty percent of his face and body when he inadvertently fired two rounds into
a partially filled propane tank, according to Lewis and Clark County
sheriff's deputies who responded to a call by a neighbor . . . blah blah
. . . apparently under the influence of . . . oh . . . Mac. Firefighters discovered marijuana cultivation near one of three outbuildings destroyed
in the blaze . . . according to Marvin Houston, MacPeters' attorney,
the forty-eight-year-old Lincoln man was distraught over the recent
death of his grandfather, to whom he was very close, and is not responsible for the cultivation since . . . since he does not own the land. . . . "

"We'll be back, Els," Joey called over his shoulder.

Elsa waved him off and watched them climb onto the Harley out
front. She knew they were good for the check.

━━━━━━━

Inside the gauze across Mac's eyes, the shooting colors and amber
flashes had finally settled into muted pulses of red. He had a sense of
feeling embalmed, wrapped in wide strips and chemical smells. There
was something cold high in his nose, but he couldn't seem to raise his
hand to push it away. Something else tugged at the side of his mouth,
and Mac could feel it extending down his throat into the center of an
agony so profound he could barely breathe around it. His arms were
tied down, he realized as he grew sickeningly aware of a catheter, IV,
and other tubes and hoses that snaked out from his body and dangled
from metal trees and monitors. He wasn't sure if he was awake or still
dreaming when he inhaled the halo of patchouli and heard her whisper, "Mac . . . can you hear me?"

He hoped it was a dream. He would rather never see her again than have her see this.

"Oh . . . Mac . . . " She grasped his hand, and he groaned out loud.

"Zheezush . . . don do dat . . . " Mac's lips were swollen and raw, and the effort of breathing to speak brought another dizzying wave of agony.

"I'm sorry," Tulsa told him. "I won't touch."

"Hey, Mac," Joey attempted, "better lay off the 'shrooms before you really hurt yourself."

Terrific. The gang's all here.

"Ged fugged." Mac barely recognized the glottal croak that was left of his voice. It was the first he'd tried to speak since he was first aware of being turned on the cool, water-filled mattress pad. He heard Joey cross to the other side of the bed where Tulsa was. He smelled the leather and motor oil and . . .

hashbrowns . . . oh, Lord, for some hashbrowns!

"Wait till you hear what they said about you in the paper, man." Joey was fidgeting and pacing.

"They called you 'Wolfgang,'" Tulsa chimed in with a less than convincing giggle. "Guess you feel like you're gonna die and afraid you might not, huh?"

" . . . uh-huh . . . " Mac fervently wished they would just go.

"Hey, Tul . . . " Joey seemed to be by the door now, calling her over in a hush. " . . . gotta get outta here . . . nothing we can do anyway . . . "

They hissed and hushed back and forth.

"Vor Crisd sake," Mac rasped, "bof of you ged de fug oudda here."

"What did he say?" Joey whispered.

"He doesn't mean it," Tulsa hissed back.

"I do!" Mac struggled to be clear, but his face felt alive with scorpions. "Ged—da fug—OUD!"

"OK, well . . . peace, man," Joey said, "and—you know, if there's anything—if you, you know . . . ah, holy shit, Mac . . . geez, man . . . "

"Uh-huh," Mac was able to nod slightly.

"C'mon, Tul."

The door swished closed, wafting a lingering breeze of patchouli. Time passed and he felt himself drift, wondering vaguely what they were pumping through the IV in his arm. Some pretty good shit, he decided, so when he first heard the Alvarez being tuned, he assumed he was dreaming.

. . . Since I met my baby . . . my whole life has changed . . .

Her voice pulled him back into the room like a silken burgundy cord.

. . . I don't need nobody . . . to tell my troubles to . . .

Mac lay alone behind the gauze curtain.

. . . 'cause since I met my baby . . .

He wanted to tell her something terribly important, but only a hoarse moan escaped his raw throat.

"What is it, Mac. . . . " She came close to him. He could feel her nearby.

" . . . doan . . . " He tried to swallow, but it hurt too much. " . . . doan stob . . . "

"I won't, Mac. I promise." Her voice was low and clouded until she cleared her throat. "Hey . . . just above these stitches in your arm, there's one little spot that still looks kind of like you. . . . "

Mac felt the silky part of her mouth there. From inside the bandages, he suddenly saw himself masked, mummified and wizened as old Pa Roy. All he wanted was the oblivion of the dripping IV.

"I'll just stay and sing for a while, OK?" she whispered.

"No . . . ged oudda here. . . . " He tried to say her name but felt his throat closing and new billows of pain rolling over him.

"Shhhhh . . . " She blew softly across his lips.

Mac's world distilled to three pure elements: pain, darkness, and the sound of her voice.

. . . the violets were scenting the woods, Maggie . . .

"White Wolf . . . come to supper. . . . "

" . . . crashing! he's crashing . . . need a respiratory cart in ICU, stat . . . "

Electronic shrilling, overwhelming pressure on his chest.

"The blood ceremonies bind us to each other. . . . " Satchi stroked his face with red. "You are a child of the Creator . . . a child of sacred origins. . . . "

satchi

" . . . fifteen cc's . . . hit him again . . . clear . . . "

"Yes, White Wolf?"

no more

" . . . one more . . . clear . . . "

She tied yellow prayer ribbons to the gnarled branches of the sarvisberry bush and IV tree, inhaled deeply from her pipe, and wafted the smoke back over her head with a graceful gesture.

Alexandra's poetry. Satchi's smoke. Tulsa's voice shifted, moved away.

"All the glorious colors of the universe and it's a beautiful day to be out boonie-truckin' around the Rockies, Joe. . . . " She was somewhere just beyond the perimeter of an oppressive heat that enveloped him.

come closer

" . . . Bloyer Chevrolet's big Halloween blowout . . . "

"Dad?"

"I don't think he can hear you, hon."

who the hell is that?

"I'm not mad anymore, Dad, so please—if you're gonna die, don't die mad at me—please! I'm sorry I said all that stuff."

Mac flinched at the undercurrents in Colter's voice: fear, pity, and pain as deep and tangible as his own.

" . . . id ogay, code . . . " he tried to reassure him, "id ogay . . . " but the effort brought another surge of agony, which brought blackness deeper than dreaming.

He awoke wondering what time it was, if the alarm had gone off or was he going to be late getting out to the Swamp.

" . . . if they can't stabilize him in the next forty-eight hours . . . "

hey colt

" . . . know it's hard to let go, love, but . . . time for his soul to travel . . . "

colter your girlfriend is a flake
" . . . other dimensions of music and light . . . free of the karmic darkness . . . "
oh yeah she's a complete stranger to reality
" . . . to unhook all that stuff . . . be better off if he just kacked it . . . "
thanks a lot colt
He surfaced from time to time to hear music: a Hank Williams tape, Three Dog Night on the radio, Tulsa singing songs she'd learned from jamming with Colter and Colter had learned from jamming with Mac long ago.

. . . blue moon over kentucky keep on a-shining . . .

He only knew he had been in blackness because he recognized himself emerging from it.
"Hey, Colter, why don't you go home and get some sleep?"
tulsa
"Why don't you?"
"I'm used to staying up," Tulsa said, but then she yawned. "They're coming to take him to surgery at six anyway."
"What now?"
"Skin grafts on his back." Mac hated how she said it so easily. "I'll just hang out till then."
"Why, Tulsa?"
"What?"
"Why are you hanging around here like this?"
"Because . . . I care about him."
"Well, take my advice—don't."
Mac started working harder to breathe, to tell Colter to mind his own goddamn business.
"*Shhh!*" she whispered. "He might be hearing you."
"Are you kidding? They keep him so tanked, he doesn't know which end is his ass."
"Would you like it better if he was lying there in agony?"
"You're just not used to it, Tul." Colter sounded weary and cynical. "Me—I know the drill. I've been here before. We wait, we cry, we take him home, and then we watch him start the same bullshit all over again."

Mac waited for her to lay into Colter, setting him straight with that nasty, wet-cat voice she got when she was really mad, but there was just quiet, followed by the rustling of Colter's down parka as she put her arms around him.

"I'm here because I care about you too, Colt." Another rustling. "Now, go on. Go home and get some sleep."

The door hushed open and closed.

" . . . tussa . . . "

"Mac! I'm here, Mac."

" . . . i . . . wuff oh . . . "

"Hmmm? Water? Here . . . go slow. . . . "

A plastic straw touched his lips, but the effort it took to draw a sip pushed him under again. He lay for a long while just beneath the all-over searing sensation, but he could almost stand it when he found himself floating in the cool stream of Tulsa's soft, expressive reading. She brought books, plays, and poems he had mentioned to her at one time or another, not knowing he mostly dropped the names to impress her and would have been happier hearing something pulpy. He became aware of her lips moving against the one small spot on his upper arm.

"' . . . soft and silent as a dream, a solitary doe. White she is as lily of June, and beauteous as the silver moon—'"

" . . . Tussa . . . "

"Colter. He's awake."

"Dad?" Colter sounded groggy and rumpled. "C'mon, Dad . . . you in there?"

Mac was pleased to notice the beginnings of some feeling in his face. His tongue was not as swollen, and even the overpowering pressure in his chest seemed to have subsided somewhat.

"Hey, Coder," he experimented. His speech was still muffled, but his voice sounded almost real.

"Hey, Dad."

"Tussa . . . "

"I'm here, Mac."

"Eighty-six da Wordsworff."

Colter laughed and Mac huffed a little, trying to join in. After that came a long darkness from which he emerged to hear her close beside the bed.

"'February 17, 1956 . . . In a place filled with people, I am dying of loneliness. . . . '" Her voice fell softer as she listened guiltily at the bedroom door of Alexandra's private thoughts. "'I lie in bed, starving for a specific embrace, envisioning the unnatural, unable to sleep until I allow this secret self to drift deep into a dark jungle of imaginings, moistened fingers frantically searching out resolution. I strain to keep still when it comes for fear of waking my husband. . . . '"

There was a sound of pages and Tulsa's deep sigh.

"' . . . The full-faced moon is a week away
Gwenn is thirsty for her dampened bed
Linda takes up a splitting maul
I see familiar dreams of red.'"

"That one's from *Belladonna*," Tulsa said absently and paged forward again.

Mac felt himself drifting downward.

I don't even want to know what that's about.

———

Time. Pain. Vague, pulsing red dreams of Satchi and Alexandra, burning timbers and voices tangled up with the Alvarez.

"Tulsa?"

"She's at work, Dad. Want me to turn it on?"

"No," Mac swallowed. " . . . ah . . . Christ—"

"Is it pretty bad today?"

"Uh-huh . . . Colt, I'm really hurting here. I need you to get something from the bunkhouse. . . . "

"Dad . . . "

"In the pie safe—there's some johnnycake."

"With homegrown in it."

"Yeah."

"I can't believe you." Colter got up and moved away from him. "Dad, there's no johnnycake. There's no pie safe—no bunkhouse! You burned the whole freakin' place down over a month ago."

" . . . oh god . . . a month?"

"You blew up the propane tank. There was a fire. Can you remember?"

"The cornfield—did the cornfield burn?"

"Yeah, right after the sheriff's department set it on fire."

"Oh, fucking son of a—is there anything left?"

"How can you even think about that now? They're talking felony, Dad. And you're talking freakin' johnnycake!"

"Shit—I'm gonna need a lawyer—I gotta get outa here—"

"Just be cool. Houston's working on it. He says because you got hurt so bad and because of your Vietnam medals and getting wounded and all—he might be able to get some sympathy and work this deferred sentencing deal where they drop the charges if you can stay out of trouble for seven years. But that's seven years of probation with no crap. So much as a joint—one joint, Dad! One bar fight, one DUI—*anything!*—you're in Deer Lodge for seventeen to twenty-one years."

Mac groaned, both out of pain and the prospect.

"This is serious shit, Dad. And Houston says this is the last time he's going up for you. I cashed in the savings bonds Gramma gave me and paid him as much as I could, but you still owe him a lot of money."

"Ah, Jesus, Colt."

"I know."

"You're a good man, Colter. I wish I could have given you more than a few funky chord progressions."

"Yeah, well . . . in that case," Colter answered, sounding like himself for the first time in a while, "can I borrow the truck while you're laid up?"

It hurt Mac to laugh, but he did anyway.

———

"'November 3, 1971 . . . J. has returned from her Detroit show bringing a string of malachite beads for me and a porcelain cow for T. . . .'"

Mac lay listening to the memories Tulsa kept like stones in her pockets: her ninth birthday, Michelangelo's David, the first time she ever won a game of Scrabble, Jeanne hugging Alexandra on the beach in Cape Cod, their skirts and shawls floating on the wind. He could

hear her turning them over in her heart, examining the precious col-
lection again and again, polishing each image smooth as an agate.

"'April 24, 1972 . . . Against my better judgment, I allowed T. to
go to the theater with a boy last night. It was a fiasco, as I suspected it
would be. She trudged in well after eleven, having obviously walked
some distance home. The piglet must have abandoned her or tried to
force something on her, but I suspect the little dullard was neither
physical nor intellectual match for her. I am furious when I see the
pain she is in. She will not speak about it. She sat in her room all day,
reading, playing the same infernal song over and over on her guitar.
We leave for Spain in two days. I plan to see an oncologist there who
has had tremendous success achieving remission through nutrition and
massage therapy. . . .'"

Tulsa closed the book. "Only we never went."

"I'm sorry, babe."

"You're awake."

"Yeah."

"Good. Because there's lots of interesting stuff in the paper today."
Tulsa rattled the pages of the *Independent Record*. "Let's see—a bear ate
a tourist up at Glacier. . . . Nancy Reagan is seeing an astrologist, and,
umm . . . you're divorced."

"Seriously?"

"Bye-bye, Beverly."

"Well, good. That's . . . solved."

"Marvin Houston rides again. He said she was just waiting to see
if there would be any money from the ranch."

"Well, I'm sorry to disappoint her. She probably earned it."

Mac began to drift less and spent most of his time waiting, listening and trying to move his fingers. They were stiff and swollen, bound
into broad white mittens of gauze. When they were periodically un-
wrapped, the air stung like acid, but Mac welcomed the sensation because it helped him count each tingling knuckle.

"Are there still ten?" he asked Tulsa.

"Well," she hedged, "eight and . . . let's call it a third. But don't
worry," she hastily added, knowing his first thought, "you'll be able to
play just fine. It's just the pinky and ring finger on your right hand.
You weren't planning to use those anymore anyway, right?" She stroked

what was left of his hand. "C'mon . . . think how convenient it'll be for flipping people off."

"Ahh . . . it only hurts when I laugh," Mac winced.

"Would that that were true," Tulsa intoned. She touched the tip of each remaining finger, and Mac flexed and extended them, imagining them strolling the slender neck of the Alvarez.

Each time they changed the gauze dressing on his eyes, his vision became less clouded; the darkness shallowed and his blurry surroundings gradually gained definition. He strained to see Tulsa's warped funhouse reflection.

"What happened to your hair?"

"You should talk! At least I had the good sense to use scissors."

"But why would you go and cut your hair?"

Tulsa laughed a little. "Trying to bully it into growing, I guess."

He asked her to bring a mirror, which she did with the disclaimer, "Be prepared. You look like a hundred fifty pounds of hamburger and you're wearing a very undignified ensemble."

"Ah, shit . . . fuck me . . . " Mac groaned at the sight of himself, raw, red, and bloated with a dark purple web across one side of his face and half his space-alien forehead extending noticeably further back than the other. He closed his puffy eyes and rang the nurse for more drugs.

Eventually he was able to stand and shuffle about. In the mornings, the orderlies took him to physical therapy, where he lifted embarrassingly puny weights, trudged for a few minutes on the treadmill, and then lowered his crawling flesh into cool, medicated water. In the afternoons, Tulsa would come. She was working middays now, and she was happy about that, hiking up to the hospital as soon as her shift ended at three, and the nurses let her stay late into the evening after Mac bragged to them that she was the one and only VA Lones.

―――――

"'And now the changelings whisper forth.'"

Tulsa traced the spring green cover of the book with one finger.

"Mac . . . are you there?"

He didn't respond, but she knew sometimes it hurt too much to talk. This was the chapter Jeanne had marked with the Shalimar-scented envelope. Tulsa chafed a little at the invasion, but she couldn't help craving the comforting place she'd always had in Jeannie's lap. She wished she still had the envelope, but somehow, the book had disappeared and Jeanne's letter with it. Tulsa had to fork over twenty-five dollars cash to get another copy off the best sellers rack at Little Professor. "'August 19, 1959 . . . Dear God, help me. I am pregnant again.'"

Tulsa clapped the book closed, her heart in her throat.

She knows.

"Mac?" There was only the steady *blip—blip* of the heart monitor. She pulled her chair over to the bed and laid her cheek against his gauze-wrapped hand. Somehow, whether he was listening or not, it was Mac's rumpled breathing close by that had enabled her to work her way this far through the life and art of Alexandra Firestein.

"'I am pregnant again. I wanted to tell C. the truth of what I am, pretending he would accept it as anything less than obscene. But now this. L. has heard of a place, fairly sanitary, not too expensive. She and I have hidden away some of our grocery money, and I will earn a little helping C's sister with her Tupperware sales. But I am afraid. If we are discovered, C. would prosecute, have me committed. He would take T. from me. To lose her would be more than I could bear; worse than my own death. Loving her is the only clear element in my life.

"'August 27, 1959 . . . L. made the arrangements and drove me into the city. There was a long hallway. Roaches, a dead skin of peeling paint, sheets on the floor, rope stirrups on a Lay-Z Boy recliner, crochet hook, knitting needle. My angels of mercy stood beneath a naked light bulb, a woman and her teenage daughter, obese and sweating in the stifling apartment. They kept the window closed in case of noise.

"'There was a rending; a tearing away, as if I were made of paper. The mother cursed and pulled a plastic garbage pail onto her lap and I lifted my head to see it all spilling out of me. I tried to scream, to beg, but the daughter clamped her hand across my mouth. Everthing was going out of me; blood, light, power, life. L. gripped my hand so tightly,

I lost feeling in my fingertips. "Sweet God, you're killing her!" The woman didn't want to call for help, fearing we would all be arrested. "Get her down to the stairwell."

"'I awoke in a sterile white room with everything gone. I will never have another child. Never feel my monthly flow, warm and emotional. Perhaps, God truly is visiting a punishment on me for my unnatural desires.

"'September 3, 1959 . . . C. came to me, grim and immovable. He had in his hands the book that held all my heart, my journal, my poems. "Who are you?" His expression shifted between anger, revulsion, and betrayal. "*What* are you? What kind of woman could imagine such *filth?*" I had no answer. He said that I was an unclean vessel, that I could never be the wife and mother God intended me to be, and knowing this was true, I could only weep.

"'Will I be charged with a crime?" I asked.

"'Your friend—" he gritted his teeth around her name—"told the police you were raped."

"'And that pleased them?"

"'I assured them you'd receive proper care for your mental condition."

"'Several days after the hysterectomy, I was moved to the psychiatric ward. Sitting on my wooden chair, day after day, I began to feel an inexorable, almost frightening calm. Deeper than morphine, silent as a nurse in the night hallway, cool and smooth as a metal examination table; it was truth, a knowing as undeniable as saltwater. Looking out from this place of calm at the tangled forests, the spiraling dance of delusion and despair around me, I knew that I was sane as any round rock, clear as words in a row. I, Alexandra, was holy, cloistered, the woman, mother, and human being God intended me to be.

"'It was agreed that, for the sake of the child, I would be given two thousand dollars, but I must take back my maiden name and leave this city and state, lest a business or church acquaintance discover my perversion. When C. handed me the money and two train tickets to Peoria, he asked, "Do you have everything?" and then clarified, "For the baby."

"'"Yes," I nodded toward the two small suitcases. "But . . . my book?"

"'"*It—is—burned!*" he answered, his only regret that he was unable to cauterize the words from his mind.'"

Mac made a low sound and Tulsa paged forward.

"'Toddle to me, Tuppy, in your patent leather shoes
and wonder why my mommy lied and why I lie to you.'"

"They called it the 'Baby's Patent Leather Shoes' speech," Tulsa told Mac when she recognized the photograph from *Life* magazine, and she held it up for him, even though his eyes were closed. It was taken that day in Battery Park, just after a protester broke through the police line and struck the genetrix in the side of the head with a wooden sign. In the photograph, six-year-old Tulsa clung to her mother's neck, mouth wide in silent screaming, but the black-and-white Alexandra appeared serene; a halcyon, bleeding Madonna in a sea of riot shields and contorted expressions.

"We are told that to break with those bonds is a crime against society and a sin against nature," Alexandra's voice echoed across the PA system. "So we bear the burden, we die or we are imprisoned. . . . "

Tulsa sat on Jeanne's lap at the back of the platform, squirming with boredom. "Are we done yet? Can we go now?"

"Terrorists who bomb and incinerate, who invoke the name of God, but undermine Her all-empowering spirit—"

"Shhh," Jeanne whispered. "Mommy's going down in history again. Then we can all go to Coney Island."

"Cloaked in self-righteousness, they butcher and strip us of our choice to give life as surely as those who let my blood and womanhood flow out into the trash. . . . "

Tulsa made two of her little cows dance together, but one dropped on the floor, and her mother turned when she heard the sound of it skittering under her foot. Here the memory turned grainy and slow in Tulsa's mind, playing and replaying like the Zapruder film.

bitch whore pervert

There was a swell of movement from both sides of Alexandra's outspread arms as security women swept forward and the protester lunged. He swung the sign and Alexandra seemed to step forward into it, as if she knew the blow would pass through her body and into the pulsating crowd like an electrical charge. People were screaming, surging. Jeanne ran forward. Tulsa scrambled beneath legs and loud voices to reach her mother, but Alexandra fought through the hands and cameras, away from Tulsa's wailing, back to the microphone.

"The hand of the tormentors is across my mouth, but I will not be silenced!"

Pinned to the ground by the body guards, the man was still bellowing.

murderess pervert bitch

"Until the day of my death, I will be heard! Until there rises a voice one hundred million women strong, crying out for justice—"

"*Mommeeee!*"

"—crying out for life—"

"*I want to go home, Mama! I want to go home!*"

Without pausing, Alexandra swept her up in one arm and Tulsa wrapped her legs around her mother's waist.

"—crying out for freedom and for sovereignty over our own bodies! And by the avenging Mother God of Abraham and Sarah, that voice shall *not—be—SILENCED!*" As the assembly rose to their feet, the voice came forward, a physical force, an unstoppable tide, and Tulsa hung on hard, trying to keep Alexandra from being swept away by it. But it was too late. When she pressed her face against her mother's neck, she could feel a pulse in cadence with the chanting.

"Tulsa?"

She looked up, startled to find herself still here and crying and all the rest gone and silent and her mother made of paper, after all.

"Shhh, it's over. It's done with." Mac reached out to her, as best he could. "It's just a book now."

"No . . . no, it's not . . . "

"It's just a book now, Tulsa. You can close it if you want to."

But she held it open against her chest.

"Set it aside for a while, babe." He laid his hand on the back of her head. "Just set it aside."

———

It snowed Christmas Day—"like the Dickens," Colter couldn't resist quipping, and Mac begged him and Tulsa to knock it off because it hurt so bad to laugh. He was sitting in a wheelchair between two rolled-up blankets, and Tulsa was pouring eggnog while Colter played the Alvarez.

"C'mon, Tul, gimme me some harmony here," Colter said, but she had to keep filling in with hmm-hmmms and la-da-da-das.

"Geez! You can sing fifty verses of 'Knoxville Girl' but you don't know 'Silent Night'?" he complained. "Who could possibly not know 'Silent Night'?"

"A Jew."

"Gesundheit," Mac supplied, and then they laughed so hard he spilled his eggnog and Tulsa had to wipe it off the front of his new robe.

"I'm not kidding, Colter, I'm Jewish."

"Seriously?"

"Tulsa Firestein Bitters," Mac corroborated, "Jewish American Princess."

"Well, OK," Colter proposed, "let's hear some Hanukkah carols, then."

Tulsa tried to think of something other than the first three words of "Dreidel, Dreidel, Dreidel," but came up blank.

"I guess Judaism was a little patriarchal for my mom," she explained, "although we did see *Fiddler on the Roof* once."

It was after ten when Colter finally ran out of carols.

"We gotta go, Dad." He set the Alvarez aside and knelt in front of his father. "Rina slips a cog if she has to stay at her mom's house too long."

"You go ahead," Tulsa told him, "I'm just going to hang out for a bit and then walk home."

"Tul, you can't walk that far in this snow."

"She could take a cab," Mac offered, but regretted it as soon as he heard how it sounded like he wanted her to stay.

"Yeah," she jumped on it, "I'll take a cab. It's a holiday."

When Colter was gone, she turned off the overhead light, pushed Mac's chair over by the window, and set about picking things up, throwing away napkins and cookie wrappers and washing out the eggnog cups. Finally she stopped fussing and sat up on the windowsill with her feet on the radiator.

"We're the snowglobe people," she said, looking out at the beauteous evening, but then they were quiet for a long while.

"Merry Christmas!" A young nurse bustled in, straightened the bed, and then studied the chart dangling from the end. "OK . . . " She flipped it over and picked up the empty water pitcher. "I'll be back in a bit for your vitals. Are you going to get him settled, Mrs. MacPeters?"

"Well, sure, but I'm just . . . " The nurse was already gone. "I guess the regular people are off tonight," Tulsa said uncomfortably.

"You should call your cab."

"Well, let me help you—"

"She said she'd be right back."

"OK, but at least let me do this," Tulsa pulled the elastic band off his ponytail, "because I brought you something."

She reached into her bag and produced a leather thong and feather. Mac didn't say anything as she brushed his hair and braided it, but as she tied off the leather, the humiliation of letting her do it was so unbearable that he pulled away and complained that her hands were cold. She was quacking on about some interview she'd done yesterday with some gimpy guy from the DAV.

" . . . to fund additional study on Agent Orange, in my opinion—"

"Nobody's interested in your opinion on Vietnam, Tulsa. You don't know anything about it."

"Well, I want to know, Mac," she solicited. "Why don't you tell me?"

"It had great beaches." His downward inflection closed the subject.

Tulsa stroked his neck lightly, kissed the top of his head, and helped him ease up onto the bed. She smoothed the blankets over him, and it was almost more than Mac could stand.

"Why don't I crank this thing down and you can close your eyes."

"*Would you stop?*" he finally erupted.

"Stop what?" she asked innocently.

"Finessing me," Mac said. "I'm nauseous enough without you turning everything to pablum and syrup."

"OK." She went back to the windowsill and watched for a bit.

"Mac?" she said, still facing the glass.

"Hmm."

"What happened?"

"I don't know, babe," he sighed. "I just got a little too much party on."

"Oh, c'mon!" She was genuinely offended. "Don't give me that crap—not when you're accusing me of turning everything to pablum."

"What the hell do you want from me? I got hammered, OK? I got fucked up. I didn't plan to die and—Christ knows!—I didn't plan for *this* to happen! I just went out and got completely, royally *fucked up!* And believe it or not, it had nothing to do with you." He pushed his hands down, struggling to sit up.

"OK! Geez—I'm sorry I asked."

"And for the record," he drove on, "I'd like to say that I'm not interested in being your lapdog or whatever it is you're grooming me for with all this saccharine nursemaid horseshit. I'll warn you, I don't feel at all obligated by it to love you or be with you or any other damn thing. In fact, I think it's time you just take your clever little mouth and your inflated theories and your droning, neurotic mother and get the hell out."

"Mac!" Tulsa's eyes widened. "Honey, you don't mean any of this—"

"Honey?" Mac derided. "*Honey?* Where the hell do you get off calling me a feeble-ass, no-dick thing like HONEY? Just save that shit for your back-East boy—or whoever you're going to be screwing ten minutes from now in your bottomless, sucking need for attention. I'm not your *honey* and I won't let you paint some face on me just because that's what you want to see."

"Oh!" Tulsa was stone-cold furious now. "Like when you call me babe or brat kid? Or VA? Admit it! You get off on the fact that I'm on the radio and I'm half your age and I make you feel like a great big stud instead of a sawed-off little cigar-shop Indian. Because for all your bull snake, cowpoking bravado, you need things from people just like anybody else, Mac—and that scares the living shit out of you!"

"Well, I sure as hell don't need your simplistic, adolescent—"

"*Bullshit!* You do need me, and you know it!" Tulsa bit off each word and spat it in his face. "Maybe you'd even appreciate it if you weren't so busy wallowing and masturbating in your ancient emotional history, making messes and expecting other people to feel privileged about cleaning them up."

"I never asked anyone to do shit for me—"

"Hah! Colter's more of a father to you than you've ever been to him."

"—and you don't know a damn thing about Colter!"

"I know you dumped on him his whole life! I know you made him afraid to go home after school! And I know that no matter how many times you let him down—no matter how many times you hurt him—like an *idiot*, he keeps loving you! He keeps trying to make things be OK. He was going to sell his pottery wheel to pay your attorney, Mac—sacrifice everything just to keep your sorry butt out of jail! And he would have done it too, if I hadn't convinced him we could get more for—" She cut herself off and turned her back on him.

"For what?" The answer was already sitting like a jagged rock in his gut. "*What have you done?*" Mac knew she owned only two things that were worth a fraction of what Houston was. "Not the Framus."

She stayed silent, arms pressed across the front of her body.

"*The Framus?*" his molten rage erupted. "God damn you! *Damn you!*"

"You're welcome."

"*You had no fucking right!*"

"I did it for Colter. You can rot in hell for all I care."

"I will not be beholden to you," he told her, teeth clenched against the intrusion. "Take the Alvarez. You take it and get the fuck out of here."

"Oh, thanks a lot! You know that cheapjack piece of crap isn't worth a fraction of what mine was!"

"Take it! You're not gonna use this to sink your talons into me!"

"So now who's *babysitting* whom?" She spun on him and leaned over the bed with a lacerating smile. "Truth is, *you're* the brat kid, Mac. Still scared of ghosts and cryin' for your mommy—"

Tulsa glimpsed the back of his hand a split second before it impacted with her mouth, but somehow she didn't immediately realize he'd struck her. She felt her head snap to the side and then became aware of a burning pressure and warm trickle beneath her nose.

Mac smashed his fists against his forehead and twisted as though a hatchet had caught him in the back. "*Ah, Christ!*" he choked. "Tulsa—" He tried to reach for her, but she scrambled like a frightened animal over the side of the chair.

"Ho ho ho! Meds for Christmas!" The nurse backed in the door, balancing a fresh jug of water and a shiny steel tray, smiling until she saw the blood on Tulsa's face. "What on earth—"

"Oh, geez, I'm the biggest klutz," said VA Lones, hastily pawing and dragging Kleenex from a box on the bedside table. "I must've—must've tracked some snow in and then—I just sort of—" she made demonstrative gestures and sound effects—"just—*wheeesh*—and then—*ponk!*"

"We'd better send you down to ER and have them take a look."

"Oh, no—no, that would be silly!" Her giggle was forced and shrill. "Maybe I could just . . . ummm . . . have some ice or something?"

While Tulsa babbled and elaborated, the nurse was characteristically quick and effective, gliding a chair over and wetting a towel.

"Hold this here." She pressed the towel to Tulsa's bloody nose. "Tilt your head back, sweetie . . . there you go. It doesn't seem to be broken, but you'll have a nice fat lip there. Apply light pressure like this . . . good girl. OK, sit tight. I'll be right back." She hurried out and the door hushed closed behind her.

Tulsa lifted her head and studied the seeping red design on the pale folds. "You couldn't stand it, could you?" Behind her shadow, beyond the glass, snow was still falling, filling up the corners of the outside ledge with a soft, white silence. "It almost felt like a family for two lousy minutes. And you just couldn't stand that."

"Get out, Tulsa." Mac's heart contorted painfully inside his ribs. "For Christ's sake—just go and don't come back."

"I said I wouldn't stop and I won't. You can't make me." She leaned forward, pale and shaking. "But, old man, don't you ever—*ever!*—"

The door swished open and the nurse was back with a butterfly bandage and blue icepack.

11

Tulsa took the long way to Saint Pete's the next day, scrunching her feet through three miles of new snow, feeling what the daily hike was doing for her body. She didn't expect she would ever be thin or willowy, but she felt stronger, and her Levis were definitely looser. She scrunched on, wondering if Mac had noticed and if he liked it; wondering if he had ever punched out any of his old wives and if they were all pretty like Lorene. Flurries of fresh snow soothed her bruised mouth, but her jaw still throbbed, and it hurt so much to wipe her nose, she resisted the impulse to cry.

When she reached Saint Pete's, she veered away from the burn unit and went instead to the OB window to look in at the babies. Some were howling, some sleeping, others just scoping out the scene, having accepted that they were in the world now and there was naught to be done for it. Proud fathers pointed out their offspring to anyone who would look, and Tulsa was willing to smile and exclaim in admiration for their benefit. She felt sorry for them in a strange way, recognizing why her mother especially loathed men when they acted all adorable and vulnerable like that.

Charles, Tulsa wondered, and his wife . . . Bertha? Wendy? Cecile? Did they have the baby girl they wanted? And how did it go over with little Skippy and Dippy or . . . whatever.

"How does it feel to be a big sister?" a grandma asked a little girl, and the timing made Tulsa laugh out loud.

Colter's stuff is special. It's gonna be worth something someday.
Did I tell you Myrtle is expecting again? Yes, we're very excited.

249

Mac—young, strong, and puffed up to bursting over his brand-new son—hooked his thumbs in his belt loops and nodded beneath the brim of his low-riding Stetson. Charles Bitters, sporting the dapper black suit he always wore in her imaginings, made *ga-ga-shoo-shoo* faces at his little girl. They stood, clapping each other on the back, tapping and pointing at the glass, commanding the future. Aaron looked over their shoulders at the source of all this manly pride: Mac's Seed Incarnate and Charles's Progeny. But he touched the glass, rested his forehead against it, a great pain evident in the reflection of his seastone eyes.

I just can't do this right now.

Tulsa suddenly saw him as one of the most courageous people she knew. Brutally brave and honest. He had forced himself—and her—to see the needing child, the storming adolescent, the dental work and car insurance. He stared beyond the innocent window toward all that cinderblock and steel without which glass cannot be framed or raised or made to be something solid.

But Mac and Charles Bitters stood there crowing and cooing and just generally being a couple of sweet, foolish daddies, the kind without whom no one would ever know what it is to snuggle with a five o'clock shadow or beg for Dilly Bars or a pony ride on the ankle of a cowboy boot or even be born at all. For them, the reflection and the innocence were all that mattered.

Tulsa pondered there for half an hour. The nurses smiled and waved, startled and curious when they noticed her disfigured face. When the weight of her parka began to press heavily on her shoulders, she turned and made her way down the hall toward Mac's room, opening the door silently, not wanting to wake him. She was surprised to see him up and sitting on the edge of the bed, wearing a set of blue-green surgical scrubs. He moved so slowly, Tulsa knew every breath must be painful yet. He put several books into a canvas bag and then tried to bend down for his guitar, made a tight sound through gritted teeth, swore, and sat back on the bed.

"Going somewhere?" Tulsa asked.

"Yeah." Mac didn't turn to look at her.

"Were you planning to tell me?"

"Didn't really expect to see you today." He tried unsuccessfully for the guitar again. "As long as you're here, though . . . "

Trying to look defiant, Tulsa tossed her parka on the nightstand and slumped into the chair with her feet up on the end of the bed.

"Get it yourself. You don't need me."

Mac set his jaw, retrieved the Alvarez, and laid it triumphantly on the bed in front of her. "Where's the case?"

"It was all charred up and smelly," Tulsa said sullenly. "I threw it out."

"OK," Mac nodded and then shrugged. "It's yours now, anyway."

"They said you crawled inside the bunkhouse to get it and that's how your hands got so bad."

"I don't remember," Mac said.

"The porch roof fell down on you, but you still kept on—"

"Is there some point to this?"

"Not really." Tulsa touched her fingertips together to form a pyramid. "Just that if you really love something, you'll risk being hurt rather than let go."

Mac sat down in front of her, but she wouldn't meet his eyes. She'd obviously cried some the night before, and the sight of her mouth dragged his heart downward; it was swollen, bruised bluish-purple on one side, the upper lip split. She had the red-rimmed look of something tipped over and spilled. She should have been protected from him, and the knowing of that swept across Mac in a way that went beyond remorse.

"Tulsa, I'm sorry. . . . " She turned away, wondering how anyone could speak so gently without rocking you like a child. "I have never in my life hit a woman, and I certainly didn't want to hurt you, of all people. God knows, you're what's kept me going since . . . all this. But I think it's time we both open our eyes—"

"Mac, please don't say any more."

"We both know this is going nowhere."

"*Please!*"

"You need someone you can make a real life with, a man who's going to love you, provide for you, have babies with you . . . "

"Don't tell me what I need," Tulsa tried to assert, but Mac spoke over her.

" . . . and grow old with you. Simple math and history says that's not gonna be me. It just isn't, Tulsa. No matter how much I wish it could be."

"Your grandfather was over a hundred—that's more than fifty years—"

"*My grandfather?*" Mac looked at her in disbelief. "Sweet Christ— If I thought I was going to grow old like my grandfather, I'd kill myself right now!"

"Isn't that what you're doing?" Tulsa flared. "Killing yourself just a little at a time, blaming it on him, hiding from me—"

"All I'm saying is," Mac put his hands down to support his aching body, "I don't want you to be hurt anymore."

"That's a copout." She waved it aside without emotion.

"I'm sick of torturing myself over Colter and Lorene and you and all the people who want—anything—everything. I have nothing for you, Tulsa."

"It's an excuse."

Mac was too weary to argue with her.

"Where are you going?" Tulsa asked after a time.

"They're sending me back to the VA hospital."

"*To the psych ward?*" Tulsa sat forward.

"How did you know—" Mac knew the answer before the question was out and, in the same instant, recognized that it really didn't matter.

"Can they do that?" she asked indignantly. "Can they just put you there?"

"They seem to think I need . . . help."

"But you don't want to be helped. You want to be euthanized."

"Oh, bullshit."

"Then don't go!"

"What else am I supposed to do?" Mac spoke as though he were already sedated. "Jesus, it's not like I have a lot of options right now. I'm broke. My land is gone. I have no job, no place to live—"

"You have me, Mac—if you'll just *have* me! Just stop all this stupidity and let yourself have me. If my apartment's a problem, we'll go rent from someone else—maybe even find a house—"

"Tulsa, it—*won't*—*work*—*out*." Mac felt like he was trying to explain the laws of physics to a five-year-old. "Have you forgotten what happened here yesterday?"

"It won't happen again. I know that."

"No, you don't. Deep down, you'd always be afraid. And with good reason."

"I don't care!"

"*I care!* And it's too late to change what I am."

"It's not what you are, Mac, it's what you do. You can change that—just don't do it! Don't hit me. Don't torture your son. Don't blow yourself to bits or smoke yourself into a bloody stupor every day!"

"I don't expect you to understand—"

"Oh, yeah, that's right! I'm just a silly little twit who doesn't know anything about life. I was never in Vietnam, I was never horsewhipped, I don't know anything about getting divorced or stoned or shot—I don't know anything about *anything* except that I love you—"

"Don't say that."

"I do!"

"*No!*"

"*I love you!* You told me never to fake it with you. You told me to tell the truth, and I'm telling you now—" Tulsa put her hands out but stopped herself just short of grasping his arms. "You don't belong there! You're not crazy. You just want everyone to think you are so they'll let you off the hook—"

"Tulsa," Mac kept trying to break in.

"—so you won't have to live up to any of the everyday expectations or obligations that everybody else in this world has to live up to. You think because of that old man and your mother and Vietnam that you're some kind of exception to the rules—"

"Enough, Tulsa!"

"—but you are not entitled to hurt the people who love you just because somebody you loved hurt you first!"

"*Tulsa!* For the love of God almighty—would you just SHUT—UP? Do you even know how to *stop talking?*"

She fell silent for a while, but Mac could tell it was killing her, and that amused him a little, even under the circumstances. He puttered

around, gathering the rest of his things, and then sat awkwardly on the
arm of her chair.

"C'mere now . . . " he said, and holding her wasn't quite as painful
as he thought it would be. Her hands were cool on his raw forearms,
and her hair smelled like winter wind. Mac breathed in as much as he
could and let it go in a long, sad sigh when Tulsa rested her head on
his knee. "You need to get going, darlin'. They'll be here soon."

"Mac, if you go there, you'll come out like Ben Sharkey—this wonderful soul lost inside some strung-out shadow of a person. Just haunt-
ing places—not even really being alive!"

"Tulsa, don't start crying," Mac begged, pushing her away. "I'm really having a hell of a day here."

"OK—OK . . . I'm not." Tulsa swallowed hard and got up to pace,
trying to be cool, to brainstorm. "Look—let's just think about your options for a minute here. You won't come with me. It's too cold to camp
out, especially given the shape you're in. What about Joey? You like
Joey. Joey's great. Joey's lots of fun, Mac, and he owes you big time—"

Mac shook his head.

"Sharkey, then. What about Ben Sharkey?"

"Tulsa, he's got his own problems."

"Well, what about—you know . . . Lorene."

"*Aagh!*" The very thought was a torment.

"OK! OK . . . that leaves Colter. You and Colter need a few days to
hang out together, right? Just a few days? You've been in here for months
and—I know you, Mac—you're starving to be outside. You are!"

She did know him, he was uncomfortable to discover; knew how
he looked out over the mountains, aching and longing, dying a little
every night he slept inside. He would open the windows and the nurses
would shut them, scolding that it was too cold, not understanding that
the indoor air was slowly asphyxiating him. Feeling exposed, endan-
gered, he struggled to get up so he wouldn't have to face her; to Mac,
pain was more private than touching himself. But beneath the dis-
comfort was a slight breeze of relief. There was no need to finesse her
anymore, and that transformed her from passing lover to blood brother.

"Just for a few days, Mac," she repeated. "Can't you just try?"

"Maybe," he wavered, "but there's still the matter of—well, let's
face it, they have good reason to believe I'm fucking nuts!"

"As long as the nuts consent, it's nobody else's business."

She said it so seriously, it took Mac a second or two to get it, and then he sat back on the bed, his growly chuckle relaxing into his old contagious hoot. He couldn't stop, even though it was agonizing, and he hoped she assumed the tears in his eyes were from the laughter or the pain.

"What a piece of work you are," he finally managed to gasp. "You spoiled brat kid—you don't let up."

"That's right." Tulsa wasn't laughing.

Mac breathed deeply and dropped his hands to his sides. "If I can't make love to you very soon," he said, "I really will go off the deep end."

Tulsa closed her eyes for a moment. "OK," she nodded, "I'm going to get Colter on the phone." She started out the door but turned back to add, "If the doctor comes in here, you act sane!"

"Yes, ma'am."

The doctor did come, and Mac adopted his old job-interview/divorce-court persona, curbing the impulse to rebel against the probing questions and patronizing tone. When Tulsa returned, the doctor glanced up at her.

"Will your daughter be assisting with your care?"

"My daughter?" Mac coughed, but Tulsa extended her hand and said pleasantly, "I'm Mac's coworker, VA Lones."

Mac teased her later for looking deflated when the doctor showed no sign of recognition.

"I see. Well, Mac, things seem to be in order for your release, but considering your history, I'm wondering if we shouldn't follow through on our original plan for continued treatment at the VA. You still need physical therapy and limited care, and frankly, I'm concerned about the pattern of chemical abuse. The VA rehabilitation program is extremely effective—"

"Yeah, I know," Mac cut in. "I've been rehabilitated there three times. Truth is, Doc, I doubt there's a program anywhere that has more impact than the one I've been in for the past few months. I feel pretty thoroughly . . . persuaded." Mac felt a twinge of guilt, an odd sense of loss, as if he'd denied knowing an old lover on the street. "Besides which," he mumbled wretchedly, "I'm on probation."

"I see." The doctor flipped Mac's chart back over his clipboard and jotted that down. "Well, it's true that you've been through a great deal in the last three months, Mac. I guess we'll see three months from now whether it had any lasting impact. Meanwhile . . . I'm willing to give you the benefit of the doubt."

Mac nodded and the doctor wished him luck, offering his hand, which Mac gripped as he thanked him very sanely. Next there were papers and forms and prescriptions, and then Mac gritted his teeth while the nurse wheeled him out to the Old Trapper Taxi. Mac's truck was parked out front of Anne Marie's, and the sight of it opened up something inside him. Colter was on the porch, stomping December snow from his boots and hanging the sidewalk shovel on its peg.

"Dad!" he waved, running back down the steps. "Oh, man . . . am I glad to see you. The doctor called here and I said no problem, and I'm really gonna watch out for you. You look great, Dad. Or at least—well, not as bad as I thought you were going to!"

By this time, Joey, Rina, and even Jack and Anne Marie were out on the porch. They cracked beers, but Mac held up his hand.

"No thanks, I'm . . . fine."

There was an awkward silence while Joey and Rina regarded the stranger in Mac's buckskin coat and Jack and Anne Marie stared at Tulsa's swollen lip.

"Dad, I've pretty much been staying up at Rina's lately," Colter spoke up, " . . . so—you know—take as much time as you want and—I mean . . . except for my work space, the place is all yours, OK?"

"Thanks, Colt." After a few more intensely uncomfortable minutes, Mac almost wished he was back in the hospital. "Well, I think I'll just head in."

"Wait a minute, Mac!" Joey reached up onto the stairway and produced a brown bag emblazoned with the Aunt Bonnie's Bookstore logo. "I know you're into Stephen King and you'll just be hangin' out for a while . . . so . . . "

"Thanks, Joe," Mac cringed, eyeing Colter's door and trying to plot the most direct escape route through the well-intentioned gauntlet.

"Open it," Joey prodded.

Mac nodded stiffly and reached inside the bag.

"Ah . . . *The Firestarter.*" He glanced up in time to see them all disintegrate into gales of laughter. Relief washed through him like a cool drink. He used the paperback to smack Joey upside the head.

"Classics are a given," Tulsa giggled, proffering a copy of Dante's *Inferno*.

"But," Colter jumped in, "there's nothing like a good movie." And Rina held up a videotape of *Blazing Saddles*.

They stood in the entryway a bit, laughing and making sick jokes about things blowing up in your face and going like a house afire. If they hadn't, Mac would have known how uncomfortable they all were, and even with the graveyard humor, he had his doubts. Finally, seeing how fatigued he seemed, Tulsa made some leading remark, and everyone murmured something about being glad he was back or whatever, and the group disbanded. She swung the Alvarez up onto her shoulder and, carrying the heavy bag of books as well, balanced both while she opened Colter's door.

"Do you think you can make it up the stairs?" she asked a little too gaily.

Mac opened the window and stared out.

"Because the day you do is the day you can make love to me." She backed toward the door, and Mac noticed for the first time that her figure was definitely more athletic these days. "So . . . start working on it, huh?"

"Yup."

"Well . . . so . . . OK?" She was looking at him uncertainly.

"Yeah."

Mac was grateful that she had the good intuition to leave him alone. He blessed her again when he saw the jeans and flannel shirt on the bed. Wandering into the kitchen, he relished the simple act of putting on a pot of coffee. He drank some, read the paper, dozed in a chair, finding new pleasure in the small freedoms. When Mac woke up, the hall was quiet. He hobbled out onto the porch and down the steps. It was dark out, and the snow made a pleasant scrunching sound beneath his feet. The mountain air cleansed his lungs, and he realized how sharp and fresh it was now that he didn't smoke anymore. It would have been pleasant, though, on a night like tonight to light up a cigarette or a pipe of homegrown.

He trudged painfully down the hill to Last Chance Gulch. When he reached the Joker's Wild Saloon, he stood outside for a bit, renewing his acquaintance with the old Bullwhacker, savoring the sounds from within, and struggling to breathe more evenly. Then he pulled the door wide and tried to look like he was just easygoing to move so slow.

"*Mac!* Oh, my Lord and petticoats—MacPeters!" Berryl looked the same; if anything, her hair was even bigger than it had been before. "Good God! You look just *awwwwwful*, you poor dog! Just hellacious! Yak! Yak! You've gotta see this! It's MacPeters, and he looks just like a goddamn *gargoyle!*"

"Mac! How the hell are ya?" Yak clapped him on the back, and Mac obliged him with a not-so-comical yelp of pain. "I told Bee, I said, Mac knew I was gonna take that bar tab outa his ass, I told her, he musta thought I wanted it barbecued first!"

Everyone on the barstools laughed, including Mac. Someone shouted to Berryl to get him a beer, but he told her coffee with a cinnamon stick in it, and then there was a round of jokes about that. Someone offered him a cigar, and before he could offer an excuse, Yak shouted, "Nah, he just got done smokin'!"

"Hey, Mac, this ain't the kind of rope you're supposed to smoke!" Brody Fox reached over and yanked Mac's long braid, adding, "Geez 'n' crow, man, you look like something right out of a sci-fi movie! What the hell were you doing up there?"

And then the tale began. Mac froze their ears with the story of his wizened grandfather and the stones around the fresh grave, old Chadwick and the boy and the Morgan named Jim Bridger. When he came to the part about the peyote, he described a wild Indian dance that ended in a blaze of glory and the snatching of the Alvarez and his own dear life from the flaming jaws of death. This was all well received, as was the exposition of scars on his chest and forearms, and Mac saying that the rest were in places too fierce to mention, which led to jokes about his wick being lit and other innuendos and entendres. Then they compared LSD and Mushroom Experiences of the '60s, each describing trips and visions more fantastically disastrous than the one before him and all agreeing at the end that it was fine back then, but Mac had better cut it out and settle down, now, just as they had back in 1975 or sooner.

"I hear you got a girlfriend," Berryl teased. "Too bad your tally-whacker got toasted."

"Hey, never underestimate the value of a good loincloth," Mac said. "And don't worry, Bee, I've always got plenty for you."

That was met by whoops and hollers and more jokes. Mac set his coffee cup on the bar and picked up his hat. He tipped it to Berryl and to Yak and to the general company, and everyone said "good to see ya." On his way out the door, he caught sight of Ben Sharkey, alone in a corner booth, and they nodded just as the door closed between them.

The walk back to Colter's was laborious and slow. By the time he reached Benton Street, Mac was stopping every ten feet or so, looking forward to a stiff dose of Demerol and a long sleep. He felt a little rankled to see Tulsa, wrapped in an afghan, out on the front porch swing.

"Hi," she said. "I was getting worried about you."

"Well, don't," said Mac.

"Did you get some supper?"

"I said don't, Tulsa."

She nodded and made room on the swing. He sat down gingerly and she moved over close to his side, being careful not to lean or snuggle too much. She nuzzled his shoulder.

"Hmmm . . . you smell like coffee. I missed that while you were wearing that sissy nightgown . . . though I did enjoy seeing your backside."

Mac smiled uncomfortably and indicated Alexandra's book in Tulsa's lap.

"Still sloggin' through it, huh?"

"Yeah," she sighed. "Pretty thick, considering she died young. And would you believe they want twenty-five dollars for this thing?"

"Should have waited for it to come out in paperback."

"Yeah." Tulsa allowed a clipped, ironic laugh. "It's my painful adolescence all over America, but while Jeanne and the political machine make gobs of money, I can barely put together the price of the book."

Mac stretched his arm along the back of the swing behind her shoulders, surprised by her bitter tone. "You told me once it didn't bother you."

"I was lying!" Tulsa declared, amazed that he didn't already know it. "Of course it bothers me. I was dumped without a dime by my mother, who got more for one lecture than I gross in six months of air-shifts! She provided scholarships to displaced homemakers, but I had to drop out. I had to learn a whole different way of life: *scrounging*. Alone." She turned over the front cover and flipped to the dedication page, which simply read "For T." "What a joke. Just like when they were reading her will, it was full of these sick jokes—the biggest of which happened to be on me. I wish it didn't bother me, Mac. But I think I know how you felt when Chadwicks inherited your land. It's the same thing—only worse, because I thought Mom—" Tulsa cut herself off, realizing she was about to say something hurtful.

"No, it's true." Mac wondered why he hadn't seen it before. "You thought she loved you. And I'm sure she did. I had no such delusions; I knew my whole life the old man hated me."

"I'm sorry, Mac. Here I am whining—"

"No. I'm the one who owes you an apology. I guess you understand things a little better than I figured you did."

"Is this mellow old age settling in," she teased, "or are you still in the midst of your midlife crisis?"

"The latter, I s'pose." Mac rested his head against hers. "I expect I will be till I can get up all those damn stairs."

_____

By springtime, Colter's place had effectively become Mac's place. Colter still spent his days at the pottery wheel in the round front room but was upstairs cooking dinner for Rina by the time Mac meandered home in the afternoon. Mac was covering the rent out of his army pension, and that made Colter happy because he was able to quit the gas station job and concentrate on the heavy bowls and goblets that were beginning to sell well at a Reeders Alley gift shop. He and Mac found a comfortable space between them, and he and Rina were happy as clams upstairs. Warm evenings were spent jamming, with anyone and everyone out on the front porch and the house full of music and laughter the way it was on Tulsa's first night.

There was even an almost easy peace with Jack after a while. The first time they found themselves alone on the porch, they were both stiff and silent until Jack said, "It's your business, Mac—you and Tulsa—but it'll be your balls if I ever see you've raised a hand on her again."

Mac went rigid, but then nodded.

"Man alive," Jack said eventually, "you shoulda seen 'em rising over at Toston last night."

"Yeah?" Mac bit the line off and tied on a swivel.

"Yeah," Jack whistled in wonder, "practically fightin' each other to get on the line." And then they sat, puttering with their reels and lures, talking about unknown riffles and secret logging roads and the best way to get access onto one stream or another.

Depending on how much production she had, Tulsa would come home between five and six, careful not to make any assumptions, always going up to her own place, never inviting Mac to have dinner with her or to come up for any other contrived purpose. Later, if it was warm, she came down to the porch with her guitar, and soon Mac realized he was listening for her step on the landing. He knew she wouldn't knock, so he left his door open so he could dodge through the front room and coincidentally bump into her in the hall and casually invite her in for a game of cribbage or chess. After a while, the evening didn't feel right unless she was curled up on his couch with a book. They sat for hours without speaking, legs outstretched and entangled. Periodically, they got up to fetch coffee and Red Zinger, and Tulsa usually took a break at eight o'clock to go next door and read bedtime stories. Mac began to notice how uncomfortably cool the room was until she came back and resettled, but he would wake up around midnight to find his book on the floor, a quilt across his lap, and Tulsa gone.

First thing in the morning, Mac shouted up to her and they walked to the No Sweat for breakfast. Then he'd see her to the radio station and continue on to the YMCA, where he was doing his physical therapy. As he grew stronger and began to look and walk more like his old self again, Tulsa wondered, he could tell, why he never climbed the stairs to her apartment. It amused him a little that she was in so much more of a hurry than he was. He couldn't explain to her that he felt

like he was driving somebody else's car; his body had changed somehow, and he was not quite used to living in it yet, not quite ready to
risk anything. He lay awake nights, watching himself make love to her,
the same tape playing over and over in his mind. The quarry, the
bunkhouse, the old brass bed. He knew every aspect of her body; it was
his own that felt foreign.

He started driving his truck again and discovered that while Colter
was using it, he had gotten the starter fixed. No more push starts. Mac
was nostalgic for about five seconds and then reveled in the crank,
thrum, and purr as the engine popped right off every time.

Summer came. He and Tulsa spent their Sundays Baja-ing over the
mountains, drinking in the clean air, and fishing the cold streams.
They started staying out all weekend as soon as it was warm enough,
sleeping close but in separate bags in the back of the truck or beneath
the stars, forming an arrowhead by the fire.

September, and Tulsa was still wondering. Mac knew that she assumed he was no longer stirred by her. But if he woke up to look at her
while she slept, he'd lie awake for the rest of the night, and when he
watched her bathing in the icy creeks or getting dressed behind the
truck, he had to look away and steel himself against the feeling. He
didn't like it that it hurt her, but even if they had spoken about it, he
couldn't have explained other than to say that it wasn't her. And she
wouldn't have believed that.

Still, she didn't stop. He finally realized he couldn't make her.

They laughed a lot and read to each other and caught fish to cook
over the fire. In the evenings, they dragged their guitars from the back
of the truck, and Mac was playing almost as well as before. Tulsa made
fun of his Hank Williams yodel, and he parodied the sad-sack lyrics of
her favorite Janis Ian Kleenex songs.

. . . I learned the truth at seventeen . . .
that snakes live in outdoor latrines . . .

But when one of them would say, "OK, OK, how about this!" and
they came together on the old ones, Tulsa lending harmony to his stri-
dent lead or his gravelly tenor backing up her clear melody, Mac would

have to shout, "Hot damn, we're good! We oughta be in by-God-Nashville!"

Relishing the last lingering chord, Mac knew he could start again, and no matter what he chose, she would be there.

"Darlin'," he told her seriously, "you are gifted with the most amazing ear for harmony." Tulsa choked on her coffee, coughing and giggling, until he asked, "What already?"

She raised her hand in a hold-that-thought gesture and went to the back of the truck. She came back with Alexandra's book, paged through it until she found the right spot, and began reading aloud.

"'T. sings with me in the evenings, sings me to sleep,' wrote Alexandra as she lay dying. 'She is cursed with an uncanny ear for harmony. No matter what I or Jeanne or the radio sings, she finds a counterpart. She sees an opening, a space, a need, and she is compelled to go there. That is a woman's ear. To harmonize, lend fullness and support, but never lead. This is what I have given her. I have owned her life and stifled her song, the same way I was once owned and stifled. She should despise me. She should rejoice that this stranglehold is almost passed. Soon she will be free.'"

Tulsa didn't go on. As she closed the book carefully and took it back to the truck so it wouldn't get dirty, Mac prepared to talk her through it, not knowing she'd already cried as much as she intended to cry over one book. When she came back, she placed her twelve-string in its case and took it and the Alvarez to the truck. Then, because it was beginning to be early-autumn cold at night, Tulsa pulled her sleeping bag close to Mac's.

"My mother," she said, "had blazing red hair and a golden voice."

———————————

Standing behind a tree, unzipping her favorite old cut-off Levis so she could tuck in her T-shirt, Tulsa glanced up and caught Mac staring at her.

"What?" she said sharply.

She wouldn't have believed him if he'd told her she looked beautiful, her hair sunstreaked with cornsilk gold, her body long and strong from all the fast-water wading and steep hill hiking. She had become a striking woman. But Mac kept that to himself, having discovered well before breakfast that she was not in a good mood and there was no possible way to phrase it that wouldn't set her off.

During the night, he had opened his eyes and found her staring into the fire. She wasn't making any sound, but tears on her face caught the flickering light.

"What's the matter, babe?" he asked groggily.

"God, you are so dense." She rolled her eyes and brushed angrily at her cheek. "If you were any denser, you'd shit asphalt."

Mac rolled over and went back to sleep. There was no point lying in the dark berating himself for the thousandth time that it wasn't right what he was doing and vowing yet again to resolve this thing tomorrow, one way or the other.

The next morning, Tulsa was puffy-eyed, stiff, and spoiling for a fight. It started with the bannock. Mac mixed up the dough like always and plopped it in the frying pan over the fire.

"Do we really have to eat that crap all the time?" Tulsa groused. "It's greasy. It's disgusting. I hate it."

"Then don't eat it. Here." Mac tossed her a foil-wrapped square. "Have some pemmican."

"Gack. That's even worse," she grumbled, but opened the pemmican and bit off a too-chewy chunk. "I don't know why we can't just buy some bread and stuff. This isn't the abject wilderness or something. There's probably a Mini Basket not forty-five minutes from here."

"Well—about two hours, actually."

"But no . . . you have to play Big Chief Scar on Butt."

"This is what I know how to do, Tulsa. It's what I learned," Mac said patiently. "If you want to go to the store, go to the store. Go to Burger King. Have it your way."

"Are you implying that's all I learned?" Dissatisfied with Mac's monosyllabic response, Tulsa kept digging. "How would you like it if I made you eat latkes and kosher pickles all weekend? It wouldn't kill you to eat some cereal for breakfast once in a while. One bowl of Captain Crunch wouldn't compromise your religion—such as it is. You're not even a real Indian, for Pete's sake!"

"Never said I was."

"At least I'm half a Jew—you're just a crummy quarter Blackfoot."

"Far as I know."

"Which means I should only have to eat this shit one weekend a month."

"If at all," Mac said amiably.

He turned the bread and studied the fire till Tulsa walked away. She went to the truck to rummage for shorts and a clean T-shirt, scuffing and swearing when she couldn't find what she wanted, and it was while she stood changing her clothes that Mac thought she looked beautiful and she caught him staring.

"*What?*"

Mac held out his keys, jingling them like sleighbells. "You wanna go to the store? Drive yourself to the store."

He meant to offer to teach her, but she thought he was ridiculing her, and the fact that she had no ready comeback provoked her even further. Mac tossed the keys and she had to abandon her zipper in order to catch them.

"Cut it out, Mac."

"I'm not gonna marry some brat kid who can't even drive."

Tulsa was no more astounded than Mac was himself. As soon as he heard the words come out of his mouth, he felt a powerful impulse to grab them back, swallow them whole, and run like hell, but before he could move, Tulsa tossed the keys back and zipped her jeans abruptly.

"Well, don't worry—I'm not gonna marry some old coot who can't even—"

"Now, now . . . c'mon," Mac cut her off, tossing the keys to her again, circling out from the truck. "What are you afraid of?"

Tulsa countered his cross and threw the keys hard so they jangled against his chest. "Driving off a cliff, for starters!"

"Yeah." Mac tossed them gently back. "Me too."

"Oh—go . . . jump in the river!"

With a swift sidearm, Tulsa pitched the keys in a silvery-sounding arc just out of Mac's desperate reach, and they *splunked* well out into the water.

"*SHIT!*" Mac lunged and lost his balance on the slippery rocks, crashing straight as a thundering redwood, face down into the stream.

Even though the water was rushing, his body made a flat, smacking noise. Mac came up coughing and sputtering, up to his thighs in the torrent, and Tulsa collapsed into an uncontrollable squall.

"Oh, that's great, Tulsa, that's fucking hilarious!" He plunged his arms beneath the surface, tossing rocks up onto the bank, frantically reaching and feeling for the keys. It was deep enough that he couldn't touch the bottom without ducking his head every time, and he stood up gasping from the cold.

"Get over here and help me, goddammit!"

Tulsa meandered over and dabbled one foot in the icy water as Mac groped beneath the choppy surface, glaring at her and panting between dives. The more he struggled and swore, the harder she laughed.

"Why don't you just stand there," Mac bellowed, "while our only transportation out of here drifts down to fucking Dillon!"

Tulsa observed him thrashing until he barked at her again, then she clambered up and looked down from a large boulder, helpfully pointing out any shiny glimpse in the creek, which meant everywhere, considering the sun was moving steadily upward and the water was sparkling clean.

"I don't *believe* this!" Body numb, eyes bloodshot and burning, Mac dragged himself up onto the bank. "I can't fucking believe you could be so stupid and childish!" He could stand the sight of her only long enough to accuse her to her face. "You fucking did that on purpose!"

"So?"

"So? So we're in deep shit here, Tulsa!" His chest was heaving, and he was close enough that she could feel his breath on her neck as she shrank back against the tree. "I hope it was worth whatever bitch-ed thrill you got out of it because you're gonna walk home right alongside me, lady. And it's a long fucking way!" He strode away and lay down on his back in the sun warmth, threw one dripping arm across his eyes, and let the other drop by his aching side.

"Fuck!" Mac struck the ground hard with a closed fist. "This is not funny, Tulsa. Do you have any idea how long it could be before somebody drives by here? *Weeks*, Tulsa—possibly more! They'll probably find our fucking skeletons here in the fall. We're two hundred miles from home—sixty-two rugged miles from fucking *anywhere*! So you'd better save some of that jocularity for when we're hiking halfway across goddam Montana without food or water or money 'cause I'm not listening to one more goddam whiny complaint." He struck the ground again. " . . . sonofa . . . goddam . . . *fuck me* . . . "

"I wish."

Mac opened his eyes and squinted into the sun. It created a brilliant aura behind Tulsa's head, and something shimmered from her hand like windchimes.

"Colter had an extra set made." She dropped the keys on Mac's crotch before he could pull his knees up. "Just in case." She stepped aside, and the direct sunlight all but blinded him. "Wasn't that responsible of him?" There was something in her voice that made him sit up and hold back some of his anger. She wasn't laughing anymore or even smiling. She leaned against the tree and kicked the trunk with her heel.

"Why the hell," he said, forcing calm, "did you do that?"

Tulsa shrugged.

"You wanted to see if I would hit you."

"Maybe."

"You wanted to punish me for hitting you!" Mac was stone-cold furious and still breathing hard.

"Maybe."

"OK . . . fine . . . that's cool." He lay back, covered his eyes again, and clenched his chattering teeth, truly, intensely hating her. "Then we're even."

"No," Tulsa said. "When I can drive—then we'll be even."

12

Mac was mad.

He drove toward Helena in granite-clad silence, even though it was only Saturday noon and they usually stayed out until Sunday evening. Every once in a while, Tulsa began giggling, thinking about him smacking the water face-out like that, or she'd get a vision of the blank look on his face as the keys sailed over his head.

not a nice thing to do to a short man

And to make matters worse, every time Mac stepped on the clutch, his boot made a squishy sound. She tried to hold it in, but it would eventually erupt in a loud snort, and then she had to laugh until her side developed a painful stitch. The first few times, he asked her to please knock it off, but that didn't mean much to her, so he decided to ignore her. He tried to tell himself it was because she was coming up on her period. He wanted it to be that simple, but he recognized the falsity of that and the futility of the whole damn thing, and after a while, he just drove. Tulsa finally managed to subdue herself, and after a long, hot, quiet spell, Mac plugged in a Hank Jr. tape.

They went on without speaking until about five miles out of town, when Tulsa finally asked, "So were you offering to teach me or just being a big jerk?"

Mac looked startled. "Huh?"

Tulsa reached over and tempered Hank's volume to a reasonable blast. "I said . . . would you please teach me to drive, Mac?"

"Not if you paid me in gold fucking bullion." He reached over and cranked the volume back up.

"Oh." Tulsa mulled a bit before she poked the eject button, spitting Hank Jr. out altogether. "So you didn't actually mean that about . . . you know . . . "

"I think I must have gotten a little too much sun, Tulsa." Mac's eyes never left the all-too-familiar road. "I'm feeling much better now."

Back at the house, he stomped up the steps with his fishing gear and the Alvarez, leaving Tulsa to struggle with her backpack, sleeping bag, books, and guitar. He was of the opinion she always took too much stuff anyway, and maybe if she had to carry it herself for once, she'd conserve a little next time.

not that there's going to be a next time . . . insufferable bitch . . .

Just as Tulsa reached the porch steps, he slammed the front door behind him. Anne Marie was sitting on the porch swing rocking a sleepy, warm Oakley.

"Trouble in paradise?"

"Mac's mad," Tulsa said.

"I could have told you that a long time ago."

"It's my fault." Tulsa sat down on the swing. "I pissed him off." She piled her gear in front of her and put her feet up. "I just want it to be like it was before. I want to talk and sing and have fun, and we do, but—if I go near him, he practically jumps out of his skin. I don't know where this is going," Tulsa sighed, "but I wish it would *go*—one way or the other."

"Be careful what you wish for, Tul," Anne Marie looked up sharply. "One way or the other."

"Hmm . . . men." Tulsa bent down and kissed the top of Oakley's head. "The Kiss Magnet" she called that spot; it couldn't be resisted. Sidling through the door, dragging the pack, rolling the sleeping bag, she flipped open her mailbox, took out a sales circular and another letter from Jeanne, and gripped them between her teeth. She started struggling her burdensome gear up the stairs, but a hand came from behind and lifted the guitar case from her grasp.

"You've got to stop hauling all this shit around," Mac grumbled, slinging her pack over his shoulder and stomping up the stairs.

Empty stomach fluttering, Tulsa clutched her books and sleeping bag to her chest and ran up after him, conscious of the fact that she was grungy and windblown from riding with the window open. When she reached the top of the stairs, Mac was leaning against the doorframe with his hands in his pockets. She looked up expectantly, willing him to take just one more step inside the door, but he didn't. He looked sideways from under the battered black Stetson.

"Miss Bitters, may I take the liberty of calling on you this evening?" he said in the courtly manner of a black-and-white Western.

Of course, VA Lones instantly responded à la Vivian Leigh

Whah, Mistah MacPetahs! Please do.

and Tulsa had that vision in her mind even as she stood there with her mail between her teeth. Mac reached up and took Jeanne's letter.

"Eight o'clock?"

"Sure."

He placed the letter back in her mouth, tipped his hat, and edged past her to make his way down the steps. She inhaled his scent and almost reached for him, but she thought of standing in the field for hours, holding a red bandana out to a shy bull elk. That sort of thing had its own rewards, he kept trying to tell her. She went into her apartment and sat stiffly on the rocking chair, plotting a direct course toward eight o'clock.

take a bath . . . shave my legs . . . change the sheets . . . diaphragm . . . diaphragm goop . . .

—————

Mac heard Tulsa come down and knock on Anne Marie's door. Their voices sweetened the hallway for a few minutes, Anne Marie called out something to Jack, and then she and Tulsa left together. It was a warm and lazy Saturday; early September in southwest Montana always offered this sort of soft, arid afternoon when the sky seemed particularly high and wide. Standing in a stream on a day like this, Mac would swear he could hear the rainbow trout slicing through the clear water, and if he lay still on the sloping bank, he could almost decipher the private communication between the stones and the deep-reaching roots of the knotted pines.

He climbed the steps and knocked on Rina's door, calling, "Hey, Colt!"

There were muffled sounds from inside, and after a moment, Colter opened the door only enough to peer around the edge. "You OK, Dad?"

"Yeah—of course," Mac said impatiently, but even as he was asking, "Wanna go fishing?" he realized Colter and Rina must have been making love.

"Maybe later." Colter unceremoniously clapped the door closed in his father's face.

Mac sat on the porch for a while and then went for a long walk. He started in the direction of the Joker's Wild but passed it by and headed up the Gulch instead. Not really going anywhere. Just walking. The tourism campaigns were always plugging "historic Last Chance Gulch" because of Big Dorothy's and the Bullwhacker and the old stone facades, but Mac felt his own history there in the pawnshops and bars and the No Sweat Cafe. When he got home, he levered off his cowboy boots and fell asleep in a chair and didn't hear Tulsa come back just after suppertime, singing as she sailed up the stairs.

———

Tulsa sank into the tub, holding her mother's book above the suds. "January 29, 1974 . . . Not much more. Thank God." The last chapter transcribed Alexandra's final journal entries, made on tape when she could no longer hold the pen. "Decisions are being made, papers drafted, all the petty preparations for funeral, flowers, and business interests. J.—my dearest, darling J.—troubles me with as little of it as possible, respecting the preparations I must make in my own heart. I have made peace with those who hurt me and whom I have hurt and forgiven myself for the moments, months, and years squandered on shame when I could have been loving, laziness when I could have been working, weakness when I could have been strong. I have seen a great many places and found the sort of love one takes into Heaven, since it extends beyond the heart and cannot be separated from the soul. I have written all the books I was fated to write, spoken and been heard—and that is a great blessing, to be allowed to imagine that I made the tiniest difference. With all this, I could go joyfully to God, see the faces of Abraham and Sarah, and know the answer to every question my seeking heart has posed. But there is T. She is not ready to be cast into a world where real Jabberwocks claw and catch, dragging young girls into checkered games of red and black. I have not told her all the things she should know. Though I have provided the applicable clinical literature, I cannot speak with her about how a man has sex with a woman. I think of my own mother, tight-lipped and sad. 'A married woman has certain duties,' she exclaimed, 'and an unmarried woman has no right.' That was the extent of my sexual education until I went away to the seashore one summer and met a boy who was only too eager to tutor me. Perhaps if that boy had been a woman, I mightn't have wasted the subsequent years, suppressing the true nature of me, believing I was an aberration, something to be spoken of in horrified whispers.

"Now, my baby will be alone. I suspect she will not stay with J., though J. loves her and has given her the closest thing in her life akin to a family home. She will go to college in the fall. I will be dead, and she will be in pain. A boy will want to teach her everything, and she has always been eager to learn. I accept that I cannot protect her from life, but in the instant of my death, with all my being, I shall will that whatever strength I yet possess should flow to her.

"I lived in my parents' home until the day I married, and then I lived in my husband's home, well fed, well cared for, unaware of my own strengths and unwilling to confess my own dreams. C. gave me the best, most noble gift ever given me the day he threw me into the street. I will not deny my daughter the opportunity to struggle, to be strong, to be the woman God intended her to be."

Tulsa turned the last page.

"On July 5, 1974," Jeanne wrote, "essayist, activist, poet, and mother Alexandra Rachel Firestein passed away quietly in her sleep."

> "I am dead, God of Abraham, well You know,
>   for it was You who called me so,
>   sorting the ranks of poets and dogs,
>   drawing me out of my stone-covered thoughts . . ."

Tulsa closed the book and climbed out of the bathtub.

"Set it aside, babe," she told herself in the mirror, "set it aside."

She put it out by the fireplace so her mother wouldn't see her primping in the bathroom, attempting to make herself desirable, scheming a man's seduction. She pulled a wide-toothed comb through her wet hair.

"You don't need a blow dryer," Mac once remarked. "Montana in the summer is as dry as a dog biscuit."

She shook her head upside down, trying to brush in some body, absently humming a Mission Mountain Woodband tune Mac had been singing lately.

. . . way down in Athens County . . .
come and have some wine . . .

"Spit and it'll evaporate before it hits the ground."
How nice. Thank you for sharing.

. . . Athens County . . . Maria and me we're doin' fine . . .

She opened the bag from Ruby Begonia's, carefully drawing out the feminine, old-fashioned gown. She'd never owned anything like it: diaphanous cotton, eyelet lace, pure white, private, and sort of expensive. Tulsa pulled it over her head, conducting a frantic inward search for Vivian Leigh, wishing she'd bought the blow dryer anyway. Standing on the cool checkered tile, she suddenly thought of the swaying train lavatory and realized that, at some point in the past three years, she had stopped despising her reflection. Now she hardly recognized herself.

"Lovely," her reflection told her. "All that's missing are the patent leather shoes."

———————

Mac jolted forward from the uncomfortable edge of dreaming just as Hank Williams extended a skeletal hand to help Sarah into his long white limo. As the uneasy sleep dissolved, it was replaced by a low, dull ache at the base of his brain.

His bathroom was equipped with a corner shower instead of a full bathtub, and he hated that; it reminded him of the army. He stood in the pulsing stream for a long time, thinking, not thinking . . . just standing. When he turned off the water, he could hear Anne Marie's children tearing around outside and Rina's fiddle meandering through the open window like a cicada. Mac braided his hair, pulled on jeans, and buttoned his good shirt, already feeling the chill of the mountain evening. He settled his Stetson, opened his door, and stepped into the hallway. The music was louder there. Colter's boot marked the rhythm of the Irish reel, stepping up the tempo, forcing Rina's fiddle to fly faster and faster.

. . . McTavish is dead and his brother don't know it his brother is dead and McTavish don't know it . . .

He didn't look back as he headed down the walk, but he could almost feel Tulsa at the upstairs window. He wondered if she saw him through the dusky pines in the yard as he climbed into the truck and drove away.

———

She saw him. For a moment, it laid her heart open like a knife, but her mind was calm and she sat in her rocker, proper and quiet as Emily Dickinson.

After great pain, a formal feeling comes.

Tulsa recognized the gray curtain descending.

The Nerves sit ceremonious.

"Guppy?" A gentle knocking on her bedroom door. Jeanne was there.

This is the Hour of Lead.

"OK, little Guppy." She knew before Jeanne's voice caught and broke that Alexandra was gone. "We're the family now, sweetie. You and me."

She sheltered the girl for a moment, and Tulsa was just about to raise her arms to return the embrace when Jeanne started sobbing and ran to the room she and Alexandra had shared before the hospice people came, bringing the situp bed and the IV tree. Jeanne locked her door and didn't come out for the rest of the day, but that night and through the following days, she was unfailingly supportive and calm. She firmly patted Tulsa's hand during the viewing and service, dispassionately handled the press conference and news release, and sat through the reading of the will, asking over and over if Tulsa was sure she didn't have any questions about it.

Weeks passed. She drove Tulsa to school, cooked dinner, spoke to people on the phone, scrubbed the sink and floor. She carried out Alexandra's wishes and went through the motions of living. She didn't cry. But she didn't laugh, either, and Tulsa would look up to find her staring with the saddest eyes at her lover's daughter.

"I feel like a widow," was the closest she ever came to complaining, "only I don't get to wear the classy black veil."

The house was resoundingly quiet, echoing the oppressive silence that fell over Tulsa's heart. She spun herself a soundless cocoon, and her next truly clear memory was of awakening on a fast-moving train to Montana.

First Chill—then Stupor—then the letting go—

"Hey, Sharkey. Long time no see."

The Joker's Wild was pretty much the same, smoky and loud and gamey, but Ben looked a little shakier than he used to, staring up at Mac, struggling through the moment it took him to recognize his blood brother.

"Mac," he finally said. "Hey, Mac."

"Hey, Ben."

"Howdy, stranger," Yak hailed. "Where ya been keepin' yourself?"

"Nowhere," Mac said.

"What can I getcha?"

"Double shot of Jack."

"Yeah?" Yak looked a little surprised. "I thought—"

"Yeah," Mac interrupted. "How 'bout it, Shark Man?" Ben nodded, Mac held up two fingers and, while Yak poured the shots, saddled up on the barstool next to his friend and leaned his elbows on the rail. They sat silent, ruminating.

Ben reached automatically toward Mac's shirt for a cigarette, and somehow Mac was just as surprised as Sharkey to find nothing there. As Ben's unsteady hand pressed against that empty pocket over his heart, Mac remembered that he didn't smoke anymore, and he desperately wished he did.

"Sorry, Shark." Mac shrugged and faced forward on his barstool. Across the chasm, beyond a brittle forest of bottles and tap handles, two empty old men stared back at him from the mirror; eyes expressionless, flannel elbows forward, not a smoke between them, and a long night ahead.

━━━━━━

At eight-thirty, there was a little tap on Tulsa's door, and she stopped breathing for an instant before she heard Anne Marie's soft mama's-here voice.

"Tul? Honey, are you OK?"

"Yes." There was a long pause but no sound of footsteps. "Go on downstairs, Anne Marie."

"Honey, I know you're hurting right now, but—"

"I'll get over it."

Anne Marie would have felt better if Tulsa had sounded even a little upset. "OK," she sighed, and she did start down the steps but turned back to add, "I'll bring some ice cream up later and we'll talk, OK?"

" . . . OK . . . "

"Häagen Dazs . . . double dutch chocolate. With Reese's Pieces on the side. I'm sending Jack to the store right now."

ok ok ok

The chair sighed an easy rhythm as Tulsa rocked, not crying, not rehearsing how she would really lay it out to Mac if she ever saw him again—just rocking, straining to hear the distant creak of the bunkhouse bedsprings, sucking on that florid memory, feeding off it like a vampire.

———

From atop the boulder beside the outhouse, Mac watched a long bull snake disappear into the shadow of a fallen tree. The sun had gone down as he turned up the road, but even in the fading light, he could make out the scars and trenches that remained eleven months after the fire leveled everything but the large stone house. That structure was impenetrable by flame, having been built by a man who was burned once. The propane freezer lay on its side, door half off, bundles of venison spilling out black as briquettes. Framed by one broken corner of the bunkhouse foundation, the twisted brass bed clawed the remains of the mattress with spiny fingers. Something akin to a lunar landscape now lay where the stable and garden and henyard had been, but yellow-green blades of buffalo grass were beginning to reach up through the loam, all fragile and innocent, determined to reclaim the true color of the mountain.

Mac threw a rock into the dark and cursed the fire for prophesying the burning since created in his belly. He cursed the sunset that wouldn't forget the color of her hair and the night that hoarded her voice. He cursed the clean air she forced him to breathe and the solid earth to which she tethered him when all he wanted was to fly away with the quail and starlings. He hurled a stone for her ignorance and another for her simplistic Jack–and–Anne Marie dreams and one more for her interminable talk—her damnable, unceasing, unstoppable mouth.

just don't do it . . . don't hit me and don't blow yourself to bits and don't smoke yourself into a bloody stupor . . . you'll be just like Ben Sharkey . . .

"Where the fuck do you get off passing judgment on me and Sharkey?" Mac demanded, but there was no reply from the bull snake beneath the rotting bark. "You don't know a damn thing about anything except—ah, *Christ!*" He slung a stone at the tree, and its occupant oozed out the other side.

"How could anyone be so fucking *stupid?*"

The bull snake slithered down the blackened path toward what was once a vegetable garden.

———

Persistent tapping woke Tulsa from the quiet plane of the wooden rocker. She squeezed the side of her stiff neck. More tapping.

"I'm fine, Anne Marie. Good night." Tulsa was not in the mood for a load of matronly advice, even if it was served up with Häagen Dazs, but the knock became more insistent. She glanced up at the clock radio, which now read half past twelve, rocked herself forward out of the chair, and yanked the door open.

"I said I'm—"

Mac's hat was there. And Mac was standing beneath it, holding a box of Red Zinger in one hand and a paper-wrapped bunch of yellow tea roses in the other. The lead weight dropped from Tulsa's chest to her stomach.

"Evening, ma'am," he said.

"I thought you were standing me up."

"I was."

"Oh, well," Tulsa shrugged.

"But now I'm . . . not." Mac held the roses awkwardly forward, and after a long moment, Tulsa uncrossed her arms and took them. They were still dripping a little, though the smiling Safeway store lady had wrapped a plastic bag around the stems. When Tulsa came back from the tiny kitchen with the roses in a honey jar, Mac was sitting stiffly in the rocker. She tossed some reading pillows on the floor and sat down in front of him. They both tried to think of something to say to break the silence, but nothing came. Eventually, Tulsa pulled over a milk crate of books and set the chessboard across it. She offered Mac both boxes of figures, and he chose the black and began to set the pieces in straight lines.

Tulsa always moved a certain pawn first. Mac started with a knight. They each made a few more half-contemplated moves. Tulsa advanced her bishop and Mac took her pawn. He couldn't stop looking at her as she rested her hand on her knight, wrinkling her forehead a little, so young and so . . . clean. The white nightgown covered her in all modesty, but it was translucent enough to brush impressions and shadows across his imagination. Her hair was thick and wavy, longer than it looked in her customary plain French braid. She moved the horseman up and over into the line of Mac's rook.

"You don't want to do that." He covered her hand with his before thinking the move through. He hadn't seen her queen standing ready.

Tulsa looked up, annoyed. "I'll play my own game, thank you very much."

"I know—I just—" Mac shook his head and started to say something else, but instead used his boot to push the board aside. The chess pieces clattered and rolled on the floor—rooks, royalty, and pawns all equal.

He gripped her hand to pull her toward him, forcing the knight painfully into her palm, and Tulsa made a small sound, "mm—Mac, you're hurting me!"

He drew back and white-knuckled the arms of the rocker.

"Babe, I'm sorry—I don't think this is going to work."

"Oh, shut up and stop thinking so much." Tulsa stood and tugged his hand until he followed her to the Murphy bed. "C'mon. We'll just talk for a while. Just talk and then . . . we'll see."

Mac lay down with his hands behind his head, and Tulsa rested her head on his shoulder. They lay listening to the pines outside the rounded window.

"Are you asleep?" Tulsa whispered.

"Huh-uh." He became aware of the pattern she stroked on his neck. "And I can remember where all my stitches were without you doing that."

" . . . sorry . . . " She tucked her hands in front of her, sounding abashed, and Mac hated himself for making it be this way. He sat up on the edge of the bed, resisting her attempt to pull him back. "Mac, just help me understand what you want! Candlelight? Baby oil? Porno movies? *What?* "

"Tulsa, I don't understand this any more than you do—it just doesn't feel right. It just doesn't feel . . . familiar."

"OK." Tulsa sat up, hugging her knees to her chest.

"I'm sorry. I shouldn't have even—"

Tulsa bounced off the bed and threw the nightgown up over her head. Mac breathed in sharply when he saw her naked, but before he had time to recover or look away, she was pulling on jeans and a flannel shirt.

"Let's go see what the coyotes have to say about it."

The night was clear and the full moon so illuminating that even from the ridge where the pickup was parked, Mac could see Tulsa sitting cross-legged on the quarry ledge below. He rummaged through the leftover camping supplies, trying to find something for her to eat. The bag ripped and one of the apples rolled under the seat, and as Mac cussed and groped the dark floorboards, his hand closed on the once-familiar shape of the silver snuffbox. He drew it out and rattled it to see if Colter had done anything with the contents. There was a shuffling sound inside, and Mac opened it to find a single joint. He remembered rolling several before he went to Townsend. That day seemed very distant now, and though he remembered that he did stop for a smoke at the Dodge House, the only image that remained was a single antelope crossing a sage-gray field.

Mac could smell the homegrown without even picking it up, rich and earthy and brown. He pulled open the glove compartment and saw the little pipe in the map light. He thought about tamping the grass from the joint into the pipe just for a toke or two. In the distance, he heard a bell-shaped howl and then another. There was an answering call, but he knew coyotes too well to think that was one. Another arcing cry went up, and this time Mac answered it himself. He scrambled back down the hill and reached the ledge in time to see Tulsa crouched on her hands and knees above the trail, moving toward one of the shadowy figures.

He started to call out to her that it was foolish and to get the hell down here right now, but he didn't want to spook the wild dog. It sat back on its haunches and tossed its head up. This time, their cries were in such harmony, Mac couldn't tell which was animal and which was woman. Then she moved a little too close, a little too quickly, and the coyote bolted, spraying dirt and pebbles onto her as it turned and ran. She covered her face and tried to stand but lost her footing and ended up sliding most of the way down on her backside.

"What the hell do you think you're doing?" Mac was half amazed at the spectacle, half annoyed at the stupidity. "It's not funny, dammit! Shit like that gets people hurt." But Tulsa was laughing, brushing off the seat of her jeans.

"Did you see that? He came right up to me! I thought I'd give you a call, and he just—he came right up to me!" Tulsa put her hands on Mac's shoulders. "I heard you, you old dog. You still know how to howl."

Mac pulled away and sat down. Tulsa threw her head back and howled again, and far away there was an answer that delighted her so much she dropped to her knees beside Mac and started snuffling at him.

"Would you cut that out? You sound like Lassie."

"Hmmmmm," she whined and panted and put her nose to his crotch, "now you know why Timmy was so upset when she ran away from home."

"Tulsa!" Mac pushed her head away abruptly. "Geez . . . c'mon—"

She bared her teeth, snarled, and bit into his shirt, grazing his arm. She shook her head, worrying his sleeve like a puppy worries an old shoe, and Mac laughed at that, so Tulsa frisked over to straddle his lap and lick his face. She threw her head back to howl again, her neck elongated, smooth and white in the moonlight, and Mac pressed his mouth to it, grazed and growled against it. She started to pull her shirt off one shoulder to accommodate him, but he was already struggling to his feet, dragging her up with him, kissing her, grappling with her belt buckle. Tulsa impatiently pulled her shirt over her head, having given up on all those stupid buttons. Her ankles were shackled because Mac couldn't get her jeans past her hiking boots, and she fell forward to her knees when he rested back and pulled her down on top of him. She braced herself, not wanting to give him her weight, but he grasped her hips and settled her.

"Shhh . . . ok . . . " Mac tried to calm her until he realized the rushing was in his own chest, not hers. "Tulsa mine . . . "

"Yes, White Wolf?" Her voice was hoarse with howling and desire, and the same old moon and stars stood just past her shoulder.

"You didn't stop."

"No, White Wolf."

She took him in slowly, easing him back into his own body like a moment of homecoming.

———————

"Just relax," Mac whispered against the back of her neck, "I'll try not to hurt you."

Tulsa nodded and let him swipe the washcloth across her deeply skinned knees. He took a body sponge from the edge of the bathtub and gently dabbed the dirt and dried blood away, then brushed more firmly at the embedded bits of cinder and gravel.

"*Ow!* Stop it, Mac! Just leave it."

"You've got to clean it up before you cover it, darlin'."

"Oh, spare me the sage advice." Tulsa hated that words-to-live-by tone. "Anyway, I remember someone saying 'least done, soonest mended', *dahrrr-luhn'*."

"And I remember someone saying you should pull your jeans up before you tried to stand because a person could easily lose their footing." Mac sounded smug and kept wiping at her wounds.

"Well, Charlie Old Fart, I guess that person would be out of touch with concepts like howling naked at the moon."

"Yeah, you were howling all right."

Tulsa slapped some water in his face and then leaned back against him. She stretched her legs in the long, low tub, trickles of red rising from her knees.

"I'll kiss them and make them better," Mac whispered.

"Mmmm." Tulsa felt her face go warm. "You think you know all my secrets, don't you?"

"Not yet . . . not ever, I hope," Mac nuzzled her hair, "but I might stumble on a few more hidden weaknesses."

"I'll tell you anything you want to know."

"What I want to know," Mac said rhetorically, "is how come I can't have a bathtub like this?"

"You can."

He cleared his throat. "Let me see your hands."

They were raw but not bleeding.

"Doctor," Tulsa asked breathily, "will I ever play the violin again?"

"Well, you play me like a fiddle."

It wasn't like the bunkhouse, they both recognized, though the Murphy bed creaked and thumped and the pines soared and hushed outside the window. They knew each other now. It was possible to let go, to be lazy and slow, to rage on but then rest for a bit, filling the quiet spaces with easy laughter and soft everyday talk. Private sounds and expressions, the rising, the dissolving. Tulsa arched and sighed, and Mac collapsed on top of her. He lay breathing for a bit and then raised up on his elbows to blow gently across her damp neck and chest.

"So does this mean we're not having the baby oil and porno films?"

"'Fraid so. But I might be able to come up with a Girl Scout uniform . . ."

" . . . hmmm . . . "

" . . . castanets . . . some chocolate pudding . . . "

" . . . ah ha . . . "

" . . . possibly a clear plastic rain slicker . . . "

Mac laughed and eskimo-kissed her, nose to nose. While Tulsa waited for one of them to say "I love you," they whispered everything but that. The words wouldn't really change anything, she knew, but she felt that aesthetically, somehow, it might have been pleasing. She began to drift on the mellow timbre of his voice, but Mac nudged her awake, drawing her back out of the haze, just being matter-of-fact, though he was still inside her and they were both pleasantly aware that he was stirring again.

"Uh-oh," Tulsa said. "We have hydraulics."

"The woman has a mind like a steel trap," Mac teased her. "Three sheets to the wind and still storing information for future reference."

"Yes, so you can imagine what I picked up in three months of you mumbling through a morphine haze." She felt him tense, and she tried to take it back. "Mac, I'm sorry."

He shook his head. "Over and done with."

"No unpleasant memories . . ." Tulsa kissed his temple and forehead as if to banish such things. " . . . no regrets . . . no bad dreams . . ." She spanned her hands wide and slid them down from his shoulders to his hips, smiling at the feel of his muscles contracting and relaxing as he moved with and within her.

It was trying to be dawn outside when they finally slept. Tulsa was aware of his body against her back; he held her, one arm across her waist, the other supporting her head. She stretched out against the whole length of him, and he shifted one of his legs between hers. She was aware of it even in her sleep, even as she began to see toy cows and wind chimes and Jeanne's lefthanded scrawl.

"He's probably breathing a sigh of relief," Jeanne said over Oakley's curly head. "He's no stranger to the one-night stand."

"That's what I'm thinking . . ." her mother said, patent leather shoes in one hand, hiking boots in the other, " . . . comfort-wise." Alexandra focused over Tulsa's shoulder toward the towering library shelves lining the lawyer's office. " . . . my entire estate to the Coalition for Feminist Action in America as administered by Jeanne Petit Compton . . . "

The lawyer's office was crowded and stifling hot. Tulsa strained to listen to her mother, but she was overridden by the seashell roar of other voices.

"Did I tell you Lorene is expecting again?" Tulsa's father said.

" . . . anything I have I would gladly give her . . . "

mama can't i have a toy cow a pretty toy cow

"Be careful what you wish for." Anne Marie scrounged for beans on the deep pile carpet. "Shall I get the scissors?"

" . . . I will not deny her the chance to struggle . . . "

i'll be good mama please mama i'll be good

"Light, tight, and bright!" Joey admonished. "Get the hell back in there!"

"Simple math and history, darlin'." Tulsa's father shook his head. "You'll need something to fall back on."

" . . . the best, most noble gift ever given . . . "

i won't stop

" . . . the opportunity to struggle . . . "

you can't make me

" . . . to be strong . . . "

"Then we're even." Mac sat up and peeled the gauze from his eyes. "You speak the truth to me."

i was lying

" . . . my entire estate to the Coalition for Feminist Action . . . and the proceeds from any future works—"

of course it bothers me

"—plus the sum of one dollar—"

"Oh, very amusing," huffed Charles Bitters. "I'd be pissed as a newt."

"—to my daughter, Tulsa Firestein Bitters."

Alexandra's green eyes connected with Tulsa's hazel ones. She extended a pale, graceful arm, offering the heavy book with the spring-colored cover.

"That's what I'm thinking."

13

Something made Tulsa sit bolt up straight. *"Mac!"*

" . . hnnn . . . " he groaned and rolled away. "No thanks, babe."

"Mac, wake up!" She shook his shoulder.

"It's not gonna happen, darlin'. Let's just get some sleep." He tried to pull her back down on the bed, but she kept dragging on his arm.

"Mac, she didn't dump me. She didn't!"

"Aaagh . . . geez!" Mac reacted like a vampire when she snapped on the light.

She seized the book from the bedside shelf and flipped to the dedication.

"Mac, *look!* 'For T.'! It's mine! She did it for me!"

"That's great, Tulsa; now can we go back to sleep?"

"C'mon . . . c'mon . . . " Thrashing through books and papers, she finally laid hands on Jeanne's letter and tore it open. *"Maaac! Oh, Maaaaac!"* She read the first line and started jumping on the Murphy bed.

"Dammit, Tulsa—" Mac was serious about sleeping and getting annoyed. "I'm going downstairs if you don't cut that out."

"Mac," she flopped down beside him and took his face in her hands, "were you just making a crummy, rotten, mean-spirited joke when you said that—that thing . . . about—if I learn to drive?"

"Can I think about it?"

"No! I told you to stop all that thinking crap."

"Ah, geez." Mac sat up and put his feet on the floor. "Standard transmission—no automatic. You learn to drive a stick or the deal's off." She nodded. "And we're not talking about some kind of here-comes-the-bride thing either, Tulsa. Just letting it be. Common law."

"OK."

"OK . . . ?"

"OK."

"OK—what? What the hell are we talking about?"

"*Money!*" She closed her eyes to savor the rapturous taste of the word. "Just look *look-look-look!* Read."

Still squinting from sleep, Mac took the letter from her as she danced by. "'Dear Guppy . . . should have known you'd be impossible. . . . '" He interjected, "no shit," and continued, "umm . . . 'Ally's daughter after all and I'm proud of you for deciding to do this on your own. . . . I understand why you haven't cashed the check for your share of—'" Mac glanced up, beginning to understand. "' . . . marked that chapter because I wanted you to know she would have understood how difficult it was for you and respected your choice to grow up before—'" Tulsa snatched the letter back, her face burning, and she waited for him to trot out the platitudes, but Mac reached for her hand and simply said, "Ah, babe."

"OK. Fine." She closed her eyes to his unbearable expression. "But there are things you don't discuss with me, and this is . . . like that—"

"Tulsa . . . " He stopped her by wrapping her in the quilt and in his arms. "I'm sorry it happened. But everywhere you've been is what brought you here—to right now. And I'm selfish enough to be glad for it." Tulsa tried to speak, but there was a warm swelling in her throat. Mac stroked the hair back from her forehead and said, "Tell me what's going on."

Tulsa took a deep breath and started in the lawyer's office the day of her mother's funeral. "She left the house, paintings, money—everything to Jeanne and the coalition, but then she added this thing about future works and—my father thought it was a joke—dead people don't have any future works, right? But she did! She and Jeanne . . . they knew she would, and—" She could scarcely breathe. "Do you know what this means?"

"You're rich." Mac didn't seem to share her enthusiasm.

"Oh, Mac!" She clapped her hands like a child. "Do you think so? My share, she said—I don't know how much that is—but the book is still on the bestseller list, so . . . "

"Well, there it is." Mac went to the window. The sun was just clearing the treetops on the far hill. "You can go anywhere you want to go now."

"Mac!" She laughed and shook his shoulders because he didn't seem to understand. "Maybe we can get your ranch back! Buy the land from the Chadwicks and then get a bunch of . . . you know—ranch stuff! Cows and things!"

"Ranch stuff?" Mac looked at her incredulously. "Tulsa, if you buy it, it won't be my ranch. It'll be *your* ranch! Christ, that would be even worse than giving it to Chadwick."

"Why?" she asked, but Mac started getting dressed, just wanting to go downstairs and back to sleep. "*Why*, Mac? You said common law, and that law is that we share everything and stay together until we die."

"Only it doesn't happen that way, Tulsa."

"No, it doesn't. You have to *make* it that way."

"And what about Colter? One of the reasons I wanted the land back in the first place was for him to have—"

"OK, OK! Wait a minute." Tulsa went into the bathroom and shut the door. Lying back on the bed, Mac heard the toilet flush, bath water running, and then a triumphant, "*Ah-ha!*" Tulsa emerged with a towel on her head. "All right, here it is: I'm investing in some prime real estate but—hey! What the heck do I know about ranching, right? I need someone to manage it for me, right? Preferably someone I love and would like to live with for forty or fifty years . . . "

"But you'd settle for me."

"It's so hard to find good help these days."

"No, Tulsa."

"We'll sign an agreement."

"No."

"You'll work for acreage instead of money . . . "

"*No!*"

" . . . and the amount you get back before you die or you dump me—"

"Or you dump me!"

"Or *whatever*—then that would be Colter's. See?"

"Oh, yeah, I see," Mac nodded grimly. "I see you holding a club over my head to keep me from crossing you."

"I'd prefer to think of it as a sword." Tulsa shook the towel from her head and started forking her fingers through her wet hair. "And not to keep you from crossing me. Only to keep you from leaving for no good reason. Or hitting me. If you hit me again, Mac—ever—I'll have the place logged off and strip mined. I'm not kidding."

"Tulsa, listen to yourself! This is not what marriage is about."

"Well, you should know, having been married six times." Tulsa raised her hand to fend off his retort. "Is it about traveling light? Feeling free to leave the minute you get pissed off or claustrophobic? Is that what marriage is about?"

"No, it's about being together to have . . . a life and—well, sex, of course . . . but more—just being . . . there and . . . *forgiving!*"

"Oh, please," Tulsa waved the sentiment aside, "I love you, Mac, but I'm not a complete moron. I'm not going to put up with a bunch of crap that requires forgiveness, and frankly, your track record for 'being there' stinks."

"And you've never been known to bolt!" Mac rejoined. "Don't forget, I watched you make Spam out of the last poor sucker who came through here."

"All right," she granted him that one, "so maybe this would help us both hang in there through the inevitable . . . difficulties. This is something I could never do without you, Mac. I would need you just as much as you would need me."

"Sweet Maria. I don't know if I'm up to this." He slumped back on the bed and pulled her down next to him. "Where were you when I was twenty-five?"

Tulsa kissed him. "You don't really want me to answer that."

"Mmmm . . . this is probably all moot, anyway. To get the ranch up and running would take a powerful chunk of change," Mac said doubtfully, "How much was the check?"

"I . . . I don't know. . . . "

"What do you mean? Where is it?"

"I don't know . . . *I don't know!* Oh—oh, no . . . " Tulsa was beginning to panic, her voice rising sharply with the dawning realization.

"OK, OK." Mac sat up and took her hands. "Relax. She said it was in the book—" He reached for the volume, but Tulsa stopped his hand.

"No, I bought that one, remember? The one she sent me—oh, shit! Mac, *I lost it!* I never lose my books, and—*I lost it!*" Tulsa collapsed onto the bed, covering her face with a pillow. "Oh, shit, shit, *shit!*"

"Just calm down."

"I've been living like a lousy pauper for five years just to pass her little test, and *I want my money!*"

"Would you *RELAX, for Christ's sake!*" Mac paced, one hand pressed to his forehead. "All right—you got the book. You were reading the book. You—you what? You . . . took it to the station."

"Some of us actually work while we're on the air."

"OK, you loaned it to—no." He knew better. She wouldn't even lend him anything but paperbacks and those only with stern words about gratuitous cover-bending. "You took it . . . *somewhere*. You left it somewhere."

"No, I never do that!"

"Then it's still in this apartment."

They bolted toward the next room, dragging boxes and crates out from cupboards, closets, and under the bed, dumping them in the middle of the room, scanning the shelves from floor to ceiling. They ransacked the place until the floors were strewn with classics, and the bed was piled high with poetry and fiction.

"Lord," Mac said dryly, "I love a woman who reads."

Tulsa sat on the rocker, looking stricken, her hair in copper tangles that spilled over the white shoulders of her rumpled nightgown, her arms full of books she had picked up here and there and was, for some reason, still clutching to her chest. Mac consciously focused on the sight of her, wanting to preserve it.

"OK, darlin' . . . " Crossing the obstacle course of books and boxes, he sat on a milk crate and pulled her head onto his shoulder. "Try to think." He stroked her hair back from her forehead. "Think back to the day you got the book."

"It was the day Aaron left."

"Did you go somewhere with him? Did you make love?"

She nodded against his shoulder.

"Did you have the book before or after that?"

"Um . . . after he left, the mailman delivered it."

"And then . . . "

"Anne Marie came out."

"Did you give the book to her? Show it to her?"

"I showed it to her . . . "

" . . . and then . . . "

"I don't know."

"Did you have it during . . . winter? At the hospital?"

"Yes . . . no—I bought the other copy. I had that." Tulsa sat up and put her hands to the sides of her head. "I was reading it and Joey and I—we saw in the paper about you, and—Mac, I think maybe I did leave it at the No Sweat. I never thought about it for weeks, and then I just couldn't find it!"

Mac was already pulling on his boots.

The No Sweat was busy with Sunday brunch people when Mac and Tulsa burst in calling for Elsa. She came out of the kitchen, but her smile faded as soon as she saw Tulsa's intense expression.

"Elsa! I left my book here and I need it back right away."

"What book?"

"*Sweet Epiphanies*—Alexandra Firestein. I think I left it here a while back, and I really really need it."

"Oh, was that yours?" Elsa asked innocently.

"*Yes!* Do you still have it?"

"Nope. Sorry."

"Yes you do. You *have* to!"

"Take it easy, darlin'," Mac kept trying to interject.

"I'm sorry, Tulsa, I don't!" Elsa exclaimed and held out her hands as if to show Tulsa they were empty. "But I'm sure it'll turn up."

"Turn up? *Turn up?*"

"Meanwhile, borrow something else. I've got everything she ever wrote."

"I don't want everything she ever wrote—I want *my* book! I don't have to borrow it, I don't have to beg for it, I don't have to prove to anybody that I deserve it—it's just *mine!* My mother wrote it for *me!*"

"Tulsa—" Mac tried to wedge himself between them. "Tulsa, you're getting nuts here. Now just—"

"Your mother? Your mother was . . . " Elsa tried to take it in, her expression one of pure reverence, *"the Tupperware Lady?"*

"Ah, geez . . . " Mac pressed his temple.

"She was not the fucking TUPPERWARE LADY, you hash-slinging book-nabbing little dyke!" Tulsa roared. "She was at *one—stupid—party!"*

"She's a little cranky . . . didn't get much sleep last night." Mac grasped Tulsa's elbow and tried to stuff her into a booth, but Elsa grabbed Tulsa's other arm and dragged her to the kitchen window.

"Stacy! Bets! Now Tulsa is 'T'!" She tapped the top of Tulsa's head for emphasis. "VA Lones *and* Firestein's 'T'—and she eats at *our cafe!"*

Mac poured himself a cup of strong black coffee.

"We're going to name a sandwich after you! Something stacked!"

"Elsa," Tulsa beseeched, "I've *got* to get that book back. It's *extremely* important!"

"Well, I got it from Betsy, and after I read it, I passed it to Ellen. . . . "

Ellen indicated Stacy, and Stacy claimed to have given it to Liz, who had gone to Safeway to buy Fleischmann's yeast and nutmeg, adding, "Maybe if it wasn't so pricy, people could afford more than one copy?" as if Tulsa had something to say about it.

Tulsa clambered out of the booth when she saw Liz passing by the painted window. Mac watched them talking outside, relieved to see Tulsa laugh.

"You're not going to believe this," she said when she came back in. "Liz gave it to Rina so she could be enlightened and dump Colter. She says you MacPeters men are trouble."

Mac jerked the truck to a stop in front of the house, and before he could shut off the engine, Tulsa was bounding two at a time up the stairs and pounding on Rina's door.

"Mac, they're not here!" When he caught up to her, she was dancing a little, waving her hands as if to shake water off them. "Where are they?"

"How the hell should I know?" Mac took a turn hammering on the door.

"He's your son!" she accused. "What kind of parent are you?"

Mac was about to tell her when a muffled voice called, "Who is it?"

"It's your father." Mac folded his arms authoritatively. "Open up."

"Go away. I'm busy."

"I don't give a shit." Mac hammered again. "Open the damn door!"

There were muffled sounds and footsteps. Mac gave Tulsa a victorious glance as the door cracked just enough for Colter to peek out.

"Wouldya get lost, Dad? We're not even—*geez!*"

Tulsa pushed past him into the messy apartment, not noticing or caring that Colter was naked. Rina was sitting on the bed amidst coffee cups and breakfast plates and a blizzard of Sunday paper sections.

"Hi, everyone." She pulled the sheet up to her chin. "Umm . . . c'mon in."

"Rina—" Tulsa was trembling, exhausted, "Liz gave a book to you. . . ."

"Alexandra Firestein . . . " Mac supported her.

"Oh, yeah," Colter said, "*Sweet Episiotomies* or something?"

"Colter," Tulsa pleaded, "that copy is mine. I have to have it."

"Actually," called Rina from the bed, "I wasn't quite finished, but—"

She held it up and Mac and Tulsa lunged, whooping and hugging the book and each other and Colter, who held July's *Rolling Stone* open in front of himself, encouraging them to take the book and go.

Tulsa staggered out to the porch swing, and Mac sat next to her.

"Please . . . please be in here. . . . " She leafed gingerly through the book.

"Oh, for—" Mac wrested the book from her and shook it vehemently by the front cover. The letter fell from the dust jacket. It was dirty and dogeared. People had used it to mark their places and jot phone messages, nibbling on the corners as they read, but beneath the scribbles and doodling and a recipe for Graham Kerr's Southwest Stew, slanted Jeanne's lefthanded script.

"*Oh!*" Tulsa squeaked.

"The envelope, please." Mac brushed it off and handed it to her.

Hands trembling, she neatly pried away the worn edges and drew out the contents. They stared for a long moment. Tulsa felt hollow. She was aware only of the sound of the trees. And zeros. Many zeros.

"Sweet Maria," Mac said stiffly.

"Is that enough to make a ranch?"

"It's a damn healthy start."

The publisher's advance and the first year's royalties, Jeanne's note explained, with additional royalties to be paid annually. And *Guppy, please*, it said, *please, don't leave my life. You're my whole family.*

Tulsa started to cry.

"I'm glad for you, darlin'.'" Mac meant it, not for the money but for the peace she had made.

"We'll call it the 'Roy-Al-X,'" Tulsa said.

"No."

"Everywhere you've been is what brought you here, Mac—even him," said Tulsa, thinking it was the name that made him shake his head. "And I'm selfishly glad." She kissed him on the chin, cheek, and mouth. "We'll build the barn and live in it while we renovate the house, just like they did. Only we'll make it be happy, Mac, and none of that stuff will matter anymore."

"Tulsa," his words were wooden, but his eyes were dark and honest, "we need to step back and think about this before we do anything drastic."

"Look," she slid back from him on the swing, "I know I'm not exactly the girl of your dreams and I'm not pretty like Lorene—"

"Oh, put a cork in it," Mac cut in, "I told you I wasn't going to dignify that self-deprecating crap anymore." He folded his arms across his chest. "I just think this might be . . . ill advised."

She shrugged, looking away from him. "It's ultimately just different ways of saying we won't be together."

"Ultimately, we won't," Mac said quietly. "Nothing you can do about it, babe. We're not going to grow old together like Jack and Anne Marie, swinging on the front porch, watching the grandkids. Sooner or later—one of us is going to grow old alone."

"So there's no point in being happy now?"

"'Now' isn't going to last, Tulsa. When you're the age I am now, I'll be almost eighty. *Eighty years old*—and I'll probably weather like an old elk turd—if I even make it that far."

"Oh, right . . . then you'd die and I'd waste away all by myself. 'Cause no other man will ever want me and you're such a devastating lover, I could never be happy with anyone else."

Mac set his jaw, trying hard to remember why a middle-aged man should not marry a twenty-five-year-old woman who loves him rampantly and has just come into a large sum of money.

"Like Miss Havisham in *David Copperfield*—" Tulsa repined upon the swing. "I would suffer my private anguish in a room of moldering wedding cake . . . never able to free myself from the impassioned bondage of my First Great Love . . . "

On the other hand, he cautioned himself . . .

" . . . haunted by lingering memories of you scratching, farting, growing hair out of your ears . . . "

. . . she can be an insufferable bitch . . .

"*Great Expectations,*" he told her.

"What?"

"Miss Havisham was in *Great Expectations.*"

"Whatever," Tulsa sighed deeply.

"And we're not having cake," he gruffed, "moldering or otherwise."

"That's OK," she smiled and shrugged, "I'm trying to cut down."

"And no kids," he continued seriously, "I want you to go into this knowing that I've been a lousy father and even worse husband. I don't know how to be a family, and it's too late to learn. And I don't dance. I don't eat canned soup or white bread or store-bought pies. No microwave. No tofu. No fuzzy cover thing on the toilet, and no flowery sheets on the bed, just plain white."

Tulsa sidled over, nodding and kissing him, item by item.

"And we're not having 'cows and things,' we're having buffalo, and you can't name them. You can't name pigs, chickens, sheep, or anything else except horses and dogs. All cats must remain in the barn at all times, and you should know that there's a dead heifer in the kitchen and I'm not dragging it out of there myself."

"Certainly not."

"This isn't something a person can do alone."

"Absolutely not."

"And you can't keep a messy kitchen the way you do at your apartment. You'll have rats the size of Buicks."

"Mac, however you want the house kept," Tulsa solemnly vowed, "I won't interfere."

"I'm serious here, Tulsa. Ranching is hard work."

"Invigorating work."

"*Mule* work. All day. Every day."

"Without fail."

"Starting at five AM."

"Can't wait."

"There's no neighbors downstairs, no Mini Basket up the street . . . "

"Screw 'em."

" . . . no plumbing, no electricity—"

"*Whoa!*" Tulsa drew back. "That will have to be negotiable."

Mac growled something about her beginning to take over his life already.

"Oh, c'mon. We could get a great big old bathtub," she coaxed, "and you don't want a snake to bite your butt at this late stage in the game."

Mac propped one boot on the porch rail. "Will you still be VA?"

"Of course. That's my . . . thing."

"What'll you be when you're not VA?"

"Well," she considered it, "Firestein's been done . . . and nobody named Bitters loves me. So I guess I'll go with the MacPeters clan, if that's OK with you and Colter."

"I'm cool," Mac shrugged, "but what would your mother say?"

"*The true meaning of liberation,*" Alexandra reminded her daughter and her daughter reminded Mac, "*is doing as you damn well please.*"

. . . if the wife and me are fussin' brother that's all right 'cause me and that sweet woman got a license to fight . . . why dontcha mind yer own business . . .

Hank blasted from the truck tape deck as they lurched and jackrabbitted up Lincoln road toward Chadwick's.

"Oh, Mac! I feel like I've sprouted wings!" Tulsa exulted. She kept shrieking through every gear-grinding curve, doing seventy or better on the straight stretches. When the road started to twist and climb,

Mac couldn't take it anymore, and he made her pull over. Not wanting to hurt her feelings, though, he invited her to get into the back of the truck with him for a while, and they arrived at Chadwicks' an hour later, looking a bit disheveled but feeling very mellow.

Mrs. Chadwick served lemonade and chatted with Tulsa on the porch, telling her all about how Michael used to come and work for them and was the most polite little fellow, always reading those poetry books and singing little songs for the Chadwick girls. Tulsa nodded and smiled, and they went in to join Mac and Mr. Chadwick at the kitchen table, looking over maps and surveys and bargaining for acreage and options to purchase more each year. They haggled over the price of Pineapple and Jim Bridger and the services of two of Chadwick's many grandsons for the following summer. Tulsa drifted back out to the porch and sat in the creaky rattan rocker while Mac and Chadwick hashed through the details. They finally emerged grinning and shook hands.

"Pleasure to meet you, Mrs. MacPeters." Chadwick offered Tulsa his leathery hand and then clapped Mac's shoulder. "Young and strapping. She'll make a fine rancher's wife."

"She'll make a fine rancher." Mac settled his Stetson on her head. "C'mon, babe. Got something to show you." He seized her hand and pulled her down the porch steps, impatient as Christmas morning. In the stable, he stroked Pineapple's nose, explained all the tack, and showed Tulsa how to saddle the mare. "We'll have to board them here while we get the new outbuildings finished, but we'll hurry. Now, you want to get up over here on this side . . . there you go. Don't pull on her head like that, darlin'. You want her to like you. That's it. . . . "

"OK . . . here I go. . . . " Giggling nervously, Tulsa climbed up on a fence rail and gracelessly clambered onto the animal's back, giddy when she felt herself up at what seemed to be a great height with the unfamiliar feeling of a huge living being beneath her. "I'm doing it! Mac, I'm riding a horse!"

"Well," he felt compelled to point out, "you're sitting on a horse. She hasn't gone anywhere yet." Mac realized as he swung up into Jim Bridger's saddle that he hadn't sat on a horse since the day of Pa Roy's burial almost a year ago, and he hoped he wouldn't make a fool of himself in front of her.

"Go, horse . . . go, pony—giddy-up . . . " Tulsa was clicking her tongue and wiggling in the saddle. "C'mon, horsey . . . let's go . . . Mac, she's not going."

OK, Mac decided, no worries that *I'll* look like a fool, anyway.

They walked the horses down to the end of the road and then started to canter. Mac ducked for a low-hanging branch and looked back over his shoulder just in time to see Tulsa hit the ground. He turned and caught Pineapple's reigns, leading her to where Tulsa was dusting off the seat of her Levis, cussing, but apparently unhurt. He knew he wouldn't have to persuade her to get back on but suspected her enthusiasm was flagging a little. He led Pineapple over to an old stump, and Tulsa managed to drape herself over the horse like a flour sack and struggle her way upright in the saddle.

"You OK?" Mac knew better than to laugh at her just now.

"Yeah, but I think this is the part where you're supposed to worship the ground I walk on."

"And sit on," he agreed.

The boundary between their land and Chadwick's lay parallel to and just over the ridge where Royal's seven sisters were buried.

"Here's us," Mac said. He pulled a red bandana from his hip pocket and tied it on a sarvisberry bush, where it fluttered in the wind like a prayer ribbon. Then he rode out into the pasture a little to survey his domain in the Indian summer dusk. To the southwest, late afternoon colors yawned and stretched on the horizon, but thunderheads arced low over the ridge to the north. Stepping his horse carefully around the silent rectangle of Pa Roy's grave, Mac went over to where Sarah and Satchi whispered through the wildflowers, and Pineapple stood waiting while Tulsa climbed down from a boulder by the aspen trees.

"Looks like the weather might be turning on us, babe," he said. "We should head back to town."

"Yeah, maybe."

"Or we could haul the camping gear up to the house and ride it out."

Tulsa wrinkled her nose. "How ripe is that cow in the kitchen?"

"Dry bones," Mac shrugged.

"Well, then . . . " She grasped Pineapple's saddle horn and actually managed to mount with a modicum of dignity. "I guess it's time to find out what kind of frontiersman I really am."

Bold and brave, Mac would tell her one day.

and beautiful

But for now, he just tugged Jim Bridger's head around and cantered down the hill toward home.

Would you run with sun warm wolves in storm

And will you wonder if you do belong

On this wild hunt and where will this moon end?

I come from mountains bearing only wind

On nights you don't know you're still alive

And still you wonder, running by my side.

Jon S. Lokowich

A NOTE FROM THE AUTHOR—I'm not sure God could create another Helena, and I know for certain I never could. That's why I chose to set this story among the true-life landmarks and locations of southwest Montana. The story and characters, however, are fiction. Yes, I did crash into Helena at age nineteen, with twenty bucks and two guitars, and I was, to my knowledge, the first female in the capital city's history to hold a full-time radio announcer's position, but—while I'm proud of that accomplishment—I hardly think it warrants an autobiography. (Besides, the characters in this story don't hold a candle to the real people I've known and loved on the true-life Last Chance Gulch.)

I have a house in Houston now, but fifteen years and three thousand miles away from my little apartment on Benton, I am still proud to call myself a Montanan. My children were born there, as were seven generations of children before me. I still have a bank account at Western Federal, my husband and I remain on the membership roll of Saint Paul's United Methodist, and I've taught the last nine summers at Grandstreet Theatre School. Helena is a hard place to leave. Her unique heart and humor have inspired me, and for that inspiration I am truly grateful.

> Robert Southwell: *Not where I breathe, but where I love,*
> *I live.*

I shall always live in Helena.

Joni Lonnquist Rodgers